MOORESTOWN LIBRARY

3 2030 00033 2394

Fiction Mas
1980
Mason
Armored giants : a novel of the

125815

Fiction
Mas   Mason, Francis Van Wyck
            Armored giants

12
12/10

Moorestown Library
Moorestown, New Jersey
08057

ARMORED GIANTS

ARMORED

F. VAN WYCK MASON

GIANTS

A Novel of the Civil War

LITTLE, BROWN AND COMPANY   BOSTON   TORONTO

COPYRIGHT © 1980 BY THE ESTATE OF F. VAN WYCK MASON
ALL RIGHTS RESERVED. NO PART OF THIS BOOK MAY BE REPRO-
DUCED IN ANY FORM OR BY ANY ELECTRONIC OR MECHANICAL
MEANS INCLUDING INFORMATION STORAGE AND RETRIEVAL SYS-
TEMS WITHOUT PERMISSION IN WRITING FROM THE PUBLISHER,
EXCEPT BY A REVIEWER WHO MAY QUOTE BRIEF PASSAGES IN A
REVIEW.

FIRST EDITION

Fiction
Mas

LIBRARY OF CONGRESS CATALOGING IN PUBLICATION DATA

Mason, Francis van Wyck, 1901–
   Armored giants.

   1. United States—History—Civil War, 1861–1865
—Fiction. 2. Monitor (Ironclad)—Fiction.
3. Merrimac (Frigate)—Fiction. I. Title.
PZ3.M3855Ar [PS3525.A822] 813'.52 80-17751
ISBN 0-316-54922-3

VB

Published simultaneously in Canada
by Little, Brown & Company (Canada) Limited

PRINTED IN THE UNITED STATES OF AMERICA

Contents

PART ONE
Quo Fata Ferunt — As the Fates Direct

	Introduction	3
1	The Convicts	5
2	Chase	12
3	At the Globe Hotel	18
4	Various Considerations	35
5	United States Consulate — Bermuda	44
6	Cross-Seas	56
7	In the Gulf Stream	64
8	The Great Wave	68
9	U.S.S. *Underwriter*	78

PART TWO
A House Divided

10	"City's Fair Jumpin' "	83
11	Roaring Town	88
12	Aftermaths	100
13	Home Is the Sailor	112
14	The Backers	120
15	Imperial French Consulate General	130
16	Letters	141
17	Crossroads	143
18	Launching Day	150
19	Celebration	156
20	Elite Tonsorial Salon	158
21	Postprandial Pleasures	164

PART THREE
Clash at Hampton Roads

22	The Blockade Runner *Staghound*	175
23	"The Invulnerable Armored Champion"	184
24	"Ericsson's Folly"	188
25	Various Intrigues	191
26	Enter Henry Dutton	197
27	The Palm Room	201
28	His Imperial Majesty Napoleon III's Sloop of War, *Gassendi*	205
29	Between the Rip Raps and Fort Monroe, Virginia	209
30	A Change of Uniform	213
31	"Gunner's Hill"	216
32	James River Flotilla	219
33	Replacements	224
34	"Cheesebox on a Raft"	228
35	The U.S.S. *Cumberland*	236
36	The U.S.S. *Congress*	244
37	Armored Duel	250
38	Critical Decision	257
39	C.S.S. *Patrick Henry*	265
40	Dispatch to the London *Telegraph*	267
41	Letter Home	269
42	News, Sweet and Bitter	271
43	Western Rivers	279
44	Kitty's Diary	283
45	Assassination?	286
46	The Western Flotilla	293
47	Battle of Memphis	311
48	Fresh Starts	328

PART ONE

Quo Fata Ferunt — As The Fates Direct

Introduction

New York, August 29, 1861

His Excellency Abraham Lincoln
President of the United States
Sir:

The writer, having introduced the present system of naval propulsion and constructed the first screw ship of war, now offers to construct a vessel for the destruction of the rebel fleet at Norfolk and for scouring the Southern rivers and inlets of all craft protected by rebel batteries ... Please look carefully at the enclosed plans and you will see that the means I propose to employ are simple — so simple indeed that within ten weeks after commencing the structure I would engage to be ready to take up position under the rebel guns at Norfolk, and so efficient too, I trust, that within a few hours the stolen ships would be sunk and the harbor purged of traitors. Apart from the fact that the proposed vessel is very simple in construction, due weight, I respectfully submit, should be given to the circumstance that its projector possesses practical and constructive skill shared by no engineer now living. I have planned upward of one hundred marine engines and I furnish daily working plans made with my own hands of mechanical and naval structures of various kinds, and I have done so for thirty years. Besides this, I have received a military education and feel at home in the science of artillery. You will not, sir, attribute these statements to any other cause than my anxiety to prove that you may safely entrust me with the work I propose. If you cannot do so then the country must lose the benefit of my services....

I cannot conclude without respectfully calling your attention to the now well-established fact that steel-clad vessels cannot be arrested in their course by land batteries, and that hence our great city is quite at the mercy of such intruders, and may at any moment be laid in ruins, unless we possess means which, in defiance of Armstrong guns, can crush the sides of such dangerous visitors.

I am, sir, with profound respect, your obedient servant,

JOHN ERICSSON

P.S. It is not for me, sir, to remind you of the immense moral effect that will result from your discomfitting the rebels at Norfolk and showing that batteries can no longer protect vessels robbed from the nation, nor need I allude to the effect in Europe if you demonstrate that you can effectively keep hostile fleets away from our shores. At the moment of putting this communication under envelope it occurs to me finally that it is unsafe to trust the plans to the mails. I therefore respectfully suggest that you reflect on my proposition. Should you decide to put the work in hand, if my plan meets your own approbation, please telegraph and within forty-eight hours the writer will report himself at the White House.

J. E.

[Comment by Author]
To this communication there came no reply whatsoever.

F. VAN W. M.

1

The Convicts

LIKE MANY ANOTHER WINTER DAY in Bermuda, 26 December 1861 broke chilly, dark, and windy over those grim, gray-stone forts, barracks, wharves, magazines, the great camber and repair wharves composing her Britannic Majesty's Dockyard, strategically vital headquarters for the North America and West Indies Station. Situated on the extreme eastern tip of low-lying Ireland Island, its powerful batteries dominated the channel into Grassy Bay and Two Rock Passage lying at its eastern end, affording this sole access by water to Hamilton, the Colony's thriving second capital — after St. George's.

By midafternoon, occasional small patches of sunlight pierced low, ragged, and fast-flying black clouds, brightening as silvery rain squalls chased one another across the Sound like playful kittens, as though to bear out the age-old Bermudian saying, "An' you don't fancy our weather, Mister, just wait a half hour."

Harry Keyes, Bandmaster of the Twenty-ninth Line Regiment, on garrison duty in Bermuda, crouched in the rain-lashed cockpit of the ketch *Fancy Free* — a former pilot boat — speedy, sturdy, gracefully designed, and only recently condemned because damage wrought by generations of teredo worms had so weakened her fabric a board of survey had declared the vessel unfit to discharge a pilot boat's often arduous and critically important duties.

Put up for auction, the ketch had been purchased and renamed by that portly, florid-faced, able man, Colonel Henry Grainger, Her Majesty's

High Commissioner in command of Her Majesty's Dockyard on Ireland Island and the formidable fortifications there.

As abruptly as it had commenced, the rain squall thinned, then raced off across the Great Sound toward Spanish Point. Soon the sky turned a brilliant blue and the sun broke through as warm and brilliant as in spring. But then, after only a few minutes, more storm clouds closed in, and sheets of rain again lashed the whole grim complex.

Under light guard, blue-and-yellow-clad convicts shuffled by. Work done about the Dockyard itself was seldom onerous. Brutal "hard labor" was performed by dangerous convicts who generally went shackled in pairs while building roads and culverts, swinging picks and mauls, cut through rock ridges and hills on the main islands.

Large rocks were broken, then conveyed in wheelbarrows to a central rock pile and used on fortifications already capable of repelling the most powerful men-of-war afloat. That these defenses were being constructed to serve as a naval base for future operations against the United States was an open secret.

Keyes's gaze shifted to the grim outlines of the great convict hulk *Medway,* tied up inside the station's camber, or long, hook-shaped jetty. With yards and rigging gone and her three masts cut off, this former first-rate ship of the line further had been humiliated through being razed down to her berth deck in order to accommodate a long, barnlike wooden structure to shelter convicts after a fashion. At present, H.M.S. *Medway* suggested what some imaginative persons compared to a worn-out but once beautiful whore.

Keyes went below and saw the girl who called herself Kitty Hamilton huddled beside the piano, damp and bedraggled in a sodden, mulberry-hued watch cloak. She was clutching on her lap a bundle of possessions secured in a faded and often patched blue petticoat.

With drops falling from oilskins and his cap's leather bill, the Bandmaster raised his voice as a sudden wild gust made the yacht's rigging rattle. "By damn, Kitty, ye were lucky to come aboard when you did. Right now it's raining fit to drown fish and frogs." He stooped, used a plump wet hand to chuck the trembling, long-limbed girl under a softly rounded chin. "Cheer up, Ducky. Likely this squall will ease up soon — sufficient to let our jailbird friends show up before long."

"Y-yes, Mr. Keyes. I-I mean Harry." Kitty Hamilton rolled large, long-lashed and slanting blue-green eyes. "I pray so too, dear."

"Don't look so damn' scared, Kit. Ain't nothin' really to worry over — so far."

Kitty's full, dark-red mouth formed a timid smile. "Thanks, Harry. I can't help it but I'm all of atwit when I think on what can happen if we get caught. Remember, I'm due on duty at five o'clock."

"Forget it. With any luck we'll be gone by then."

About a month earlier, plump Harry Keyes had become Kitty's "protector," a privilege she'd earned by having once or twice briefly granted him a few mild intimacies, just enough to stimulate his yearning for further explorations.

An especially furious blast of wind set the ex-pilot boat to bumping hard against the Commissioner's private dock fashioned of Aeolian sandstone — inaccurately termed "coral" by native Bermudians.

Harry Keyes was finding it even more difficult to remain calm and self-controlled. An acid taste invaded his mouth; 'twasn't every day, he thought, that a man deserted his family, abandoned his career, and then risked liberty by pirating a High Commissioner's yacht and, even worse, by aiding and abetting the escape of convicted felons.

Most of all, the Bandmaster yearned to glimpse the long, horselike features of one Giles Healey, an ex-sea captain convicted of barratry — the crime of deliberately sinking his vessel for insurance purposes. An Admiralty Court had sentenced him, guilty or not, to transportation for a term of twelve years. Keyes knew that of all the fugitives, only Healey might be able to navigate to the American coast with any degree of success; the Bandmaster was no more than a self-taught amateur at the art of navigation.

As for Kitty, she was beginning to realize that within the next few hours events were about to take place which undoubtedly would shape her destiny. But she had made an irrevocable decision. Thanks to her naturally sunny disposition, and because she had granted the ultimate favor very seldom and even then selectively, she was determined to gain security from some gentleman of breeding and substance who would protect her.

Bandmaster Keyes, among others, had long been aware of Kitty's acting ability; the girl certainly could sing, dance, and mimic far more ably than any amateur he'd watched. Of course, her ability might be noticeable in a tiny place like Bermuda, but not count for much in such big towns as Boston, New York, or Philadelphia. Ever since she'd been hired as governess for the Commissioner's gawky daughter, he had noticed Kitty avidly reading about those cities.

Recently, Kitty had become possessed of a mounting sense of self-reliance. Right or wrong? Well, she would soon find out. For one thing, it seemed likely that in a huge country like America, no one would suspect her of being only three-quarters white. Long ago, Kitty had adopted the surname of "Hamilton" with no better justification than that this was the place she'd been born.

Bit by bit Kitty had learned from her mother that presumably her father had been Major Ian Drummond, a dashing and socially prominent officer of the Cameronian Regiment, at that time on garrison duty in Bermuda. Major Drummond, a recent widower, had for several years employed her mother, a handsome, pale-complexioned and delicately built mulatto, as his "housekeeper" — a liaison which had endured over several years, until the Cameronians had been transferred to duty in Canada. What fate might have befallen Kitty if her mother hadn't perished in a yellow fever epidemic shortly after the gallant Major's departure, leaving her an orphan at the awkward age of twelve, she could no more than imagine.

Listening to the sharp slap-slapping of waves beating along the *Fancy Free*'s beam, Kitty recalled what *did* happen — a succession of miserable foster homes, the worst of which had been the first to employ the skinny, big-eyed orphan. The master of the house had been a brutish ship's carpenter who, with his loud and drunken harridan of a wife, had cuffed or beaten her for any real or imaginary cause, meanwhile working her to the limit of her strength.

Next, she had served as scullery maid at the Weathercock, a sordid pothouse on the road to St. George's. There, although barely nubile, she'd had to endure slobbery, whiskery kisses, and pinches which left on her meager buttocks constellations of blue-black bruises.

She might have perished from malnutrition but for the buxom and generously mustachioed wife of elderly and morose George Marchant, the Chief Warden responsible for hundreds of convicts confined in the fetid prison hulks moored at the West End. While marketing one day, Mrs. Marchant, in a rarely generous mood, had taken pity on this emaciated, yellow-haired waif with such large, black-rimmed, blue-green eyes and fine-boned features, and had bought her services, taking her out to the Chief Warden's comfortable quarters on Ireland Island.

For more than two years, Kitty had served willingly and cleverly as housemaid, waitress, and cook. Nobody could honestly deny that the Marchants hadn't treated Kitty Hamilton with anything but kindness; indeed, the Chief Warden's childless wife had even taught this pretty adolescent how to read, write, and even to understand simple arithmetic.

That happy interlude had continued until the Marchants were ordered back to England. Just before departing, Mrs. Marchant had recommended Kitty to Colonel Grainger's wife to be upstairs maid in the Naval Commissioner's unusually handsome mansion; she was also to act as governess for a ten-year-old daughter.

Interrupting the flow of memory, Kitty glanced outside the *Fancy Free* and saw that the pelting rain had once more subsided. Soon, to Bandmaster Keyes's great relief, he recognized the tramp of heavy boots advancing along the Commissioner's private dock.

Peering out of the companionway, and to his infinite relief, Keyes recognized two of the three men upon whose various skills he was most dependent.

Clad in a convict's half-blue, half-yellow jacket and trousers of coarse brown Holland cloth, the foremost arrival, Christian Pitcher, was bent under a length of spar the other end of which was being supported on the shoulder of a huge Irishman, Dion O'Dea, whose long, blue-black hair dangled, dripping and snakelike, from beneath a wide-brimmed tarred straw hat.

Anxiously, Keyes scanned the nearest guardhouse while the two were advancing along the dock. Pitcher must have stolen a length of rope and, as an added bit of camouflage, was wearing it looped over a shoulder something like a military aide's aiguillettes. The convicts dumped the spar beside the *Fancy Free*, and then, at Keyes's quick gesture, clumped aboard, dropping below and out of sight.

Kitty, glancing up, felt an icy dart stab her as she recognized the man she dreaded most, Christian Pitcher, an apprentice pilot and a fellow Bermudian. Kitty had encountered him only once or twice, and even then at a distance, but there loomed the possibility that he might have heard something about her mulatto mother.

She rallied. Quite possibly Pitcher might not have heard about that; there seemed nothing alarming in this rangy, unshaven young fellow's manner. Covertly, she studied his thin, hawk-shaped nose, high-cheekboned features, and coarse, blue-black hair. Besides, there were such pronounced coppery tones in his sunburned skin that she felt convinced this convict must have more than a trace of American Indian blood in his veins, which wasn't to be wondered at since, especially around St. David's Island, there were descendants of Pequot warriors defeated and reduced to slavery at Stonington in Connecticut by Captain John Mason during the Narrangansett War, waged far back in 1677.

Proud and fierce warriors, the Pequot captives had threatened to eat dirt and die rather than toil as field hands or to perform other menial tasks. Most owners soon discovered these captives were such excellent seamen, fishermen, whalers, pilots, and shipbuilders that they encouraged their copper-skinned chattels to breed with plump, shiny black-skinned girls imported from the West Indies for the purpose, thus creating the so-called St. George's Indians. For some reason these half-breeds, on being emancipated in 1834, had mostly elected to settle on that scattering of islands constituting Bermuda's East End.

The other convict, Dion O'Dea, stood an even six feet and somehow had remained muscular despite the miserable prison diet. Heavily, he descended the companionway ladder, clumsy boots squelching and oozing water. As soon as the big Irishman noticed Kitty, crouching fearfully beyond a piano, which the Bandmaster had brought aboard, the better to entertain the Commissioner's guests, the Irishman's heavy black brows merged and he snarled, "Now by Mary and all the Saints, here's a female aboard! 'Tis a damned unchancey cruise ye've let us in for! Ye should know, Harry, 'tis nearly as bad cess as to have a priest or a rabbi along of us."

O'Dea's face was flattish and smooth-looking, with an overlong upper lip. His snub of a nose had been broken in some fight and poorly set, and one of his front teeth was broken halfway off. His long black hair, though soaked, remained as wavy as that of a wet Labrador retriever.

Keyes snapped, "Quit such talk, you dirty Roman Catholic harp, and look alive! There's oilskins in the forepeak, see if any will fit your inches. If not, stay below! Pitcher! Get into weatherproofs, follow me on deck, and prepare to cast off the instant Healey shows up."

Pitcher, a recent deserter from Her Majesty's Thirty-ninth Regiment of Foot for reasons of his own, strained eyes toward the *Medway*'s great, ugly outline.

By fast-fading light Pitcher read the hour as a quarter past four on a clock printed on one of two towers rising midway above the principal administration building. Hell! In midwinter and with foul weather blowing, the sky might turn pitch-black within half an hour. At best, this venture seemed as likely to prove a near-run thing.

To the portly Bandmaster's immense relief, he sighted through diminishing rain the slightly built figure of former sea captain Giles Healey tramping out along the Commissioner's dock. Under an arm, he was lugging a parcel; he moved slowly, as if dispatched on some unwelcome errand.

As soon as Healey got within earshot, Keyes shouted, "Pitcher! Quick! Cast off the stern line!" The new arrival tossed his bundle into the cockpit, then stalked forward unhurriedly to free the *Fancy Free*'s bow line.

Following a course long since plotted in painstaking detail, the Commissioner's yacht first would run past Sober Island, then veer as if making for the naval boatyard on Boaz Island, then put about till the *Fancy Free*'s bowsprit swung toward Stag Rock and that narrow passage between Spanish Point to the eastward and Ireland Island, with its massive fortifications, to the west.

2

Chase

BANDMASTER KEYES BREATHED more easily as the *Fancy Free* eased away from the dock under a jib and a stained little mizzenmast sail, and there was no visible reaction either from the batteries or aboard the *Medway*. Possibly this was due to the fact that yet another rainstorm was obscuring Grassy Bay.

Ex-captain Giles Healey, having donned a set of dingy oilskins, appeared and, looking more cadaverous than ever, seated himself beside Pitcher, who was handling the tiller. Once he'd studied the set of the sails, he snapped to Keyes, "Mister, once we get past Stag Rock, hoist the mainsail the fastest you can, then cast loose the missen sheet's reef points — need the best speed we can coax out o' this tired old bag of sea worms."

Before long Pitcher put the *Fancy Free* about and, fighting down sickening fears, steered for a low-lying line of batteries and gray-white buildings visible on the extreme tip of Ireland Island. Skillfully manipulating the mainsheet, Giles Healey thought back to that day more than two years ago when he'd stood in the dock of the Vice Court of Admiralty in Liverpool and, stunned, had heard himself found guilty of barratry and sentenced to twelve years at hard labor in one of Her Majesty's penal colonies.

Quite clearly he could recall the glowering white-wigged judge intoning: "Captain Giles Healey, the worst crime a shipmaster can commit is deliberately causing a vessel entrusted to his command to be lost for the sake of her insurance."

Again Healey could hear his own voice pleading: "Your Worship, by all that's holy, I swear I am *not* guilty of this charge! 'Fore God, I'd no part in the loss of the *Griffin!* For generations my family have been shipmasters and have served in the Royal Navy with never a black mark against our name!"

"Nevertheless, you have been found guilty as charged. Guards, remove the prisoner."

The ex-shipmaster quickly erased the whole scene from a mental blackboard. Best to employ his wits to figure out what were his chances, in midwinter, of navigating an ill-found little ketch to some port along the American coast, despite icy gales and mountainous seas in the Gulf Stream.

He glanced at Keyes. "You found a sound chronometer?"

The Bandmaster blinked. "No. Had no luck in that direction, though I tried my best; all I've got is a fairly accurate pocket watch."

"Oh God! What about a sextant?"

"Bought one last year from a junk dealer."

"Reliable?"

"Think so. It'll have to do."

Heart sinking, the ex-shipmaster ducked under a sheet of spray vaulting the old pilot boat's bows.

"How about charts?"

"They're old but they were drawn by the Royal Navy, so they ought to serve. Once we're clear of the reefs, Healey, you will be in command from then on. Now get you below. Pitcher will take the helm; 'twouldn't do for lookouts to note this cockpit crowded on such a day. They might wonder why the Commissioner's yacht should be putting out fer a pleasure cruise with such a lot of people aboard."

Healey obeyed immediately, visualizing spyglasses fixed on the reeling and spray-smothered ex–pilot boat.

Bracing clumsy boots against a thwart, Christian Pitcher presently brought the sloop into the wind before allowing her to fall off on a starboard tack which should carry the *Fancy Free* close to the tip of Spanish Point and as far as possible from heavy guns mounted on Ireland Island.

With his blue-and-yellow convict's jacket giving off pungent odors, Dion O'Dea meanwhile crouched beside Kitty's neatly curvaceous figure, feeling his spirits rise when the girl made no effort to avoid the muscular arm he'd slipped about her shoulders as if to steady her softness against the *Fancy Free*'s wild plungings and rollings. 'E faith! This voyage might not prove dull after all.

To his surprise, the girl glanced up at him. "Say," she inquired, "aren't you Dion O'Dea, the fellow who almost succeeded in deserting the garrison?"

"That I am, m'dear, and Satan's blackest curse on the bugger who betrayed me for a few shillin's so the ship I'd stowed away on was stopped and searched off St. David's Head."

Kitty forced herself to appear sympathetic. In her fix it wouldn't do to offend anyone. "You poor fellow! How come they heard you were deserting?"

The Irishman sucked hard through a half-broken front tooth. "Like I said, I was betrayed by Corporal Toby Jennings. 'E owed me ten bob. Believe me, someday I'll spill his guts for that!"

An especially vicious squall filled the yacht's nearly spotless canvas (the Commissioner had recently purchased a brand-new set of sails) and heeled her so far over that water foamed over her lee rail till Pitcher expertly eased the helm. He was feeling better. Thanks to such weather, Grassy Bay now seemed devoid of shipping beyond a few fishermen scudding for shelter. Better still, not a single man-of-war lay at anchor off Dockyard.

"Not a bad-riding craft, this," grunted Healey, knuckling water from dark, deep-set eyes amid the gloom deepening in the *Fancy Free*'s small cabin. "Wonder how she'll handle in really heavy seas?"

Keyes nodded, ginger-hued side whiskers fluttering in the wind. "For all I'm an amateur, I know this boat can sail five points closer to the wind than any craft I've ever steered."

All at once the rain let up again, the breeze slackened, and then, with the suddenness of a magician's trick, the sun appeared, pallid and dipping low, breaking through hurrying clouds. Healey growled from the companionway where, with O'Dea, he lurked out of sight. "Damn! Now the lookouts will get a clear view of us."

The Bandmaster attempted to sound reassuring. "To be sure but don't worry. The Commissioner's yacht is well known hereabouts."

"Maybe so," O'Dea grunted, "but why in hell would the Commissioner go out for a pleasure jaunt in such bollixy weather?"

Keyes laughed shortly. "He wouldn't; so I took care to tell the harbor master I'd be taking the yacht this afternoon down to pick up some gear at the Watford boatyard."

The *Fancy Free* scudded by so close to Spanish Point that the Irishman cried, "What in hell you doin'? Aim to drive us onto the rocks?"

"Take it easy. Pitcher's a Bermudian," Keyes yelled. "He's done a lot of piloting in these waters."

The course was altered, but without undue speed, for certainly, glasses were being leveled from the fort as well as from aboard a pair of small supply ships undergoing repairs in the lee of the Dockyard's camber.

Pitcher, after shifting position in the stern sheets and gripping the tiller's handle with fists gone white-knuckled, called below to where Kitty crouched nervously, knotting and unknotting her kerchief's ends. "We're near opposite to the near batteries," he called, "so keep out of sight everybody while I shape a course for the Northwest Channel."

Healey, staring through a porthole at what seemed like acres of rocks boiling and creaming ahead, queried, "Any ships of war due?"

"No," answered the Bandmaster. "Yesterday I looked at the list of men-o'-war due in around this date. None expected to show up inside the next two days."

The afternoon sun began to touch the horizon even as the *Fancy Free*, pitching and rolling, plowed past the camber. Union Jacks flown from various staffs still were streaming stiff and straight, but it seemed to Pitcher the wind's velocity was beginning to slacken.

No signal to heave to had been flown, nor a warning gun fired from the batteries on Ireland Island, but this pleasant realization vanished as Pitcher suddenly shouted: "Look! For Christ's sake, look! There's a sloop o' war following the North Shore Channel inbound!"

"About how near is she?"

"Off Admiralty House. Blasted headland's kept her hid till now."

Plans crashing about him, the Bandmaster unloosed a volley of curses. "Think she'll bother to chase a little boat like this?"

Indianlike features gone rigid, Pitcher said, "Perhaps not, lest the forts signal an alarm. Now, all hands stop cussin' an' start prayin'; we're about to cross a mess of rocks close to the Northwest Channel's south entrance." Wind whipping long blue-black hair about his eyes, he added, "Don't nobody fret too much. Me, I've fished, whaled, and hunted wrecks 'mongst these coral heads ever since I could piss over a gunwale."

Breathless, taut silence descended upon the *Fancy Free*, relieved only by the hissing of spray and the gurgle of water flowing freely along the yacht's scuppers. Again and again the *Fancy Free* heeled dangerously far over, but always righted smartly when Christian Pitcher expertly eased the tiller.

The Bandmaster, O'Dea, and Kitty couldn't resist the temptation to thrust heads out of the companionway to see how matters stood.

"Down, damn it! Down!" rasped Healey. "Spyglasses over there still can sight us, clear. Should them forts fire alarm guns, yonder bulldog still can catch us before dark so I — I'll...."

The words died on his lips when the wind-dulled report of a signal cannon sounded from astern. No doubt someone in authority finally had come to wonder why, at this unlikely time, the Commissioner's yacht should be sighted outward bound and headed for the Northwest Channel.

Everyone breathed a trifle easier when the sloop of war, under easy canvas, continued up the North Shore toward Grassy Bay. Had her commander mistaken those cannon shots as salutes to his flag? Apparently so, because the inward bound man-of-war fired only one signal gun in acknowledgment. But the respite proved only momentary. Several hoists of bright, varicolored signal flags could be seen hauled, flapping wildly up the Dockyard's principal flagstaff. At once, the sloop of war, a vessel of a class especially designed for swift reconnaissance work, shifted course away from Ireland Island and, despite fading light, crowded on canvas and started in pursuit. Soon it became inescapable that, although the ex-pilot boat was uncommonly swift considering her size and rig, her pursuer was considerably faster.

Darkness was closing in with encouraging speed, and Giles Healey was amazed at how Christian Pitcher, without hesitation, picked correct courses among a succession of murderously spouting reefs. Just how the Bermudian could recognize one boiler from the next passed comprehension. All the same, the ex-shipmaster told himself, God alone knew what might happen once true darkness descended.

Since there was no longer any point in remaining out of sight, Kitty, O'Dea, and the Bandmaster climbed up into the cockpit and in silent apprehension watched the long, low outlines of Ireland Island become lost to sight even as running lights commenced to glow aboard the pursuing man-of-war.

3

At the Globe Hotel

ABOUT MIDAFTERNOON in late December of 1861, passengers commenced to debark from the transatlantic brigantine-rigged paddle steamer *Coral Queen,* and landed on Furbert's Dock in St. George's, Bermuda. Onlookers agreed the mail steamer must have experienced some uncommonly severe weather during her passage from England; her foretopmast had been carried away and her single, long, and rust-flecked funnel was canting to port, reminiscent of a drunken sailor clinging to a lamp post.

Because it was midwinter, the Royal Mail steam packet's passenger list had been brief. On it were the names of Lieutenants David Dexter and Ira Thatcher of the United States Navy.

The Purser, who'd touched in St. George's on several occasions, suggested to them and to a few other favored passengers that they patronize the Globe Hotel. " 'Tis easy to find. St. George's isn't what you might call an important port, for all these ships you see." He pointed to a mass of shipping anchored or tied up to the few docks.

"Why are so many vessels in this small place?" Lieutenant Thatcher wanted to know.

" 'Tis all on account of that war that's been going on in America since last spring; both sides think Bermuda's a handy place to refuel, transfer cargo, and take on water, fuel, and supplies."

He broke off, "To find the Globe, go uphill from King's Square till you see St. Peter's Church at the top of a long flight of red brick steps. The hotel lies almost directly opposite the church." He grinned briefly. "The Globe's accommodations don't look much like those in some fancy London place or a big-town hotel, but the bugs there ain't too bothersome. Food is mostly native seafood, middling-well cooked; liquor's cheap. There's plenty of American whiskey, Jamaica or Barbados rum. I'll send up yer luggage soon's I hear you've found space — it just might be a mite crowded this time of year."

Once they had left the freight-heaped dock, Thatcher laughed. "Good Lord, if only the ground would quit heaving under me I'd feel more like ordering a decent dinner. Always takes a little time for me to find my land legs."

"Yes, I still feel the ship's motion," Dexter agreed.

Clutching tall hats, the two Lieutenants bent heads against a rising wind, crossed King's Square, then continued along a narrow street crowded with roughly dressed blacks and seafarers, more than a few of whom appeared well gone in drink.

Following the Purser's advice, both men had donned civilian clothes, for, according to that worthy, Federal-blue uniforms might cause trouble. A vast majority of Bermudians were violently pro-Southern in the war that was spreading, and growing more violent. Such partiality, the *Coral Queen*'s Purser had explained, was due to the fact that, right from the start, Bermudians had had historic ties first with Virginia and the Carolinas, then later with the other cotton-growing States.

Bermuda's uninhabited Islands had been discovered back in 1609 by Sir George Somers, after he was blown off course by a hurricane while on a colonizing expedition to Jamestown, Virginia. Shortly afterward, the Islands had been settled by disgruntled immigrants, refugees disgusted by the perils and hunger prevailing in poorly situated and unhealthy Jamestown. Even now, some older Bermudians still referred to their country as the "Somers" or "Summers" Isles. Otherwise, Bermuda geographically served as an ideal way station or entrepôt for the transportation of Southern exports to Europe, especially because few Southerners owned ships capable of completing an uninterrupted transatlantic voyage; that their steamers should refuel here was imperative.

"Guess the Purser was right," David Dexter remarked as they made their way to the Globe. "We'd better not wear uniforms. Stupid to get involved in some senseless scrape."

As they sauntered up the short, cobbled street toward venerable St. Peter's Church — claimed to be the most ancient Episcopal church in North America — Thatcher was reminded of Europe by the many small, overhanging buildings and the narrow, winding streets of this old port, which until 1793 had been the Island's capital.

Privately, Dexter was pleased it hadn't seemed advisable to wear a uniform until he had arrived at a formidable soul-searching decision. Northern-born-and-bred in Beverly, Massachusetts, at Phillips Academy, in Andover, he'd first encountered Ira Thatcher, a slightly built, studious, attractive young Virginian. Against the influence of his father, but strengthened by the bright mind and seductive natural charms of a certain Louisa Cable Ridgely, David had been, since then, fighting a battle of conflicting loyalties. Louisa's family had owned for several generations a notable estate, "Gunner's Hill," near Culpeper, Virginia; knowing her, and them, had much to do with his miserable uncertainty.

About the convictions of his father, Daniel Snow Dexter, Captain, U.S.N., retired and recently become a shipyard owner, David had no doubt whatever. The Captain's dedication to preserving the Union was fanatical. Nevertheless, David had kept silent, even to Ira Thatcher, about the possibility of resigning his commission and heading south. From all he'd heard and read in England, great numbers of senior officers in the United States Regular Army, after resigning, had departed to fight for the Confederacy, full of enthusiasm.

On the other hand, why had so few officers of the Regular Navy proved eager and ready to exchange Federal blue for Confederate gray? Possibly, David had reasoned, this might be explained by the fact that shrewd naval officers who'd seen anything of the world abroad had come to understand the South's greatly inferior manpower and serious lack of mechanical and mineral resources. They must have been well aware, too, that major shipyards, aside from those in Norfolk, Virginia, and New Orleans, were few and of limited capacity for the construction of modern men-of-war.

Dexter fell to speculating on where Thatcher's secret loyalties might lie. Ira, he knew, had been born and reared in Norfolk. Moreover, his father had been a Virginian to his fingertips and had been posted to duty at Gosport Navy Yard until, only two years ago, he'd been stricken by a fever which had carried him off only a few days after Bull Run — that ignominious rout of Federal troops after a savage battle fought between two overconfident amateur armies, about twenty-five miles south of Washington. Northern newspapers called their defeat "Bull Run," while jubilant Southern journalists referred to this clash as the "Battle of Manassas."

Had Pa lived, Ira reckoned, as a Virginian he would likely have supported the new-born Confederacy, but his mother, née Emmeline Peabody, hailed from Portsmouth, New Hampshire, where Pa had met her on a training cruise and had fallen so desperately in love they'd married two months later. Tall, severely handsome, and tactfully upright, Emmeline Peabody Thatcher had never spoken or written to the contrary, but Ira felt convinced his mother remained quietly, deeply loyal to the state of her birth. And the Federal government had paid for Ira's Annapolis Academy education; Virginia had not. As for Ira's friend Dexter, he was beginning to realize that his day of decision could not much longer be postponed. He wondered whether other passengers booked for New York on the *Princess Royal,* to which he and Ira would be transferring, were undergoing similar soul-searching. Their new ship was a screw-propelled steam brigantine plying between Liverpool and New York, with a stopover in Bermuda to recharge her coal bunkers against the second leg of the voyage to New York.

The two young travelers could see that the usually sleepy little port of St. George's had come into prosperous times. Not a single vacant shop, shed, or storehouse was anywhere to be seen; many stores were displaying a wide variety of expensive foreign merchandise. Mounds of cotton bales, sometimes with contents bursting through hempen bindings like snow, lay on all the docks, completely exposed to the elements. Local warehouses were crammed to capacity.

Gangs of sullen black laborers of varying hues and conditions were loading bales onto wheelbarrows, carts, and drays, or onto lighters for transfer to ships of many rigs and tonnages, moored or anchored out on the harbor's placid, bright-blue waters. These vessels were flying flags of several nations; some were Dutch and a few French tricolors were to be seen. There were even a few rakish, slovenly appearing Spanish merchantmen. But nowhere did Dexter or Thatcher sight the Stars and Stripes displayed.

As the two Lieutenants were nearing the Globe's entrance, a familiar voice hailed them: "I say, chaps, hold on a moment!" It was Lionel Humphrey, a fellow passenger aboard the *Coral Queen*. This long-nosed Englishman was lanky, red-faced, and affected drooping blond mustaches and generous yellow sidewhiskers.

During the voyage, in an unguarded moment, Humphrey had let slip that he was a newspaper correspondent for the London *Telegraph*, assigned to cover the ever-expanding and bloody war being fought in America. In Ira's opinion, Humphrey's diffident manner, stylish clothes, and fastidious love of creature comforts didn't fit the conception of a war correspondent. However, the fellow possessed a redeeming dry sense of humor and produced a bulging purse whenever drinks were in order.

Only the evening before, while flashes from Bermuda's Gibbs Hill light were being sighted, Humphrey, over a third glass of fine old brandy, admitted to having served for two years as a reporter during the recent Crimean War. He had, he said, covered the Battle of Balaklava as well as that ghastly siege of Sevastopol, so efficiently that the *Telegraph*'s editors had granted him a byline plus a slight raise in pay — complimentary, but inadequate to say the least, he remarked.

Now, clinging to Humphrey's arm, was another ex-passenger — a sprightly young Frenchwoman listed on the passenger list as "Mlle Arlette Louise d'Aubrey." Vivacious and charming, she had proved to be an uncommonly good sailor even during winter gales. She kept her generous mane of heavy, chestnut hair neatly dressed and netted in simple but stylish fashion. Mademoiselle d'Aubrey spoke an almost completely unaccented English.

During the latter part of the voyage, she and Lionel Humphrey were seen together with increasing frequency, usually after dark — a fact which did not escape the notice of Ira Thatcher. Dexter, however, paid the French girl little attention; the image of Miss Louisa Cable Ridgely always interfered.

Every evening David made fresh entries in a long, continuing letter to his beloved. *Why* had he heard nothing from her in weeks? She must have written, care of his family. A gold-framed miniature of the girl, painted on ivory, always stood beside his bunk. It depicted Louisa with golden brown hair, a wide, graciously curved mouth, and large, blue-black eyes which, at times, appeared to be violet. Granted half an excuse, David would expatiate on Louisa Ridgely's accomplishments, wit, and charm. Ira thought that if even half of what Dexter claimed were true, then Miss Ridgely indeed must be a paragon of beauty, virtue, and intelligence.

He was recalled to the present by the Englishman's question: "I say, where are you lads headed?"

Ira told him, "To the Globe's so-called taproom."

"D'you mind if we join you?" The correspondent moved with unexpected speed to protect his companion from splashes raised by a passing carriage. "Good. I have been informed the Globe is the cleanest hostelry in this country."

"Let's hope that's so," Dexter said. "Thanks to the Purser's advice, Ira and I hope to obtain quarters there until the ship for New York is ready."

"So, you also are departing on the mail packet *Princess Royal?*" Mademoiselle d'Aubrey smiled sweetly. "What a pleasant coincidence. By chance, Monsieur Humphrey and I also have booked passage on the *Princess.*"

During the voyage from Liverpool, Lionel Humphrey had gradually ascertained that Mademoiselle d'Aubrey purported to be a *modiste,* a dress designer of *haute couture,* and that she was hopeful of establishing a salon of her own in New York where, by all accounts, certain classes were growing richer by the hour.

Only a few patrons paid any attention when the quartet entered the Globe's crowded, hot, and smoke-filled taproom. Voices, heated by liquor, made it difficult to talk in normal tones. When, with the correspondent's assistance, Arlette d'Aubrey unhooked a dark-gray coaching cloak, she revealed a modish bolero jacket of dark-green velvet and dark-red hoop skirts. Conversation faltered momentarily.

To Dexter's astonishment, seated at a nearby table were two men clad in Confederate-gray uniforms. How, David wondered, would Louisa like to see him wearing such colors. She had always claimed navy-blue was especially becoming to his deeply tanned complexion, long and luxuriant pale brown hair, and impressively tall figure; he stood an even six feet tall. But how did Louisa *really* feel about this war? For all her undeniable beauty and fluttery manner, she had a discerning and practical mind. She had never appeared overly impressed either by martial glitter or the rantings of perfervid politicians. Possibly her strong-minded mother might provide an explanation.

A few shillings covertly bestowed by Humphrey on a perspiring and round-bellied black headwaiter secured the four of them a table just vacated by a pair of well-dressed civilians and two British officers wearing the Queen's scarlet.

The Englishman hung up his opera cloak and spread his coattails preparatory to taking a seat. "Fancied we couldn't gain admittance lacking the use of a shoehorn," he observed.

With a flourish, Dexter pulled out a chair for the Frenchwoman. When she seated herself with a fluid grace, several nearby wind-burned and whiskery faces turned to stare.

"Ma foi!" Arlette commented, "Is it not pure delight to be off that cramped and most uncomfortable vessel?"

"Aye," Humphrey agreed. "Let us make the most of this Bermuda layover, especially since we may not greatly enjoy the last leg of our voyage."

Thatcher's gaze sharpened. "Why so?"

"Because I've just heard our ship to New York, the *Princess Royal,* is screw-propelled. So she lacks the stabilizing, steadying effect of paddle wheels. Yes, I fear she'll probably pitch and roll far worse than the *Coral Queen* ever did. True, Mr. Thatcher?"

Ira's narrow, dark-brown head inclined. "I fear so. I noticed the unsteadiness of a propeller-driven ship during the short cruise I made aboard the *Gloire.*"

"You agree?" Humphrey turned to Dexter. "And what about the *Warrior?* You've been aboard her?"

"Yes. When she came into Southampton for supplies I was invited aboard and managed to get a good look at her engines. They're sited below the waterline, which is more than sensible."

"Why?" Arlette d'Aubrey unexpectedly put in.

"Because a single well-aimed shell exploding in a ship's paddle-wheel housings in her exposed engine room would put her out of action at once."

One of the Confederate officers, a small, dark-complexioned fellow affecting long, spike-pointed mustaches and a goatee rendered fashionable by Napoleon III, arose from a neighboring table and drew nearer, his gait a trifle uncertain. Formally, he bowed to Mlle d'Aubrey, then to her companions. "Pardon me, Ma'am — gentlemen — but I chanced to overhear your remarks concerning propellers on men-of-war and the advantages of their use."

Tucking a napkin under his chin, Dexter settled back. "Sit down, sir. I assume you agree that screw propellers are the most efficient means of propelling vessels — especially warships?"

"Indeed I do, sir. May I present myself? I'm Lieutenant Mark Wister of the Confederate States Navy." A double row of well-polished brass buttons winked on his gray tunic when he bowed in Arlette's direction.

To Thatcher's surprise, another Southerner arose and drew near, hand outstretched toward Ira. "Suh, am I mistaken or didn't we serve together in the *Congress* on a cruise to South America some time ago?"

"Yes. You're Ernest Dupuy from New Orleans — and a Rebel, aren't you?"

"Guilty as charged." He smiled. "So is my friend here." He indicated the man with the Napoleonic mustachios.

Thatcher said, "This lady is Miss d'Aubrey from Paris, and this is Lieutenant David Dexter, U.S.N., and this is Mr. Lionel Humphrey of the London *Telegraph.*"

The first Confederate drawled, "As I've said, I'm Mark Wister, late of the United States Navy and presently on my way to England."

A small tremor descended Dexter's back over the thought that just possibly he might be wearing a uniform like Wister's before long. The Lord above only knew what "the Captain," as he always addressed his father, would say or do if he turned his coat — this Captain who came from Boston and had served in the Navy since 1820.

Arlette Louise d'Aubrey treated both men in gray to an especially dazzling smile as Lionel Humphrey made a wide motion, saying smoothly, "Won't you gentlemen join us — provided you can find any chairs."

Once the Confederates had seated themselves, Ira remarked, he hoped quite casually, "I trust you gentlemen can give us some accurate news about what's going on at home. You see, my friend Dexter and I have been on foreign duty abroad for almost two years, so we don't know anything beyond what appears in the English and French newspapers. And they're so biased in favor of the South, we've been wondering how much of the war news they print is anywhere near true."

Wister lifted his glass. "You can believe most of what you've read. The

Yankees are half-whipped already. Here's to a quick and complete defeat of all Abolitionists!"

Neither Ira nor David more than touched lips to their glasses, but Dupuy and Wister both took deep swallows.

Increasingly loud and broad Bermudian accents began to dominate the babble of conversation. How curious, Ira thought, that so many locals were given to substituting the letter w for v, or vice versa.

Glancing casually about, he noted that many Bermudians were expensively, if not smartly, dressed. Some were sporting heavy gold watch chains draped across loud-colored waistcoats, suggesting they had only recently come into a lot of money. Much talk could be heard about the impending departure for New York of the *Princess Royal*. Some were debating her chances of being stopped and searched, for recently a powerful Federal steam frigate had been sighted, apparently on blockade duty, but well off Bermuda.

"Ah, so M. le President has created a blockade?" Arlette demanded, delicately sipping coffee from a heavy, earthenware mug.

Wister laughed. "Don't be fooled, Ma'am. The Federals have so few seaworthy warships that when they're strung out along our seacoast, near three thousand miles long, they cruise so far apart that what old Abe has established is no more than what European powers term a paper blockade, and so ineffective that legally it isn't worthy of notice."

Dupuy nodded, twirled the well-waxed tips of his mustachios. "Ever since the start of the war, British and other foreign flags have been entering Southern ports almost at will."

"What do these neutrals import?" Humphrey inquired, wrinkling his nose over a glass of inferior sherry.

Lieutenant Wister laughed easily, "Why, sir, they bring in medicines, field guns, siege cannon, percussion caps, and all manner of small arms and ammunition for them." He winked. "They also import highly profitable but nonmilitary items such as ladies' bonnets of the latest fashion, fine laces, corsets, silk stockings, dresses, and ball gowns, not to mention thousands of bolts of silk, satin, and velour and other high-priced yard goods."

The other officer in gray laughed. "Yes, Ma'am, reckon a clever dressmaker could soon make herself a tidy sum by catering to fashion-minded Southern ladies."

Thatcher inquired softly, "And how do the Confederate merchants manage to pay for such imports?"

"Through the sale of sugar, tobacco, and, most of all, cotton. European spinning mills are near to starving for raw cotton and ready to pay almost any price for it; you needn't doubt that within six months at the most, King Cotton will finance and end this 'second war for American independence,' as we call it."

"Oh, come now, Ernest," Wister objected, color rising. " 'Twon't be that soon; don't forget those damn Yankees outnumber us."

Thatcher cast Dexter a glance at the use of "damned Yankees," but David seemed occupied in downing a rum swizzle. Surprising, Ira thought, that Wister hadn't also mentioned the South's critical shortage of steel-rolling mills, foundries, and up-to-date shipyards, save for that great U.S. Navy Yard the Confederacy captured at Gosport, lying only a short distance up the Elizabeth River from Norfolk. Of course, the inexplicably easy seizure of this yard had yielded to the South immense stores of fine modern cannon, ammunition, and stocks of naval stores of all descriptions.

Aside from that, Norfolk, for Virginians, constituted a strategic base of operations from which they could threaten the entire eastern coast, from Washington and New York clear up to Boston, and at the same time protect Wilmington, North Carolina, Charleston, Georgia, and Florida.

A stumpy, yellow-bearded individual approached through the smoke haze. It soon appeared that this was the Chief Pilot for the Colony. He slapped Mark Wister on the shoulder, and grinned vacuously at his companions. Obviously, he'd been drinking, but seemed to be carrying his liquor fairly well. Said he, "Shay, Mark, just heard two pieces o' interestin' news. For one, a big U.S. Navy sloop called the *San Jacinto* has been stationed to closer blockade duty off Bermuda. She's supposed to search and snap up vessels carryin' contraband cargo to the Yankees. So far, she's only been patrollin' the outer reefs."

Lionel Humphrey paid no apparent attention, but he made a note in his remarkably retentive memory. Unlike most newspaper correspondents, he made written notes of possible significance only at the end of the day, after having winnowed a few grains of true news from a chaff of speculation and rumor.

Thoughtfully, Dexter remarked, "I pity the *San Jacinto*'s master — whoever he is."

"Why?" Arlette d'Aubrey asked softly.

"Because," the Chief Pilot told her, while leering down her well-curved bosom, "he don't stand a chance of a snowball on a hot shovel of snappin' up many blockade runners; ocean 'round here's mighty sizable."

"How very true. But you mentioned other news, did you not, Monsieur?" the Frenchwoman queried.

The yellow-bearded Bermudian's brown hand failed completely to smother another resounding belch. "Sure did, Ma'am. Just this afternoon I overheard a British prison varden say a party of convicts have escaped from prison hulks out at Ireland Island, so it's out o' the fryin' pan and into the fire for them there willains."

"Why so?"

"Because them desperate rascals stole the Commissioner's own yacht and last vas sighted shapin' a course for America. Bloody idiots don't stand a chance of getting avay, 'specially in midvinter."

Humphrey, absently stroking his fluffy sideburns, remarked, "One wonders why even hardened criminals would run such a risk."

A Bermudian at the next table, picking his few remaining teeth with a grubby forefinger, said, "Ye'd too, if ye knew what it's like aboard them rottin' prison hulks."

A sweating, pale-brown mulatto waiter staggered in under an enormous tray and distributed steaming bowls of conch stew, plates of "Hoppin' John," made of rice and black-eyed peas, followed by servings of huge, spiny lobsters, along with side dishes of cassava pie.

Lionel Humphrey dabbed his mouth with a none-too-clean napkin while considering the mustachioed Confederate opposite him, then remarked casually, "I say, shortly before leaving England I heard rumors that you Confederates are in the process of building a brand-new kind of warship — something like the armored floating batteries we used during the Crimean War."

Unexpectedly, Mlle d'Aubrey held up a slim hand, a small emerald ring glowing with the gesture. "You have seen such, M. Humphrey?"

The Englishman finished drying his whiskers. "Yes. I've watched several such batteries in action."

"They proved effective?" Thatcher inquired.

"Very. I watched heavy Russian shells and solid shot bounce off their casemates like hailstones from a barn door. Only weakness with such batteries is that they lack propelling power of their own; they have to be moved by tugs to shift to new positions. Incidentally, a good many such tugs were either sunk or crippled by Russian gunfire."

Thatcher turned to the Englishman. "Did you hear whether this Reb — er, Confederate ironclad will have engines of her own?"

"Indeed yes, suh!" The officer called Dupuy spoke so emphatically people turned to stare — and some to listen. "Our naval engineers have successfully raised a big new Federal steam frigate called the *Merrimac*, forty guns. During the great fire at Gosport Navy Yard last spring, she burned clean down to the water's edge, but we've raised her and have her in dry dock for reconstruction."

The speaker looked proudly about. "Some folks claim us Southerners have no inventive talent fit to match that of the Yankees. Don't you believe it! We've put her in dry dock and razed her clean down to her berth deck. At this very minute her hull's bein' rebuilt to carry a powerful battery, protected by an armored steel casemate — or citadel, as some call it. The *Merrimac* — officially she's been rechristened the C.S.S. *Virginia*, but for some reason the name ain't caught on — will prove invincible against the biggest wooden men-of-war afloat."

"In what state are her engines?" Humphrey asked casually.

"Oh, they're still sound, or so they say," Wister almost shouted. "Yes, gentlemen, once the *Merrimac* — I mean the *Virginia* — is commissioned, she'll be able to sink the most powerful men-o'-war in the Union Navy, or in all the world for that matter."

People within earshot burst out laughing.

"If you wasn't wearing Rebel gray," somebody called from the back of the smoke-veiled taproom, "I'd say that be just a fine example of Yankee brag!"

Wister whirled, glowered at the speaker. "Call me anything you like, suh, but don't you *ever* call me a Yankee!"

So many patrons burst into applause that Ira Thatcher was astonished; Dexter and Humphrey looked thoughtful. This noisy fellow sounded damned sure of himself.

The hubbub had begun to subside when a large, well-dressed individual entered, wearing a stovepipe hat and an imposing, well-filled waistcoat of flowered tabby velvet. Many wavered to their feet, raising mugs and glasses to the moon-faced new arrival, who, bowing right and left, made his way toward the crowded bar with the ease of a snowplow parting drifts.

Humphrey's steel-gray eyes roved the room when shouts of "Here's to King Cotton and the Confederacy!" and "To hell with Abe Lincoln!" reverberated through the smoke-filled air.

Smoothly, Arlette d'Aubrey inquired of Ernest Dupuy: "Please, Monsieur, who might that so popular gentleman be?"

"Yonder, Ma'am, is Major Norman Walker."

"Is he a high government official?"

"Why sure, Ma'am, he's the Confederate Government's principal agent in these islands."

Quickly, patrons, merchants, insurance underwriters, sea captains, shipbuilders, and businessmen of all descriptions began to collect about the rotund, semibald, black-bearded Major.

From the end of the taproom a deep voice bellowed, "Hi, friend Walker! Just landed two hundred bales of prime long-staple cotton, ready to ship soon's you find me cargo space. I'm ready to pay top freight rates. Boy! Fetch this gent and me some of yer best rum swizzles."

The din increased until the Confederate agent, in danger of being mobbed, raised pudgy, liberally beringed hands. "Easy, friends, easy, please! Day after tomorrow come one, come all to my office in Queen Street over in Hamilton, where we can talk business; but ye'd best hurry for I've just learned there's a fast steamer, the *Penguin,* due any day. Better you should just talk to the *Penguin'*s agents, Trott and Astwood, and settle on the freight rates; if you get together, I warrant there'll be plenty of space to be found for cotton bales in good condition."

A gaunt fellow with stringy gray whiskers and a jaundiced complexion yelled through cupped hands, "Get my cotton on the way to Yerrup this week, Major, and I'll hand you a bonus fit to make yer eyes pop!"

Mlle d'Aubrey's slim hand, mitted in black lace, brushed the correspondent's knee beneath the table. "Please, *mon ami,* can we not somehow escape so much noise and insufferable smells?"

"A sound suggestion! I'm also fed up with this place. Suppose we try the lounge in the Grand Hotel, where I've reserved lodgings for the two of us."

She flushed. *"Nom de Dieu!* Not together!"

The correspondent chuckled. "Of course not, m'dear. That would never do — in Bermuda. Too small."

The Frenchwoman murmured in sibilant undertones, *"Bon.* It would be most unfortunate were certain people to suspect we have become good friends!"

"You will accompany us?" the Englishman asked of Ira Thatcher, who also had risen to his feet.

"I think I will, if you don't mind. Need a few breaths of air after the heat of this stokehold." To Dexter, he said, "Dave, please take care of my share of the shot. See you later."

The three were preparing to leave when comparative quiet descended on the taproom. Patrons turned to face the entrance, and conversation almost died out as a tall, gaunt, and clean-shaven individual wearing a gray stovepipe hat and a frock coat of the same hue entered. He unslung a long black cloak, then sharply addressed the headwaiter, "Jamison, you have reserved my usual table?"

The innkeeper spread apologetic hands. "Sorry, Mr. Allen, tried my best but once those people" — he glanced toward a group of obviously British merchant officers — "heard the American Consul had reserved it, things being as they are, couldn't prevent them from taking over."

Without hesitation, Charles Maxwell Allen, United States Consul in Bermuda, walked stiffly over to the table in question, announced in a flat, incisive voice, "I fear you gentlemen have made a mistake. This table has been reserved for me. Kindly depart."

So saying, he stared evenly at them while a few catcalls sounded in the background. The merchant officers glared a moment but, accustomed to yielding to authority, ended by rising and, carrying half-emptied mugs of ale, mingled with the crowd.

The Consul calmly seated himself, looking quite unruffled, and was promptly joined by a couple of men who appeared to be Yankee skippers.

Once Dexter's former shipmates had disappeared, David invited Mark Wister and Ernest Dupuy to join him, along with a trio of Bermudian shipping agents. Swizzles (brandy and rum of various sorts) had been served in swift succession. Dexter had experienced little trouble in directing the conversation toward the still not very risky business of exchanging and transshipping cargoes of cotton, tobacco, and sugar to Europe in exchange for ships, munitions, and all manner of military and medical supplies.

David, feeling his liquor a bit more than usual, ordered a further round before inquiring of Nathaniel Butterfield, an important, comfortably plump and prosperous-appearing local shipping agent, how he expected such a traffic might best be implemented — as though he didn't already know plenty about the subject.

"You spoke of ships being among the supplies most needed by the South?"

A slightly pop-eyed Bermudian named Gosling beamed, exposed numerous gold teeth. "Why, friend, I know about charters already let to English shipyards for the constructing of a number of wery fast and low-lyin' steam sailers 'specially designed to run the Union blockade — if ever the Yankees can establish a real one. Such blockade runners on their vay from Europe vould have to put in here to recharge coal bunkers, and then run on southvards vith cargoes for the Confederacy. On their return woyage they'd put in here again to refuel and take on cotton bales — and our sheds and varehouses are close to burstin' vith 'em."

"But why take on cotton here? Surely there must be plenty in the South?"

"Yes," Butterfield admitted, "but for some strange reason the Rebel President has forbidden the exporting of cotton, as a form of blackmail so's he can get recognition for the Confederate States, since French and British spinning mills have about used up their reserve supplies."

"Indeed a clever notion," Dexter was surprised to hear himself say. "But don't you imagine, sir, the United States Navy soon will be able to establish more than this inefficient 'paper blockade'?"

Another Bermudian, Mr. Musson, an auctioneer, slapped the dripping table hard. "Not in a month o' Sundays! Say, Mister, speedy vessels can be built in England and other foreign countries much faster than even the best Yankee shipyards can do it."

During a break in the conversation, a black banjo player at the taproom's far end struck up a catchy new tune called "Dixie's Land," whereupon many patrons jumped to their feet and began singing badly off key, but making up for that in volume.

Dexter remarked casually to Lieutenant Wister, who'd grown so weary of drinking and singing that his long, black mustachios drooped, "Say, friend, whilst I was in London I heard rumors about you Southerners building an ironclad ram so powerful she could sink any and all warships the Union might send against her. Isn't that a considerable exaggeration?"

Lieutenant Wister raised a tousled black head and focused bloodshot eyes. "Dunno much 'bout it, suh, 'cept I've heard high-rankin' officers swear the *Merrimac*, I mean the *Virginia*, will be proof 'gainst the heaviest weight of shot or shell yet known."

"Um. Haven't the Yankees anything fit to stand against her? They're an inventive lot."

"Not by a damn sight!"

"Is it true she's being rebuilt in the big dry dock at the Gosport Navy Yard?"

"Yep. We made one mighty handsome haul when the Federals got burnt and chased out of there."

Further questioning made it evident that, even after downing another glass, Lieutenant Wister could provide no details of value about the reconstruction of the burnt remains of the U.S.S. *Merrimac*, except that her wooden hull had remained undamaged below the waterline.

After settling his bill, David Dexter, his mind a bit fuzzy, shoved his way out into the chilly street, thinking that if this armored vessel Wister had described as a ram could accomplish even half of what he'd claimed, there would remain few doubts that the French, British, and other European powers would quickly recognize the seceding states as an independent power and grant the rights and privileges of a belligerent nation.

Moving uncertainly along the narrow street, Dexter again debated the true meaning and implications of that word "loyalty." How could a well-bred man draw a straight line between duty to the service and devotion to lovely, trusting Louisa Ridgely? Lord! Lord! Lord! At the very thought of her, his being thrilled, craved her nearness, her beauty, quick wit, and undeniable physical attraction.

Entering King's Square, Dexter drew several deep breaths in a vain effort to clear his head. Incredible how, whenever he came to think of Louisa, other problems appeared insignificant. With her Tidewater Virginia background and ancestors, one of whom had been a signer of the Declaration of Independence, the notion of her marrying an out-and-out Yankee would certainly be incredible. What in God's name could he say when he reported to Naval Headquarters in New York City, as inevitably he must?

A sharp clicking of heels preceded a hail of "Hi! Hold on, will you?" Turning, he saw the glinting of Lieutenant Mark Wister's brass buttons only a few paces behind.

"How about having a drink with me, suh? I owe you several."

" 'Twould be a pleasure, sir. But not tonight. My head's already buzzing like a beehive."

"Then let's make it tomorrow afternoon around five at the Bull's Head Tavern in Hamilton. It's easy to find, right handy to Major Walker's office."

"Why not? Thatcher and I've been talking about visiting that port for a couple of days. Thank you and good night."

4

Various Considerations

For Bermuda — those supposedly tropical but really subtropical islands — the night was growing extremely chilly, thanks to intermittent rain squalls and a humid gale howling out of the northwest, which bowed palms and other trees like participants in a minuet. Lionel Humphrey shivered and increased the pace while escorting Mlle d'Aubrey toward the Grand Hotel, a modest establishment to say the most. Again he was reminded of his conviction that the more pretentious a hostelry's name, the less elegant the place proved to be.

Skirts billowing, Mlle Arlette d'Aubrey tucked her bonneted head in against his shoulder and clung to the correspondent's lean and wiry arm till they were practically blown through the hotel's front door. Dripping, the French girl shivered, and said, her teeth chattering slightly, "As you may recall, *mon cher* Lion-el, I possess a bottle of Napoleon's own cognac? I think we should revive ourselves with a taste, *non?*"

"You are very kind — thank you." The correspondent, grinning, wiped dampness from flowing side-whiskers. "Thank God for this quiet."

The receptionist was slumped over his desk and snoring loudly. Undoubtedly he'd also absorbed a deal of liquor against the cold.

Humphrey's curiosity was piqued as never before. During the voyage on the *Coral Queen,* somehow he'd sensed that this luscious but aristocratic-appearing young Frenchwoman, whom he judged to be about thirty years of age, quite possibly might be something more than just the fashionably dressed and successful *modiste* she professed to be.

In the Globe Hotel's taproom, he'd noticed that although Mlle d'Aubrey had found little to say, her large, greenish-blue eyes kept darting back and forth about the room, like swallows over a meadow at twilight. Um. Why had they lingered most frequently on the United States Consul, a dour-appearing individual if ever there was one? Hardly anyone else had devoted much attention to him. Who *was* Arlette d'Aubrey? He had yet to form a tenable explanation, although aboard the *Coral Queen* they'd exchanged a few quick but inconclusive embraces.

Once in her room, Arlette excused herself, saying she was soaked to the skin, and soon returned, wearing a filmy, lace-collared, blue-silk peignoir. Smiling over her shoulder, she said, "And thus, *mon ami,* do we banish boredom! One trusts you will enjoy this impromptu séance, especially since I do not think it will bear repetition.

"Believe me, Lion-el, except on very rare occasions, I really am a most discreet and serious individual, aware that she must travel long distances before she can attain the goals she has set for herself. So, *mon cher,* tonight is tonight, period."

"To put it diplomatically, you don't calculate that Lionel Humphrey is sufficiently qualified to advance your personal and private ambitions?"

"Oh, no, it is nothing like that!" she cried, and pressed velvety lips against his. "It is only that one knows so little about your influence and — and your connections. For me the vast influence of the press — your *Telegraph* and the *Times* especially — are a great and unsolved mystery!"

Smiling, Arlette loosened the negligee about small, coral-tipped, and well-formed breasts, glimpsed briefly as she bent to slip off a pair of white satin mules adorned with tufts of blue-dyed maribou feathers. "*Alors,* let us make the most of these indiscreet moments."

They did. Soon he was amazed and enchanted by the versatility and ardor of her erotic abilities.

When at last Lionel resumed damp clothing, Arlette yawned prettily. "*Hélas,* Lion-el, *mon ami,* I must take rest and try further to recover from our so stormy voyage and those miserable foods and wines on the *Coral Queen.*"

"I sympathize. Wines and cuisine both have been English, and therefore abominable! You don't know how lucky you were to have been born in France."

"Tiens, mon ami, before we part, let us now enjoy one more *soupçon."*

"A pleasure and a privilege, Ma'am." He lifted his cognac, and without taking his eyes from her, swallowed a quick sip.

The correspondent fixed a penetrating gaze on this lively young woman. "Tell me, Arlette, why is it that during our voyage I've formed a strong impression that I've seen you before? Now where could that have been?"

To his surprise, Arlette d'Aubrey smiled like a drowsy kitten and, glass poised, seated herself on the foot of her bed. "Lion-el, recently you have lived in Paris, no?"

"Why, yes, my dear. Once that idiotic war in the Crimea ended, I was assigned to our Paris desk to investigate some little-known but politically important aspects of that unpleasantness. But it was quite some time ago, so it couldn't have been in Paris. Feel positive I've seen you recently in or about London — perhaps at some diplomatic function?"

The young Frenchwoman's expression remained unchanged, yet he sensed a wariness in her manner. "No. That is impossible. In London, I do not often move in, *comment le dire,* high society."

Except, perhaps in bed, Lionel thought, but he said: "Let us hope our next ship proves more comfortable. I was eaten alive by bedbugs on the *Coral Queen."*

Delicately, Mlle Arlette d'Aubrey sipped the last of her cognac. "And you? What will you be doing in America?"

"I? Oh, I'm supposed to be a war correspondent on much the same assignment as my friend William Russell, of the *Times."*

"The *Times* of New York, or of London?"

He bristled a little. "My dear, there is but *one Times."*

"And your friend, Mr. Russell, what of him?"

"Only that nowadays he's become known as 'Bull Run' Russell on account of his excellent coverage of that absurd and bloody battle last July. He has achieved an enviable reputation. You can have no idea how deeply concerned the British are growing over the outcome of this American war."

"And which side do your people favor?"

"Well, the aristocracy, the upper and middle classes, such as spinning-mill owners, manufacturers, bankers, and the Government — they all favor the Southern States."

"But why?"

"Our industrialists don't enjoy competition from Yankee — that is, Northern — manufacturers who are becoming more important trade rivals and so they pose a threat to that most tender of their concerns — their pocketbooks. You see, m'dear, European spinning mills realize the immense importance of American raw cotton; lacking it, most will have to close down and allied businesses will be forced into bankruptcy. No doubt you have heard that Mr. Lincoln, the Northern — no, the President of the United States — has proclaimed a blockade which at present is a pathetic and inefficient effort. Recently, Russell reported that the Yankees — the Northerners, that is — are arming tugboats, river steamers, and merchantmen, even yachts, almost anything that will float, in order to present the semblance of maintaining a genuine blockade."

"How very interesting. Please, Lion-el, let us have a trifle more of cognac, *non?*"

Bushy blond brow wrinkling, he refilled the glasses from her dusty green bottle. "Mr. Lincoln's blockade had proved so ineffective that the British, French, and other European governments are preparing to declare it only a paper blockade and therefore they can ignore it."

Humphrey took another sip, and continued, "Strictly between us, m'dear, I suspect the real reason behind my being sent to America is because the Lords of Admiralty repeatedly are receiving reports from presumably reliable sources that the seceded states are engaged in building an ironclad warship capable of single-handedly smashing the Yankee blockade at the entrance of Chesapeake Bay."

Lips parted and eyes intent, the Frenchwoman clasped arms around knees revealingly drawn up beneath her peignoir. "Please to tell me more."

"Sorry, my dear, that's all I've heard on the matter save that my managing editor told me he's heard a number of reports that, as a retort to the Southerners' threat, the Yankees are building an ironclad of radical design."

"Tell me, *cher* Lion-el, have you heard more concerning this mysterious vessel the Unionists are supposed to be constructing?"

"Nothing but that she's been designed by some Swedish-American fellow by the name of John Ericsson which, my poppet, explains why I am on my way to discover what more can be learned about this curious craft. Many call it an experimental freak. Now that I have informed you, suppose you tell me what further motives might lie behind your ambition to design stylish raiment for wealthy American ladies?"

Pushing an errant curl into place, Arlette smiled demurely. "If you imagine such a thing, *mon ami,* you are mistaken. I have no ambitions other than to open a fashionable salon of *haute couture* for ladies of *ton.* As a well-regarded Parisian *modiste,* would I not be foolish if I failed to capitalize on such special knowledge and taste before it becomes too late? After all, one is no longer exactly a *poussin."*

"What nonsense! My dear. Right now you are nearing the summit of a lovely young female's charms."

Lionel Humphrey was too experienced a correspondent to pursue at this moment even the subtlest line of inquiry.

"I say, isn't it fine to be off that wretched, heaving paddle steamer and to enjoy even half-decently prepared food again? In fact, I am becoming impressed by Bermudian cuisine. What do you think of the food here?"

"Some dishes are memorable, especially the seafoods. I find the yellowtails, amber fish, and *langouste en beurre,* or lobster, as they call them here, most delectable. So, *mon cher,* let us drink to the future. One wonders what perils you will encounter during the American war."

The Englishman laughed. "Judging by what William Russell writes, there will be more dangers than I'll enjoy. Still, they can't be any worse than those I met during the Crimean War, which incidentally was no lawn party for anybody, especially war correspondents, who were forced to work as close to the firing lines as commanding officers would permit."

Arlette d'Aubrey's bosoms lifted to a sigh. *"Mon Dieu.* Modern war has become so terrible one grows almost to despair. I lost one dear brother at the Battle of Balaklava. Surely this American conflict must soon be over if, as you say, the Yankees cannot enforce their blockade."

As she talked, Humphrey suddenly remembered where first he'd noticed this intriguing female. It had been at the French Embassy in London, at a ball given not long ago in honor of the visit of the Prince Imperial, heir of Napoleon III, Emperor of the French.

Arlette, to her surprise, was forced to admit she was feeling the brandy. Normally she limited her drinking to a few glasses of light wine, followed on rare occasions by a liqueur. She gave a small wriggle, and allowed ivory-smooth and slim legs to slip over the bed's side before, with eyes half-closed, she briefly inserted a vibrant tongue between his lips.

"Your room — is it so comfortable as this one?"

"Far from it!" he said, responding to her tongue. "Must once have been some inferior servant's kennel."

"So? Therefore would it not be foolish to spend the night in so miserable a place?"

"Indeed so, my poppet."

"I must not allow you to suffer needlessly, but remember to disarrange your bed convincingly — and don't keep me waiting. I am growing sleepy."

"I won't, dear. I'll be back quick as I can find a nightshirt." He hurried out the door.

Clenching her teeth, Arlette thrust bare feet between chilly and rather damp sheets, pulling the covers up to her chin. What consummate liar had assured her Bermuda was tropical? *Dieu de Dieu!* And what had come over her? Possibly the atmosphere of this New World possessed peculiar properties? Why was she, usually so self-controlled, about to bed this undoubtedly handsome and well-bred gentleman, but knowing less than nothing about his financial, official, or social standing? Subconsciously, she was hoping Lionel would prove more accomplished than the very few other Englishmen she had bedded in hopes of obtaining information on some subject of importance.

Yawning, she stretched long and slender arms, once more recalling that lovely autumn day, clear and crisp, in Paris along the Champs-Elysées, when she'd accompanied Papa, Baron Albert Marie August d'Aubrey, indigent member of the old noblesse and at present holding a post of secondary importance in the Imperial Ministry of Marine. The Baron d'Aubrey and his loyal but practical semi-invalid wife had seen to it that their only child should receive the best possible education and training the Baron's meager salary permitted. He and Adelaide had tacitly agreed that their daughter constituted their only asset against a bleak future. Tired and disillusioned, the Baron's principal ambition was that his daughter should meet as many as possible rich and influential noblemen — even if she were forced to settle for a title of Napoleonic creation.

How subtly clever Papa had been about securing invitations for her to attend, duly chaperoned, a series of select *soirées, salons,* banquets, and even a few *bals masqués,* where she might encounter some eligible and wealthy nobleman who would at least protect and keep her in luxurious style if he could not be persuaded to marry her.

Well, she guessed she hadn't entirely failed to fulfill Papa's hopes. She smiled, recalling that glittering *bal masqué* where she first encountered the Marquis Edouard de la Villette, then Chief Commissioner for Naval Supplies, garbed in the panoply of a Roman general. Coached by Papa and dressed as a dainty, lovely shepherdess, she'd succeeded, after dancing several numbers, in titillating and inflaming that jaded and middle-aged nobleman's interest so that as the consequence of a few discreet rendezvous, the Marquis had hinted delicately that she would be welcome to become his *"maîtresse en titre."*

Papa, hounded by creditors worse than ever, hadn't objected too long to this arrangement, aware as he was of the influence exercised by Edouard de la Villette now that he was Assistant Minister in the Imperial Ministry of Marine.

Before long, the Marquis had installed Arlette in a neat little elegantly appointed apartment close by the Porte de Neuilly, and provided her with a generous "dressing allowance," three servants, and even a glossy phaeton drawn by a pair of perfectly matched grays.

Some little time elapsed before she'd perceived the tired old Marquis's true motives in supporting her. Matters had continued well enough until, one evening after an especially delightful frolic, Edouard quietly suggested she might serve the Ministry of Marine by undertaking a mission requiring considerable tact, charm, and intelligence. The suggestion had intrigued her.

"It will be as you wish, *mon coeur*," she'd murmured.

"Bon. I will inform you about this mission at the proper time."

Only a week later the blow — if such it might be described — had fallen. She could recall every moment of the evening when the Marquis had strode into her tastefully furnished salon, chilled and with great flakes of snow clinging to his cloak.

Once she'd poured him a measure of Armagnac, his favorite brandy, he'd suggested that, in the best interests of His Imperial Majesty, Napoleon III, she would shortly depart for New York City in North America and there discharge a delicate mission of the greatest importance. When she'd voiced genuine alarm, her protector, as they lay in her huge Louis

XV bed, confided: *"Ma petite Arlette, you should enjoy this voyage as a vacation from this glittering, but I fear decaying, society. Most Americans are incredibly naive; after a few drinks and with suitable encouragement, most readily will satisfy the curiosity of a fascinating lady. Ah, what sacrifices do we not make for our beloved country! I shall miss you greatly, chérie."*

"But — but this mission, what is it, Edouard? And why should I be selected for it?" Fervently, she hoped she had not sounded too diffident. *Bon Dieu!* Could he possibly have heard gossip concerning her passing dalliance with a certain Austrian Colonel of Cavalry? Or possibly with Captain Bates, on duty with the British Admiralty? Oh no, certainly not! Edouard would have dismissed her the minute she was detected in such indiscretions.

She'd heaved a sigh of relief when he had resumed, "You are required, *ma petite,* to proceed to New York and there discover everything possible concerning a strange ironclad vessel we know to be under construction there for the Federal Government. Thus far, we have received but the vaguest of descriptions of her armor, guns, and estimated speed. You will arrive at the truth about such matters. Also, we must learn about a so-called ironclad ram being built by the Southerners somewhere in Virginia."

Of hardheaded Norman descent, Arlette had sufficient wit to accept the inevitable gracefully, at the same time managing to look pitiful. "Ah, so I no longer amuse you. Is that it?"

"Non pas, bien aimé!" Edouard had declared with convincing vehemence. "That anyone of taste could ever tire of your versatility is impossible! I shall pray for your safety in America and your swift return to my arms.

"Incidentally," he had added playfully, spearing a gleaming chestnut ringlet with his forefinger, "do not doubt that I shall bank your — allowance for so long as we remain parted."

"A thousand thanks, beloved. How long do you think I must remain abroad?"

"Surely you will return before the leaves begin to fall in the Bois de Boulogne next autumn. That fumbling American war must soon end."

Edouard had sounded entirely sincere — she'd have risked her life on that. At the same time, to her great surprise, she felt a curious readiness to observe political independence firsthand, as well as a yearning for unfamiliar new scenes and values.

"Tomorrow," the Marquis informed her, "you will appear at the Ministry at eleven *au point*. We will discuss a new identity for you and prepare the necessary documents to substantiate it. I will leave it for you to decide what best should be your most convincing new profession." Suddenly, his expression had so hardened she'd been appalled. "Remember this. Under *no* conditions are you to approach our legation in Washington. However, you must report upon arrival to Baron Robert Lebel, our Consul General in New York. Is that clear?"

"But naturally, *mon coeur.*"

He had embraced her, nude as she was, and peered earnestly, almost sadly, into her strongly boned but still enchanting pink-and-white features. "Please remember that I part from you, *only* out of my sense of duty, *ma petite*. We must find out all about these warships the Americans are constructing." Then his voice had rung out like the clash of steel blades. "Never again shall we allow the accursed English to rule the oceans unchallenged!"

A soft knock at the door abruptly ended Arlette's reminiscing. Lionel Humphrey slipped in, wearing a rust-black boat cloak which, ludicrously, failed to conceal the hem of a nightshirt and reddish bare toes shrinking from contact with the cold, red-tile floor.

United States Consulate — Bermuda

THE PLEASURES of St. George's were largely limited to drinking, brawling, or wenching with females of various shades of skin hues by indiscriminate crews and some officers.

Next morning David Dexter suggested, "Maybe, Ira, your suggestion of moving over to Hamilton isn't bad. I'm told 'tis only a short trip by sea provided the weather's agreeable, but if it isn't, we're in for a bone-wrenching coach ride to the capital over crude roads. Isn't the *Princess Royal* supposed to sail from Hamilton?"

"Yes. How big a town is Hamilton?" Thatcher asked.

"From all I've heard, they've a population of near thirty-five hundred people. Hamilton isn't near as old as St. George's, but it's got far better anchorages and greater docking capacity, I hear. They say the water along the length of the harbor front there is enough to accommodate deep-draft vessels and let them tie up to wharves, so the expense of lightering freight back and forth is saved."

Later, thanks to a moderate sea, a battered ferry sloop discharged Ira and David, with other passengers, at the foot of Queen Street on a cluttered dock paralleling the waterfront. The two officers, still in civilian clothes, found accommodations in the unimaginatively designed but clean-appearing Hamilton Hotel.

After checking in, they sauntered along Front Street over a splintery wooden sidewalk. "Things look a damn' sight busier here than they do in St. George's," Dexter observed.

It was indeed apparent that people here seemed more smartly dressed than at the East End. Pedestrians included a good many stiff-backed, scarlet-jacketed and gold-laced officers of the Thirty-ninth Regiment of the Line. More numerous were blue-clad naval officers and other ranks ashore from a huge, third-rate ship of the line, swinging to her anchors off Darrell's Island. Thoughtfully, Thatcher's lively, dark-brown eyes considered a small forest of masts and spars raking the sky.

David was right. The tempo of life here in Hamilton *was* considerably livelier than in St. George's. For example, an amazing number of shops and large stores were advertising a surprising variety of foreign-made goods.

It didn't take the two Americans long to deduce that here on these lonely, lovely little islands the British had established a base capable of supplying even the most formidable battle squadrons assigned to the American and West Indies Station.

At the moment this fleet was absent, patroling the Canadian coast and within easy striking distance of New England's most important ports. Soon they learned that this squadron included the flagship H.M.S. *Nile,* mounting ninety guns; and the *Hero* and the *Aboukir,* of eighty-six guns each. Such a force, if concentrated and well-directed against the presently weak and dispersed United States Navy, undoubtedly could blast the latter out of the water.

Shipping agents' signs showed names on the second floors of many buildings along Front Street. Other activities also were advertised by placards and posters. For example, Gilbert R. Frith, Jr., a real estate agent, stood ready to sell any number of commercial or private properties. The Phoenix Insurance Company, Ltd., of London was prepared to insure almost any vessel against fire, shipwreck, piracy, or barratry — but *not* against hurricane damage!

Augustus W. Meader announced himself able to extract all manner of painful teeth; next door, and probably not by accident, was located the office of one R. S. Musson, a "Specialist in the Creation and Insertion of Artificial Teeth"!

A large grocery store was announcing the arrival of a consignment of "Worcestershire Sauce" — a spicy new condiment concocted by Messrs. Lea & Perrins; also of Major Grey's East India Chutney and Frith's Bermuda Hot Pepper Sauce.

Against the background of rain-stained, wind-torn old notices fluttering on a sizable billboard had been tacked a fresh placard advising that the steam sloop *Racer* was due from New York any day now. Streams of traffic kept moving to and from the docks; many vehicles were creaking under heavy loads of cotton bales. What chiefly attracted Thatcher and his companion's attention was a big notice announcing that the Royal Mail steam packet *Princess Royal,* flying the Cunard Line's house flag, was expected to depart in about two days' time, resuming her regular run between England, Bermuda, and New York.

Always a light sleeper, Ira Thatcher awoke to the realization that a pallid winter sun was rising in the general direction of St. George's. Yawning, he rolled over and cast a glance at David Dexter lying on his back, sound asleep and snoring like a buzz saw striking a knot. He was occupying a lumpy folding cot that the hatchet-faced assistant manager of the Hamilton Hotel had produced, once a suitable tip had changed hands.

Ira grinned because David, a generous six feet tall, had his bare feet sticking out from under the blankets, with pink toes cramped tightly over, thanks to the chilly and very humid atmosphere. Yawning again, Ira stretched, got up, and went over to yank the pull bell for hot water. Since neither had duties beyond reporting their presence to the United States Consul, there seemed no point in rousing Dexter, especially since his last night's indulgence in several drinks "over the nines." Moodily, and in no great hurry, Ira shaved, dressed, and made his way below to a breakfast of scalding hot coffee, fried amber fish, corn bread, and a generous slab of tough native ham.

Presently, his gloom began to lift — until he began to recall certain remarks and reactions in the Globe's taproom. He experienced a growing sense of uneasiness. If *only* he could feel a shade more sure about his classmate's innermost convictions about this war. He recalled an oval, gold-framed ivory miniature of Louisa Cable Ridgely, of Virginia, which invariably reposed close to Dexter's bedside. Might she be the cause of his classmate's seeming diffidence about what might occur in New York?

A discarded copy of the *Royal Bermuda Gazette* lay on a nearby table. He propped it against his coffee pot and quickly discovered it to contain news items which must have been received before the *Coral Queen*'s arrival. It reported that Her Majesty Queen Victoria remained prostrated by grief at Windsor following the death of the Prince Consort. Passionately, Her Majesty had vowed to wear mourning forever in her dear Albert's memory. Gentlemen of the court had been ordered to put away gaily colored and fashionable garments and to wear only black for an indefinite period. None of them, while complying, could foresee that, much to the dismay of fashionble tailors and to the great relief of a good many slender pocketbooks, well-bred men on all formal occasions for generations to come would continue to wear funeral black full-dress "hammer-claw" coats or somber short-tailed jackets, later to become known as "dinner coats," on less formal occasions. Keeping up with court dandies could be hideously expensive.

Moodily, Ira turned the page and read that Mr. William Bluck's bookstore had received a generous supply of religious tracts, novels, and stirring new romances written by Sir Walter Scott, as well as an assortment of elegant stationery. He scanned, without interest, announcements of local importance, such as the fact that a Mrs. John F. Burrows had given birth to a baby boy, while Mrs. William F. Zuill recently had been blessed with a daughter.

He found it equally uninteresting to read that various merchants were now able to offer cake cannisters, mousetraps, bellows, horse collars, paste strainers, loaf sugar, and, slightly more important, a supply of medicines, including an Essence of Paregoric, Balm of Syriaticus, and Perry's Concentrate of Copaiba.

Thatcher's thin, ruler-straight lips tightened on suddenly encountering a brief article reporting that Union forces had suffered another defeat, at Harpers Ferry in Maryland. Although apparently it had not been a big battle, yet the loss must be serious. Harpers Ferry was the site of one of the most important Federal Government arsenals in the East.

David was still audibly asleep. Ira pulled on a cloth traveling cap — his expensive London-made stovepipe hat being reserved for special occasions — and set off down Queen Street. With half an eye, anyone could tell how greatly Bermudians were profiting from this war. Every few minutes, it seemed, the eerie moaning of conch shell bugles announced the tying up of still another ship to the freight-heaped docks along Front Street.

Chancing to glance up a side street, Ira noticed a small crowd congregated before a large, pink office building which, as usual, had housekeeping apartments occupying its upper two or three floors. Curious, he turned up Reid Street and quickly discovered the explanation for this early gathering. Above the building's entrance hung a freshly patinaed sign reading: "Commercial Agent, Confederate States of America."

Further up the street he could see an American flag dangling from a second-story window. His pulses quickened as beneath the flag he saw an oval metal plaque: "Consulate of the United States of America," and just below it the name of Charles Maxwell Allen. Ira's thick gold-washed pocket watch showed the hour to be eight-thirty. Um. Though it might be a mite early, perhaps he could risk presenting his respects. From recollections of happenings in the Globe's taproom, he somehow felt confident that even at this hour the American Consul might welcome a friendly caller.

As was customary, most Consuls occupied living quarters situated either above, or very close to, their official offices. When Mr. Allen appeared, still setting a cravat, he looked somewhat forbidding, what with his long, faintly hooked nose, piercing blue eyes, high cheekbones, and a narrow, jutting jaw to which traces of shaving soap were still adhering. He had "New England Yankee" written all over him.

"Please take a seat, sir." Mr. Allen waved the caller to a straight-backed chair placed before a desk piled high with documents of various colors. "Well, now, Mister, who am I addressing?"

Ira clicked heels, stood stiffly to attention. "Sir, Lieutenant Ira Thatcher of the United States Navy reporting."

The Consul's thin, pale-pink lips made an effort to form a smile. "You are welcome, sir, but where is your friend, Mr. David Dexter, who is also a naval officer, I believe?"

This Consul seemed to be remarkably well-informed.

"Sir, I'm sure Lieutenant Dexter will report later. When I left him, he was still sound asleep."

The hard blue eyes bored into his. "Ah, I see. Did you enjoy a pleasant voyage on the *Coral Queen?*"

"Hardly a pleasant one, sir, but uneventful." Uncertainly he gazed at that spare figure sitting so erect beneath a shield displaying the Great Seal of the United States.

"May I ask, sir, how you learned that we arrived aboard the *Coral Queen?*"

The Consul shot well-starched cuffs and held up a sheet of paper. "I have here a complete list of passengers. You see, we have some useful informers, although not near as many as the Rebels — an unfortunate situation I am working to remedy. Do I take it correctly that you and Lieutenant Dexter are proceeding to New York for reassignment?"

"Yes, sir, such is the fact."

"You both have been Naval Attachés — you in Paris and Dexter to the Court of St. James's?"

"Aye, aye, sir."

"Glad to hear it. Our country stands in serious need of regular naval officers, especially those with foreign experience."

Ears flapping, a beagle puppy came bounding in, eyed the newcomer and, barking and nuzzling, jumped up and down till Mr. Allen patted the intruder before firmly ejecting him. "Mr. Thatcher, what was your assignment abroad?"

"Sir, I served as assistant to the Naval Attaché at our legation in Paris; I've specialized in engineering."

"I presume you found your duties instructive and socially agreeable?"

Thatcher flushed to the roots of his wavy, dark-brown hair. "Yes, sir. Paris is a delightful place. Very different from any city I've ever visited."

The Consul readjusted steel-rimmed spectacles, then squinted at the passenger list. "Hum. I notice here the name of a Miss Arlette d'Aubrey of Paris. Tell me, was the fact that you were traveling on the same ship entirely accidental?"

A deep flush stained Ira's features. "As far as I am concerned, such was the case, sir. Of course, once on board we became quite good friends; she has a vivacious and engaging personality."

"This friendship, was it in any way — intimate?"

"No, sir. She appeared largely occupied with an English journalist."

"Mr. Lionel Humphrey of the *Telegraph?*"

"Yes, sir." Ira was staggered. Who could have furnished the Consul with so much detailed information? No telling.

Steepling fingers under his chin, Allen deliberated momentarily. "During your tour of duty in Paris you must have encountered many important officials, naval or otherwise?"

Sweat began to bead Ira's forehead. "Why, yes, sir, quite a few — mostly engineers or naval architects."

"Learn anything of note?"

"Not much, but I could, with time..."

"Time is just what we're desperately short of." Wintry sunlight, beating through the window, drew flashes from the spectacles Mr. Allen had just replaced on his hawk's beak of a nose. "Paris is indeed a charming city, so expert in catering to a wide variety of tastes. And what were your duties there?"

Ira felt miserably flustered. Was he duty-bound to describe details of his mission for the Navy Department, to learn how much could be ascertained about the design, armament, and thickness of armor of an armored steam frigate named *Gloire?* Should he inform this minor official that, following the great effectiveness of armor-clad floating batteries during the siege of Sevastopol, the Imperial French Government had decided that if such batteries had possessed motive power of their own, they undoubtedly could have accomplished far more destruction?

Need Mr. Allen be informed that the French had designed a new kind of warship, built along the lines of an ordinary wooden frigate, protected from prow to stern and from water level to gun deck by bands of heavy armor at least four inches thick? Wouldn't going further into details constitute a breach of security? "Sir, I was ordered to make only an unofficial visit to Le Havre and view the new warship," he said, deciding to be evasive.

"You boarded her?"

Thatcher hesitated. Had Mr. Allen been a senior Naval officer, matters would have been different. "No, sir," he lied, "I only viewed the *Gloire* at a distance, but to my mind, sir, she appears a very formidable battleship. Experts assured me she could easily sink the largest wooden man-o'-war afloat."

Mr. Allen again steepled long, tobacco-stained forefingers under his chin, and vented a short, mirthless laugh. "I believe, Mr. Thatcher, you are attempting to pull my leg. I'll bet my bottom dollar you *have* been aboard the *Gloire*. Please tell me the truth."

Ira shifted his gaze up to the Great Seal above Mr. Allen's desk. "Sir, I'd greatly like to satisfy your curiosity, but I have received strict orders to divulge nothing concerning the *Gloire* save in an official report directed to the Secretary of the Navy."

To his astonishment, Mr. Allen extended a bony hand across the desk and said quietly, "I understand and respect your reticence, young sir.

Wish to God there were more like you in our services. Can you, in all propriety, confide anything more upon the subject of ironclads?"

"No, sir, only that the British were deeply alarmed over reports about the formidable construction and armament of the *Gloire* which reached the Admiralty some two years ago. Only recently we learned in Paris that the Royal Navy not long ago had completed the *Warrior,* as a counter to the *Gloire.* They now are in the process of constructing two similar ironclads; one is to be called the *Black Prince,* I believe. I am convinced nearly every sea power in Europe knows about the *Warrior's* thickness of armor, her armanents, and speed."

"How so?" Mr. Allen queried. "I thought details of her construction had been kept very secret."

"They were, sir, but effective security is almost nonexistent in both French and British navy yards."

"I fear," Allen said, "because of an unfortunate tendency of our people to brag, effective protection of our yards at home will prove even less efficient."

Allen went over to peer down the narrow street through a none-too-clean window. "I notice that the office of my esteemed neighbor, Major Walker, is being besieged — as usual." He uttered a barking little laugh. "Won't find many seafarers and merchants lingering in front of this consulate. Thank God the seceding states haven't yet been recognized as a sovereign nation. Until that happens, which God forbid, Walker won't dare to display the Confederate flag."

From upstairs young voices sounded, and a woman's clear voice directed, "Edgar! Sit up straight. Billy, you aren't starving. Compose yourself until the toast is served, then eat your eggs tidily."

"My wife," Mr. Allen smiled, "is a firm but gentle despot — couldn't do without her."

The Consul folded hands before him, and then, leaning forward, lowered his voice. "As I said previously, Mr. Thatcher, I respect your reticence concerning the matter under discussion. Would to God more of our people in high and responsible offices would remain close-lipped."

"Is loose talk all that common, sir?"

"I have been reliably informed that almost anybody can wander anywhere they please about our construction yards — also down South, thank God. Visitors are almost never required to produce credentials. Alas, too many of our officers and officials are eager to achieve social, military, or political advancement through disclosing secrets. Others are even more keen to make money that way.

"Mr. Thatcher, will you be good enough to inform me how much is known in Europe concerning the mysterious ironclad the Rebels are reported to be constructing at Gosport in Virginia? You know the place?"

"Ought to, sir. I was born in Norfolk. My father was stationed there a long time."

"What rumors have you heard abroad?"

"Only the wildest sort of yarns — few are worth a second thought."

The Consul waved toward a comfortable armchair. "Seat yourself, sir, and join me in a glass of sherry, though ultra-pious folk back home might not approve."

Once he had filled a pair of small, gold-rimmed glasses, Mr. Allen reseated himself and took a modest sip. "Can't tell you, Mr. Thatcher, how very comforting it is to talk with a fellow Yankee — I mean Unionist. I forgot you stated you were born in Virginia. Anyhow, I do thank God to see a friendly face! Believe me or not, you can't conceive how greedily most Bermudians lean toward the Southern cause." His angular features tightened. "Twice within the past two weeks I have been insulted and almost mobbed on the street."

Fixedly, the Consul regarded his guest. "Where do your true sympathies lie?"

"As I've said, my father is from the South and served with distinction in the United States Navy for over twenty-five years. My mother is from New Hampshire, and so, sir, I'll have to wait till I get home before making a final decision about which way I'll go. Sorry not to give you a firm answer."

"I admire your honesty, young sir. What can you tell me about the United States frigate *Merrimac*, which I'm told the Rebels have rechristened *Virginia?*"

"Just what would you like to know, sir? My friend David Dexter should be able to inform you, since he served aboard her on a Mediterranean cruise about three years ago."

Mr. Allen made a note under the name "Dexter" on an officially headed document. His deep-set, steel-gray eyes sought Ira, sitting uncomfortably upright with his sherry still untasted.

"Tell me this much, if you can." He tapped the paper. "Here is a report stating that the *Merrimac* displaces around thirty-five-hundred tons and is about one hundred and seventy feet long. Is this correct?"

"I believe, sir, that is approximately correct."

"We also have learned she is being designed to mount a total of ten guns — a pivot gun fore and aft and four Brooke rifle guns on each side."

"As to that, we've heard nothing in Paris, sir." Almost too quickly Ira asked, "Does this report you speak of mention gun calibers, sir?"

"No. I presume the marine architects who are reconstructing the frigate can take their pick of all those fine cannon in the Gosport Navy Yard when it was set afire and captured by Virginian troops last spring."

Although the puppy continued to scratch and whine at the door, Mr. Allen only settled deeper into his chair, thoughtfully fingering an imposing seal suspended from a heavy gold watch chain.

"By the way, have you breakfasted?"

"Yes, sir."

"Nevertheless, please join me in a cup of coffee which, I might add, is brewed marvelously well in these Islands." The Consul tinkled a small brass bell whereupon, almost suspiciously soon, it seemed to Thatcher, a gaunt black woman appeared, wearing a blue bandanna knotted around her head.

If the Consul was aware of this remarkable promptness, he said nothing but, "Josie, fetch coffee and some cinnamon buns for this gentlemen and myself."

In the street below sounded the rasp of iron-tired wagon wheels upon cobblestones, the clopping of hoofs, and an ever-increasing hubbub of street cries mingled with the despairing squawks of fowls being conveyed to market.

The Consul offered a china jar filled with slim, dark-brown cigars. "Care for a seegar?"

"No, thank you, sir. Don't smoke." He tried to grin. "No minor vices."

Ira fought a mounting desire to escape those steel-gray eyes peering so relentlessly from behind rectangular lenses. Next came the question he'd been dreading all along.

Settling back in his chair, Allen remarked, "Seemed to me during my arrival in the Globe's taproom the other evening that I noticed quite a difference between your attitude toward me and that of your friend. His name's Dexter, isn't it?"

"Yes, sir. David Holcomb Dexter. He was born in Beverly, Massachusetts, and is descended from an old China trade family."

"His mother?"

"I believe she was a Miss Belle Stevens, born to a family socially prominent in New Haven, Connecticut." He hastened to amplify: "Dexter's father was a captain in our Navy during the war with Mexico."

"So? Is this Captain Dexter still in the Service?"

"No, sir. He became disabled by rheumatism and retired some years ago. He now lives in New York City, where I believe he is now establishing a shipbuilding concern."

The Consul again went over to peer down the street, observing the crowd thickening before the Confederate agent's office. Over his shoulder he invited, "Please, Mr. Thatcher, kindly inform me further concerning your friend. I really must know, since in the Globe Hotel I saw the pair of you seated in company with two officers in Confederate uniforms."

"Perhaps so, sir. But I have no reason to doubt where Dexter's true loyalty lies."

"That's no answer, is it? North or South?"

"With the North, sir," Ira replied without hesitation. "I'm completely confident of that. David is a Yankee born and bred and educated at Phillips Academy, and later in the Academy at Annapolis. We were classmates."

"Um. Very interesting. I will bear this in mind while making out a certain report. All the same, I noticed that your friend was conversing affably with Major Walker. Wonder whether he really will call here."

"He will, sir! I'll stake my career on it."

"No need to risk so extreme a step."

The Consul asked, after blowing loudly on the huge cup of coffee Josie placed before him, "I believe you said he once served aboard the U.S.S. *Merrimac*."

Miserably uncomfortable, Ira left his steaming coffee untasted. "Yes, sir, he did, at the same time as I served on the *Congress*."

"And then?"

"I was posted to our legation in Paris as engineer-assistant to the Naval Attaché. David was ordered to duty in London."

"Any notion of what Dexter's duties were in England?"

"I suspect his assignment was much the same as mine."

"Which was . . . ?"

"To learn, from an engineering point of view, everything possible about those newly constructed foreign ironclads — design, engine power, speed, and the thickness of their armor. In David's case, the ship was the H.M.S. *Warrior;* in mine, it was the *Gloire.*"

"Good," Allen said. "I hope you both learned a great deal. I have been unofficially informed that should the French and English governments decide to ignore the President's proclamation of blockade as being ineffective, either of those two armored steam frigates you've mentioned should be able to sink our heaviest men-o'-war."

Mr. Allen's gaze sought the floor of well-polished cedar. "This would allow floods of war materials of all sorts to enter Southern ports, which certainly would lead to *de facto* recognition of the Confederacy as a sovereign nation, with all the rights on the high seas of a legal belligerent."

Such a possibility had been nagging at the back of Ira's mind ever since he'd first heard about these ironclads being discussed in Parisian political and social circles. Good God! How ghastly the fate of a wooden man-of-war's crew would be — to see their heaviest shot glance ineffectively off an armored enemy, while their own ship was being riddled into helplessness. Now that it was almost certain the Southerners were about to complete such an ironclad, what would be the result? Such a warship might appear insignificant in tonnage, but her potential for destruction would remain gigantic!

He was recalled to the present by Mr. Allen's clipped, precise tones. "Mr. Thatcher, would you and your friend Mr. Dexter care to take supper with Mrs. Allen and me tonight? It would be a great pleasure for us to entertain not one but *two* officers of our Navy," he added, with subtle but unmistakable emphasis.

Ira stood, and offered a head bow. "Sir, I am *certain* we both will be honored to accept your kind invitation."

6

Cross-Seas

It was ten o'clock by the thick, gold-plated watch David Dexter's father had given him to commemorate his graduation from the Naval Academy. The room was chilly, so after ringing for hot water he ducked back under the bedclothes until a fuzzy-haired, full-breasted colored girl, wearing a scarlet-and-yellow bandanna turban, appeared lugging a bucket of slowly steaming water.

David pulled on a dressing gown of silken brocade over a frilled and long-skirted nightshirt purchased in Bond Street. Strange, he thought, that so many English gentry were obsessed by the importance of the cut and smartness even of undergarments. Of one thing Dexter felt proud: his dark-blue naval uniforms had all been cut from the best materials and expensively tailored in Savile Row. How much would they eventually be used?

The chambermaid mumbled, still staring fixedly at the floor, "Please, Masta, yo' frien' next door, he done gone out."

"Say where?"

"Yassuh. He say he goin' look up Misto Allen."

"Mr. Allen?" Dexter muttered, knuckling hot and sleep-swollen eyes. "Who's he?"

"Why, Misto, he de pun-top Yankee officer in Bermuda. He what dey calls a counciller."

"Consul, don't you mean?"

"Yas, Misto, that's hit." Grinning, the girl set about kindling a fire of cedar sticks.

When she had finished, Dexter extended slightly trembling hands toward the little blaze in the fireplace. "Please fetch up some breakfast."

"Yassah. I brings up a real 'Mudian breakfast.'"

"What's that?"

"Cream codfish and fried bananas, suh," she grinned, and shuffled out.

God's love! He must have tucked away plenty of liquor last night; his mouth felt like a last year's bird's nest. Although he had learned to calculate to a nicety his capacity for brandy, whiskey, and heavy wines, he simply must learn to go easy on rum-based drinks. Since Ira had already gone to report, he'd better hurry to pay his respects at the United States Consulate.

Only gradually was he coming to realize that at least a part of his conduct in the Globe Hotel's taproom might have aroused suspicions. In his present situation, what a great fool he'd been to be seen in public fraternizing with men wearing gray uniforms.

After stirring up lather in a steaming mug, he opened a handsome morocco-bound case containing seven razors, one marked for each day of the week. These had been presented as a farewell gift by certain convivial junior officers of the Royal Navy. On the ivory handles of each of these deadly sharp blades had been etched a brightly colored American eagle clutching an effective but heraldically incorrect national shield.

A sense of uneasiness mounted in him, partly due to his hangover, no doubt, but nonetheless he felt more than ever beset by amorphous doubts.

Would it be honorable to resign a commission for which the nation had paid to train him? True, many fine senior naval officers like Matthew Maury, Josiah Tatthall, and others had already seen fit to resign and go South to serve their State. But, dammit, as far as he knew, all were Southern-born. He wasn't, but in his case, there remained the problem of Louisa Ridgely, child of the Tidewater aristocracy.

Wiping off traces of lather, David felt more uncertain than ever. His misery increased when he went over to study the delicate oval and gold-framed miniature of Louisa on the nightstand beside his bed. He remembered how radiant she'd appeared last autumn in London, on their last evening together at the Duke of Winterbotham's stately, glittering ball.

How rapturously they'd shared any number of waltzes — a new dance step becoming increasingly popular despite the severe disapproval of Queen Victoria. Never had Louisa appeared more exquisitely lovely, her golden-brown tresses dressed in modish side ringlets, and with a lovelock swaying over her left shoulder. A large chignon at the nape of a long and very white neck was impaled with a sturdy pin, tipped by a heart-shaped ruby. As they whirled around and around, her bouffant skirts swaying and lifting just high enough briefly to expose shapely ankles, he'd come to realize for the first time that Louisa's eyes really weren't dark blue, but a very deep and exciting shade of violet.

He could see himself, too, wearing a brand-new dress uniform and kid white gloves. His thick brown hair had been carefully combed but was marred by that ever-persistent cowlick from which he still suffered, despite what British hairdressers — as barbers were called over there — could accomplish toward curbing that unruly strand.

Once he had been a visitor to "Gunner's Hill," the Ridgely's somewhat pretentious pillared plantation house near the lovely, sleepy Virginia village called Culpeper. There, no one hurried even on cold days; dogs were said to be too lazy to scratch fleas. Following retirement, Major Ridgely had planted fine Burleigh tobacco there with considerable success, and small wonder, since for three generations the Ridgelys of "Gunner's Hill" had been cultivating the weed.

Again his mind reverted to the Duke of Winterbotham's ball, when he'd suggested, "Shall we go sample some fresh air?" Without waiting for a reply, he had conducted Louisa onto a secluded balcony, where he'd clasped her tightly and awkwardly but convincingly declared his undying love, devotion, and intention of marrying her.

Louisa, with a reassuring lack of hesitation, had accepted him and for the first time had permitted him to kiss her mouth; previous polite pecks of lips brushing her cheeks didn't count. Soon their engagement was announced to a few intimate friends, and letters disclosing this breathtaking news were dispatched, although weeks would pass before they could hope to reach America.

By now he'd learned that Louisa's older brothers, Francis and Charles, for some time had been wearing gray uniforms. Peter, the youngest and handsomest, aged fifteen, probably would have stayed on at the Virginia

Military Institute, but he might have been recalled to help manage "Gunner's Hill" if all other males had gone off to war.

Perpetually florid-complexioned, Major Marcus Ridgely was a rabid pro-secession fire-eater from "way back." So, beyond any doubt, he'd never consent to Louisa's marrying a man wearing Federal blue, no matter how well-connected he might be.

Buttoning up a checkered shirt, David stared out over irregular rows of stepped and white-washed roofs, which, he now knew, had been so designed to catch more effectively whatever rain fell, there being no freshwater ponds, creeks, or springs of any description on any of the Bermuda's almost innumerable islands, reefs, and islets — three hundred and sixty-five of them, one for each day of the year, some said.

Dexter paused after selecting a flowing gray silk four-in-hand necktie. Oh, hell! What to do? Again, family traditions must be taken under consideration. Dexters had commanded privateers during the War for Independence and the War of 1812 and a regular sloop of war during those ignoble hostilities with Mexico. Three granduncles on his mother's side had held commissions in the United States Army and had served, some with distinction. One, Granduncle Benjamin, had earned a Major-General's commission, the highest rank possible in the Regular Army. Another had held the amorphous grade of "Commodore" in the United States Navy. Why had a Government, which thought nothing about commissioning generals by the dozen, never appointed anyone, no matter how worthy, even to the grade of Rear Admiral? Only recently had it yielded to pressure — and necessity — by creating the new grade of Flag Officer, supposedly ranking equally with a Major-General.

Father's family, of course, had been in the China trade for time-out-of-mind, which explained, perhaps, why he'd been brought up in a fine big house on the outskirts of Beverly, Massachusetts. The family's wealth, however, had never been flaunted. Should a Dexter care to parade riches, he'd better move to New York, Richmond, Chicago, St. Louis, or New Orleans.

Sighing, David picked up a small, slightly dented silver flask but put it down. Small point appearing in the Consul's office with liquor on his breath. With care, he knotted his silk cravat, at the same time wishing he dared wear his smart, dark-blue uniform, but from what he'd seen and heard here and in St. George's, the risk of getting pelted with mud and horse manure was all too great. Instead, he donned a pair of Scottish plaid trews, a black frock coat, and a canary-yellow satin weskit which might have attracted favorable comment in some of London's elite social clubs, such as White's and Boodle's.

Thoughtfully, David rubbed specks of dust from the toe of a shiny black shoe — must do the old Service credit. Then, setting a gray top hat at a jaunty tilt, he went below to inquire of the desk clerk where the American Consulate might be located.

The fellow gave him a startled look. "American? Say, Mister, don't you mean the Confederate States Agent's office?"

"No. I mean the United States Consulate."

Once the clerk had jotted down the address, David Holcomb Dexter, Lieutenant, United States Navy, marched rather than walked out of the hotel.

Few people in Bermuda — officials, government employees, tradesmen, or ordinary citizens — suspected that easygoing and invariably courteous Charles Maxwell Allen, United States Consul to Her Majesty's Government in Bermuda, was so efficient and such a shrewd observer of what might be going on.

Smiling thinly, Mr. Allen arose from behind his desk, and offered a bony hand to this tall and straight-standing young fellow with wide-set hazel eyes and luxuriant dark-brown hair. His caller's long and deeply tanned features appeared open enough, Allen thought, but experience had taught him that one shouldn't be guided too much by first impressions.

"Well, sir?"

"Lieutenant David Dexter reporting, sir."

The Consul, without appearing to, listened with acute interest, paying special attention to Dexter's description of his duties as Assistant Naval Engineer Attaché to the United States Legation at the Court of St. James's. He made and underlined a mental note that, as Thatcher had implied, this handsome young Lieutenant *had* made a cruise as observer aboard the H.M.S. *Warrior,* England's formidable new steam frigate. Questioning him about details of the *Warrior*'s dimensions, the thickness of her armor belt, and the caliber of her guns, Allen soon became aware his caller sometimes gave him devious or evasive replies.

"And her maximum speed?" Allen demanded mildly.

"Why, sir, her Chief Engineer boasted the *Warrior* can turn up fourteen to sixteen knots under steam and all sails set."

Allen steepled together yellow-stained fingers under his chin. "Very interesting. And is the Admiralty planning the construction of more vessels of the same design?"

Somewhat disconcerted, Dexter admitted, "I — well, sir, at the Legation we came to suspect that others in her class are being laid down in secret."

"How many more?"

"Two, sir, possibly three. Sorry, sir, but when I left there was no definite information on that score to be had." Dexter's gaze sought the Great Seal of the United States on a metal plaque above the Consul's desk.

Abruptly, Allen switched the subject. "Your father still alive?"

"Yes sir."

"Served in the Navy, didn't he?"

"Aye, aye, sir. He was a Captain when he was forced to retire on account of crippling rheumatism."

"Pity. As I told your friend, we stand in grave need of veteran officers. What did Captain Dexter do after retiring?"

"Father turned his attention to shipbuilding. He and some partners have just completed a sizable shipyard in New York."

"I take it your present orders are to proceed to New York for reassignment?"

Dexter barely succeeded in keeping his voice level. "Yes, sir, guess that's about the size of it."

"Somewhere I've heard that you, your friend Thatcher, a French lady, and an English newspaperman all have booked passages to New York on the mail packet *Princess Royal.* That true?"

Startled, Dexter managed to reply evenly, "Yes, sir, I expect so, though such passages call for expensive bribery."

The Consul went to look down the street once more, and noted that the crowd before the Confederate Agent's office was still increasing. Over his shoulder he said, "I believe Lieutenant Thatcher stated you once served on our steam frigate, U.S.S. *Merrimac?*"

"Yes, sir. On a short cruise to Malta. I worked with her engineering staff."

"How sound were her engines?" Mr. Allen's voice had acquired an edge. "Were they capable, reliable?"

Dexter hesitated. "Not very. So much so it was decided to replace them as soon as the *Merrimac* returned for refitting at Gosport Navy Yard."

"Do you know why?"

"Only that the engines lacked sufficient power to drive the *Merrimac* at her designated speed of twelve knots without sail, which was a great disappointment to the Navy's Engineering Board since although she, the *Cumberland,* and the *Roanoke,* her sister frigates, all lacked engines, they were the pride of our Navy."

Mr. Allen inserted another note into a mental file he'd begun compiling once Ira Thatcher had quit his office. He arose from behind his desk and gravely offered his hand. "I wish you and Mr. Thatcher and the rest of your party a speedy and pleasant voyage to New York, but I fear you won't enjoy the weather over the Gulf Stream in January; it can prove mighty uncomfortable."

Dexter took the outstretched hand, finding it as cold as any haddock on a marble slab. "Thank you, sir. Have you any reports, dispatches, or letters you wish delivered to New York?"

Allen's gaze wavered aside. "No, thank you all the same, Mr. Dexter. I am giving a small dinner tonight. Your friend has accepted, and for you, too."

"Aye, aye, sir." David Dexter smartly clicked his heels before departing into unseasonably bright sunshine.

Charles Maxwell Allen listened to his caller's receding footsteps, and then, from his window, watched the big, broad-shouldered figure swing down the street toward Major Walker's office, hesitating for a perceptible moment in front of the Confederate Agent's office before continuing down the street.

The Consul returned to his desk, locked hands behind his head, and stared into space. Damned if he could make up his mind about this young fellow named Dexter. He'd appeared likable and seemed impatient for reassignment; yet . . . Reaching into his desk, Allen sighed and pulled out a preliminary draft of his regular monthly report to the State Department.

After dipping his pen in a cast-iron inkwell shaped like a bullfrog, Allen scribbled: "Just now have received calls from two U.S. Naval Officers — both lieutenants returning from diplomatic duty abroad. One,

Lieutenant Ira B. Thatcher, has been on duty in France; the other, Lieutenant David H. Dexter, served in England. The first I judge to be trustworthy; about the other, I am not altogether satisfied. I may well be wrong, and I hope I am, for he is such an engaging and intelligent young fellow."

7

In the Gulf Stream

CAPTAIN NEWBOLD, Master of the Cunard steam packet, the brigantine-rigged *Princess Royal,* tugged at a plentiful spade beard and lingered on his bridge, watching the blue-gray outlines of Bermuda merge with the horizon.

A pilot who greatly favored some Pequot Indian ancestors buttoned a salt-stained pea jacket, rolled up charts, and, tucking a spyglass under an arm, drawled, "Well, good luck, Cap'n. Best watch out fer that Yankee blockader. She was sighted a few days ago, patrollin' 'bout fifty mile offshore."

"This time o' year, about how soon can we expect to encounter foul weather?" Captain Newbold inquired.

"Well, Cap'n, anytime once you enter the Stream, but you just might strike an easy spell — which ain't usual." He touched his cap's peak, then clumping in his heavy seaboots, made his way below to descend a swaying Jacob's ladder to the pilot boat, a larger version of the *Fancy Free.* Her sails filled at once and with lingering lacy clouds of spray over sharp bows, she scudded off over a bright blue and comfortably moderate sea. All fifteen passengers lining the rail flourished scarves or waved hats.

"Wonder how many of us will sight yonder islands again?" Dexter remarked.

"D'you know," said Lionel Humphrey, "I've an idea some of us will, and not before too long, either."

"Why so?" Thatcher inquired.

"Well, from what most of us have noted, shouldn't wonder if Bermuda doesn't become the most strategic and commercially important port off the North American coast before this wretched war is over. Presume you've all noticed how many fast vessels were putting into Hamilton and St. George's?"

Lord, thought Thatcher, how many hundreds if not thousands of brown-and-white bales of cotton hadn't he watched being lowered into the holds of vessels about to clear for Europe, mostly into English bottoms.

Significantly, during the length of his stay on the island, Ira couldn't recall seeing more than two or three Stars and Stripes displayed anywhere. So, beyond reasonable doubt, most Bermudians, as always, were keeping an eye on the main chance and clasping the nascent Confederate States to ever-hungry cash boxes.

Dexter darted a smile, devoid of implications, at Arlette. "Let us pray for fair weather, especially while we're crossing the Gulf Stream. I've heard the seas there can be really frightful."

Arlette nodded. "But yes! Our voyage from Europe seemed as an endless nightmare. I lost so much weight that few of my dresses fit properly — a terrible calamity."

Thatcher didn't feel called upon to point out the depressing fact that the *Princess Royal*, being screw-driven, would likely prove even less stable in a hard sea than a side-wheel steamship like the *Coral Queen*, whose paddles helped somewhat to stabilize her motion.

Arlette drew a few quick breaths of crisp salt air, and pointed upward. "See how graceful are those birds." Terns were swooping, wheeling, and screaming about the packet's topmasts as though reveling in the sheer joy of being alive.

The smile faded on Arlette's discreetly tinted lips as she wondered what fate might be in store for her in the vast reaches of the young and raw United States. Would she be able to remain sufficiently subtle, discreet, and charming to advance the interests of Marquis Edouard de la Villette?

Fervently, she hoped that Mme Charles Antoine, the *modiste* she'd been ordered to notify upon her arrival, would prove to be agreeable and knowledgeable about local affairs and facts of a practical nature. Long since, she had memorized Mme Antoine's address, Number 15 Cheslea Street. Pray

God it would prove to be in some decent, if not fashionable, neighborhood.

Her naturally ebullient spirits soaring, Arlette steadied herself on an arm deftly offered by the polite and well-dressed Dexter.

"And what at this moment can you be thinking about, Miss d'Aubrey?"

"You cannot imagine, Monsieur, how thrilling the excitement I experience at the prospect of dwelling in a great new city like New York. All too many of our big towns in France appear so old, dull, and weary! Nowadays, only in Paris, Marseilles, and Lyons can one enjoy a true *joie de vivre.*"

"It's lucky you're so eager to adjust yourself to a raw country. I trust you won't be too disappointed. We Americans are a very different and varied lot, even among ourselves."

"*Merci.* What nice things you say."

"Think I heard the dinner gong sound," Thatcher said.

Humphrey advanced over the tilting, well-holystoned deck. "May I escort you below?"

Both of them played their parts well. No one possibly could suspect their intimacies in the Grand Hotel.

"But of course, Monsieur Humphrey," Arlette responded. "Perhaps we shall become better acquainted during the latter part of our voyage."

One thing rankled Thatcher. During the voyage from Liverpool, he had noticed that the young Frenchwoman, whenever she appeared between the spells of seasickness which kept her below through the greater part of the voyage, had appeared more than friendly with Lionel Humphrey. Now he heard her saying:

"One feels confident that New York will prove an exciting place. Will many painted and feathered savages be seen?"

Thatcher laughed out loud. "Not a chance, Mademoiselle, lest you see a parade of Tammany braves decked out in their regalia."

"Tammany? Is that a tribe?"

"No. Only a political party which pretty much runs New York City. Most of 'em are crooked as a dog's hind leg. And where will you be staying?" he quickly added.

"Of that I do not as yet know, for sure, Monsieur Thatcher. A Madame Antoine is supposed to have engaged suitable lodgings for me. And you? Where will you be quartered?"

The deftness with which the Frenchwoman diverted conversation didn't escape Lionel Humphrey's attention, although he appeared engrossed by a school of porpoises disporting themselves alongside.

"Don't know yet either, Ma'am," Thatcher said, deciding to be evasive himself.

Arlette turned to David. "And where will you stay, Monsieur Dexter?"

"I presume I'll put up with my family. I hope my friend Thatcher will accept an invitation to stay with us as long as he remains in New York."

8

The Great Wave

THE MORNING AFTER the *Fancy Free* left Bermuda — to the vast relief of everyone aboard the stolen yacht — the sky turned a rich light blue and, better still, a moderate-to-stiff breeze began blowing steadily out of the southeast. Indeed, it seemed as though Providence was really smiling on them at last as, hour after hour, the horizon remained blessedly devoid of topsails or steamer smoke. All they sighted were a few brown, triangular sails, typical of local fishermen, making for Bermuda.

Following a breakfast of tea — boiled until it resembled varnish — stewed codfish, cassava pone, and chunks of bread, Bandmaster Keyes summoned all hands into the tiny cockpit. They sat there slouched on the coaming. All three convicts, in order to conserve civilian clothing, were still wearing filthy remnants of blue-and-yellow prison garb. For once, Kitty appeared nearly as bedraggled as her companions.

Harry Keyes, chunky body yielding easily to the *Fancy Free*'s gentle roll, spoke softly but forcefully. "Now, friends," he said, "let this be clearly understood. Until we set foot ashore, don't forget for one moment that *I* am the Captain and the Law aboard this ketch!"

Successively, he looked each of the gaunt, haggard, and unshaven wretches steadily in the eye. "Now, because I know I don't understand navigation near as good as Giles Healey here, I'm appointing him First Mate, Navigator, and Second-in-Command. We'll divide into two watches. I'll stand the starboard watch with Pitcher and Kitty. I'll teach her how to steer and to make herself useful. Healey, you and O'Dea will stand the port watch." His voice grew emphatic. "Now, listen well! You have got to forget Kitty's a female. She's just another seaman except when — when she's got natural matters to attend to private-like."

Indeed, seclusion aboard this fifty-foot ketch approached the impossible; the yacht's only "head" was a small closet situated beneath the forepeak, equipped with a pierced seat and a wooden bucket.

"The rest of us," he continued, "will hang our butts over the rail as usual, save in stormy weather."

Below, four narrow bunks lined a compartment built forward of the galley and the saloon, a cramped living-and-dining space. On the Bandmaster's orders, a hammock for Kitty was rigged in the main cabin to minimize the chances of intimate explorations being conducted after darkness closed in.

Keyes turned to Giles Healey, whose iron-gray hair was so long and greasy it stirred only reluctantly under this light breeze. "As a former licensed master of oceangoing vessels, I rely on you to plot our course. While I've picked up considerable knowledge, I still don't understand over much about deep-sea navigation."

He steadied the tiller against his knee. His previous free-and-easy manner was fading with the realization that since yesterday afternoon he'd become as much a criminal as any of these convicts.

The morning grew so warm that black-haired O'Dea ripped off his stained convict's jacket and, spouting obscenities, flung it overboard to float briefly amid patches of bright yellow-brown gulfweed. "And that, b'Jasus, marks the death of Dion O'Dea's first life." He leered at Kitty. "So, m'darlin', willing or not, ye've been midwife to a newborn human bein'."

When Pitcher also started to unbutton his convict's coat, ex-Captain Healey growled, "Quit that, you bloody fools! Remember, we're sailing almost due north and we're bound to strike plenty of freezing weather this time of year. Keep every rag you own!"

"Captain" Harry Keyes, as he now termed himself, had had enough foresight to purchase several more or less worn civilian coats and trousers at one of Bermuda's innumerable charity fairs. Scarcely a month passed without some bazaar being conducted for the benefit of some worthy cause.

O'Dea, hunching wide, muscle-corded shoulders, tucked a grimy undershirt into shapeless prison pants of brown Holland cloth. He was deciding that the rotund Bandmaster must be considerably smarter than he'd appeared. Yep, Keyes is aimin' to keep us from sharin' his dolly. Grinning, he winked at Kitty. She looked pretty and exciting even though huddled, pale-faced, beneath a thick shawl of Irish wool.

Just how he could get to her, O'Dea couldn't foresee right now, but he *would*, come hell or high water, he promised himself. It had been three long years since he'd shagged a female. Matters being as they were, 'twouldn't be long before his fellow fugitives would also appreciate the runaway nursemaid's attractions. From a fellow convict who had once acted as a footman at the Commissioner's house, he'd learned that Kitty could sing right sweetly and also could play lively tunes on an ocarina. "Captain" Keyes and that wiry Bermudian named Pitcher he figured to be the ones he would have to outwit.

Under strong gusts of wind, the former pilot boat heeled well over and spurted ahead, flinging lacy flecks of spray over her bows. Pitcher was thinking that this shanty Irishman's jabber hadn't been too wide of the mark when he'd claimed to have been "born again" — kind of.

What would America be like? In common with most seafaring Bermudians, Pitcher had heard a good many opinions, generally conflicting, about that vast country. Most people said that through the use of gray matter and plenty of sweat, a man could satisfy reasonable ambitions; so, equipped as he was with seafaring knowledge and an undeniable skill at shipbuilding and engineering, Christian Pitcher should make out all right, provided his criminal record remained concealed. Who aboard just might spill the beans?

He glanced sidewise at Kitty. The girl had reason enough to keep quiet. Right now, no one but himself was aware of that "lick of the tar brush" in this cheerful and full-blown wench's background. Certainly, when one considered Kitty Hamilton's light, olive-hued complexion, curly, golden-brown hair, and large, widely separated blue-green eyes that showed tiny splinters of gold in them, who would suspect her of being a quadroon — three-quarters white and one part black? Fortunately for her, her nose was fairly long, thin, and with small, flat nostrils. The only hint of the flaw in her background was her wide and rather thick dark-red lips. Christian figured a man would have to study the girl quite a while to take notice of this, because her figure was pleasing, thanks to gentle curves in most of the right places.

The first time Christian took notice of Kitty had been more than a year ago, about the same time he'd become an apprentice pilot. He recalled her standing and staring through a shop window at a display of spurious but tastefully designed jewelry.

As for "Captain" Harry Keyes, Kitty had held a peculiar attraction for him ever since he'd first noticed her tending the Commissioner's small daughter on the porch of the Mansion.

Since he'd been placed in charge of the *Fancy Free,* it had been easy to visit the Commissioner's residence and strike up an acquaintance which had culminated in a few discreet trysts, one of which had ended in passionate surrender, but seemingly against the young woman's will.

Bearing this in mind, Keyes had bought a midshipman's jacket and a pair of white duck pants he'd figured would be of about the right size, remembering her nude body. Tonight, Keyes decided, he would order Kitty to don those trousers and never, under any conditions, unbutton them, save when Nature called. Yes, the girl readily could pass for a slim young man, provided she bound her breasts flat enough. He felt sure she was eager to cooperate in that; she'd already braided her fair, shoulder-length hair into very tight braids and tucked them under an officer's peaked cap she had snitched off a hat rack in the Commissioner's mansion.

Christian Pitcher, however, had been around long enough to know that if a fellow got really heated up, neither breeches nor pants would prove a hindrance. The young Bermudian stretched, and watched porpoises frolicking alongside. How fine it felt to be free again! He made up his mind to die sooner than return to a foul-smelling, vice-ridden convict hulk, where sodomy prevailed and young prisoners were in such demand that quite a few murders occurred every few months.

As for former Captain Giles Healey, he also had silently vowed he would never go back to prison. Dammit, he *hadn't* been guilty of barratry! He was sure he knew who had, one dark night, opened seacocks on the steam brig *Brighton* and sent her to the bottom for a share in her insurance money. Unfortunately, he hadn't been able to prove his suspicions. Hollow-cheeked, with iron-gray bristles standing out like teeth on a fine-tooth comb, Healey wondered how Bella, his wife, and their twin daughters might be faring. Possibly not too badly; Bella's family owned a prosperous ship chandler's warehouse and dockyard hard by Bristol harbor.

But his present and most urgent problem was how to keep this worm-eaten tub afloat and sailing on the correct course; scanty supplies of food and water precluded a long voyage. At the nearest Healey could calculate, this trip would require about two weeks, granted fair weather, but God help all hands should wintry blizzards begin howling out of the west to drive the *Fancy Free* far off the American coast.

That Healey indeed was an expert navigator became evident as, patiently, he explained to the Bandmaster, after he had studied faded old charts, how he plotted the general course, allowing for bad weather and the Gulf Stream's powerful currents.

In the late afternoon of the fourth day out of Bermuda, the fugitives became uneasy when over the horizon astern appeared the tops of a tall ship undoubtedly traveling under steam, since a sinister trail of coal smoke streaked the serene sky from a tall funnel set between her fore and mainmasts.

God help us, thought Healey, if this stranger was a man-of-war. She was coming up so fast she'd find no trouble in overhauling the *Fancy Free* long before darkness could conceal the yacht.

Kitty tried hard to relieve the mounting anxiety by singing a few gay songs.

Spouting curses, Christian Pitcher felt his stomach beginning to churn. To occupy himself, he started whetting the already razor-sharp sheath knife Harry Keyes had bestowed, growling, "An' we get took by a Britisher, this time I'll be takin' some bloody bastards along."

Color drained slowly from the Bandmaster's rotund and roseate features as he threw several hitches about a large ballast stone. Then he fashioned a loop into which he intended to thrust a foot should the stranger indeed prove to be a British man-of-war. He asked Healey, while he gripped the tiller with bony hands, "Can't anything be done?"

"No. If yonder proves to be a bulldog, the best we can do is to show British colors and hope to God her skipper will think us such small fry that we'd not be worth the time lost through heaving-to and lowering a boat."

Kitty turned to Pitcher, her blue-green eyes very round, yet she spoke with surprising calmness. "If people come aboard, tell them I'm your promised bride and we've been eloping to escape Pa's wrath."

"Worth a try and we just might get away with it. Harry Keyes claims you're able at dramatics." Christian cast a look astern and saw that the stranger's hull had lifted into sight. She was a steam brigantine with a black hull, bearing along under snowy canvas, with spray flashing far from beneath sheer bows.

"You'd best go below, Kitty," Keyes said, "and climb into female duds fastest you can."

"Wish I was better at it, Christian," she smiled on the Bermudian, "if you get us out of this, I'll be ever so grateful. Just you wait and see."

He cast her a half-grin. "See that you do. Funny, I've just remembered something about you which I might forget if you treat me right."

Kitty, staring, felt her throat constrict. Then this fellow must know about her background. But she gave no sign of apprehension.

Almost as quickly as though the little ketch were lying into the wind, the steam brigantine raced closer — closer — so fast that Healey calculated grimly she must be turning up at least twelve or more knots. Once the black-hulled stranger had closed to within two miles, Healey, who had been studying her through a verdigris-speckled spyglass, suddenly uttered a resounding gasp over his shoulder. "Take heart, everybody! Whatever she is, she's no man-o'-war." He squinted again through his long glass. "Yep, she looks to me mighty like a screw-driven mail packet. Pitcher! Break out the Union Jack real quick!"

The steamer continued to thresh nearer, a dainty sight save where her lower canvas had been blackened by soot from her single funnel.

Pitcher suddenly cried, "Hey! I recognize that vessel! She's a Cunarder — a Royal mail packet! Usually runs from England to Bermuda and on to New York. Disremember her name though."

Quickly Keyes added, "No matter — just pray hard nobody aboard her recognizes this as the Commissioner's yacht."

The packet boat closed in rapidly and everyone held breath until, while still a half-mile distant, the swift vessel altered course toward the northeast. Her skipper apparently had decided that this ketch was not in distress — and he even had the courtesy to dip his flag before racing onward. Her name, painted large across her stern, presently became visible. In large gold letters it read, *Princess Royal of Liverpool.*

That night everyone felt so relieved that "Captain" Keyes removed the piano's cover and played accompaniment to Kitty's singing.

Early next day, the *Fancy Free*'s company suffered a more severe shock. Another ship was sighted astern, and Healey averred that, from her lines, this tall ship looked like a man-of-war. Could this possibly be the

American cruiser reported to be on blockade duty off Bermuda? he wondered. If so, what a futile gesture, when one considered the hundreds of square miles she was supposed to patrol.

After a little while, O'Dea growled, "Ain't no use prayin' this time. Look at all them gunports; least of her battery can blow us out o' the water. Sure an' our luck's run out!"

Everyone stared at that long row of white rectangles running along the frigate's black-painted side.

"Any use showing colors?" Keyes demanded.

Healey flicked a nod. "No harm in that." So the ragged Union Jack once more was broken out.

The stranger proved to be a big sail-and-steam frigate, which, deviating only a little from her course, ran out a few guns and came bearing down on the rolling, pitching little yacht.

Suddenly Healey shouted, "Maybe Satan's takin' care of his own. Whatever's her nationality, yonder vessel don't look like a Britisher!"

Pitcher demanded hoarsely, eyes very white and round in his dark features, "How can you tell?"

"By her lines and the cut and set of her canvas. Seen enough to know!"

The ex-skipper's identification proved correct. Less than a half hour later, the man-of-war rushed by, trailing angry clouds of jet smoke and flying a blackened and weather-beaten Stars and Stripes from her signal gaff.

After she had passed, Harry Keyes succeeded in reading her name: *San Jacinto*.

The ex-Bandmaster grunted, "I'll be damned if she ain't the very same warship what damned near started a war."

"War with who?" Kitty wanted to know.

"Betwixt England and America. As I recall, yonder *San Jacinto* on the high seas stopped a British merchant steamer called the *Trent* and took off two of her passengers, both Confederate States diplomats. There was plenty of angry talk for a while about England's going to war over such a flagrant violation of international law."

"Who were them high-mucky-muck diplomats?"

The Bandmaster furrowed heavy brows, and scratched at a balding head. "If I recall correct, they were named Mason and Slidell. Yes sir, we damned near went to war over that business. 'Tis said if the Prince Consort hadn't cooled down Her Majesty the Queen, and her Prime Minister, Lord Palmerston, we'd be fighting right now. As it turned out, Abe Lincoln, the Yankee President, apologized at once and ordered the seized Southerners surrendered and sent on their way. So, thanks to Prince Albert, God rest his soul, we're not at war with the United States — yet."

For the next two days, the *Fancy Free* continued to enjoy amazingly mild weather — so much so the piano was used again and again, and Kitty was able to comb some sort of order into her bright and wavy golden-brown locks, while the men shaved or trimmed beards and whiskers. This done, all hands picked lice from clothing, then ran a candle's flame along seams in the infested garments before boiling them to make doubly sure.

Pitcher, existing in a rising state of confidence, made increasingly bold advances toward Kitty, but was tactfully thwarted. More than once Keyes opined, "The Lord sure must be on our side. Never even heard tell of such a long spell of mild weather in the Gulf Stream durin' January. Ain't it grand to feel the warm sun on your back?"

"Yez can say that again," O'Dea laughed; he had been taking a brief swim. "I been feelin' dirtier'n Mother O'Leary's pig in a wallow after a rainstorm."

Spirits rose, especially whenever Kitty fetched on deck well-seasoned hot victuals, at such sharp variance from the tough and tasteless rations issued aboard convict hulks.

For several days longer, the unseasonable weather continued. Mornings, Healey instructed Keyes on the art of shooting the sun, and then marking the *Fancy Free*'s presumed position on a wrinkled map. Wiping a bow-pen's point, Healey said: "Right here is about where I figger we ought to lie now — maybe. I say maybe 'cause I've had to figure by dead reckoning. Pity, Harry, you weren't able to lay hands on a chronometer. That pocket watch of yours, though, seems like a real good chronometer. It *may* be off by a few seconds, which out here can make a whale of a difference in calculating longitude."

"My turnip's one of the best," the Bandmaster assured, "so we mayn't be far off course. How soon do you figger we'll sight land?"

"With a bit of luck, tomorrow or the day after — might raise land somewheres along the coast near New York, if we're lucky."

O'Dea exposed gapped and amber-hued teeth in a wide grin. "An' that be so, Saints Christopher and Patrick must be straddlin' our bowsprit!"

"Don't say such things till we're anchored in New York City," Giles Healey rasped, shoving aside a lock of iron-gray hair from a deeply furrowed forehead. "As it is, with a female aboard, even a pretty soiled one, we're fair tempting the Fates."

"Shut up, you ugly jailbird!" snapped Keyes. "Kitty's proved worth her salt time and again. Maybe she may appear a mite sloppy right now, like the rest of us, but 'twill all be different once we get ashore and cleaned up."

During the next day, an increasing number of coal-smoke clouds and snowy sails began to dot the horizon, but none seemed to be steering parallel, allowing the *Fancy Free* to continue along the course Healey had plotted.

All at once, O'Dea, for the moment holding the tiller, quit pulling on a foul-smelling clay pipe long enough to yell, "Hi! What's that thing coming up our left?" He pointed at an apparently limitless straight barrier of white-crested black water.

"Hell, 'tis only an odd-shaped ray of sunlight," Pitcher commented. "Nothin' to get yer balls in an uproar about."

"Like hell!" snapped Healey. "Saw just such a streak on the Indian Ocean years ago. Look again! If that's what *I* think it is, you'd best start prayin' hard and fast."

"What is it?" Kitty squeaked.

"Looks like a damn tall quake wave, that's what!" Healey shouted, his features working.

Rushing toward the *Fancy Free* at appalling speed was what appeared to be a towering battlement of water rising out of a wide expanse of normal dark-blue waves.

"Where would such come from?" quavered Pitcher, convulsively throwing an arm about the cockpit's coaming.

" 'Tis a great comber raised from the sea's bottom by an earthquake somewheres."

With uncanny speed, the huge, foaming line raced nearer. Healey shouted over a thunderous, ever-increasing tumult, "Bring her into the wind! Quick! Quick!"

Keyes, O'Dea, Pitcher, Healey, and even Kitty hauled frantically on the jib and the mainsheet lines, but before the old pilot boat could be brought to head more than a few degrees to confront the menace, the endless, towering comber, easily fifty feet high, curling and white-crested, roared up, up, and up until, amid a stunning smother of spray and water, it engulfed and rolled the little *Fancy Free* onto her beams' ends.

At the last instant, Kitty had followed Pitcher in plunging down the companionway and was overwhelmed by a wild, roaring confusion such as she'd never imagined could exist. She was flung over and over amid a wild tangle of smashing furniture, bedclothes, supplies, and surging icy water. She only half felt the yacht's fabric shaken like a toy in the grip of a giant. Then she was flung, spinning about the cabin, her eyes, nose, and mouth full of spume until her head cracked so hard against a stanchion that she all but lost consciousness.

Dion O'Dea, clinging with a death grip to the base of the mainmast, was only dimly aware of the cabin's ports smashing and of whole sections of the bulwarks being ripped away. Then, when the ex–pilot boat again was driven onto her beams' ends and rolled bottom-up, he swallowed so much water that he came close to drowning. But somehow he clung onto the mast's broken, splintering base. The *Fancy Free* kept on revolving until she righted herself after a fashion. Vaguely, Dion heard a fearful, grinding crackling of timbers and of heavy, crashing noises.

Keyes, half-drowned, was swept overside to the end of a lifeline he'd rigged at the last minute. Then, by some freak of the quake wave, he was washed back onto the wrecked cockpit, only to have spray and spume close in and half smother him again.

Once more the yacht rolled completely over until he was completely submerged. Then, for a third time, the well-built old pilot boat managed sluggishly to right herself and float with deck awash, the stumps of her masts stabbing a serene blue sky like jagged spearheads.

Of the Bandmaster, there was no sign.

Once O'Dea had done puking up what seemed like gallons of seawater, he peered dazedly about. He saw Healey's sodden body lying beneath the tiller's handle, with a lifeline still wound about him, limp as any puppet with its strings cut. Then O'Dea heard sounds from below suggesting that Christian Pitcher and the girl might have survived. What most shook O'Dea was a growing awareness that if Healey and the Bandmaster were gone, no navigators remained.

9

U.S.S. *Underwriter*

A LOOKOUT ON THE BRIDGE of the former New York Harbor ferryboat *Gowanus*, recently rechristened the U.S.S. gunboat *Underwriter*, reveled in the unseasonably mild weather. This side-wheeling, speedy ex-ferryboat was now a unit in what had come to be derisively nicknamed "Abe Lincoln's soapbox blockade," composed as it was of steam-powered tugs, yachts, revenue cutters, freighters, pleasure boats, and even Hudson River liners — or for that matter, any craft capable of mounting one or two cannons, usually wheeled field pieces.

The *Underwriter* was unusual in that she was large enough to carry a pair of ten-inch Parrott rifled guns, bow and stern, plus a pair of smoothbore eight-pounders amidships. Of course, as her crew was aware, should the U.S.S. *Underwriter* (whose former name was still visible amid gilded scroll work, even through a coat of barn-red paint too hurriedly applied) ever encounter a real man-of-war, she'd stand less chance of survival than an icicle in a furnace.

A lookout perched on top of the wheelhouse bellowed, "Hi, down there!"

The officer on deck, glowering, yelled back, "Say deck ahoy! you damn hayshaker."

"All right, Cap'n."

"What do you sight?"

"Dunno," yelled down this scrawny individual, wearing a bright red-and-white-checkered shirt. "Looks like a big hunk of wreckage."

"Where does she lie?"

"Off'n our bow, kind of southwest, I'd hazard — sir," he added hastily.

Acting Lieutenant Fremantle, in the *Underwriter*'s ornate pilothouse, leveled binoculars disinterestedly to study a distant, half-submerged brown-black object. He sighted what commanded his instant attention — there were people aboard that derelict. Somehow, they had rigged a tattered jib to the stump of what must once have been the vessel's foremast.

"Quartermaster!" called Fremantle. "Steer for that wreck."

Once the wheel was ground down, the blockade ship's huge sidewheels churned froth and the *Underwriter*'s low, rounded bow swung southward.

Fremantle emitted an exasperated sigh. Dammit, because there were survivors on that wreck, under the law of the sea he was duty-bound to examine her, although the half-submerged craft couldn't possibly be a blockade runner — too small. Now, valuable time must be consumed in taking off survivors and determining whether the wreck was worth salvaging. His crew, as he was, was burning with impatience for shore leave after two dreary months of patrolling the entrances to sounds along the coast of the Carolinas.

Not much time was required for the former ferryboat to close in on the wave-lashed wreckage. The *Underwriter*'s crew, eager for a break in the monotony, hoisted out a lifeboat once the *Underwriter*, lifting, with dipping huge paddle wheels, and still churning slowly, came about and headed into a rising northeast wind.

"She worth towing, sir?" Fremantle's second-in-command, a midshipman out of the Regular Navy, asked.

"Doubt it, sir. Such a mess of wreckage never would pay fetching her into port."

"Order the coxswain to bring those survivors aboard fast as possible, then we'll exercise the gun crews and sink the wreck as a menace to navigation."

"Aye, aye, sir," said the pink-cheeked midshipman. "But did you notice, sir ... there's what looks like a female among 'em."

Fremantle readjusted his binoculars' focus. "Ye're right ... looks like a pretty piece. Shove off right away."

PART TWO

A House Divided

10

"City's Fair Jumpin'"

A LIGHT SNOW WAS THICKENING into a howling blizzard, whose whirling flurries nearly obscured both shores of the gray, floe-choked East River. Brooklyn, starboard of the U.S.S. *Underwriter,* remained visible in more detail than the jagged roofs and spires of Manhattan, lying to port. The gunboat's helmsman therefore had reason to repeat a series of strident whistles; so many vessels of varying sizes and descriptions abruptly were looming into sight. The first to appear was a tug chuffing hard to pull against an incoming tide a string of barges deeply laden with what appeared to be field guns and caissons. Next appeared a gunboat ferry which, like the *Underwriter,* carried on her bow and stern wheeled field guns, inadequately protected by a double row of sandbags protected by a curved strip of one-quarter-inch rolled iron plate. She was churning downstream, no doubt on her way to take up station in the blockade's inner line.

"Damn this snow," rashed the sergeant in charge of the converted ferryboat's forward cannon. "On a clear day, 'tis a real sensation to view all them tall buildings over on the Manhattan side — there's more'n a hundred of 'em. Yessir, quite a few stand even ten stories high or better." He waved a mittened hand. "Yep, the city's fair jumpin' these days. See how all them wharves are jam-packed with freight? Stevedores are busier'n foxes with fleas in their ears."

Under a borrowed blue army overcoat, Kitty Hamilton stared in incredulous wonderment and didn't realize she was shivering violently. Lord! In all her born days she never expected to experience such icy blasts; neither had Christian Pitcher, also wearing a borrowed boat cloak, the long skirts of which whipped furiously about his legs.

Every now and then the dull chunk-chunk of the U.S.S. *Underwriter's* big paddle wheels slowed, stopped to grant some other vessel the right-of-way, then picked up speed again. When for a space, the blizzard thinned, a wide lane of dirty gray water, not at all reminiscent of Bermuda's sparkling waters, opened among jagged, grimy ice cakes. The sergeant in charge of the forward field piece, his full beard flecked with snowflakes, pointed to a shipyard off to the right, topped by cranes of various sizes and descriptions.

"Yonder's Tom Rowland's Continental Ironworks, about which you'll no doubt be hearin' plenty before long."

Despite the storm, several blast furnaces and open-hearth forges glowed, sending streamers of gray smoke whirling away. A swarm of workers could be glimpsed at work under a ship house on what appeared to be the hull of a long, flat-bottomed vessel apparently being constructed solely of iron.

"What's that?" Pitcher yelled. "Never sighted such a craft before. Is it an iron water barge, or what?"

"No one rightly knows," the sergeant admitted; his breath was instantly whipped away. "Seems she's some kind of contraption a crazy Swede inventor named Ericsson is building under Government contract. Been at it hammer and tongs since late October because she's got to be ready for acceptance inside a hundred days or forfeit the Navy's contract — or so they say."

"What's her use?" Pitcher queried.

"Nobody knows for sure. Nor could anyone guess when we sailed on blockade duty six weeks ago."

The fugitives from Bermuda glimpsed a double row of huge iron ribs standing stark as fence posts in a snowy cow pasture. To them, it appeared a crew of ironworkers were busy driving red-hot rivets into what looked like very heavy sheets of iron. Fires, built to warm laborers, flared and burned fitfully. One of the gun crew commented, "B'gravy, Rowland's have got a lot done since we sailed."

Using a huge and hairy paw, O'Dea shielded his eyes from snow and asked incredulously, "You mean all them there piles of scrap iron are supposed to make a ship?"

"So they say," the sergeant grunted. "Reckon they're crazy. You'll find plenty of gamblers right now ready to give long odds that there contraption won't ever float — not under the weight of the guns, shot, and armor she's supposed to carry."

Pitcher felt inclined to agree. A series of strident blasts on the *Underwriter*'s whistle saluted the appearance of a beautifully designed steam sloop standing down the East River, with Stars and Stripes flying briskly from all her mastheads. She kept sounding her steam whistle continuously, as if to demand attention.

The sergeant explained, "That'll be one o' them new steam-screw men-o'-war. Must have a reg'lar Captain aboard. Look how smart her yards are braced." He squirted tobacco juice over the bulwarks. "Pray God before she's done she'll send plenty of Reb raiders to visit Davy Jones."

With half an eye, anyone could sense that the ex-ferryboat's volunteer crew were itching to set foot ashore and enjoy themselves at home — or with other comforts. Acting Lieutenant Arthur Fremantle felt the same way, although he couldn't hope to reach his home over in Manhattan until the following morning. There'd be inspectors to inform, too many official reports to fill in and convey to the Commodore at the Brooklyn Navy Yard, where at least four large wooden men-of-war were undergoing repairs or alterations.

O'Dea, peering in all directions, was astounded at the sprawling vista of New York and Brooklyn and their surrounding suburbs. Although he'd seen Manchester, Dublin, and Liverpool, none of these places could hold a candle to what he was looking at right now.

He was thinking, so this is what bragging Yanks call the land of the free and the home of the brave? Possibly New York town might prove to be just the ticket for Moira O'Dea's erring son to take refuge here and try to earn an honest living. He'd have to; right now he had exactly one shilling and sixpence to bless himself with. Just to keep alive might present problems, but thanks to his experience in the ring, he oughtn't to make too bad a prizefighter.

As an escaped convict, it would be a good idea to change his name and work out a fictional but plausible past. How about "One Round Tim

Murphy"? Not bad, although he'd never yet knocked out a pug in the first round of any official match.

Under the lee of the *Underwriter*'s pilothouse, he swung arms to warm himself and tried to devise a plan of action, which didn't come easy to an illiterate bog-trotter. Pitcher, he knew, was as penniless as himself, but he guessed Kitty had saved her wages and just might be carrying a few pounds somewhere on her person — possibly beneath her underpinnings? To stick with Christian Pitcher seemed wise. The Bermudian was a glib, fast-thinking rascal, he figured, who would likely fall on his feet, no matter what chanced, especially if pert and pretty Kitty Hamilton remained alongside.

Apparently, the two had struck up a bit more than a casual friendship. What about his fellow fugitives? Beyond doubt, considering the ex-pilot's shrewd, narrow face and restless eyes, he reckoned Christian Pitcher wouldn't be above doing a bit of pimping if worse came to worst.

Long since, the Irishman had become aware that this runaway nursemaid possessed more than a passable voice and could do some fancy dancing if occasion offered. How different things would be for her had the Bandmaster survived, if, in truth, he really had had those useful theatrical connections in New York he'd sometimes mentioned.

As for Kitty Hamilton, she grew more and more frightened by the minute. She was overwhelmed by the size of this huge city, looming so gray and ghostly through snow squalls. As far as the eye could reach, buildings loomed beyond piles of jagged, broken ice lining both shores of this fast-running and dirty East River, dotted by floes interspersed with patches of semifrozen slush.

What was going to happen once she and her companions were set ashore? Briefly, she regretted having abandoned the snug if dull security of the Commissioner's mansion. If only she'd been able to save a little more from her meager wages! Five pounds, six shillings wouldn't last long, despite the most rigorous economy. She'd felt she'd been right about playing up to Christian Pitcher; had to, didn't she? He held the dread secret of her breeding. She'd been inclined to favor Dion O'Dea, but something forbidding lay beneath the hulking Irishman's ebullient good nature. She suspected that, whenever he could, he would drink heavily, which likely might bring to the surface some violent streak in his nature.

Like the voice of doom, the shout of an officer sounded from the *Un-*

derwriter's bridge: "Stand by to tie up. Passengers, go below and get yer dunnage ready."

That so insignificant a craft should attract little attention among a handful of people standing on the ferry's slip was scarcely surprising. No whistles blew or bells clanged a welcome to the dark-red ex-ferryboat when, responding to a six-foot steering wheel expertly handled by a bushy-bearded harbor pilot, the little gunboat was eased into her berth. Only a few seagulls screamed while the *Underwriter* crunched her way between ice-coated pilings into the slip and came to a halt. Immediately, dense white columns of steam roared up from her exhaust pipes.

The *Underwriter*'s crew and the shore gang knew their business; within minutes, the blockader was made fast. Acting Lieutenant Fremantle vented a whistling sigh of relief, then grinned with the realization that he had fetched his first command home safe and sound and, better still, he would be able to report she had not only captured a medium-sized blockade runner, but also had made prizes of two Rebel schooners loaded to the guards with cotton bales, which should fetch a pretty price in Port Royal, South Carolina, the new Navy base, where he'd ordered them sent under prize crews.

He turned to his first officer, Midshipman Rogers, of the Regular Navy. "Don't expect we'll win medals from Congress, but I allow we might at least get a letter of commendation from the Port Commandant, once he's read my report."

"What about those civilians we've got below, sir?"

Fremantle shrugged snow from his boat cloak. "Don't know and don't care, except that I'll have to account for the rations they've consumed."

His second-in-command, buttoning up his overcoat, glanced sidewise and remarked, "Sir, if it's all right with you, I'd like to sign on the big Irishman we took off that wreck. He'd make a fine gunner — all muscle and few brains, but maybe because he's a British subject there might be objections."

"Probably not. We've already signed on plenty of foreigners and, before this war is over, I expect we'll be glad to enlist anything in human form that's got two good eyes and sound limbs."

11

Roaring Town

ON THE LAST DAY before the U.S.S. *Underwriter* was due to put into New York, it had appeared only sensible for the *Fancy Free*'s survivors to agree to stick together upon landing in America. Kitty, however, was secretly determined to rid herself somehow of Pitcher's company at the earliest opportunity. For a while she had deceived herself that he was ignorant of that stain in her background. Only once, while making her submit to being fondled intimately, had Pitcher explicitly let on that he knew her to be a quadroon, but thereafter the Bermudian had made few further attempts to capitalize on this knowledge, and she had successfully managed to keep him under control, since opportunities for indiscretions aboard the crowded and uncomfortable former ferryboat had been few. But, once ashore, his attitude very well might change.

As for O'Dea, the big Irishman unexpectedly had assumed the role of her protector against advances not only from Pitcher but from others of the gunboat's company.

A stark fact remained: two of three of the yacht's survivors would have been flat broke except that Acting Lieutenant Fremantle, warmed by a double tot of bourbon, and some of the gunboat's crew had passed the hat for a collection which, when split three ways, amounted to roughly five dollars apiece. Kitty, of course, made no mention of the precious five pounds and six shillings she had somehow managed to conceal from fumbling, explorative fingers.

During the afternoon, the snow diminished and, when it stopped, disclosed an apparently endless series of structures — docks, wharves, warehouses, shipbuilding houses, and stores of all descriptions, stretching as far as one could see, lining both shores of the turbulent East River. A number of distant steeples lent reassurance that this bewildering complex was, indeed, a Christian country.

While the 23rd Street ferry began to discharge throngs of roughly clad, ill-smelling and foul-mouthed mechanics, laborers, and carpenters, O'Dea announced, "Now then, me friends, let's stay close together whilst I find cheap and maybe decent lodgings for the lot of us. Maybe there'll be a rooming-house keeper who'll let us in with no advance payment — especially if Kitty treats him to some of her sweetest smiles.

"Nah then, Kitty, just you and Pitcher hang onto me arms but let go quick if I give the word and have to start swingin'." He eyed Pitcher. "You been to sea. Know how to use your dukes?"

The slightly built Bermudian shook his head. "No, but I've got me a knife that's a bloody good equalizer when it comes to fighting out of a tight corner."

"Fine," O'Dea said, "but don't get too free with that blade — English and Americans despise knife work in place o' fists toward settlin' a rookus."

Jostled by weary, homeward-bound laborers, and occasionally slipping on icy cobbles, the three turned left off 23rd Street and soon found themselves on 22nd.

Never had any of the *Fancy Free*'s survivors beheld such dense throngs of humanity, of all colors and descriptions. Most numerous after the laborers were soldiers. Some, wearing colorful and foreign-looking uniforms enlivened the dark-blue worn by Federal troops and seamen.

Heavens, thought Kitty, why is everybody here in such a hurry? Women in swaying hoop skirts, some of them the worse for wear, hurried along. Ragged, pinch-faced newsboys shrilled their wares, presumably the latest editions of such important newspapers as the *Times*, the *Tribune*, the *Herald*, and the *New York Post*.

O'Dea and his companions were about to enter a broad street marked Second Avenue when, somewhere in the near vicinity, a deep-toned church bell began to ring, and soon more bells of varying degrees of pitch and resonance began to clang. Most of the hurrying crowd halted, trying to determine what was amiss and where. " 'Tis a fire!" someone yelled. "Sounds like it's somewheres on Twentieth."

"Mebbe 'tis some warehouse storin' fancy goods or booze!"

"Let's go see!"

A surge of yelling, cursing, shaggy, and shabbily dressed humanity quickly flooded the street. Windows banged open and heads emerged, yelling for information; more and more ribby curs raced about, setting up an excited yapping. The *Fancy Free*'s survivors were swept, unwilling, in the direction of an increasingly dense pillar of gray-blue smoke rising perhaps half a block away. Presently a brisk wind began to drop increasingly thick showers of sparks and brands. Residents ran out of doors, pulling on scarves and coats. So rapidly did the crowd thicken from all directions that O'Dea and his companions were hard put to keep arms linked and maintain footing. More bells joined in, raising the tumult; billows of acrid, eye-stinging smoke thickened as the deafening cacophony increased. If there were any police on duty in the vicinity, they were nowhere in evidence.

"Hell, where's the blaze?"

Then someone started blowing continual, ear-piercing blasts on a trumpet and a big ruffian yelled, "Hey! Fire's in the house next to Harvey Dillard's liquor warehouse!"

"Is it afire, too?"

"Yup!"

"Who's pumpin'? What engine's that?"

"Hose Company 21. They'll be racing Valley Forge's Number 60 hook and ladder. Both of 'em want to show up first so's they can claim the insurance money."

Shouts went up. "Start her lively, boys! Let's go!"

A tall, red-nosed figure bellowed, "If Dillard's grog shop is really burnin', let's go cut the hoses. I'm drier'n a charity sermon."

More bugles and trumpets began to shrill from various directions, swelling the din.

O'Dea pressed Kitty flat against a warehouse door as a dumpy little man wearing a tall top hat and a scarlet coat appeared, panting and pausing only long enough to blow on a red-ribboned cornet, meanwhile bellowing, "Jump her, boys! Jump her; damn you! Fire's spreadin' fast!"

More fire companies appeared, only to fight a losing battle with the mob. Their little engines and wooden pump handles appeared absurdly inadequate, Christian Pitcher thought, pressed as flat as the others against an iron-bound warehouse door.

Soon it appeared that this was no ordinary fire. Clouds of smoke thickened, as increasing numbers of the blazing brands and sparks billowed along the street. Terrified carriage and dray horses snorted, reared, and plunged, dragging wrecked vehicles. Some of the animals broke loose, trampling and charging aimlessly about the crowd.

O'Dea watched two heavy freight wagons lock wheels and remain immovable while their drivers, howling obscenities, lashed at the crowd, at their horses, and at one another. More people of all ages and descriptions — many of them Negroes, others shouting in foreign languages — appeared to spout out of alleyways onto the frozen pavement.

Never in all her life had Kitty Hamilton, clinging to Dion O'Dea's massive arm, been anywhere near so terrified. Then she remembered something frightening. In her haste to disembark, fearful she might become parted from her bundle of clothing, she'd ripped the banknotes free of her corsets and tucked them into her handbag. How could she hang on to it in all this violent confusion?

Pitcher, wiry but slight of build, grabbed a stick from the pavement and struck out savagely whenever a threatening move was made in his direction. It was reassuring to know his eight-inch sheath knife remained strapped to his belt over the small of his back. However, recalling O'Dea's warning about the misuse of steel in this country, he determined not to use his blade except as a last resort.

More surges of ravening humanity poured out of side streets and collided with the mob rushing out of 19th Street. Amid howls, yells, and the pounding of feet it became apparent that this was a conflagration of major proportions. Three other big buildings had started to ooze smoke before flames burst through their upper windows.

Unluckily, a sign stretching across the front of the nearest warehouse read "H. Dillard & Son, Dealers in Liquors and Fine Wines."

By their speech, many of the rioters were Irish, so O'Dea, shoving off his companions, slugged away and cursed in broad Gaelic so effectively they fell back momentarily, thus sparing himself not a few blows. But then a new gang closed in, led by a pug-nosed giant lacking both front teeth. He charged like an enraged bull, forcing the ex-convict again to wrench arms free of Kitty's and Pitcher's convulsive grips.

"Arragh! Here's for ye, ye sister-seducin' spalpeen o' Satan!" the attacker shouted, aiming a vicious swing. But O'Dea, balancing on the balls of his feet, ducked expertly, and straightening, put plenty of weight behind a savage uppercut into the other's jaw. The bone broke as he reeled back and fell into the arms of other bellowing toughs.

A small space opened before him, and O'Dea, roaring, snatched a shillelagh from someone, charging single-handedly. He drove the mob back, leaving his assailant lying unconscious on the snow and manure-speckled cobbles.

Meanwhile, amid the roaring crackle of flames, there were ringing yells of "Dillard's grog shop's aflame!" and "Come on, boys! Wet yer whistles afore the fire beats us to it!"

Free fights were taking place everywhere. A handful of blue-clad policemen, sufficiently brave or foolhardy to confront the rioters, were promptly battered, knocked down, and kicked into unconsciousness to join other fallen figures on the filthy pavement.

Women, most of them painted, wild-haired, and drunken harridans, retreated into doorways, clutching bottles, shrieking, or squealing as though all the demons of hell were about to assault their long-lost virtue.

More fire-fighting engines and operators appeared, but got nowhere amid the billowing, choking smoke and flying brands. Looters promptly hacked through what few hoses had been connected.

"Let 'er burn! Free booze, boys! Free booze."

"Come on!"

All manner of hand carts, barrows, and lighter carts were overturned, blocking streets. More dray and carriage horses, breaking loose, blundered about, knocking down people and trampling shrieking figures.

Once Christian Pitcher's hold on O'Dea's arm was broken and the Irishman went to charge the mob, the ex-pilot snatched Kitty's arm and, while he lurched about as though participating in some rough country dance, he noted the weight of Kitty's handbag when it bumped his arm. As a fresh wave of shouting rioters closed in, Pitcher finally pulled his sheath knife and, finding his companion's bag straps in the way, slashed them through. Once he felt the released purse's weight, he crammed it into his jacket front and, blade glimmering, slashed furiously about. Shrill cries of pain resulted.

"Damn you fer a bloody Dago!" someone shouted, but gave way once Christian started in his direction.

Suddenly he was free of the worst of the crowd and started to run in the opposite direction, but where he didn't know.

Kitty felt herself spun about, screaming as she never had before. She staggered to and fro, her ears numbed by voices reeking of liquor. Instinctively, she raised hands to protect her face from flying cobblestones, flat irons, beer mugs, chamber pots, and other missiles. What had become of Dion and Christian? She had no idea — likely they were now being trampled by this bestial, insensate mob. "Oh, God Almighty, what shall I do? What shall I do?" she sobbed.

The tumult swelled anew as more rioters gained access to Dillard & Son's liquor supply.

Sailors and foreigners drew stilettos, Bowie knives, even curved Oriental daggers, and slashed wildly about. Streaks and splashes of bright blood spattered the pavement. As in an all too vivid nightmare, the terrified girl saw men and wailing women and tatterdemalion youths sag onto their knees before collapsing, to be trampled under heavy boots of workmen, soldiers, and seamen.

Kitty had begun to blubber a prayer when a huge, dark-skinned Negro gripped her wrist and started to haul her toward a nearby passageway, but a bearded, red-faced soldier, wearing neat white cross-belts, brought his musket barrel down hard on the attacker's head. Her rescuer panted, "Sis! Get over to that doorstoop and hide under it till . . ." The soldier got no further because a hard-flung cobblestone knocked the kepi from his head and dropped him, quivering, in his tracks.

Terrified, Kitty squirmed, bent, twisted, and plunged toward the stoop. Her clothing was sadly ripped and torn by the time she dove into a small space under a short flight of steps leading up to some private dwelling's front door. There she crouched, trembling, face buried between palms. Her breath was terribly hard to catch. Worst of all, she discovered that her handbag containing the all-important five pounds, six shillings had vanished; only the severed ends of its supporting strap remained in her hand.

For a long time, Kitty, weeping wildly, crouched there, panting like some vixen gaining her burrow after barely shaking off pursuing hounds.

She listened to the pandemonium increase — if that were possible. Male rioters and hideous, harpylike females were prancing back and forth to the blazing liquor store, fortunately ignoring that small space beneath someone's door stoop where she hid.

How long she crouched, panting and running sweat in rivulets, Kitty had no idea until a lock clicked, the door behind her opened, and a woman thrust out her head, beckoning sharply. "Whoever you are, come in here quick."

Sobbing hysterically, Kitty Hamilton flung herself into the arms of a pleasant-looking middle-aged woman dressed in a neat brown gown. Her carefully dressed iron-gray hair was drawn smoothly back and knotted into a tight bun over the nape of her neck. Instantly, she locked the door and shot home a brace of stout brass bolts.

"There, there, my dear, quit weeping; spoils your looks and won't help a bit. You're safe now, lest some of those drunken bastards break in before the troops arrive."

"Bastards?" Even in the depths of her hysterics, Kitty noticed the incongruity of the word employed by this plain but decent-appearing female who smelled of violets.

"I'm Adah Markham, Mrs. Henry Markham," the woman said. "I've been a lone widow since my husband got killed in some senseless battle at a place called Bull Run, which I'm told lies close by Washington to the southward."

Kitty grabbed the woman's hand, and convulsively pressed it to a tear-streaked cheek. "Oh, thank you! Bless you, Ma'am! But for you I guess I'd be dead by now."

"Probably not dead, my dear, but something worse could have happened."

"Worse?"

"No telling what can happen to a young girl during the course of a riot. We've had quite a few lately here in New York, especially since the Rebels now appear to be winning the war."

Kitty began to sob again, recalling that every stiver of her money had vanished. Only then did she remember Pitcher drawing his sheath knife when a huge rascal had hurled himself at Dion O'Dea. Sure enough, when she examined the remains of that light strap she'd used to secure her handbag, she found it had been neatly severed. She doubted whether she would ever again lay eyes on the ex-convict.

Still, come to think of it — no great loss without some small gain. In disappearing, Christian also had taken along with him the knowledge of her tainted ancestry. What with her smooth pale-olive complexion, short, straight nose, not too generous lips, and wavy, golden-brown locks, who would suspect?

Mrs. Markham rose her to her feet, saying, "Come along, dear, and we'll have a cup of tea in the kitchen. Do I presume correctly you mightn't mind a tot of brandy in it?"

"Bless you, God bless you, Ma'am!" Kitty's large and slightly oblique gray-green eyes filled. "I—I'm so eternally grateful I'll do anything in the world for you."

Mrs. Markham blinked, averting her gaze. "A fine sentiment, my dear, about which we shall presently converse. I think General Brebner might be pleased with your fresh young charms."

Kitty thought that a rather odd remark.

The riot continued to rage until a half-battalion from the Sixty-ninth Volunteer Infantry doubled into the street and fired a warning volley into the air. They deployed and trotted along the littered street behind fixed bayonets and made use of brass-covered musket butts so effectively that soon the last of the mob able to walk or crawl was scattered and driven away, shouting obscene threats and leaving the street before the burning warehouses, occupied only by crippled horses, sprawled bodies, and smashed vehicles.

The tumult had faded and had nearly died out before Kitty was led upstairs, where Mrs. Markham brought her bread and butter, hard-boiled eggs, and a cup of a somewhat bitter tea. It must be a local favorite, Kitty told herself. She was too polite to ask for sweetening.

To hear female voices somewhere upstairs seemed reassuring. Nearing the point of utter exhaustion, disheveled and ragged, she allowed Mrs. Markham to lead her up a steep, well-carpeted staircase. There her hostess proudly indicated a tin-lined bathtub. "That's one of only five in this whole block. Now, my dear, you look badly in need of a bath, so I'll order Moses to fetch up some pails of hot water." She opened a door across the hallway from the bathroom. "Best rid yourself of those rags and tatters."

"But — Ma'am . . ." Kitty stammered. "I-I have no money."

Mrs. Markham summoned a pale smile, and folded hands over a flat stomach. "No matter for the moment, my dear; 'tis a real Christian's duty to aid those in distress."

Kitty, increasingly drowsy, made only halfhearted attempts to bathe her bruised body before wrapping herself in a big towel and approaching the room before which Mrs. Markham was waiting, a faint smile on her plain but not unattractive features.

"Mercy me! You look like a new young lady. By the way, what's your name?"

Kitty Hamilton told her just before collapsing onto the bed. She was sound asleep long before her protectress had finished gathering up the last of her soiled and badly torn garments.

Despite being continually hit and jostled, once he'd managed to stuff Kitty's purse inside his coat, Christian Pitcher bent low so as to offer a minimal target for flying debris and whirling clubs while working toward the crowd's edge. He couldn't help coughing spasmodically, because acrid-smelling smoke clouds were thickening. Suddenly he was menaced by a pair of hairy, tough-looking youths, against whom he knew he didn't stand a chance at fistfighting. Ducking, and in the same motion, he again unsheathed his knife.

Experienced in this kind of fracas, Christian slashed rather than stabbed at his attackers, who would be stung rather than badly hurt. One tough screamed, whereupon his companion, seeing blood streaming down his fellow's grimy features, wheeled and disappeared.

Finding himself truly on the fringes of the mob, Pitcher heard another detachment of soldiers fire a warning volley into the air. He broke free, and weaving, ran so swiftly that he soon outdistanced all except a few drunken men and shrill-voiced sluts capering pointlessly about. Keeping a sharp lookout, the Bermudian trotted toward where he guessed the waterfront might be. There he might at least feel less disoriented. He was sad to be parted from Kitty; she might have become a great asset, as long as he kept his mouth shut.

As soon as he dared, he slipped into an alley and rifled Kitty's handbag, in which, to his sharp disappointment, he discovered only a few trivial baubles, her five dollars from the crew's donation, and her small savings. Not much, but 'twas better than a poke in the eye with a sharp stick when added to the five dollars that Acting Lieutenant Fremantle had handed him on debarking. So, for the immediate present, there was no need for him to go hungry or lack shelter of some description. Before nightfall, he had found lodgings in a shabby rooming house on First Avenue.

Only then did he find time to conjecture briefly about what might have chanced with Dion O'Dea. In all probability the big Irishman would have survived the free-for-all without getting seriously hurt. The last glimpse he'd had of him was just before the first detachment of troops had appeared, and he had glimpsed his fellow ex-convict exchanging punches with a tough almost as tall and burly as himself.

He couldn't know that, unaware of the approaching infantry, O'Dea had landed another haymaker on his opponent's jaw, so powerful it knocked the fellow clear off his feet. The man had fallen heavily and struck the back of his head hard on the cobbles, splitting his scalp and cracking his skull so badly that a puddle of blood mingled with gray streaks of brain matter which began at once to form beneath the fellow's shaggy head.

A sergeant trotting in advance of his men shouted out, "Halt, there, you! Halt! Halt!"

Dion O'Dea, having already had enough of soldiering for one lifetime, stooped and picked up a heavy billet of wood, hurling it at the sergeant before turning and plowing his way through the retreating mob with the ease of a bull overtaking a flock of sheep.

How long, O'Dea wondered, would it be before his description might appear in newspapers and on various police blotters? Arragh! *Why* must he always play in such muddy luck! What to do? What to do? He started walking rapidly, not running, up Second Avenue toward the 25th Street ferry slip. Long since he'd discovered the wisdom of following a familiar if dangerous line of retreat rather than risk blundering along some possibly easier and safer route.

In a saloon located close to the ferry slip, a gang of workmen were grounding tool bags. One, better dressed than his fellows, sang out, "Hey! Feller! Wasn't you once Number 14404 on Ireland Island in Bermuda?"

Icy fingers explored Dion's spine as he recognized a fellow with whom he had served on a chain gang a year or so ago.

"Hell, no! What in hell you talkin' about?"

"You and me was on the convict hulk *Medway,* remember?"

"Ye're crazy! Get yerself a pair o' specs. I ain't never even been close to Bermuda!"

The other stared a moment and, then, apparently satisfied, he appeared to back down. But still — but still — gnawing fears nipped at O'Dea's mind. There were rewards for turning in escaped felons.

"Ye're mistook, Mister, and I don't fancy that kind of a mistake." He balled fists, towering over the other. "Shut yer mouth or I'll close it with a bunch of fives."

"Sorry, guess I was mistook." The man gulped the last of his beer and hurried out.

Apparently no one had noticed the incident. A man better dressed than the average joined O'Dea at the bar. "Hey, Mister! Want to earn good pay on a steady job in a hurry?"

"Aye, that I do!" the Irishman admitted. B'grabs, maybe here was a good way out of escaping the past.

The labor recruiter took another look at the big, muscular figure. "Reckon you'll do. No hernias?"

"No."

"Then come along and sign up. We're building faster than fast a queer craft some goddamn Swede has designed for the Navy. His contract allows but a hundred days to completion and we're runnin' behind schedule so we're workin' night and day."

"Can I find lodgings in Brooklyn?"

"Sure, plenty of 'em — cheap and dirty; tarts workin' Greenpoint are the same. Ain't nothin' like so fancy as ye'll find over in Manhattan."

A little later, O'Dea found a grimy little room not too far from Rowland's Continental Ironworks, then literally slept the clock around.

Once he'd escaped the riot, Christian Pitcher, being young, felt surprisingly fresh and clear-headed while lingering at the entrance to Poppy Smith's Saloon, which appeared to be uncommonly well-patronized. After all, he had a little money, a sharp knife, and quick wits, a combination which should carry him far, provided he didn't make some damn fool mistake — and that was exactly what he did.

On the afternoon following the fires and riot on 22nd Street, he returned to Poppy Smith's place, which was presided over by a rotund German whose imposing mustachios were as wide, curved, and pointed as any Cape buffalo's horns. Christian entered and indulged in a few tots of Barbados rum; he didn't deem it wise to sample aquavit, whiskey, schnapps, or any other unfamiliar tipple.

"By the look of you, *mein Freund,* you are seafaring, *nicht wahr?*" the jovial bartender inquired.

"Aye. Used to be a ship pilot." Unashamedly, he omitted the word "apprentice."

"So? Und vhere vas dot?"

"Never mind where."

The big-bellied bartender nodded and chuckled. "No matter. Now iss time I giff trink on der *Haus* of one special fine rum because, *mein Freund,* I hope you come back here soon und often." From a thick, squat bottle he deftly poured half a glass of yellow-brown liquid which, chuckling louder than ever, he called *"Rhine Mädchen Milch."*

This bottle, he explained, he kept beneath the bar, reserved for favored customers. The florid, round-faced bartender paused momentarily, lowering the bottle out of sight. Then he filled a similar glass and lifted it to touch Christian's. *"Prosit!* Und as they say here, 'Over *mein* teeth, 'tween *mein* gums, look out guts, here she comes!' "

People banged beer steins or glasses on the slippery, froth-covered bar, and yelled for a fresh round.

"Goot. Come, I fill you up quick," chortled the big mustachioed bartender, following a vast stomach over to work the draft beer pump handles.

"Nun," he said to the Bermudian, "now you buy two *Rhine Mädchens* for us, und ve make vun fine chug-a-lug."

"What's a chug-a-lug?"

Someone spoke up. "God, ye're a real greenie, Buster. Means ye've got to finish yer drink 'thout taking the glass from yer lips or ye'll have to buy 'nother round."

"Here we go," chanted the patrons, "Chug-a-lug, gug, gug! Chug-a-lug-gug-gug!"

Christian Pitcher had just managed to choke down the second chug-a-lug when the floor flew up and hit him so hard he lost consciousness.

12

Aftermaths

Soon after Christian regained consciousness, gradually and painfully because of a fiercely throbbing head, he knew at once he was aboard a vessel of some sort — and at sea. The rhythmic rushing and beat of waves alongside removed all doubt on that score.

Gradually, he became aware of lying sprawled on a lumpy, fetid-smelling mattress on a bunk in what he recognized to be a typical merchantman's foc'sle. Christ in the foothills! What could have happened to him? What was today? Where was this craft headed? From her motion he judged her to be fully laden, a sailing ship, and of around four hundred tons displacement.

Christian Pitcher blinked, then stared unseeingly into dim light cast by a heavy glass deadlight set into the deck directly above his head.

Gradually an appalling realization dawned on him. That damned Dutch bartender's "trink on *das Haus*" must have included a good measure of what along most waterfronts was termed a Mickey Finn, or knockout drops.

Lord! His temples pounded as if all the devils in hell were belaboring them with sledgehammers. How could he have been so careless, especially when merchantmen all along the Atlantic Coast were known to be desperately hard up for seamen.

Gingerly, Christian began to test fingers and limbs for breaks; next, he explored his rib cage, but even on his scalp, his groping fingers discovered no lumps. He reasoned that since he'd been effectively rendered senseless, there'd been no point in beating him up.

As from a great distance, he heard an English voice shouting something, then the ship's bell sounded, summoning the next watch. Presently, six figures in grimy, shapeless sea clothes clumped down the foc'sle companionway ladder to extend stiff hands toward a small potbellied stove clamped hard onto the foc'sle's deck.

To the Bermudian's astonishment, these men didn't much resemble the rioters of yesterday — for all that they were unshaven, with hair dangling in heavy, greasy locks over their foreheads. They bore no bruises, and looked no better or worse than ordinary merchant sailors.

Pulling off dripping sou'westers, they noticed that the shanghaied hand's eyes were open. The boatswain's mate, a thin, black-haired, red-faced Yorkshireman named Bott, said not unkindly, "So, me gradley younker, ye've decided to return to life and for you 'tis more than a pity."

Pitcher could only moan. "My head, my head! Water, please, a sip of water, for God's sake!"

One of the watch offered a half-full tin cup. "Too bad. Old Albrecht must ha' slipped ye an extra-stiff dose."

Others gathered above Christian's narrow bunk. "By God," one commented, "Ain't much to this feller. Can you lay aloft in a stiff blow?"

Surges of nausea kept Pitcher from replying beyond gurgling, "Think so."

"Hope ye're right. I've seen cabin boys look more able, and us so damned shorthanded we'll be standing double watches afore we sight Cape Fear, *if* we do."

Cape Fear? Where in God's name was such a place? A stocky young fellow wearing a slim gold ring in his left ear was kind enough to offer an earthenware mug of lukewarm coffee. Christian gulped and hung on, although he still felt like vomiting.

"Now," said he with the earring, "how're ye called?"

Christian was too confused to contrive an alias, so he told the truth. Bott, the big round-faced Yorkshireman, said, "'Fore you sank to this level, what did ye do for a living?"

"I was a 'prentice pilot — Bermuda waters."

"Why'd you leave such a pretty place?"

Now that his head had cleared somewhat, Christian mumbled, "Figured I'd do better in America."

A short and skinny fellow, face deeply pitted by smallpox, observed, "Then you bein' seafarin' and a helmsman to boot — if ye're not lyin' — that should stand ye in good stead. Cap'n Varick's short of good helmsmen; maybe he'll sign you on as able seaman, pay and all."

To the Bermudian's astonishment, these uncommonly brawny crewsmen appeared friendly, possibly because he'd turned out also to be a British subject?

The ship heeled sharply as she was smartly put about on a course heading straight out into the wide Atlantic. Pitcher noticed, and wondered why this particular lot of sailors didn't seem in the least downhearted; most crew members hated the prospect of beginning another voyage which might entail weeks or even months spent at sea. Gradually, Pitcher learned he was aboard a fast, recently completed sail brigantine named the *Staghound of Bristol*.

Normally, he was told, she plied to various ports scattered along the long Eastern coast of the United States, and that a majority of these ports lay southward of New York.

"This here trip is special," the big Bosun's Mate explained. "According to the Northerners, our cargo's mostly contraband, which good, patriotic New Yorkers aim to sell at high profit to the Rebels — medicines, sheet iron, mechanics' tools, fine duck canvas, and a few field gun barrels, amongst other things."

Weakly, Pitcher propped himself up on an elbow. "Please, where are we cleared for on this voyage?"

"For Bristol — but only durin' three days' sailin' time." The Bosun's Mate bent and jerked off sodden kersey trousers. " 'Course that ain't our real port of call, at all, or so the First Mate let drop whilst I was at the wheel. Once we slip through the line of blockaders — there are two such lines, the inner and the outer cruisin' farther offshore — it'll be different. Neither amounts to a pinch of dog shit right now, but later on I reckon we'll see a considerable change. 'Make hay while the sun shines,' or so say the Yankee smugglers. Yep, this blockade's only thinly enforced by a few Federal men-o'-war and the Rebel coast, they say, is above three thousand miles long and full of bays and inlets. So, after three days, if all goes well, we'll come about and head for a port called Wilmin'ton, behind Cape Fear."

"Where's that?" someone asked.

"In one of the Rebel states called North Carolina. Once we get near the inner line of blockade and the goin' gets sticky, Cap'n promises all hands will draw double pay till we tie up in Wilmin'ton."

Pitcher recalled conversations overheard aboard the *Underwriter,* indicating that President Lincoln's blockade right now was as leaky as a coarse-meshed sieve. Fresh appreciation of his position sank in, and at once he realized that should he play his cards right, knowledge he'd acquired or heard about in Bermuda concerning certain tricks and dodges useful in blockade running might persuade Captain Varick to let him sign articles not as an A.B. but maybe as assistant quartermaster — provided he hinted about his store of special knowledge skillfully enough.

Steadily, the *Staghound* left astern the dim outline of America and flying an unnecessarily large British ensign from her mizzen gaff, headed for the open sea. Toward midday, Christian staggered up on deck in time to watch the Union Jack dipped thrice. Not a half-mile away was steaming an ugly side-wheel gunboat which might have been the U.S.S. *Underwriter*'s twin.

If Dion O'Dea had ever witnessed work going on, uninterrupted, hour after hour, it was here in T. F. Rowland's Continental Ironworks, located among several other such shipyards in Greenport, Brooklyn. There was the hammering, sawing, and never-ending clang, clang of rivets being driven home and the continual noise of long and heavy rolled-iron plates being unloaded at all hours, by day or by torchlight. Big, heavy-footed, sweating draft horses were hauling drays, wagons loaded with boxed oversize rivets and pieces of mysteriously complicated machinery for discharge onto wharves running parallel to the ship house sheltering that strange vessel about which everyone was guessing.

By day, chuffing tugs nudged barges nearly awash under the weight of long lengths of rolled sheet iron, most of it four inches thick. However, experts pointed out that some of these were an astonishing eight inches in thickness. Others were fetched by rail and deposited on a platform along that yard in which Mr. Ericsson's "Iron Monstrosity," as the *New York Times* described it, was taking shape with unprecedented speed.

After all, under the Navy's "within one-hundred days" contract required for completion or no payment need be expected, no time remained for horseplay, celebrations, labor disputes, or political bickerings.

Day and night, gangs of blackened, marvelously profane artisans, engineers, and ironworkers toiled long past normal quitting time, and even lingered long enough to explain to a fresh shift what had been done and what most needed attending to.

Once Dion, during a barroom brawl, had in succession knocked flat three towering, brawny, and pugnacious steelworkers and thereafter was regarded as unofficial boss of the Number 2 Plate Ironworker's gang.

Simply because of his enormous strength, skill, and willingness on occasion to work overtime, it wasn't long before the hulking Irishman became second assistant to Mr. Rowland's armorer in chief — with pay to match.

Only a few fellow workers noticed or conjectured about why O'Dea, on an occasional day off, never crossed over to Manhattan. No point in admitting that he retained a vivid mental impression of the fellow he'd knocked crashing over backward to spill blood and brains over filthy cobblestones.

Here in Brooklyn, and now an enlisted man in the United States Navy, he figured he'd remain reasonably safe, at least until this curious ship, for which he entertained a curious and growing affection, was finished. Once she was afloat, although many were willing to bet she'd sink like a stone the moment she left the ways, he figured to sign on the *Monitor*. Having helped to build her might stand in his favor. The *Monitor* had been so named by the Secretary of the Navy, Gustavus Vasa Fox, at John Ericsson's request. The name, before long, caught the public's fancy, and that of the press — Lionel Humphrey included.

One editor wrote: "Ericsson's revolutionary warship, although tiny in size, will prove *a severe monitor* to chastise monumental Rebel arrogance over an armored ram known to be under construction in Gosport, Virginia."

Originally, the ram had been the U.S.S. *Merrimac*, pride of the American Navy, until it was half-burnt, when Gosport disgracefully had been allowed to fall into Rebel hands. Southern newspapers reported this warship to have been rechristened the C.S.S. *Virginia* and predicted that their armored vessel, although small in tonnage, would exercise a gigantic effect upon the navies of all the world.

There were so many of Dion's compatriots in Mr. Rowland's shipyard that they became known as the "Bog Trotters," or more commonly, as the "Shamrock Troublemakers." Rapidly, Dion's reputation as a rough, tough bruiser circulated through that once pleasant and lovely suburb of New York called Brooklyn. Come a Saturday night, he usually allowed himself to be coaxed by his gang into a ring improvised in the near vicinity of the ship house. Following a few impressively successful fights won as "One-Round Grogan," he commanded ever-larger purses, most of which were spent in drinking and occasional sprees, ending in some "leaping parlor" — the local term for whorehouses. These were mostly owned or controlled by ward heelers, municipal politicians, and high-ranking police officers.

Why he never contracted a venereal disease was only because, as he put it, "The Devil's lookin' out for his own." All in all, he was feeling pretty "high on the hog" these days, but retained sense enough to realize that, before long, the *Monitor* would be ready for launching, and with her completion, this pleasant phase of life would end unless he succeeded in bribing some paymaster's assistant to order him to duty aboard "Ericsson's Folly." Only once in a great while nowadays did Dion's thoughts revert to those evil-smelling convict hulks.

What might have happened to Kitty Hamilton during and after the fire? he wondered. Strange how often the girl's lively, light olive-hued features and shapely figure intruded, unbidden, into his imagination. Much less frequently he conjectured the fate of Christian Pitcher. Smart, fairly well-educated, capable in his profession, and able to wield a useful knife, the Bermudian ought to have survived.

As it was, Dion soon settled down to bossing his "iron gangs" and working harder than any man. Meanwhile, he was alarmed by the almost total lack of security maintained by police and Marines ordered to chase away newspapermen and other unauthorized visitors, who were left to wander freely about, to inspect progress, and even to make sketches of the iron hull as it took shape. As anyone could see, the *Monitor* was flat-bottomed and designed to stretch only 172 feet overall, her beam being about 41 feet at its widest point. Her designer, who made no secret of this important fact, figured that even fully laden, armored, and armed, his experimental craft shouldn't draw more than ten and a half feet of water.

She had one obvious drawback, and a serious one, however, which only a few experts noted. John Ericsson had designed bunker space for *only eighty tons* of coal! How far could this iron machine steam on such a miserable supply of fuel? Certainly, she could never travel any great distances; and otherwise she appeared definitely unseaworthy. Only God knew how her crew could be expected to survive when they were forced to live entirely below the waterline.

Gradually, "One-Round Grogan" experienced a growing sense of identification with this weird craft's construction. Convict Number 14404, Dion O'Dea, was no more. He now called himself Dennis O'Day — an identity he had assumed the day he'd enlisted in the United States Navy; legally, he was still a British subject enrolled in that service. That he was Irish offered no obstacle to a recruiting officer, for, as the war progressed, more and more foreigners were being enlisted by both sides in this ever-expanding fraternal conflict.

So utterly exhausted, mentally and physically, was Kitty Hamilton, and so effective had been the mild sleeping potion Mrs. Markham had thoughtfully administered in her cup of tea, that she never woke until noon of the next day. Only by stages did she discover that she was lying beneath the covers of a clean, not uncomfortable bedstead, with brass head and footboards. With a start she sat up, and only then realized she was naked as any new-fledged jaybird. To collect her fuzzy recollections and arrange them in proper sequence proved most difficult.

She, Dion, and Christian must have been caught up in a fire-inspired riot. Yes, this must be so; a long scratch across the back of her hand and numerous black-and-blue marks about her body proved it. But she did not grasp the full import of what had happened until she looked about for her garments. None were visible in this small but clean-smelling bedroom! The dresser and a chest of drawers appeared of good or fair quality and, of all things, a cross-stitched sampler reading "God Bless Our Home" hung above her bed. The motto looked as though it had been executed by a schoolgirl.

Then occurred a reassuring thought: kindly Mrs. Markham must be washing and mending her clothes. Relieved, Kitty relapsed into a light doze until she heard a knock. The door lock clicked, and Mrs. Markham entered, a broad smile on her pleasant, only lightly rouged features.

"Well, my dear, and how do we feel this morning? A bit bruised and battered, shouldn't wonder."

"Yes, Ma'am, I slept fine, but I'm hungry as a nursing shark."

"We'll tend to that soon, but first," Mrs. Markham said, "we'd better come to a bit of an understanding." She seated herself and quite deliberately scrutinized, or rather appraised, the slight, large-eyed, bedraggled and wild-haired figure clutching sheets under her chin. "Suppose you tell me — truthfully, mind you — just who you are, where you're from, and how you came to get mixed up in that riot."

To manufacture some sort of a logical statement without giving away vital secrets seemed impossible, yet Kitty managed, after a fashion, to convey that she'd been born into a respectable family in Bermuda. When her father, "George Hamilton," had died of yellow fever, she'd been forced to seek employment as governess in a distinguished household —and certainly the Commissioner and his wife were so qualified. But because opportunities were so few in those tiny, isolated, little islands, she'd decided to voyage to America to improve her status, since (she added nervously) not only was she an accomplished seamstress but could dance and sing pretty well.

Mrs. Markham nodded encouragingly. "I take it, then, you have no friends or relatives here?"

"No, none, Ma'am. I've only a note to a Mrs. Schroeder, a boardinghouse keeper I heard about aboard a gunboat which picked us off the wreck of the ship I sailed on, but I fear I lost it because my purse was stolen during the riot."

"What was this vessel's name?" Bright blue eyes across the footboard became as penetrating as gimlets.

"She was named the *Fancy Free,* Ma'am. She was only a small ketch which got wrecked by a terrible great wave. Only three of us got picked up by a Union blockade ship."

"Indeed? You poor girl! You have had a miserable time of it." All the while Mrs. Markham's eyes never shifted from Kitty's. "You talk and act like a sensible, decent girl. Do you read and write well?"

"Oh, yes, Ma'am — oh, and I can play a pianoforte fairly well."

"Oh! And where did you learn such an accomplishment?"

Kitty almost said, "At the Commissioner's house," but stopped short in time. "At school in Hamilton."

Her hostess was silent for a long moment. "You appear to be an uncommonly attractive, well-spoken, and practical young woman, even though not quite to the manor born, so I'll not beat about the bush any longer."

A subtle alteration in Mrs. Markham's tone prompted Kitty to gather fallen bedclothes again tightly about her smooth, lithe body, unaware that the outlines of her high, full breasts had become evident.

"Yes, Ma'am, it's as you wish. Please, how soon can I have my clothes back?"

Mrs. Markham said evenly, "Alas, Miss Hamilton, I fear they have been ruined beyond repair."

Kitty gasped. "But — but what can I wear?"

Mrs. Markham sat straighter. "I'll find something after a bit. Now, my dear, you've said you aim to better yourself. Is that true?"

"Yes, Ma'am."

"Then we shall see that that comes about." She paused. "Provided you act sensibly and do what you are told — and willingly. If you do, I'm confident I can find means of winning for you everything you desire — within reason, of course — such as creature comforts, stylish clothes, and maybe eventually a wealthy husband with social position or important political power somewhere in America — but *only* if you promise to obey my wishes and play your part with enthusiasm, sensitivity, and imagination."

Sensing what might lie ahead, Kitty's eyes grew larger. Mechanically, she smiled and pushed aside a stray lock of greasy hair. "Ye-yes, Ma'am. I-I'll do my best to please," she said, much as she had when she was engaged by the Commissioner's wife.

"That remains to be seen. However, somehow I feel you're to be trusted," Adah Markham said, in flat tones. "I am a professional hostess specializing in providing polite but exciting entertainment only for select gentlemen of financial quality or high-ranking military officers. Yes, Kitty, I've taken the notion that you can learn how to please the choosiest of them." Unexpectedly, she winked. "I believe you're smart enough to understand on which side the bread of survival in this cruel world is buttered? You're not a virgin, I take it?"

The bed seemed to rock under Kitty. "No, Ma'am, but I — I've not had much experience." This was true enough. She had granted ultimate surrender to only three men — the late Bandmaster; Christian Pitcher, to buy his silence; and, the first, an arrogant British diplomat who, visiting in the Commissioner's mansion, had stealthily invaded her room and yielding to drunken urgency, had forced her, none too gently.

Adah Markham commented crisply, "I can guess what's going through your mind right now. Do you realize you could have fared far worse than to find yourself offered — employment in Mrs. Markham's Elite Hairdressing Establishment for Gentlemen? You see, my prices scare away all but very well-to-do patrons. Quality, not quantity, has been my motto ever since my husband got killed and I, coming from a pious but small and impecunious family, had to fend for myself. Being untrained but appreciative of carnal talents, I elected this profession."

Expertly, her eyes appraised the satin-smooth, fresh young shoulders and breasts again momentarily exposed by an involuntary gesture. Here, really, was the choicest peach she'd come across since — well, since she'd taken up "hairdressing."

"Well, Kitty, by your expression I can tell you are not about to fly off into some silly tantrum, claim virtue, and a wealthy family somewhere. Truth is, I credit you for being just an unusually pleasing, clever, and ambitious little piece. Isn't that true?"

"Yes, Ma'am, if you say so." Now Kitty allowed the bedsheet to rest where it had fallen, drew a deep breath, and forced a timid smile. "What do you expect of me to advance my ambitions?"

The older woman looked startled. "Now, I declare! In all my life I've never encountered so sensible a female of your age. I judge you able to face facts, pleasant or otherwise, and not delude yourself with romantic or fanciful notions. Wish I could find more like you. My other young ladies, of which only two live in, are pretty, empty-headed, and lascivious chits, but well-mannered at all times. If they forget their manners, I can and do warm their pretty bottoms with a switch as a reminder — which I'll admit I enjoy doing."

Somehow, this straightforward discourse restored a measure of color to the naked girl beneath the coverlets. "Thank you for your encouragement, Ma'am, but how many gentlemen will I be expected to entertain?"

Mrs. Markham arose and commenced to walk back and forth, dark-blue skirts softly rustling. "Not many. Only the most attractive and affluent of my clients. Kitty, believe it or not, I do feel for you in your predicament.

You see, I come from a good family in a middlewestern city and was well educated, as perhaps you have noticed by my diction. I, too, for a time was as desperate as you at this moment."

She seated herself, after placing a stick in the tiny fireplace. "Don't know why I tell you this, but my husband — whose name wasn't Markham, incidentally — was a struggling lawyer before he joined the Union Army and got himself killed at Bull Run, which left me rich in memories but with a flat pocketbook and little else. I came East because here is where the money is and flows. I granted only — well, let's call them worthwhile favors — to such gentlemen as appreciated my background and seemed able and willing to finance my intentions.

"As you will soon discover, my dear, as I've said I have only two girls as permanent boarders, but I do have connections with a few refined but complacent ladies who live close by and are ready to please first-class clients."

Her voice changed, sounding plain and businesslike. "Play your cards right, Kitty, and I will take my Bible oath that inside of a few months you will have fine lodgings of your own, servants, and a wardrobe most hoity-toity society ladies would envy. Yes, you may even take the air in a cabriolet of your own. This war has turned society upside down, many old rules and standards are being forgotten. Smart people learn to bend with the wind. Do you understand?"

"Y-yes, Ma'am, I think so."

"Of course, if you choose to ignore my advice, at the snap of my fingers I can turn a pretty girl like you over to operators of half-a-dozen brothels where you'll be cheated, mistreated, and worked so hard your looks and your health will be ruined in short order. Now, give me your solemn word, for your benefit *and* mine, that you always will prove willing and trustworthy and will do exactly as I tell you. Have I your word?"

All of a sudden tears filled Kitty's eyes. She couldn't believe such luck. Mrs. Markham was so genteel and soft-spoken. "Yes, Ma'am."

"Don't ever call me 'Madam,' " snapped Adah Markham. "I may be one, according to some envious people, but I don't want to be reminded of it. Always address me Mrs. Markham. Understood?"

"Yes, Mrs. Markham. I promise to try to please any patron you ask me to entertain."

Best of all was the fact that this elegant-talking lady could have no suspicion that she was a quadroon. Even though Christian Pitcher had cut her purse, Kitty now felt infinitely relieved to be shut of him and his ruinous piece of knowledge.

Home Is the Sailor

Since he had never visited New York, Ira Thatcher felt overwhelmed by the hurly-burly and bustle that seemed to prevail everywhere. Nobody sauntered, and everybody appeared in a hurry for some reason, important or not. While the hackney carriage conveying David Dexter and himself rattled away from the ferry landing and down a crowded street, Ira again blessed David for having so forcefully insisted that he must visit at his family's home until they were reassigned to duty.

The young Virginian had roamed about the great, teeming cities of London, Brussels, and Paris, but none could compare with this superenergetic metropolis. Everywhere there was visible a variety of uniforms, some of them quite picturesque but mostly plain dark-blue, as soldiers picked their way among handcarts, barrows, drays, army wagons, horse omnibuses, and a plethora of private vehicles of various descriptions.

A sigh of relief escaped Dexter's guest as the hackney pulled up in front of a handsome five-story dwelling built of brownstone on the northwest corner of Lexington Avenue and 35th Street.

"Is this your home?"

Dexter smiled. "Yes. 'Tis a humble hut to be sure, yet it serves to keep the rain off our heads. Wait while I ring and find out whether that damned messenger boy I hired has given warning of our arrival."

It turned out that this information indeed *had* reached the Dexter mansion — it could hardly be called anything less. After tilting his top hat to a jaunty angle, David pulled a bell knob of silvered glass and the door opened immediately. A lean, gray-haired, sallow-complexioned individual wearing a butler's livery appeared.

At first glance, Ira guessed the butler must be either a mulatto or, because of his large curved nose and mahogany complexion, a native of some South or Central American country. Until he recognized the tall figure of David Dexter climbing the steps, the servant's manner remained impassive; then his white teeth flashed in a wide smile. He bowed almost double. "Welcome, Señor. *Teniente, bien venuda!* Welcome home, Señor!"

"Thank you, Manuel. How are you?"

"I am fine, Señor, and pray you are the same."

Surprisingly, David put out his hand; the butler hesitated, shook it gingerly at first, then harder.

Once the cabbie had finished unloading a small pile of much-traveled luggage, David almost ran up the steps and into a warm and spacious vestibule floored with blue-and-white tiles. In the background hovered two foreign-looking maids wearing black uniforms, frilly white aprons, and neat little caps; both curtsied deeply, gracefully, as David strode indoors.

"*Bien venuda*, Señor Dextair."

Recalling more elaborate estates down South, Ira thought, Can't be too many places like this around crowded, rough-and-ready New York.

"Manuel, is the Señora at home?"

"No, Señor." Manuel's expression became set, dispassionate. "The Señora's father has been taken much sick. Yesterday, the Señora and Señorita Abigail departed for New Haven to attend him."

"When is my mother returning?"

"No telling, Señor. El Capitán might know."

"Is my grandfather very ill?"

"I do not know, Señor, but he must be, else the Señora would not have departed so fast and taken your sister with her."

Ira was impressed by the number of prints and engravings decorating the walls. Most of them pictured famous United States men-of-war in action — the U.S.S. *Constitution* versus the H.M.S. *Guerrière;* the U.S.S. *Constellation* pounding the H.M.S. *Java;* the U.S.S. *Wasp* blasting the H.M.S. *Frolic;* and so on. Along the walls was displayed an exotic collection of trophies from as far away as China, the East Indies, and South America.

Slowly, David slid his arms out of his coat, which Manuel stood ready to remove. "And how is my father?"

"Fairly well, Señor. Only that his sickness is not improving. His rheumatism is most painful. It nearly broke El Capitán's heart when he became so crippled he was forced to retire just before this war broke out."

"Can't the doctors do anything?"

"No Señor, and he has consulted the best *médicos* of this country."

Even before he had last been ordered abroad, David remembered hearing his father, the Captain, occasionally complain of pains in his extremities. What could the Captain (since he was a small boy he'd always thought of his father by his rank) be doing? It wouldn't be like him to lie about, a querulous, useless invalid.

"Where is my father now?"

"Señor, he should be on his way home from the shipyard that he and his *amigos* have built up the river; only recently has it been completed."

"Tell me truthfully, Manuel, how bad is his rheumatism?"

The butler hesitated. *"Pues,* Señor, it must cause him great pain. He complains seldom even though he must use two canes in order to walk. Even in good weather, El Capitán orders his carriage for the shortest of journeys."

Lingering in the background, Ira grew steadily more disturbed; with the Captain so sick, he probably shouldn't stay here. But when he broached the subject, David snapped sharply, "Nonsense! I'll not hear of it, nor would the Captain. You'll damn well stay here till you get your reassignment!"

David directed his attention to the butler. "What is the name of this shipyard my father is interested in?"

"Señor, it is named Dexter and Son Ironworks."

"You said 'Dexter *and Son'!"*

"Si, Señor."

And Son! This must refer to himself; he had no brothers, only his sister, Abigail. Dexter and Son! So the old man must have remained as proud as ever over his son's career and confident of his future in the service. Aye, but which service?

David indicated the luggage. "Have it fetched up, Manuel. Which room will Mr. Thatcher occupy?"

"The one next to yours, Señor. It is prepared."

Once the butler had departed, Ira said, "Say, what is he? Mexican?"

"No. A Venezuelan. My father had him as a steward and body servant aboard his commands for years."

About five o'clock of that bright, wintry afternoon, David heard the front door bell jangle three times, then once, the Captain's private signal. Half-dressed, he descended the stairs three at a time. In the vestibule he halted, gulped, and found it difficult to credit that this bent, round-shouldered figure could be the father who had always held himself straight as an arrow. Manuel was supporting the old man once he had tottered indoors and impatiently thrust one of two walking sticks into an umbrella rack set next to the entrance.

"Reporting aboard, sir!"

"David!" Captain Dexter straightened a trifle, but still had to look upward to see into his son's bronzed countenance. They embraced quickly, David's face averted to conceal the quivering of his features.

About the only things which hadn't changed about the Captain, he quickly decided, were the length of his flowing side-whiskers and a certain penetrating quality in his small, wide-set, steel-blue eyes. "Oh, Pa, to hell with formality. I-I wish I could find something encouraging to say: can't there be any hope for improvement?"

"Not likely. I guess you can say that Dame Nature has hulled me, like the *Constitution* did the *Guerrière*. Take heart, lad, we Dexters are a hardy lot — always have been. I'm not done for yet, far from it. There's too much to do with this cursed, senseless war. I fear it will prove long, bloody, and cruel. We must remember that the rebels are our own people, and they can be just as tough and ingenious fighters as we are."

Supporting his father by an elbow, David conducted him into a little library situated off the end of the vestibule. He'd heard Ira's footsteps hesitate on the stairs and then retreat. Silently, he blessed his classmate for his tact in remaining aloft.

The Captain pulled off a long, red merino muffler before collapsing into a chair beside the glowing sea-coal fire Manuel had hurriedly stirred up. "Stand over yonder, David, and allow me to inspect my newest partner. Did Manuel tell you about the Dexter and Son Ironworks?"

David struggled not to show his emotion, managing to keep his voice under control. "Yes, sir. I-I feel undeservedly honored."

The old man stroked the snow-white hair which brushed his collar, and chuckled softly. "You've made it easier for me by being my only son. Wouldn't it have been hell if there'd been two or three other boys around to complicate matters? For one thing, this damned war can't last forever. After it's finished and I've gone to my reward — such as it may be — you can take over the shipyard and enjoy an assured future, provided you manage things smartly. There'll be plenty of competition."

"May that day never come, sir! Can't anything be done about your — condition?" David asked anxiously once more.

"No. I've consulted the best sawbones in the land and they can do nothing. But don't fret yourself. I figure I've still got time left to see the defeat of the Secessionists and an end to this war." He extended brown-splotched hands toward the flames, and said over one shoulder, "Describe your service abroad and your voyage home."

David complied. Omitting unnecessary detail, he told in full of his fruitful — from an intelligence point of view — cruise aboard the H.M.S. *Warrior*, as he had not to Mr. Allen in Bermuda. He watched his father's interest mount.

"Is she an all-iron man-o'-war?"

"Not quite, sir, but the *Warrior* is armored with four-inch plate iron down to her waterline and along both beams from just aft of the bow all the way to her stern."

"Humph. What's her armament?"

"She mounts around thirty-six heavy guns, some of them rifled and some on pivots. Venture she could blow any ordinary man-o'-war, even a ship of the line, higher than a kite."

The old man murmured, when David fell silent: "Now isn't that interesting! Makes a body think hard." Again he held grotesquely misshapen hands toward the fireplace. "Reckon we'd better figure out an answer pretty quick. Heard tell the Rebs are building an iron-plated steam ram or something very like that."

"Is her hull of iron, too?"

"No. It's wooden, actually, like that of the *Merrimac*, which they've razed down to her berth deck."

As if on cue, Manuel appeared, bearing two hot rum toddies — cinnamon, lemon peel, and all. Captain Dexter took such a long swallow that his snowy side-whiskers swayed like abbreviated gull's wings.

"So far so good, son. What have you heard concerning that so-called French ironclad named *le* or *la Gloire* — or something like that?" Languages had never been his forte.

"I'm sure Ira can explain that in detail, sir. He made a cruise on her in the Mediterranean. I've invited him to stay with us till he's assigned to duty — is that all right?"

"Of course. Recognized him straight away. Wasn't he a classmate of yours at Annapolis?"

"Yes, Captain."

"And recently?"

"He's been doing at our Paris legation pretty much the same as I've been doing at St. James's — a bit of genteel spying, as it were. We both have learned a good bit about modern marine engines and armoring of men-of-war."

"Damn it, David, why didn't you inform me of this before? Manuel! Manuel! Run upstairs, present my compliments to Mr. Thatcher. Tell him I wish him to report below at once!"

When Ira appeared, doing the last button on a stylishly cut waistcoat of brown velour, he stiffened to attention and clicked his heels. "Sir, Lieutenant Thatcher reporting."

The old man laughed. "At ease, Mr. Thatcher; you forget I'm retired. Take a seat and try some of Manuel's justly famous rum toddies."

Once the drinks had been served and sampled, the Captain remarked, "If things are anything like they were in my day, I expect that for the next few days you young roosters are going to be almighty occupied socially. It's providential you've shown up today, so both of you must be free to attend a small dinner party I'm giving tonight in honor of Mr. John Ericsson, the Swedish-American genius who has invented more truly practical machines for use on land or water than there are fleas on a mongrel's back. You'll accept?"

"Of course, sir," David said. "We feel unduly privileged to meet so distinguished a guest."

"Oh, one thing. Mr. Ericsson won't be able to dine with us since, for some time, he's had an important appointment with the famous cannon designer, Captain John Dahlgren, whose influence with the Navy Department can't wisely be ignored. Therefore my ingenious Swedish guest can only arrive in time for coffee, liqueurs, and cigars. Still, there should remain ample time for constructive conversation."

David recalled something. "So sorry, sir, to hear that mother and Abigail have had to go up to New Haven. Is grandfather seriously ill?"

"I fear so. If I remember right, Abner Stevens is a mere cockerel of seventy-two; but then, most of the Stevenses, like us Dexters, live to disappoint our heirs."

By the way father tilted his head to one side and mildly stroked his side-whiskers, David foresaw what was coming. "Of course there is our family's *very private* motto, which is 'Hang for rape at eighty.' A high mark to shoot at, true, but a few of us Dexters have made it — or so they say. Of course, I'll not be one to score that honored distinction — with this blasted rheumatism."

To simplify matters for Ira and David, Captain Dexter ordered the guest list for dinner sent up, along with an armful of newspapers from which Ira, in particular, might identify some of the important guests. The foremost certainly must be Cornelius, nicknamed "Harry," Delamater, whose Novelty Ironworks were reputed to build the best and most powerful of steamboat engines. Two of these were of the horizontal type, each developing 320 horsepower, and presently being installed in the *Monitor*.

Listed also were Cornelius H. Bushnell, owner of a railroad and a foundry up in New Haven, Connecticut; and Thomas F. Rowland, of the Continental Ironworks, on Calyer Street, in whose huge ship house the iron hull of "Ericsson's Folly" was taking shape. Some newspapers termed Ericsson's invention a "floating steam battery"; others derisively dubbed it a "tin cheesebox on a raft."

A member of the Ironclad Board was quoted as saying that nothing like it had ever been seen on earth and predicted she would capsize on launching.

The dinner list concluded with I. W. Merrick, of the Aetna Ironworks, a Charles Delany, and a Mr. Griswold, to whose name no identification had been attached.

Ira spent the rest of the day attempting to discover whether any postal or telegraphic connections still existed with Virginia, only to learn that they did not. But somehow he must advise his mother that he'd returned to

America and would inform her of his whereabouts the moment he was reassigned. Probably she was still living in Norfolk, where his father, Captain Scott Thatcher, a Virginian and a native of that city, had returned seven years ago for retirement, only to die early in 1861 during an epidemic of typhoid fever.

A letter from his mother, bearing these sad tidings, had reached him in Paris and proved to be the last he'd received from her. If she was still living in Norfolk, these must be perilous times for her, since both of his brothers, the last he heard, were holding commissions in the Regular Army's Corps of Engineers. Well, until he found out about these matters, there was nothing to do but report and offer to make his engineering skills and other experience available. Why shouldn't his special knowledge of the machinery, engines, and ordnance of foreign navies serve as a step toward promotion?

With great care he was brushing at a rebellious cowlick in his thick dark-brown hair when Manuel knocked. "Señor, El Capitán and Señor David would be pleased if you would join them for a drink before the guests arrive."

14

The Backers

SINCE MORNING it had been obvious that tonight's dinner party would prove an affair of no mean importance. Why else should so many grocers' and vintners' carts and caterers' wagons keep pulling up in an alley behind the Dexter mansion? Manuel could be heard issuing orders, not loudly but effectively, as to what should be done.

Both Ira and David, still somewhat unsettled by the sea voyage and slow in regaining their "land legs," decided to postpone until the morrow reporting to Naval Headquarters in the Brooklyn Navy Yard, situated on the East River not far from Greenpoint. As Ira pointed out, both of them needed time to read recent newspapers and orient themselves, after a fashion, to whatever situations prevailed in the country. Much of this reading proved unpleasant; Union defeats, small ones, but nonetheless discouraging, had been frequent. Some engagements, no more than skirmishes in reality, had been fought out in the Middle West and at various points along the Mississippi River.

But what again and again struck the young officers were various reports and articles published which disclosed abundant details of the ironclad ram, the C.S.S. *Virginia*. Apparently, reporters must have been allowed to rove at will about the dry dock in which the ram was nearing completion, and could obtain answers to any question which came to mind; enthusiastic Southern braggarts evidently felt free to vouchsafe critically important information. In sum, the rebuilt *Merrimac*, now officially the *Virginia*, appeared to be nearing completion with dangerous rapidity, but not without serious delays in procuring vital equipment. However, most newspaper reports were in conflict over such crucial details as estimated speed, the caliber of her guns, and the thickness and placement of her armor. Both Ira and David, from their experience abroad, were well aware that should the *Virginia* be completed soon, no ship, or ships, in the United States Navy could hope to defeat her.

Both of them well knew that by now France had two semi-ironclads in commission and more under construction; England, not to be outdone by her ancient foe, already had commissioned three somewhat similar ironclads, the H.M.S. *Warrior* and the H.M.S. *Black Prince;* it was also rumored that four more had been laid down.

All manner of rumors were being circulated at the Battery Hotel, ever a favorite rendezvous for journalists of all sorts, concerning the iron vessel presently taking shape in the capacious ship house of Rowland's Continental Ironworks. Derisively, some reporters had labeled this unconventional craft "Ericsson's Folly," "Mousetrap of a Ship," or simply, "Ericsson's Death Trap."

Somewhere among the newspapers his father had supplied, David had read that a Captain Davis, of the Navy Department's Ironclad Board, when shown a cardboard model of Ericsson's invention, had commented acidly, "Take this little thing home and worship it, which would not be idolatry because it is in the image of nothing in the heavens above, or on the earth beneath, or in the waters under the earth!"

Cornelius Bushnell, the thick-bearded railroad magnate from New Haven, long had maintained a close friendship with Gideon Welles, Secretary of the Navy. It was he who persuaded Welles to take, and personally present, the cardboard model of the ship for President Lincoln's inspection. After carefully examining the model and listening to Bushnell's enthusiastic description of the proposed man-of-war, the President had remarked, with a dry chuckle, "Gentlemen, all I have to say about this is what the fat girl said when she put her foot into the stocking, 'It strikes me there is something in it.' "

Studying an old and wrinkled copy of the *New York Herald,* Ira was reminded again that when the contract for the *Monitor* had been signed in early October, it had included a proviso that she must be completed within one hundred days!

The reporter had written: "Here in the North we are supposed to be pretty efficient, but I doubt whether the Archangel Gabriel and the Twelve Apostles plus all the labor they cared to summon could accomplish such a miracle in so brief a time."

The article went on to report that, under contract, this radical craft must be able to turn up minimum speed of eight knots. There must also be a guarantee that men serving in the turret would be safe against shot of any weight or description, otherwise none of the contract money — all of the magnificent sum of $275,000 — would not be paid by the Government to Ericsson, his partners, and the subcontractors.

By eight o'clock, nine well-dressed and sometimes liberally bejeweled gentlemen, boasting a wide variety of hairy chin adornments, except for Ira and David, seated themselves at Captain Dexter's glittering and handsomely appointed mahogany table, reportedly fashioned by Sheraton himself for Sir Joshua Reynolds. Tall candles set in a pair of graceful Sheffield candelabra reinforced illumination afforded by an elegant French crystal chandelier to cast a mellow light over the table, the bottle-laden sideboard, and the gleaming silverware.

It seemed curious to Ira that when the guests arrived, not one of them was wearing a uniform! A pity, since he and David had been bursting to show off their brand-new, foreign-tailored full-dress blues.

Ira listened hard and contributed little to the conversation except when he overheard guests discussing various types of steam engines. Apparently, several sorts were to be installed aboard the *Monitor*. The main driving power was to be a pair of horizontal vibrating lever engines, mounted below the waterline, each developing 320 horsepower, and capable of driving a huge, single-screw propeller to attain a maximum speed of at least ten knots. Then there were also several lesser engines designed to drive ventilator fans; others would supply forced drafts for the boiler's fireboxes, and would pump the bilges. There was even a small engine Ericsson had designed to hoist shot and ammunition from the magazine into the turret, but what particularly amused the guests was the great inventor's design for flush toilets!

Mr. Griswold demanded, "Now, why in God's name would anybody want such things, even if practical? Space below is already jam-packed."

"Well, my friends," Captain Dexter observed, "we all must remember one very important thing concerning Mr. Ericsson's invention. Aboard the *Monitor* her entire crew must eat, sleep, and otherwise exist *below* the waterline! Therefore, there would be no way for a man heeding a call of Nature to go on deck to relieve himself."

Sitting at the head of the table, Captain Dexter laughed so hard that candlelight created brief golden speckles among his ample white side-whiskers. "Thank God I was born when a sailor while relieving himself could enjoy God's sunlight and find space to scratch his balls without banging an elbow."

Manuel and two maids deftly removed course after course, consisting of delicacies from terrapin à la Maryland to canvasback duck and filet mignon, along with salads, savories, and desserts. The rank of gleaming wine glasses of varying shapes and sizes ranging before each guest gradually shortened. Voices grew louder.

Cornelius Delamater, affable and standing straight despite a very well-filled vest, tapped an empty tumbler and raised a glass of wine. "Gentlemen, here's to our host, Daniel Dexter! Always has been a fine officer, a good friend, and a true patriot, but who would ever have suspected him of rivaling the Roman Emperor Lucullus as a connoisseur of fine wines and such rare fine victuals!"

Everyone arose and drank. David, feeling his drink a little, added, "And to the finest father in all the world!"

"David, I fear you exaggerate," the Captain protested, peering upward. "Old failing of yours, but thank you all the same." He looked enormously pleased and proud.

Talk centered on the *Monitor* and the slowing progress in her construction. It appeared that quite a few essential parts and materials, due to wintry conditions, were arriving late or at unpredictable intervals, by boat, barge, and railroad from towns and foundries as widely separated as Nashua, New Hampshire, Buffalo, New Haven, and Baltimore — not to mention plate iron and port lids from Rensselaer and Albany, New York.

Inevitably, conversation shifted to the South's ironclad ram. As both David and Ira had already perceived from the newspapers, and judging by a plethora of articles and artists' sketches appearing in journals and magazines such as *Harper's* and *Leslie's Weekly*, security precautions around Newport News and the Gosport Navy Yard certainly must be as lax or possibly even more slipshod than those prevailing in the North. Consolidating their sum afforded a fairly accurate picture of the Rebel's progress in arming the ex-U.S.S. *Merrimac.*

Everyone knew that this once magnificent frigate had been razed down to her berth deck and then topped by a massive, barnlike casemate sheathed in iron, built along its sides to an angle of forty-five degrees and protected by rolled plate iron. She was to be armed with ten cannon: two seven-inch rifles were mounted, one at the bow and the other at her stern; two six-inch rifles and six nine-inch smooth-bore guns constituted her broadside. In other words, the "ram" (as she was designated by the press because of a cast-iron beak four feet long fixed under her bow) carried ten of the most modern and efficient guns capable of firing heavy projectiles with impressive penetrating power.

Someone inquired about the state and strength of her engines.

Cornelius Bushnell dabbed a spot of wine from a neatly pointed beard and observed, "By all reports, she's to be driven by the same engines that propelled the original frigate."

"Yes," nodded the red-haired, bearded John T. Griswold, who had just come down from his foundry in Buffalo to straighten out a mix-up of some sort, "so far as we know, that's our enemy's weak point."

Captain Dexter added quietly, "Most of us know that both the *Merrimac*'s engines and her boilers were condemned before she was burned and the Rebels captured her. That's so, isn't it, Delamater?"

"From what I've learned, the Rebels have been working day and night to restore those engines to good working order."

Pursing his lips over a goblet of Napoleon cognac, Merrick, of the Aetna Ironworks, queried, "D'you think they're being successful?"

Across the table Tom Rowland, from the Continental Ironworks, shook a balding head. "We've no way of knowing about that till the ram undergoes some trial runs, but as an engineer, I venture she won't prove fast, not with her overall length of one hundred and seventy-two feet and all the weight of armor, guns, ammunition, and fuel we've been informed she is supposed to carry."

"Of course, speed, plus an ability to maneuver briskly, will make all the difference in her effectiveness," Rowland commented. "So if she proves even moderately speedy, I can't at this moment see any way of stopping her." He selected a bonbon and revolved it before popping it into his mouth, licking his fingers like a small boy. His glance ranged down the table to the two young officers, who were eating heartily, but listening hard. "I presume you all have heard there's a tide of panic beginning to rise over the *Merrimac*'s threat to Washington. Even here in New York some important people are a little anxious."

Delamater nodded, "So I've heard. Some intelligent people claim that if the *Merrimac* succeeds in sinking our squadron of powerful men-o'-war blockading Hampton Roads, the ram would then be free to harry and place under ransom Eastern ports all the way up to Portland, Maine."

Captain Dexter signaled Manuel to circulate coffee and cigars before commenting, "All the same, one can't help wondering how seaworthy this ram would prove, considering her radical design and carrying so much armor."

A slight pause followed, while the guests dabbed at finger bowls.

"Probably she'd be no more sea-keeping than the *Monitor,*" Cornelius Delamater conceded. "Outside of this room I wouldn't say it — and I count on all present to give their word not to repeat me when I say, in strictest confidence, that I entertain grave doubts about the seaworthiness of our little vessel. In fact I . . ."

He broke off as a big voice boomed from the far end of the dining room's main entrance. Now it was filled by the towering, broad-shouldered figure of John Ericsson, inventor *par excellence* of many sorts of practical machinery from locomotives to caloric engines and flush toilets. Color in his squarish features flowed unusually high to those who knew him best. "About that," he almost roared, "none of you need to lose sleep. Correctly, I have calculated my vessel's probable buoyancy. She will float, all right, and will prove entirely seaworthy for short voyages along the coast! I vass . . ." a trace of Scandinavian accent made itself evident whenever Ericsson got angry, which he often was ". . . not paid to design a deep seagoing man-o'-war."

Everyone at the table became aware that this celebrated man still was seething as a result of what must have been a monumental row with someone of importance. Captain Dexter started to signal Manuel to serve *Branntwein,* which, Delamater had confided, was the inventor's favorite liqueur, from a frosted dark-green bottle nesting in a hole carved out of a solid block of ice, but checked himself. John Ericsson appeared too enraged to be placated so easily. Advancing into the dining room, he didn't bother to nod to or greet any of the several important guests he knew very well.

David and Ira registered impressions of a tall, broad-shouldered individual with a boxlike face, broad chin, receding hairline, and icy-cold blue eyes. "Muttonchop" whiskers on either side descended his cheeks, appearing to reach up as though to touch the ends of a pale, wide, and uncompromising mouth. The eminent Swedish-American's nose was straight and short and his eyebrows so scant as to be barely perceptible.

Cornelius Delamater, who knew him best, got up, and patted his shoulder. "Easy on, John, this is a friendly dinner party, not a Navy Board meeting. We are all friends here."

"Don't mention the goddamn Navy Board!" bellowed Ericsson, so forcefully the candle flames on the table wavered. "Enough of those conceited idiots I haff had too often!"

"What's happened this time?" Bushnell — the other Cornelius — inquired, exhaling a puff of fine Havana smoke.

Ira thought that if this late arrival had been a bull, he would start tossing his head, snorting and pawing at the carpet. "My Gott! To inspect my invention the Board sends this Commander David Porter, a fancy, high-and-mighty officer, all gold braid and brass buttons flashing. I ask him what he wants. He says he has been ordered to conduct a survey of my ship for the Navy Department."

Guests pushed their chairs back from the gleaming table. To most of them John Ericsson's mercurial rages were nothing unusual, but this was a beauty! T. F. Rowland, who knew all about Porter's inspection, sighed and devoted his attention to clipping precisely a long cigar.

Bushnell inquired, "So what that's so bad happened, John?"

"This *gentleman*," Ericsson's tone implied that Commander David Dixon Porter was anything but one, "ranges all about your ship house, Rowland, talking to himself. He called my ship an 'iron piss pot' and those beautiful engines which are to revolve the turret 'common coffee grinders'! He even insulted one of my most valuable engineers by naming him a huge sham with bird brains!"

The big Swedish-American — he had become naturalized long years ago — almost spat. "I vass ready to explode when, too late, this gilded fellow suddenly laughs and says, 'Forget all I've just said. In my opinion this ship, properly handled, can destroy any vooden man-o'-war afloat.' "

The inventor remained red-faced, bright blue eyes glaring. "Whether dot damn fool meant that or not, I don't know and care less. Pray Gott such a idiot never gets sent abroad on a diplomatic mission of any sort!"

Cornelius Delamater raised a placating hand. "Hold hard, old friend, and simmer down. It's well known David Porter has a perverted sense of humor, but don't forget that he himself is a master designer, and more important, wields considerable influence in Washington. Personally, I believe he really meant that last comment of his."

It seemed a propitious moment for the host, peering up through frosty brows, to signal Manuel to serve the *Branntwein* — a sizable noggin of which was poured for the late arrival, who had accepted a chair next to Captain Dexter and appeared to be calming down somewhat. Ira watched Ericsson's high color gradually fade once he had gulped a big swallow of *Branntwein.*

David's father, on occasion, had heard descriptions of this genius's varied and generally successful inventions. Born in a log cabin at Langbanshytann in central Sweden, of a mining inspector and a Scottish-Swedish mother, young John had served in the Twenty-third Rifle Corps of the Swedish Army and even then had been experimenting with model machines.

Through the influential backing of one Robert F. Stockton, he'd arrived in America in June 1839, and had continued to design machinery of real and lasting value. It was he who had designed the hull of the U.S.S. *Princeton,* an unlucky ship from the start. On it a great cannon called "the Peacemaker," with which he'd had nothing to do, had exploded, killing the Secretary of the Navy and seriously wounding John Tyler, President of the United States, and Cabinet members of an official inspecting party.

Treacherously, Robert Stockton had quickly placed the blame on Ericsson, although soon it was proved that responsibility for the disaster lay, in fact, with Dahlgren, a famous designer of heavy artillery who for once had failed to cause sufficient white-hot iron bands to be shrunk around to reinforce this monster cannon's breech.

Gradually tension relaxed while billows of gray-white cigar smoke began to curl and drift toward the chandelier. For those who didn't care for *Branntwein* — which much resembled *aquavit* — sherry, cognac, or extra-aged bourbon whiskey was offered.

David, studying the bent figure of his father, sensed that he had something of importance on his mind. During a lull in the conversation, Captain Dexter turned toward Ericsson, lounging on his right and puffing equably at a long-stemmed meerschaum pipe. "I presume," he said, "you're too occupied to have heard that some friends and I have recently completed an open-hearth forge and foundry not far up the East River. I'm aware this is late in the game, but if Dexter and Son can do anything to speed the *Monitor*'s completion, we would be pleased and honored to offer contract bids."

Ericsson passed the back of a huge ink-stained hand over a sweaty, receding hairline and answered quietly. "Thank you, my host, for your offer. We can use all the help we can get. Would you care to contract for special designs for some small engines I haff drawn?"

"And what might they be?" Delamater queried. "Thought we've engaged all the subcontractors we can use."

"How many engines have you already called for?" demanded John Griswold.

"My plans at present call for fifteen," Ericsson replied. "I need badly two blower engines for forced drafts into the fireboxes; also, I need a small machine to operate the flush toilets."

A ripple of laughter broke the tension. "Flush toilets! Surely," Tom Rowland chuckled, "you can't mean that."

Ericsson gulped the last of his colorless iced liqueur, and yawned. He looked dead tired. "But I do. Aboard a ship designed like this, the crew's health is of more importance than ammunition. I must have some flush toilets on time. Since the whole ship's company must eat, sleep, and work below the waterline, there can be none of the usual heads or latrines on the foredeck. I doubt whether any of us would enjoy using a head over the *Monitor*'s bows, which will be covered with water most of the time."

Ira was astounded by how quickly David's father said, "Sir, if you can furnish detailed designs for such, and the blower machinery too, in a hurry, I will accept that responsibility."

"It will be done," Ericsson promised, "but they must be ready for installation inside of two weeks."

Cornelius Delamater shook his head. "Wish you good luck. You're going to need it by the jugful."

Once the guests had departed and the clink of china and glassware being washed below stairs became audible, David sipped the last of his brandy and turned to Ira. "I expect we'd better report to the Naval Commandant for this district tomorrow." He turned to his father. "Sir, where are these Headquarters located?"

"In the Brooklyn Navy Yard — it lies not half a mile away." He raised bushy white brows. "I presume both of you have already made up your minds about what kind of assignment you'd prefer?"

David was surprised to hear Ira say, without the least hesitation, "Sir, should you find me qualified, I will request assignment to duty at your shipyard, provided I can work on the machinery and put to use my engineering experience which, with all modesty, is rather specialized and extensive."

"Even to flush toilets?" smiled the old man.

"Even to mounting flush toilets. You see, sir, I really want to work on the *Monitor*."

"Why so?"

"Because I've a strong premonition that although she may prove of uncertain value as a sea-keeping warship, she will have a great impact on the navies of Europe, and small as she is, will prove a very formidable warship. Will you accept my services, sir, if the Department agrees?"

The Captain drew a long, slow breath. "I'll have to sleep on that, son. Hope you don't mind my calling you such. You see, I've always wanted David to have a brother." He half smiled. "It has long been a rule in our family, when we face an important decision, to sleep on it. I will let you know in the morning." He glanced at his son. "What about you?"

David put down his glass, and said carefully, "Well, sir, with all due respect, as soon as possible I'd like to be sent to duty off Fort Monroe."

The veteran's shaggy white brows lifted. "Oh, would you now? Then I expect you'd prefer orders for service with our blockade squadron off Hampton Roads?"

This wasn't exactly what David had in mind, but he thought it better not to say so. "That would suit me very well, sir."

"I'll see what can be done. I have some contacts in Washington who possibly might accomplish your preference."

15

Imperial French Consulate General

THE FIFTEENTH OF JANUARY proved so astonishingly mild and pleasant that Mademoiselle Arlette Louise d'Aubrey, tucking small feet shod in green leather *bottes* under her, settled onto a bench in a small park located behind the Battery, where a wide variety of activity was taking place. Her appointment with the French Consul General, Baron Rémy Lebel, was not until ten, and it was only twenty minutes past nine. That was because she had quite unexpectedly succeeded in hailing a hackney cab close to Madame Antoine's salon, and for once had encountered little traffic during a long ride down to Manhattan Island's southernmost tip.

Absently, Arlette stared unseeingly ahead, oblivious to her bustling surroundings, until, to a brisk rat-tat-tat of drums, a column of blue-clad infantry bearing long-barreled muskets and muffled in heavy overcoats tramped into the park. Briefly, these troops halted until, in obedience to shouted commands from their officers, the measured tramp of heavy boots divided itself into two units. Amid a mist of breath vapors, one detachment set off toward one of several New York–New Jersey ferry slips. The remainder, meanwhile, turned off to the left and disappeared in the direction of the East River.

Noticing her puzzled expression, a pipe-smoking soldier seated beside her, a sergeant as advertised by his triple stripes, explained good-naturedly, "Ma'am, them there are replacements for our Ninth Regiment, headed south."

"But, sir," Arlette queried, "why do the men move off in different directions? Have they quarreled?"

"Lord love you, no, Ma'am," the noncom explained, "they ain't mad at one another; 'tis only because the First Battalion — them that are headed toward the ferries — have been ordered south to defend Washington; the others are going off to board transports headed for Hampton Roads."

"Hampton Roads? Where is that?"

"Dunno for sure, but it's somewhere down in Virginia, they tell me. Likely they're going down to reinforce Fort Monroe or some other fort close by Norfolk where the Rebels have a great big naval and ship-building base."

When an officer, a captain, called out, the sergeant tapped dottle from his pipe and, grinning at this pretty little lady, brushed his kepi's beak, " 'Scuse me, Mum, but the Cap'n can't nohow fight this war 'thout me." He swung off toward another knot of infantry falling in along the square's far side.

It had come as no surprise that when Arlette called on Madame Thérèse Antoine, evidently one of New York's leading fashionable *arbitre elegant*, she had ascertained in short order that she was not about to enter the smart garment trade. Vividly, she recalled presenting credentials enclosed in an imposing heavy linen envelope bearing the blue wax seal of the Emperor Napoleon III's Ministry of Marine and duly signed and sealed by her protector, the Marquis de la Villette.

Reading the message, Madame Antoine, a handsome, middle-aged woman with large and vitreous jet eyes and blue-black hair, had registered surprise, remarking cheerfully, *"Alors, ma petite,* one ees mos' pleased to welcome you to thees City of New York. It ees noisy but much moneys ees to be made here now — by one means or another."

From the rear of Madame Antoine's reception parlor sounded a rising chatter of female voices: "Oh, zos seely weemen!" She arose and in something like a parrot's screech, called out, "Be quiet, zee lot of you!" Silence descended.

"Upon zee receipt of certain instructions," Madame continued, "I have obtain' a room for you een a *pension* across zee street. 'Ave no fear; it ees a clean and proper establishment." Softly she added in French, "For us to be heard conversing in our own language might cause risks there is no point in taking."

Arlette was delighted to know that she wasn't expected to stitch and sew, a skill which, since childhood, she'd always abhorred.

"*Mais non, ma petite,* two days I weel grant you to accustom yourself somewhat to thees violent country. You 'ave friends here?"

"No, Madame, only an Englishman, a journalist I met aboard the ships which conveyed us from England."

Madame Antoine's manner underwent a curious change. Shrewdly, she asked, "A newspaperman, *hein?* How ees he called?"

"Mister Lion-el Humphrey of the London *Telegraph.*"

"I presume," Madame Antoine inquired quietly, "you know where thees gentleman ees to be found, *non?*"

"*Oui,* Madame. When we parted, he told me he intended to spend a little time in New York."

"*Bon.*"

To Arlette's considerable surprise, Madame Antoine, looking pleased, produced a handsome silver case, and of all things, offered her a cigarette. Smilingly, Arlette refused. She had tried a few of them, but had experienced no pleasure beyond the pleasure that came with appearing *à la mode.*

Taking Arlette aside, the proprietress of Modes Parisiennes whispered, "I wish I could tell you about your duties here een America, but since I know only a little, I must leave thees to our distinguished Consul General, Baron Lebel." Delicately, Madame Antoine lifted her cigarette to thin, lavender-hued lips, and puffed gently a few times. "*Ma chérie,* I hope I may be of assistance once you undertake your new duties."

"Can you tell me nothing at all of their nature, Madame?"

"If I could, perhaps, but I dare not; that will be Monsieur le Consul Général's responsibility."

Forgetting that on shipboard she had given Lionel Humphrey Madame Antoine's address, she was both astonished and pleased when Madame handed her a hastily scrawled note from Lionel Humphrey, noting that he had taken a room in the Battery Hotel and hoped that some evening soon she might join him for dinner and the theater. She still carried his note in her reticule.

Arlette wondered whether her proud but indigent Papa would be pleased with his daughter's conduct thus far? Perhaps, but what next was going to happen? No telling. Probably that problem would be resolved in the Imperial French Consulate General's handsome offices just off Wall Street.

With a flattering lack of delay, Mlle Arlette d'Aubrey was escorted into the presence of Baron Rémy Lebel, whom she discovered seated behind a huge Louis XV desk. With him was a thin, large-featured, clean-shaven individual, who sat at one end of a well-polished table. She could feel his gaze taking in her aristocratic bearing and modish costume, from little balmoral boots and Spanish lamb's wool blouse to her bonnet of brown bark, secured by a gay plaid ribbon.

Gracious as only a French diplomat could be, Baron Lebel quickly put his caller at ease and introduced his guest as André de la Pléignière, a Capitaine de Vaisseau in the Imperial Navy.

"Mademoiselle, one is pleased to find you so well-bred and so ravishingly attractive," he said smiling, alert pale-blue eyes busy. He consulted a note. "It is a considerable asset that you speak English so perfectly. *Non?*"

"It is faultless, I am told, Monsieur le Baron, save during an excess of emotion."

"A weakness you must conquer if you are to be of real service to the Empire."

Arlette was conscious of subtle appraisal on the part of Capitaine de la Pléignière who, because of a long, thin, pointed nose and small, alert, dark eyes, suggested a heart-broken greyhound.

The Consul General then planted elbows on the table, laced fingers under his chin, and admitted that the French Government knew more than a little about the *Monitor*'s construction. This was largely because, a few years ago, a surprisingly similar vessel had been designed by one Puy d'Lôme.

"Even now," Baron Lebel commented, "we have three agents actively and discreetly employed at the Continental Ironworks, learning details of Monsieur Ericsson's curious invention."

Capitaine de la Pléignière spoke for the first time. "A positive genius, this Swedish-American; but how practical his radical ideas will prove in battle remains a conjecture."

The Consul General nodded. "But what will be required of you, Mademoiselle d'Aubrey, is to obtain, as discreetly as possible, all manner of information, even minute details, concerning the *Merrimac,* possibly the *Monitor*'s rival. This is a matter of the first importance, since the ram those gallant Southerners are building now nears completion, or so we are informed."

"I understand, Monsieur le Baron. How am I to proceed on this mission?"

The Baron told her. "Mademoiselle, you will at all costs delicately, tactfully, ingratiate yourself with certain foreign and native war correspondents who, due to the nature of their profession, specialize in noting significant facts and plans."

Smiling sweetly, Arlette straightened on a fragile gilt Louis XV occasional chair. "In that case, Monsieur le Baron, I think I am already in a position to obtain information of this nature."

"How so?" demanded Baron Lebel.

"Monsieur, on the steamer coming from Europe I encountered a celebrated English war correspondent, Lion-el Humphrey, who described many major conflicts during the Crimean War."

To her astonishment, she found herself genuinely excited over the prospect of resuming contact with gangling, humorous, and unexpectedly sensitive Lionel Humphrey; but of this she naturally said nothing, only studied the Baron's sharp features. "Monsieur, may I enquire what is the exact nature of the information you wish to obtain?"

"Anything concerning this ram's armor, armament, and more important, the condition of her engines." He held up a slim, blue-veined hand. "What we especially need to know, for certain, is how close the *Merrimac* is near to completion. Some Yankees — Northerners — are terrified by the threats presented by this ram's very existence. Already heavy defensive batteries are being thrown up in this city and on nearby islands."

The two officials discussed details of the Rebel ram's expected attacks, most of which Arlette could not comprehend. Then Capitaine de la Pléignière leaned forward, "And where is this English newspaperman friend of yours staying?"

From her reticule Arlette drew out Humphrey's note. "At the Battery Hotel, Messieurs."

"*Bon.* Fortunately this Battery Hotel lies nearby," the Consul General said. "Although every *pension* and hotel in this city at present is filled to overflowing, I personally will ensure that you, Mademoiselle d'Aubrey, will be accommodated in the Battery Hotel this afternoon. From the moment you receive your instructions" — he was sufficiently tactful not to say orders — "from Monsieur le Capitaine, who is of His Imperial Majesty's intelligence service, you will follow his instructions to the letter." For a moment the Baron's pointed and ascetic features tightened. "Apparently there is no need to warn that the use of the utmost discretion to acquire this information is required. Should you say or do something likely to jeopardize the success of your mission, there are very unpleasant means of punishing a thoughtless agent."

De la Pléignière smiled, like a friendly wolf. "One feels convinced, Monsieur le Baron, that we need expect no breach of security on the part of this so attractive young lady. Once she secures her accommodations in the hotel, I will remain in touch. From all we learned, little time is left to spare. Matters are approaching a crisis, since today it has become known that this Southern ram is nearly ready for sea. Only the failure to arrive in Gosport of certain important elements of her machinery is delaying her sea trials."

To Arlette's surprise, the Consul General patted her hand, saying, "One is aware that this is a task of the most difficult. You will take *déjeuner* in my company in order that possibly I may assist in helping you to avoid errors."

It was astonishing, Arlette reminded herself, how smoothly problems of all natures could become resolved by the use of money, power, or both. Despite a biting wind off the Hudson River, she glowed from having seemingly obtained the Baron's good opinion. Entering the Battery Hotel, she advanced through a jam-packed lobby and inquired of a desk clerk for Mr. Lionel Humphrey. To her acute disappointment, she was informed that he was not expected to return until after noon.

Seating herself at a small writing desk, Arlette wrote in a handsomely shaded script:

Dear Lionel, prepare yourself for a shock. The stars in their wisdom have determined that I shall patronize this hotel from this afternoon on, for an indefinite period. Would I appear ill-bred if I admit I anticipate a renewal of a most agreeable friendship? In haste, but with anticipation, Arlette Louise d'Aubrey.

Scanning Arlette's note, Lionel Humphrey experienced a surge of pleasure inspired by something beyond recollections of a few bedtime frolics. How curious that this appealingly beautiful young woman should usually retain such aloof self-possession, but was also able to plunge rapturously into complicated throes of passion. How could she so unerringly sense exactly what her companion wished her to say — or to do.

With astonishing clarity, he could visualize Arlette's wealth of rather coarse but naturally wavy chestnut hair, her sensitive mouth and large, lively, gray-green eyes, set in gracefully oval features, marred only by a faint suggestion of hair along her upper lip. How *chic* was her clothing. He could visualize her as he had one evening beheld her, wearing a white worked muslin gown supported by a conservative hoop skirt adorned with seven graduated flounces and full bell sleeves.

What in God's name, he inquired of himself while stretching out in a deep armchair, could Arlette really be up to here in New York? From the start, instinct had warned him that here was no practiced, seductive adventuress. Certainly this young woman was well-born and educated, but she retained a genuine gaiety and radiant warmth lacking in all too many of his own countrywomen.

The reception clerk informed him that he expected Miss d'Aubrey to occupy her room about three o'clock. Surveying the jostling, overcrowded lobby, his hearing affronted by the continuous traffic noises and the more distant shrilling of steam whistles out in the harbor and the hurrying of feet along the sidewalk just below, Lionel again realized that this New York was unique, for all he had visited and even lived for a space in several foreign countries. Although the United States was foreign — had been since early 1789 — people spoke English here, although sometimes with odd inflections, just as they did at home. Nor was the atmosphere alien to an Englishman. Small wonder: basically, both countries observed many similar laws; both believed in the value of the given word, in fair play, and in sound currency.

Most Americans, however, with some few exceptions, lacked polish and dressed unfashionably. He was beginning to decide that the essential difference between the two nationalities was that here in America almost everybody of any social class appeared to be driven by an intense eagerness to succeed financially and socially, and otherwise to better themselves and their families.

What in the world could have motivated Arlette's voyage from France? Again he pondered; long ago his reporter's instinct had advised him that her tale of coming to New York to become a *modiste* was implausible. One had only to note the soft shapeliness of her white and delicate hand and fingers — neither suggested those of a professional seamstress.

Lionel settled back in his chair and lit a slim cheroot. They had really fine ones over here, he'd discovered. A considerable challenge to his correspondent's ingenuity it would be, he thought, to discover what lay behind this lovely creature's motives in so promptly reestablishing their friendship? Since it was nearing two o'clock and it was another hour before Arlette was expected, the Englishman decided to patronize the hotel's bar, where possibly he might pick up a few newsworthy items.

Before a pair of Negro porters deposited her baggage in a small but moderately comfortable room in the Battery Hotel, Arlette d'Aubrey's parting with Madame Antoine had proved surprisingly warm — and possibly genuine.

The older woman had said, in her slightly Provençal accent, "It grieves me, *chérie,* that our connection has proved of such brief duration. How I enjoy listening to your pure Parisian speech."

Impulsively, Madame Antoine had held her hands briefly between hers. "Always remember, *ma petite,* if things should go wrong, as they often do in this rough country and in such troubled times, you have only to communicate with me." Tears momentarily dimmed her black, bird-quick eyes. "Oh, how I long to return to France, but in America — remember this — dwelling is not at all difficult provided one learns to adapt and not to be critical of — well, strange manners, speech, and more important, thoughts."

Once more or less settled in her room, Arlette sent a note by a bellboy to number 620, Lionel Humphrey's room, adding her own room number 714, then continued to unpack her luggage. God in Heaven! How mussed and rumpled were these priceless gowns, robes, and dresses — products of the best salons in Paris.

Flatteringly soon there came a rap on her door and a voice, unmistakably that of Lionel Humphrey, inquired, "I say, my dear, may I intrude?"

"But of course. Please enter, *mon ami.*" She unlatched the door, stepped back, and quite failed in her attempt to suppress the thrill she experienced in once again beholding this lanky, red-faced, towering Englishman.

If Humphrey experienced similar reactions he concealed them by drawling, "Fortunes of war sometimes turn out for the better, eh what?" He started forward, opened his arms, and then lowered them.

Ah, these *sacré Anglais*. She'd expected him at least to embrace her, but then she reminded herself that under present circumstances, he must not be allowed to take anything for granted, despite certain delightful moments in Bermuda and on the *Princess Royal*. "Ah, my dear Arlette." He merely kissed her hand.

After a brief discussion as to what might have happened to their erstwhile shipboard companions, Lionel produced and placed a monocle over his left eye.

At her startled expression, he pulled flowing, yellow-brown side-whiskers and winked. "It's only ordinary glass, of the windowpane variety, but I've already discovered that many upper-class Americans — can't imagine why — appear to respect an Englishman who sports an eyeglass. So, since it may serve to smooth the progress of one's work, I've adopted this silly thing."

Considering Arlette, he wondered how that delightful young woman had managed on this occasion to appear so smartly attired in a walking costume consisting of a black pelisse over a light gown of black silk. Her eyes, he noted, were shaded by a stylish "jockey cap," bearing a trio of pheasant's tail feathers attached above its brim and to one side. On a chair at her side reposed a little muff of silver-gray chinchilla.

Following their separation after landing, it had occurred to Lionel that Mademoiselle d'Aubrey quite possibly might prove useful in turning up useful bits of information such as a man might hesitate to confide to another. Aye, such a clever young female, properly handled, very well might prove of use in that unscrupulous jungle of journalistic rivalry in which he'd been schooled.

Gracefully, Arlette smoothed full, wide skirts. "And so, *mon bon ami*, how do matters proceed in your direction?"

"Not badly, except that the *Telegraph*'s editors have engaged a new accountant who's written complaining that my expenses are exorbitant. Don't know who this blighter might be, except that apparently he can't comprehend the validity and importance of certain important but expensive items listed on my expense account."

Lionel laughed softly, went over and kissed her cheek — like an uncle. "Now, my sweet, let us forget such sordid details. Half an hour from now I am about to treat some journalistic friends to drinks in the café below. Do you care to join us?"

"Why not, *mon ami?* Who will be present?"

"William Dade of the *New York Herald,* Alan Simmons of the *New York Tribune,* and also Mr. Charles Farnham who, for a change, is a popular artist-illustrator covering the war for *Leslie's Weekly.* Don't ask me how accurate his drawings are — people like them."

Arlette entered the names in a mental notebook: Simmons, Dade, and Farnham.

"Now," Lionel drawled, after allowing the useless monocle to drop to the end of its ribbon, "I think the fellow we should devote especial attention to is Joseph Hayes, a leading and popular correspondent on the *Washington Evening Star.* Already I suspect Hayes really knows more true facts about the *Merrimac* than anyone else I've encountered. Unfortunately, Hayes is returning to Washington in a day or two, but I'm confident he'd enjoy meeting such a tastefully dressed, intelligent, and otherwise appealing young French lady. I'm convinced Joseph Hayes might prove to be a most valuable source of information about this Rebel ironclad, which everyone here feels so fearful of. Knowing this, my dear Arlette, that I'm really working, may I still count on your presence in the café?"

Arlette managed a slight, yet somehow intimate smile. *"Mon cher,* only big bears and many wolves could keep me away." Suddenly, she flung her arms about the startled Englishman. "Oh, you can have no idea of how good it is to behold a trusted face once more." Lightly her lips again brushed his cheek, crisscrossed and tinted by many tiny red veins. *"Alors, à tout à l'heure."*

"Good. It will afford me a vast pleasure to boast our friendship, and . . ." He started to continue, but broke off, jerked a half-bow, and was gone. For so tall a man, Lionel Humphrey could move very quickly and quietly.

Once the door had clicked shut, Arlette stared at the ceiling. *Nom de Dieu!* She had been assigned to collect — God knew how — all possible information concerning this Confederate vessel called *Merrimac* and had wondered where to begin when, *pouf!* all of a sudden what promised to be a rich source of information had offered itself, and with no effort on her part!

Even after so brief a stay in New York, she was aware that Washington must be the place to acquire intelligence of any real value. And Joseph Hayes came directly from Washington!

16

Letters

As usual, Ira Thatcher had beaten David out of bed and gone downstairs for breakfast. It was typical of him to go early to report to Commodore Gregory, the Commandant of the New York Navy Base in Brooklyn, as early as possible. Ira felt all aglow now that Captain Dexter had virtually assured him of an assignment in some way directly connected with the *Monitor*'s construction.

Back upstairs, David awoke sufficiently to consider the multiple and difficult problems presented by his engagement to Louisa Ridgely. For months memories of Louisa's innate sweetness, intelligence, and cultured beauty had almost constantly occupied his leisure-time imagination. Sitting up in bed, he reached out, and pulled the bell cord for Manuel.

Today, he realized, he would have to face up to the gravest decision of his life. How deeply his conscience was taxed, but whatever the cost, he *would*, by God, have Louisa to wife. But how to accomplish this? By altering his allegiance? It was so terrible a price that even now he couldn't make up his mind.

Should he join the Confederate Navy, no matter how this war ended, he would never dare face any member of his family. Mother in particular was bitter in her open contempt and hatred for those who were attempting to rend a nation so slowly, so painfully united.

Manuel appeared, bearing a small tray complete with coffee, sweet butter, jam, and crullers. "By the way," David inquired casually, "have there recently been any letters addressed to me arriving here?"

The butler dropped his gaze as if caught prying. "Only two *cartas*, Señor, and they arrived many weeks ago."

"Where were they postmarked?"

Manuel, looking most unhappy, said, "A city called Richmond, Señor. That is in Virginia, no?"

"Yes. What happened to them?"

"The last I saw of them was when la Señora, your mother, took them, saying she would readdress and forward them to you in London."

If suddenly a pail of ice water had been spilled over his head, David couldn't have been more shocked. Could Louisa's letters have been read and then destroyed? Oh Lord, why did mother have to be away in New Haven now, of all times? As if to compound David's agony, a telegram had arrived only that morning reporting that her father's strength was receding slowly.

"You saw the letters yourself, Manuel?"

"*Sí*, Señor. Both were written by a lady using most beautiful handwriting."

"Do you recall anything else about these letters?"

"No, Señor. Only that El Capitán observed that they must have been fetched North by Federal officers returning from the front. There is — what you say? — no regular postal service remaining with Southern States."

Never before had David felt so wretched. Those letters from Richmond *must* have been written by Louisa. Why had he never received them? The tragic likelihood occurred that Mamma, a passionate Unionist, had read Louisa's letters and then had destroyed them lest they damage her son's career.

17

Crossroads

It was a spacious but sparsely furnished and uncomfortably chilly office occupied by Commodore Francis H. Gregory at the Headquarters of the Navy Department in Brooklyn. Its austerity resembled that of some hard-line commanding officer's cabin aboard a ship of the line, first rate. Perhaps because yet another blizzard was raging, hammering noises and the clang of armorers' mauls could not be heard.

David, clad in his best English-tailored undress uniform, stood to rigid attention before Commodore Gregory's wide desk, feeling lonely and unhappy.

The Commodore shoved aside a pile of papers, saying in a curiously high-pitched but penetrating voice, "I've just finished examining your fitness report, plus an account of recent activities at our London legation. They appear to be in order."

"Thank you, sir."

The Commodore looked up with an odd expression on his lean, brownish features. "Mr. Dexter, I am very pleaséd to see you. Because of a strange mischance, I had deemed you dead."

"Dead, sir? I don't understand."

"Humph! I presume you must have been aware for a long time that there is another David H. Dexter carried on the Regular Navy List?"

David vented a small, relieved sigh. "Aye, aye, sir. For some time this coincidence on occasion has caused me embarrassment. I have received orders intended for him, and vice versa. The officer you have mentioned graduated some three years ahead of my class at Annapolis."

Gregory's high, smooth forehead creased. "Mr. Dexter, in the future you will refer to that institution as 'the Naval Academy.'"

At last the Commodore motioned to a chair and, speaking over the sudden whine of saws, the clang of hammers, and the din caused by plate iron being riveted into position, said, "Please be seated, Mr. Dexter. Tell me, how is your esteemed father faring these days?"

"Not very well, sir," David said stiffly. "Apparently there is little hope of his condition's improving."

Some of the hard lines in the Commodore's features softened. "Grieved to hear you say so. In the old days, he and I were shipmates on several long cruises. Pray, present him with my best regards when you see him next." He settled back, eyes fixed on the ceiling, and fingers laced over a concave belly. "Now, I wish you to inform me precisely concerning your duties and experience as Assistant Military Attaché in London."

Once David had concluded his report, the Commodore's chair creaked softly as he shifted his weight forward. "Good! I'm more than pleased to hear what you've had to say. You can be of special use to the service at the present moment."

"Yes, sir, I very much hope so."

"In regard to the matter of reassignment — had you a choice in that matter, what would you prefer?"

Caught unawares, David fumbled, "Why — why, sir, I'd like to serve wherever action promises to be the most immediate."

"I gather," the Commodore remarked, "you would prefer an assignment possibly near Fort Monroe? Undoubtedly you are aware our North Atlantic Blockade Squadron is on duty in Hampton Roads, Newport News, and off Norfolk. Would you like that?"

"Oh, yes, sir!"

Commodore Gregory grunted. Tugging thoughtfully at a neatly pointed black goatee streaked with gray, he said, "Got any friends in the Richmond or Norfolk areas?"

David struggled to control his voice. "Aye, aye, sir. I have — or had," he instantly corrected himself, "several good friends and classmates coming from both those places."

"Good. Good." The gaunt officer rose, began to pace back and forth, halted a moment, and spoke in a flat undertone. "Mr. Dexter, what I'm about to propose to you *must* remain a secret, even under torture."

"Torture, sir?"

"Not a few Rebels are Indian or have Indian blood in them. Do you give me your sacred word of honor?"

"Aye, aye, sir. May I ask the nature of this mission?"

The Commodore went over to gaze at the wintry scene beyond a window, hands joined under coattails. "Shortly you will *pretend* to resign your commission in this Service and convince people your Southern sympathies are too strong to be denied any longer."

Like the deck of a ship tossed in a heavy seaway, the well-polished floor seemed to sway under David's feet. "Sir, do you require a real resignation?"

"No. Only a pretense of committing such an ignoble deed. However, I will be forced to let it be known in certain quarters that you have turned your coat."

Emotions whirled about David's mind like pinwheel fireworks in some Fourth of July display.

As from a distance, he heard the Commodore say, "As a man of honor, I know you will be deeply hurt by this seeming change of sides, but some of our best officers in the Old Service have chosen to do so — 'Deep Sea' Maury, Franklin Buchanan, and Josiah Tattnell, among others, if that is any comfort."

Returning to his desk, the Commodore selected a document and read a few minutes. "This letter is from the office of Gideon Welles, Secretary of the Navy." Squinting through hastily donned spectacles, Gregory read:

> It is most urgent, I stress the word *urgent,* that an officer of undoubted loyalty shall at once pretend to resign from our Service then proceed as fast as possible to tender his services to the so-called Confederate Navy. This Department deems it essential to post a reliable agent in the Gosport Navy Yard who, using an expert's eye, can inform us of *exact* details concerning the *Merrimac*'s armament, armor, estimated speed, and the size and quality of her crew.

"In other words, Mr. Dexter, you are prepared to accept a Rebel commission? Can you manage this, convincingly?"

"Yes, sir, I believe so."

"You understand, of course, you will be executed down South the moment the truth of your mission becomes exposed."

Incredible! So many soul-searching doubts appeared on the way to resolving themselves. Visions of Louisa momentarily blanked out other perceptions.

"Well, sir?" The Commodore's voice grated. David became conscious of that officer's sharp features and shrewdly penetrating black eyes. "Mr. Dexter, are you prepared to make such a sacrifice?"

David drew a long, deep breath. "Yes, sir, but on one condition."

"Which is?"

"That my father be informed of the truth of this matter; for him, to believe that I'd serve the Rebel cause undoubtedly would kill him."

"Upon that you have my word of honor," the Commodore assured him quietly.

"Thank you, sir." David hesitated again. "There's that serious matter of my namesake."

"Serious?"

"Aye, aye, sir. You can have no notion how often orders and signals intended for David Howard Dexter, Class of '51, of Niles, Ohio, have been forwarded to me at the Academy and vice versa. To complicate matters, David Howard and I must physically resemble one another to a certain degree. Although during my service at home and abroad I've attempted several times to meet my namesake, I've had no luck."

The Commodore jerked a few nods. "Now I understand several matters. Were you aware that this namesake of yours proved so competent that, despite his age, he was put in command of the U.S.S. sloop of war *Argus*, and early last year was ordered to patrol duty off Santo Domingo to suppress the slave trade?"

For a moment nothing further was said, then Commodore Gregory, having adjusted a pair of steel-rimmed spectacles on a long, beaklike nose, read the detailed report. "I note you've spent quite a few leaves down South. That so?"

David flushed scarlet. "Yes, sir. As a result, Miss Louisa Ridgely, of Culpeper, Virginia, and I are affianced."

Gregory's heavy, rattan-backed chair creaked as he settled back. "Ever since your name came up yesterday, I have been conjecturing about something."

"Something, sir?"

"Yes. The newspapers, some months ago, in early September I believe, reported that during a violent tropical storm, the U.S.S. sloop of war *Argus* was lost with all hands off Santo Domingo. Later, official sources verified her loss."

David choked. "Sir, did these reports identify me instead of David Howard as missing?"

Gregory picked up a strip of newsprint. "This clipping is from the *Richmond Inquirer,* but other Southern papers ran the same:

> It has been confirmed that the U.S.S. sloop of war *Argus,* commanded by Lieutenant David H. Dexter, was lost last month with all hands off Cape Macao, Santo Domingo.

The Commodore's curiously high-pitched voice returned David to present considerations. "I assume that neither you nor your family and friends have even heard of this report?"

"No one has — including my father."

Gregory grimaced. "What a pity your gifted father became a cripple. At this time our country could employ his services far better than by his establishing a private shipyard."

Sitting stiff-backed before the desk, David, lips clamped tightly, wondered whether this gimlet-eyed Commodore might have heard rumors of the possibility that he had been having more than purely romantic interests lying south of Washington?

What was Commodore Gregory saying? "Mr. Dexter, because of your engineering background, I feel convinced that you must sense the enormous threats raised by completion of the *Merrimac*. Every day we receive all kinds of reports of her structure and armament; many are contradictory or inconclusive. All we know for certain is that this Rebel ram is very near completion. When this event may take place is a matter of critical importance to the Government. Some say that once this armored steam battery, as some war correspondents describe her, is completed, she will be able to destroy our blockade at Hampton Roads, and once this occurs, what can be done to prevent her from steaming up the Potomac and shelling the Capital into submission?

"Personally," he went on, "I doubt this will prove possible, but there are plenty of frightened old women wearing pants around Washington who even now are clamoring for more troops and ordnance to defend the Capital." The Commodore banged his desk. "Damn! Such forces could far better be used in front of Richmond."

He settled back, looking David steadily in the eyes. "Possibly, Mr. Dexter, it may have become apparent that I'm about to invite, no, *require* you to make a great personal sacrifice."

David, sitting straight, experienced unhappy premonitions. "Yes, sir. What is required of me?"

"As I've said, you will pretend to resign your commission in our Navy. I promise to see to it that no more than a very few discreet officers hear the truth about this. You will then, by whatever means you can devise, immediately travel South. On arriving in Virginia, you will give out that you have sent in your papers and are ready, like all too many others, dammit, to accept a Confederate commission, which, I'm convinced, will readily be offered. Then, tactfully of course, you will devote your *entire energies* toward securing some post aboard the *Merrimac*. Do I make myself clear?"

David gulped on something intangible, about the size of a goose egg. His head was spinning. God above, thus being offered a foolproof opportunity to travel southward passed all credulity! Within a few days he ought to be able to claim Louisa, but a big question was included in that decision. How much time would pass before the Confederate Navy Department realized it had been tricked? On the other hand, he felt a measure of reassurance. Suppose things went wrong in Richmond or Norfolk, what was there to prevent his quitting the Rebel service to resume his rank in the United States Navy? Possibilities seemed too varied to prove altogether foolproof. Ah, well, only time would furnish the answers.

Commodore Greogry's high voice penetrated his inner turmoil.

"Mr. Dexter, you will have only a very short time in which to straighten out your affairs. I trust you will give your word of honor that nobody excepting your father shall know the truth of this situation."

"Yes, sir. As I've said before, I'm sure it would kill the Captain were he to believe that I really would turn my coat. How much time do I have?"

"Day after tomorrow you will take a ferry over to the New Jersey shore and engage passage to Norfolk aboard a schooner named *Viper*, which we know to be a contraband goods runner, unless you can devise a better plan.

"Tomorrow, the paymaster on the deck below will furnish you with funds adequate for your mission, and you will be instructed as to how, when, and in what form your reports are to be forwarded through a certain agent of ours, Joseph Gurley, who is a newspaperman on the *Richmond Inquirer*. He has means of communicating with us when necessary. In Norfolk, you will make contact with a Mr. John Duncan, in the wholesale hay, grain, and feed business. He will insure that once you have secured a commission in the Confederate Navy, you will be assigned to duty aboard the Rebel ram."

Commodore Gregory's narrow, clefted jaw jutted and his voice flattened. "No doubt this matter has struck you hard — like a cannonball landing amidships — but I feel you appreciate the great trust this Department is reposing in you and your reports. Were you not Daniel Dexter's son, I would never have agreed to place such confidence in one so young."

He produced and passed over the desk a long, heavy linen-paper envelope. "Mr. Dexter, enclosed is a letter tendering your resignation from the United States Navy." The older man's voice deepened until it almost broke. "Once it is signed, I undertake, upon my sacred word of honor, to see it destroyed once this matter of the *Merrimac* is settled and you are able to return to duty."

After David had scribbled his signature, the Commodore, smiling a little, offered a bony hand. "Good day, sir, and good luck."

18

Launching Day

DION O'DEA, who no longer was experiencing trouble in answering promptly to "Dennis O'Day," was like most everybody else who'd labored long cold weeks on the *Monitor*. He looked forward to getting gloriously drunk this evening, but not so drunk as to be incapable of rolling a pleasing dolly later on. Many, including Dennis O'Day, felt as though they'd spent half their lives driving home heavy, red-hot rivets eight inches in diameter and eight inches apart into iron plates delivered from Delamater's Novelty Ironworks, designed to armor the *Monitor's* massive turret. Laborers, coughing and cursing, shuffled out of the Continental Ironworks' huge ship house onto one of two cluttered wharves paralleling the stocks within.

On the icy afternoon of January 30, 1862, a small crowd of onlookers had collected along the shore or shivered aboard tugs and private boats. Loudmouthed gamblers, muffled to the ears, were offering two- or even three-to-one that, when launched, the crazy Swede's all-iron ship would not float and would sink of her own massive dead weight.

Dennis O'Day, standing a good half-head taller than his companions, noticed that not very many Union flags or the usual festoons of gay red, white, and blue bunting were in evidence. To be sure, this hardly was the sort of weather that sensible folk would quit a warm home to go and stand about on such a bone-chilling day.

From the start, Dennis O'Day somehow had clung to an inexplicable faith that John Ericsson and his subcontractors must know what they were about, but many more stood ready to contradict. All the same, Dennis and a handful of fellow laborers and mechanics risked their bottom dollars — at very favorable odds, to be sure — that this ugly little armored monstrosity indeed would float.

To the crack of many mauls knocking out props and shores, the new vessel's stern gradually appeared jerkily out of the ship house, whereupon knowledgeable mechanics and shipwrights exclaimed over the extraordinary diameter of this craft's single bronze propeller. God above! It was all of nine feet in diameter! Moreover, along with a balanced rudder, it was completely shielded within a cavity situated well beneath the *Monitor*'s probable waterline.

Now whistles aboard tugs, river steamers, and freighters tied up along both sides of the East River commenced to tootle and scream. On the dock a small and shivering Army band struck up patriotic tunes while, foot by foot, more of the new vessel's black hull became visible. A ringing shout arose when her big rivet-studded turret with two great gunports became visible. Smoothly, the *Monitor* took to the gray, ice-filled water and floated free!

Everyone could see John Ericsson's solid figure, top hat and all, standing like a living statue beside a Union flag streaming from the stern, proof of his unshakable confidence in his extraordinary man-of-war.

Even before chunks of the yellow-gray tallow which had been used to grease the ways began to bob about, many of the gamblers vanished, but O'Day and his friends managed to collar enough of the slippery rascals to reap substantial harvest from their bets.

Everywhere resounding cheers were arising on this unforgettable January day, even from those who had lost bets. People yelled themselves hoarse. Forgotten were arguments that she was too heavily equipped after several small secondary steam engines were mounted in addition to her propelling gear and the weight of two enormous eleven-inch guns.

In Jim Murphy's loud and smoky tavern, long the new Dennis O'Day's favorite saloon, excitement reached a fever pitch. Its roughly clad patrons, men with calloused hands, busily drained glass after glass of whiskey or mug after mug of beer until even the weary, tired, old, and raddled drabs began to resemble angels straight from Paradise.

As for Dennis, he shouldered his way through the crowd toward Rosie Springs, a sprightly, red-haired girl whose favors he'd received — and paid for — on numerous occasions. He had enjoyed this dolly greatly, not only for her accomplishments in bed, but also for her lively sense of humor. Moreover, not only was Rosie much slimmer than most competitors peddling their dubious charms along Brooklyn's waterfront, but she was very pale-skinned and wore a wistful, shy expression, as though wholly dependent on her escort of the moment for protection and courtesies.

Across the saloon sat "Diamond" Teddy Butcher, a fancily turned out pimp who boasted of connections with Tammany Hall and, by consequence, enjoyed considerable immunity from the heavy hand of the law. On previous occasions, he had made note of O'Day's preference for Rosie Springs, a favorite protégée. Only three days before, "Diamond" Teddy had smacked her bottom, and his big diamond ring had jabbed painfully when he'd chucked her under her lovely little dimpled chin. "Kiddo, if you want to keep healthy and good-looking, just you steer clear of that big black Irisher. I know his sort; they breed nothing but fights and start trouble. Besides, they seldom pay well."

Rosie seldom saw this master pimp, however, except when he ordered her to participate in some rowdy party.

"Drink up, boys!" a big foundry man shouted. "I'll be jugged if that damned queer ship ain't actually afloatin'!"

Someone yelled, "What size are her guns? Seen only two of 'em so they must be goddam heavy."

Dennis bellowed, "Eleven-inch smooth-bore Dahlgrens, Bub, that's what!"

"Then why in hell when them guns goes off won't the recoil and concussion blow the turret apart and kill the crew?" demanded a slender well-dressed fellow with a cigar dangling from his mouth. By his accent, he definitely was a Southerner, and seemed soberer than most of Jim Murphy's patrons.

While Rosie Springs, in wide-eyed admiration, clung to his massive arm, Dennis roared, "Won't nobody get hurt in that turret because that smart old Swede has rigged up a friction slide of some sort to take up the recoil."

One thing led to another, and pretty soon the din became deafening —

dangerous, too, as more or less friendly fights began breaking out. Rosie's grip tightened on Dennis's arm. "Please, dearie, let's clear out of here. I'm startin' to get scairt."

"Aye, me foine colleen, 'tis right yez are." Dennis reverted to native inflections, "So let's enjoy a frolic of our own. But where?"

Her painted lips whispered in his ear, "To my own place. Saving one, you're the only man I've ever invited there."

Dennis didn't believe that, for all this trollop sounded really sincere. "Thanks, dearie, let's get shut o' these noisy shenanigans."

To his surprise, it came as a relief to relax in the quiet and comparative cleanliness of Rosie Springs's little flat, located fairly close by. It smelt not too strongly of patchouli toilet water. He noticed a cheap ebony crucifix suspended above the big bed's headboard. "Oh, so ye're Roman, too?"

"Aye," the girl replied, starting to unhook her bodice, "though I'm a poor one, but, maybe I can please some of the handsome young devils when I get down to the Hot Place."

Of all the expertly erotic evenings Dennis could recall, this one so far had to rank among the "pun-tops." Weeks of hard, physical labor, uncertainty about the future, and the fact that, legally, he was now an enlisted man in the United States Navy and therefore subject to orders and discipline, served to heat a simmering cauldron of uncertainty in the Irishman's mind.

Never before had he been prepared to spend an entire night in a whore's bed, yet with the warship safely launched, he felt so full of high spirits and inspired by Rosie's versatility that he decided to stay, finally sinking into a deep sleep, no longer aware of the girl's soft and fragrant body relaxed beside him.

He had no idea what hour it was when, all of a sudden, the door burst inward and a towering black-whiskered fellow wearing a jaunty jockey cap roared, "Now b'Jesus, Rosie, I've finally trapped you — you damned disloyal little bitch!"

Slowly Dennis rolled over — and saw a whole constellation of shooting stars following a shrewd blow on his ear. By the dim light cast by a night lamp resting on a little table beside Rosie's bed, Dennis, warding off further punches, identified this outraged fellow as "Diamond" Teddy

Butcher, boss of nearly all pimps and whores operating in this vicinity.

Half-dazed, the Irishman instinctively rallied and rolled sideways, snatched a heavy earthenware pitcher from the wash stand, and hurled it into Butcher's face with such accuracy that the intruder lurched and stumbled, then collapsed with crumpled face and forehead spouting bright streams of gore.

"Oh, Jesus, my beads!" screamed Rosie. "Ye've done gone and kilt poor Teddy!"

"An' I hadn't hit him first, he'd of kilt me, and you too," Dennis mumbled, staggering over to the chair on which he'd dropped his dark-blue seaman's uniform donned in honor of the launching.

"Shut up, you slut," he snarled when Rosie started to wail. As she kept on screeching, he dealt her a smart clip on the cheek. Rosie slumped back, unconscious and bleeding from the nose. Meanwhile, Dennis struggled into a shirt and heavy, bell-bottomed trousers. Next, he went over to the recumbent, blood-spattered figure on the floor and pressed an ear to Butcher's chest, but heard nothing. He tested the pulse, and still felt nothing. No doubt about it, "Diamond" Teddy Butcher had pimped for the last time.

Rosie Springs, roused again and wild-eyed, prepared to utter a scream, but Dennis's open hand again clipped her, sending her rolling across the room. To make sure she'd raise no further alarm, he kicked her in the crotch — hard. She lay sprawled motionless.

"Sure and if this ain't a extra dirty mess ye've got yerself into this time — so, me boy, ye'd best clear yer head and think fast."

A frigid dawn was breaking when Dennis O'Day, wearing his uniform, sought his barracks. When none of his fellow seamen roused, he quietly grabbed his duffel bag and, after donning a flat, round cap and heavy overcoat, tiptoed down into the blessedly deserted street and instinctively headed toward the waterfront — the area he knew best. He was hurrying, parallel to the river, when, in the near distance, he heard the trampling of many feet, which, to his relieved surprise, was caused by a brief column of blue-clad seamen on the march. They also were carrying duffel bags slung over one shoulder. Some were more or less drunk.

A petty officer sang out, "Come along, me lad, come sail in the *Congress*. She's ever been a lucky ship, and we're short only three men for these here replacements."

LAUNCHING DAY 155

Instinct advised Dennis to fall in near the end of this straggling column. "Fine, I'll come along," he said.

What class of warship the U.S.S. *Congress* might be, or where she might be stationed right now, Dennis had no idea, nor did he greatly care so long as she lay berthed somewhere comfortably removed from Brooklyn and its vicinity.

19

Celebration

IT CAME AS NO GREAT SURPRISE that, thanks to Captain Dexter's unostentatious but forceful influence, Ira Thatcher presently found himself assigned to serve as Third Assistant Engineer aboard the *Monitor,* that exceptional warship which, it was hoped, would soon be accepted and commissioned into the Navy of the United States. Of course, there remained one proviso — and an important one. She first must undergo and successfully complete sea trials and other tests.

On the same day that Ira achieved his ambition, David appeared wholly delighted by the receipt of orders instructing him to proceed to Washington, where further instructions awaited him. Ira had known his classmate for so long and so well that he sensed an indefinable element of satisfaction in his friend's bearing, but made no comment.

On parting in the vestibule, they exchanged bear hugs, but David, smart in his English-cut uniform, failed to look his friend squarely in the eye as he said, "Very best of luck, Ira. Wouldn't be surprised if we'll both need plenty of it before we meet again which, let's hope, will be before long."

Looking solemn and impassive, Manuel lugged the Lieutenant's sparse baggage down to a hired sleigh; a succession of blizzards had so clogged New York's streets that most wheeled vehicles had been rendered temporarily useless.

"When do you report for duty?" David asked as they descended the freshly scraped granite steps from the Dexter mansion.

"Tomorrow. Tonight there's going to be a supper party given by Henry Busby, a State Senator and a powerful politician in New Jersey, or so I've been given to understand."

"Where? In the Astor House?"

"No. It'll take place in what the Senator described as a fashionable but little-known private establishment."

Momentarily, David's rugged features relaxed. "Hell! And to think by that time I'll be bumping along in a railroad coach headed for Baltimore. They say we have to change trains there for Washington."

Impatiently, the withered-looking sleigh driver pulled back a robe of thick, brown-black buffalo hide. "Say, Mister, get aboard, if you aim to travel along of me and Annabelle." He indicated a dejected, scrawny-looking beast drooping between the sleigh's shafts.

Presently, with jingling of bells, David disappeared down the street.

That morning, to his disgust, Captain Dexter suffered a bad day and decided to remain in bed. Ira was stricken to note how grimly the old man suppressed recurrent spasms of pain, which even liberal doses of laudanum could not alleviate.

"Captain, sir, isn't there *anything* I can do for you?"

"No. This pain's been worse before," the old man grimaced. "All the same, I feel better on account of your assignment to serve aboard this — well, nautical freak that Ericsson's designed."

"Can't thank you enough, sir, for having arranged this matter. I solemnly promise you will never find cause to regret this step in my behalf, if I can prevent it."

"I gather," the invalid remarked, "that there's to be something of a celebration this evening. Henry Busby invited me, assuring me that only a small but select company of influential gentlemen will be present." He spread thin, blue-veined hands. "Alas, 'twill be impossible for me to attend."

"Shall I wear uniform, sir?"

"Don't know — no harm. I gather there'll be a few ranking officers present, so polish your buttons; also, it impresses the ladies no end. Think of me when the party really gets going." He sighed. "Ah, me. When I recall some parties in Marseilles, Havana, and Tampico, not to mention a few other foreign ports, I could weep. Penalty of growing old, no doubt. For my sake have a fine time."

20

Elite Tonsorial Salon

By the second day after Kitty Hamilton had been accepted as a "boarder" in Mrs. Markham's Elite Tonsorial Salon, she had become fairly well acquainted with the two other young women who lived on the premises. That afternoon, Mrs. Markham, wearing a crisp white collar and a dress of severe black bombazine, summoned all three of her "apprentices," or "boarders," as she sometimes called them.

Kitty was nervous but remained outwardly placid. Not so a giggling young female calling herself Jill McAdams, who had pale-pink, heart-shaped features, fetching long blonde curls, and innocent-appearing wide blue eyes. And then there was Peggy Laverne, a tall and quietly handsome girl, whose heavy but gleaming blue-black hair had been arranged with such skill and imagination that Mrs. Markham was careful to compliment her.

Once these ladies had collected in the Markham office — or "study," as she termed it — they were instructed to seat themselves, after which Mrs. Markham addressed them, mostly in Kitty's direction.

"Now, young *ladies*," she emphasized the word, "I want you to know that I have just received an important communication which, if well acted upon, can earn you and me a very tidy reward."

Her listeners paid full attention, shifting eagerly beneath frilly, transparent voile and challis negligees as Adah went on, "Our guests tonight will be a small but most select company of important and influential gentlemen; four in number."

Listening intently, the girls uncrossed legs and leaned so far forward as to afford a generous display of shapely breasts. Kitty drew a deep breath, appreciating how incredibly fortunate she'd been in New York — thus far, at least. Yes, Mrs. Markham's establishment almost reeked of respectability. At the Commissioner's house, she had heard gentlemen in their cups brag about certain curious amusements which took place in such high-toned bordellos as this. Possibly they had exaggerated. Certainly in this salon no muscular pimps lounged about, ready to enforce what some termed "keeping order."

What was Mrs. Markham saying? "Our host tonight will be a Mr. Arnold Busby, who is President of the Acme Ironworks, over in New Jersey. He is reported to be very rich, bluff, and a little noisy late in the evening. Now, remember this: Mr. Busby doesn't like wine, he prefers old bourbon to champagne. His guest of honor on this occasion will be Brigadier General Carl Brebner, of St. Louis, Missouri. Now don't laugh if he sometimes speaks with a German accent, for all 'tis said his family has lived in Missouri for quite a while.

"I know only that this General is very well-to-do and owns one of the most important shipbuilding yards along the Mississippi River. He is now building ironclad rams for an Army Engineering officer called Colonel Eads. Carl Brebner holds his rank of General in the Missouri Militia Volunteers — beyond that I know nothing about him, except that he has powerful political connections in Washington."

When she heard the next guest's name, Kitty's heart seemed to stop beating. "The last members of this party will be a Mr. Dunbar and a Lieutenant Ira Thatcher, who has just returned from Europe and Bermuda and is here awaiting assignment."

Had the floor collapsed, Kitty couldn't have been more terrified. How long could this Lieutenant Thatcher have stayed in Bermuda? How many people might he have seen or talked to? Characteristically, she suppressed panic and took a grip on herself. Don't go imagining things, you silly baggage, she told herself. There isn't one chance in a thousand this gentleman has heard of my existence.

Carefully, Kitty crossed her legs because an unwanted warmth in her private parts was increasing, and her breasts had been swelling and growing tender. Absently, she shifted a stray lock from her neckline, listening intently.

"Oh!" Mrs. Markham exclaimed, touching her forehead with the heel of a hand, "I near forgot! Since I need another lady guest, I have invited a near neighbor, a Mrs. Linda Weaver, to attend. She is quiet, well-bred, and the widow of a soldier who fell at Bull Run. I shall expect you all to treat her kindly — just as if she was a regular boarder. Understood? I know the three of you will behave discreetly, be inviting, but nothing more until after the dessert and liqueurs have been served."

Three heads — two blondes, and one brunette — inclined. Adah Markham produced a strip of paper from the front of her dress. "This is the order in which you will pair up — unless the gentlemen decide differently. Kitty, you will devote especial attention to General Brebner; Jill, forget to giggle and direct your most subtle charms to Mr. Busby. Peggy, you will be Mr. Dunbar's partner, and Linda Weaver will entertain Lieutenant Thatcher, who, I gather, is about the same age. Does everybody understand what is expected?"

She paused to straighten a curved tortoiseshell comb set in iron-gray hair. "I shall not be present, but I will be watching dinner through a peephole, so behave yourselves accordingly or you'll rue it in more ways than one. Now get on to your preparations."

After dinner, which as usual was served in the middle of the day, Mrs. Markham directed, not unpleasantly, "Go to your rooms, young ladies, and after you have done your hair and selected what you propose to wear, repose yourselves so that you may appear fresh and alluring."

She turned to Kitty. "For you, I have selected an expensive green silk ball gown, which on you I think will prove decidedly fetching. Now, one more thing — all of you pay special attention to Mr. Busby; after all, he is the host. Make him feel lucky to have patronized our establishment. So, girls, go pretty yourselves up, and whatever the temptation, don't drink too much or allow yourselves to get moist or untidy in any way — anywhere. Tonight is of great importance to all of you." She might have added, "And to me," but didn't.

The boarders, giggling, started for the staircase, but Mrs. Markham signaled Kitty to linger. Her little black birdlike eyes narrowing, she sighed. "Don't know why, Kitty, knowing you for so short a time, I place so much trust in you, but I've decided you possess brains besides your unusually charming personality, so I therefore deputize you to represent my best interests, for, of course, I shall not be present at the supper table."

"Thank you, Mrs. Markham. Is there anything special you want done?"

"Yes. The only two unknown quantities are Linda Weaver and Lieutenant Thatcher, who, I'm told, are younger than the other guests. Keep an eye on them and anticipate any misunderstandings. And all of you must concentrate on pleasing General Brebner."

There it was again! Ira Thatcher had been in Bermuda. What if, by some strange quirk of fate, he recognized her? Firmly, she resolved under no condition to betray her origin by slipping into a Bermuda accent.

No one, not even the most finicky of critics, could have found fault with the dining room's arrangement. Holly branches ablaze with scarlet berries occupied silver urns at either end of a fine old mahogany Scottish hunting board doing duty as a sideboard; clumps of mistletoe traced the small chandelier dangling above.

Bitterly, Adah Markham lamented that at this season natural blossoms were as scarce as virgins in frontier dance halls. After careful consideration, she plotted a seating arrangement and wrote out place cards to be positioned as tactfully as possible.

Privately, she debated whether she had been wise in pairing Kitty with General Brebner. Maybe she should have partnered Mr. Busby? Odd, that she should have selected her newest boarder for this all-important responsibility, but somehow Kitty had a sort of presence, as though she had been in the company of important people before. From all she had learned about Mr. Busby, silly, lighthearted Jill should suit him right down to the ground, or in this case to a fourposter.

Mr. Dunbar presented something of an enigma. He had the reputation of being a selective *bon vivant*. He just might take to darkly lovely and sultry Peggy Laverne like a drake to water.

"I'm not experienced at this sort of thing, Mrs. Markham," Kitty said, pausing at the stairway, "but you can be sure I'll do my best — and thank you so much for the lovely gown." She smiled. "Do you wish me to sing or dance?"

"By all means sing, but you won't be able to dance. No room for musicians in the dining room. Now, get along."

As Kitty turned, to her pleased surprise, she was patted on the buttocks so briskly they were still stinging when she reached her room where, fervently, she prayed that "the flowers," which, as nearly as she could tell, were due at any moment, would hold off until tomorrow.

Portly Carl Brebner, of the Missouri Volunteers, obviously had tarried at some bar and exuded the joy of living as he deftly goosed the giggling maid who took his military cloak to hang it, along with other cold-weather gear, in the hall closet.

Before the party arrived upstairs, Mrs. Markham's girls, all aglow and hopeful, were already seated at their designated places when, one after another, the guests appeared in the dining room door, laughing and in high good humor.

Arnold Busby had a naturally large voice which magnified in intensity until it made the whole dining room resound. (Well before dessert was served by a pair of plain but efficient Swedish serving girls, hired for the occasion, he was seemingly oblivious to all that transpired.) "I hope," he said, "that you'll join me in presenting our compliments, and making a toast, to our excellent hostess, Mrs. Markham. Now, come on, let's eat. I'm close to starving."

Mr. Busby and General Brebner, the buttons on whose ample chest glowed as though heated, led the way toward a round table, glittering with silver and glassware. At their heels appeared country-bred Mr. Dunbar, looking rather ill at ease against the tasteful background, of a kind he had thus far never experienced.

Buttons also winked on the chest of Ira Thatcher's tunic when he appeared in General Brebner's wake, looking rather like an observant student following his professor into some significant lecture — which in effect was the case.

To reassure herself, Kitty glanced sideways at Linda Weaver and drew courage from the way this almost stately young widow — if she really was one — held herself, smiling sweetly at the guests, but retaining a certain indefinable reserve.

Mr. Busby, arms linked, led in General Brebner, whose gold-mesh belt encircled a considerable girth. His heavy epaulettes glittered as he advanced beside his host, his large and pale blue eyes shifting from one to another of the females.

Arnold Busby boomed, "I've always admired Adah Markham's elegant taste, but tonight I feel she has surpassed herself." He conducted General

Brebner to a seat opposite his. "Well, here's your partner, Carl. I'd say you are in luck."

Kitty forced a smile and managed a half-curtsy behind her chair, saying softly, "Good evening, sir." But slowly her smile faded; this well-upholstered General was staring at her as if upon some ghostly apparition. Quickly he recovered himself and offered a deep bow.

"Such a pleasure, *meine Liebchen,* you are so lovely, so *zaftig!*"

"Glad of that," Busby observed. "For a moment I fear you weren't pleased."

"*Ach, nein,*" the rotund officer protested. "It is only that this young lady so much resembles *meine* late daughter."

"Daughter?" Busby queried.

"Yes, *mein* friend. For me, this has been a most sad year. First, *mein* only son dies of a disease called typhoid in his training camp; a few weeks later his twin, Hildegarde, perishes in childbirth." He blinked, shook his blond head, and rallied. "Forgive me, my good friends, and I will speak no more of sorrow now that I have met this so pretty Miss Hamilton."

21

Postprandial Pleasures

WHEN THE LAST of the gentlemen, varying considerably in age and appearance, had entered the dining room, they found the boarders were waiting expectantly behind their place cards. Their colorful flowing gowns suggested the brilliance of pheasants, tanagers, orioles, or canaries.

Mrs. Markham paused, the image of dignity and propriety, as she left them, "I wish you all, ladies and gentlemen, a memorable repast. Rest assured you will not be disturbed, now or later, in anything you care to do — short of violence."

She offered a graceful little curtsy in the direction of the already perspiring Mr. Busby. He acknowledged her genteel gesture by bowing as much as an ample belly would permit; a thick gold watch chain, heavy with seals and other ornaments, swayed well away from his vest of buff nankeen.

Ira had attended many formal dinners in Paris and elsewhere, but this occasion promised to be unique — a polite orgy, perhaps? The guests circulated the sparkling table until each found the proper place card; all appeared satisfied with their prospective partner.

Having stopped off en route for drinks with a friend, Ira was feeling in wonderful form, to say the least. He halted by his place and, after reading the cards, said, "Ah, Miss Weaver. Am I not the luckiest of mortals?" With a flourish acquired in Paris, he kissed Linda's slim hand, smelling faintly of violets. Its unblemished whiteness was emphasized by a bow of narrow, black velvet ribbon. "Allow me to present myself. As you can readily tell, I am the least important among my companions. I hope you don't feel put upon."

Linda Weaver treated him to a dazzling smile, framed by her full dark-red lips. Her face was long, but not unattractively so. From beneath flaring jet-black brows she raised large brown eyes. This young woman couldn't have been much more than twenty, he decided. "Thank you, sir, I am honored to be partnered with you. May I say I've seldom seen a more handsomely cut uniform than yours?"

Ira flushed. "Why, thank you, Miss, I mean Ma'am." He had just noticed that the prefix of Linda Weaver's name was "Mrs."

The other couples also were introducing themselves. Mr. Busby and pretty, flighty Jill McAdams occupied the places of honor immediately before the entrance. The iron magnate, beaming and beginning to perspire, was remarkably turned out in a dress coat of midnight blue, with a pearl-gray waistcoat of watered silk and buff drill trousers.

Through her peephole Adah Markham peered anxiously and sighed in relief when Kitty managed a fairly graceful curtsy. La! This wench certainly *must* have been around high society sometime, somewhere. What gave her pause was the expression on General Brebner's bronzed and craggy features. His buttons and epaulettes aglitter, the General stood staring at Kitty a long moment and drew a deep breath before jerking a curt bow. That Mr. Busby's friend was of German descent there could be little doubt. Thinning blond hair on a head which seemed to have no neck, but arose straight from his collar, had been clipped short so that it stood on end like silvery bristles. His mustache, too, had been trimmed very short. His eyes were small and a very pale blue.

Fear seized Kitty about what had prompted that strange look, of which no trace now remained on her partner's round countenance.

Once the company had seated itself, Arnold Busby heaved himself erect and raised a champagne glass. "Ladies and gentlemen, I propose a toast to our friend, that amazing patriot and engineering genius, John Ericsson! God grant him health, happiness, long life, and every success with his newest invention."

Laughing, the company arose and drained glasses. For a moment, Ira wondered if they would follow the English custom of smashing glasses from which a solemn toast had been drunk. Apparently that prodigal fashion hadn't yet crossed the Atlantic.

Although Carl Brebner was sufficiently broad in the stern to force Kitty to hitch her chair a few inches to one side, even so, their legs remained in contact clear down to the floor.

Mrs. Markham remained apprehensive about whether Mr. Dunbar, of the ginger-hued and flowing muttonchop whiskers, would take to Peggy Laverne, but very soon they were engaged in a laughing, low-pitched conversation, leading to arch expressions on Peggy's part and a well-beringed broad hand reposing on her knee.

Her next concern was how Ira Thatcher and Linda Weaver were faring. She was sure the Lieutenant had enjoyed a noggin or two before arriving at her place; he didn't appear to be a young man who would normally act so free and easy.

By the time the delicious-smelling green turtle soup had been served and the sherry poured, Adah Markham uncrossed her fingers and only vaguely wondered when Kitty would follow instructions and raise her rich if untrained voice in song.

What with the candles and the heat emanating from a hot-air register, it was growing so hot in the dining room that, more or less surreptitiously, the gentlemen began to ease collars and waistcoat buttons. But for the life of her, Kitty couldn't understand General Brebner's attitude; not that he acted in the least hostilely, but he appeared distraught — as though he had something of deep importance on his mind. Was it the thought of his dead daughter? Desperately, she offered talk on various subjects — and some mildly risqué jokes — but they failed to capture this hard-bitten Middle Westerner's attention.

Course after course was deftly served and cleared away. By the time the claret was poured, Jill had Mr. Busby roaring with laughter while he caressed her back, starting at the shoulders and pausing far below. He said, "Now that we've begun to know one another, our hostess tells me Miss Kitty has a rare fine voice; let's have her sing."

Trembling, Kitty got to her feet and looked brightly about. "I don't know any very American songs — would 'Annie Laurie' do for a starter?"

Everybody applauded, and after accepting a quick sip of wine offered by the General, Kitty arose, looked about the now disordered table, drew a deep breath, and filled the heated dining room with such melody that even before she had done, everyone began clapping and calling, "Bravo! Bravo! More!"

Ira's hands squeezed Linda's. "I say, dearie, can't you too sing?"

"Wish I could," she dimpled, "but when I try to sing, song birds in the trees fall off in a faint."

"Give us another song, Kitty," Mr. Dunbar, growing red-eyed, demanded. "How about 'Love's Old Sweet Song.' Know it?"

Happily, Kitty nodded, whereupon comparative silence descended upon the dining room.

Ever so slightly, Linda's head came to rest on Ira's shoulder. He wished he dared kiss her, but long Service training restrained him. With Mr. Busby and the General present, one of them might frown on such a departure from decorous behavior — unless, of course, one of the civilians set a precedent.

While Kitty's rich contralto concluded the final lines of "Love's Old Sweet Long," she was amazed to watch tears suddenly well from Carl Brebner's pale-blue eyes and trace silvery lines down his cheeks. "Oh, my dear," she bent low to him, "what have I done to distress you?"

"Nothing of your fault, *Liebchen,* it is just that you look almost the image of my daughter who died not long ago. She, too, used to sing dot song."

"Oh, General, I'm so sorry."

He chucked her under the chin. "You may call me Carl, little one." He heaved a sigh.

Unwilling to risk the approval she had won, Kitty was very gently stroking the General's hand when Arnold Busby boomed, "Hey, dearie, ever hear of a song called 'Lorena'?"

Kitty managed a little nod. "Yes, I've heard it sung by Southern people, but since it's a Rebel air, is it fitting to be sung here?"

Busby's hand smacked the table. "Stuff and nonsense! When it comes to music, there ain't," he corrected himself, "there isn't any national barrier — not that the seceding states are a nation or ever will be. So by God! girl, go ahead and sing!"

Curiously enough, to Kitty's infinite relief, the girl calling herself Peggy Laverne also knew both the air and the words, so she joined in. Nobody applauded longer or louder than Carl Brebner; the crushed look had vanished from his sweating, red-brown features.

Mr. Dunbar's restraint abruptly vanished. Stooping, he fumbled briefly under the table cloth, and then straightened, flourishing one of Peggy

Laverne's fancy garters — pale blue, edged with lace and decorated with a circlet of brilliants.

Swaying a little, the contractor called out, "Hi, Arnold! Let's have one more song, 'Yankee Doodle,' then this garter goes to the best singer."

"Hell's bells, no!" roared Busby. "You can give that pretty thing to Miss Kitty right now. We'll find a consolation prize for Peggy."

He tossed the garter across to Kitty but, with a speed surprising in one of his dimensions, Carl Brebner intercepted it.

"Stand up! Stand up!" shouted Dunbar. "Let's see that dainty thing put where it belongs."

There was nothing for it but that Kitty should leap up gaily onto a chair, extending a shapely leg over the table so Carl Brebner could push the trophy up, up, until it encountered her own garter of bright green silk.

By now, Ira Thatcher, adrift and vastly enjoying a pleasantly unrealistic world, felt possessed of unfamiliar recklessness. He got to his feet, swaying just a trifle, "Gentlemen and ladies, I feel it would be unfair to allow my gracious partner and brilliant conversationalist, Linda, to remain unrewarded. Who will offer her a tribute?"

To no one's great surprise, Mr. Busby captured one of Jill's garters — a gaudy affair of red satin trimmed with little ostrich feathers.

"Oh, dear. Ira, please steady me." Ira took Linda's hand as, amid a frothy swirl of petticoats, she thrust an ankle over the table far enough to reveal a considerable length of snowy thigh, and the prize traveled a bit higher than was necessary. Ira had never been so thrilled, although the room seemed to tilt slightly now and again.

Voices grew still louder, the girls giggled and laughed — Kitty loudest of all. She so wanted to please the General, since he seemed to have relapsed into some private apathy. His head inclined, he remained slumped in his chair until, laughing and giggling, couples started for the door.

Ira just managed to reach the top of a staircase leading to the second floor when suddenly his legs buckled and something suggestive of a warm black velvet blanket descended, and he knew nothing more until the next morning, when he roused to find Linda's fragrant dark head on his bare shoulder. She was asleep and breathing softly. Their garments, he presently realized, lay scattered about or had been heaped in confusion on a small sofa at the foot of the bed. Much must have happened during the night, but for the life of him, he could recall only delightful sensations.

Squinting through the peephole the evening before, Adah Markham was relieved there had been no disputes, no broken chinaware, except for inexpensive champagne glasses she had furnished in anticipation of an initial toast. In fact, the whole company appeared to have gotten along like pups in a basket, save for that one couple lingering by the light of guttering candles in the disordered dining room.

Whatever his other qualifications, it would appear that General Brebner was no headstrong lover; it was only after the last of the others had departed more or less ceremoniously, to enjoy postprandial pleasures that the German-American beckoned Kitty to occupy his lap. Even then he only kissed her once or twice on the cheek, while keeping his hands under control. Why? Mrs. Markham wondered. Certainly, Busby's good friend appeared to have enjoyed his dinner, and the evening's more or less circumspect goings on. Obviously, he was more than just a trifle beguiled by Kitty's company. What could be wrong? Why hadn't he, like the rest, taken her off to bed?

By now the General had not only loosened his collar and his waistcoat but had unbuttoned a heavy blue dress uniform jacket and was sipping only an occasional swallow of schnapps. Moreover, he didn't press any liquor or wine on Kitty — strange conduct on an occasion like this. Even after a clock somewhere had struck twelve sonorous notes, this strangely assorted couple lingered in the dining room, much to the annoyance of servants, impatient to clear away the round table.

Finally, and just in time, Carl Brebner lifted Kitty off his lap, saying gently, *"Nun, Liebchen,* to bed like a good girl. Mrs. Markham no doubt has an extra bed somewhere that I can sleep in. In the morning, we will talk further on what I decide is to be done."

Just in time, Kitty darted into her room and closed its door, panting and infinitely lucky, for only a few moments later, she was flooded by the "Curse of Eve."

Why did this General, who apparently had been so deeply attracted to her, not elect to come to bed? Did he have some venereal disease which he was too decent to communicate? There was so much of it around, and many Army units had become so infected they were seriously under strength.

Once Kitty had hurried upstairs, General Brebner got to his feet and went over to bang on a hurricane glass until it tinkled like a crystal bell. "Service! I vant service!"

Almost before the words had escaped him, Adah Markham appeared, stately and severe in her dark gown. "Yes, General, you want something?"

"*Ja*. Please to sit down, *meine Frau*. With you I must seriously speak."

Odd, noted Adah, how much more accented the General's speech had become at this hour.

Folding her arms as primly as any schoolmistress, Mrs. Markham seated herself and surveyed her guest with great but imperceptible care, and wished she knew much more about the last of Mr. Busby's guests. But she need not have worried. He only poured out two small measures of champagne, and offered her one. To her own surprise, Adah accepted it.

"*Und* now, *meine Frau*, seriously, ve must talk."

Adah Markham's handsome, long-lashed eyes widened. "Tell me, sir, is this a complaint? Has not everything been satisfactory? I have been very well paid and so have been my boarders. Why do you look so serious? Mr. Busby's fee was most generous."

The General's blond lashes batted quickly. "Now, *meine Frau*, let us move into your parlor. I vant no one should overhear our talk."

Once they had ensconced themselves in comfortable armchairs, Adah Markham was still attempting to guess what was afoot. Brebner quickly spoke out. He explained that he was one of the richest men in St. Louis and, now, thanks to Mr. Busby and others, he had signed contracts which should make him still richer. His pale blue eyes suddenly filled as he repeated once more the story of the death of his son.

"Dear me," Mrs. Markham murmured, "how dreadful that he could not, like my late husband, have perished in the heat of battle."

"*Ja*. Ve Brebners for generations vere of the Army, fighting against Napoleon, then the Austrians, and then the Danes and others. Against the French I fear ve vill haff to fight once more. This Napoleon the Third is but a silly, dangerous actor trading on his uncle's fame."

Then, in detail, Carl Brebner again described the death of his twin children, beginning to weep as he did so.

Adah never forgot his expression when, using a perfumed handkerchief, she gently blotted away his tears. "I, too, have known sorrow," she told him. "What do you want of me?"

Through a palpable effort, Carl Brebner pulled himself together, and spoke clearly, "Thank you, *meine Frau*, for your compassion. Now it iss that your lovely boarder, Miss Kitty, so greatly resembles my dead daughter I cannot take advantage of her at this time. To do so vould be like — incest. *Ja,* incest. Later on, perhaps, but now I cannot part with her. Do you understand?"

Mrs. Markham's own eyes were filling. After all, she didn't enjoy being a madam, but she had to exist and knew no other way of making a living.

"Sir," she said, "I honor your sentiments. What do you propose?"

"It iss late. If you can find me a bed, I vill sleep here until morning, and then ve vill talk again, with Kitty present. This is what I haff in mind: if all goes well, I vill fetch Kitty back to St. Louis, where I haff a big, comfortable, but cheerless house. I vill present her as my niece, easily because she so much resembles *meine* daughter. She vill become my hostess and housekeeper. In other words, *meine Frau,* I would intend, in a manner of speaking, to adopt Kitty. Perhaps later, if things go vell, I might — vell, possibly I might take her to vife. I am still too full-blooded to live like a hermit — not for a long time yet."

Adah blinked. She'd grown used to surprises — most of them unpleasant — but this surely topped the lot! What was this virile-appearing gentleman in the disordered uniform saying?

"I vould like to take Kitty avay tomorrow, but," he waggled a forefinger, "there are several official duties I must first attend to. I know that when Kitty leaves your establishment, it vill cost much. Vat vould you require as compensation for releasing her from your — service? Vould three thousand dollars be sufficient?"

Deep in Adah's being began a struggle. None of her girls, except possibly Linda Weaver, had Kitty's deportment or her gift for singing. But rapid mental calculations told her that many weeks, if not months, would be required for a girl even of her ability to earn anything like such a sum.

Gently, Mrs. Markham stroked Carl Brebner's hand. "You make this decision most difficult for me, General, for in a short time I have become extremely fond of Kitty. However, let's not quibble. For three thousand silver dollars I will release her into what I feel, General, will prove to be trustworthy hands."

PART THREE

Clash at Hampton Roads

22

The Blockade Runner *Staghound*

WITH MIXED EMOTIONS, Christian Pitcher perched on a lower limb of a huge live oak and watched the side-wheeler *Staghound*'s slender gray funnel begin to belch increasingly dense clouds of pitch-black smoke. Definitely, the Bermudian sensed that her departure was marking another turning point in his life. Through a thick pendant of Spanish moss — or "grandfather's beard," as it was called back home — he concentrated attention on a row of small docks built along the tan-hued river below Elizabeth City.

At these a surprising number of blockade runners of different sizes, designs, and nationalities were tied up, charging or discharging mounds of cargo. Swarms of black stevedores, sometimes chanting a variety of songs, many plaintive or downright doleful, crammed holds and even decks with precious brown-and-white cotton bales.

Watching the trim blockade runner back out into the sluggish current and then gradually swing until her bowsprit headed downriver, he was torn again by doubts about whether what he was doing was the wisest course; but after a bit he reckoned he'd done the smart thing by jumping ship.

It would be a long while before he got over that terrible scare he'd suffered when a nondescript Federal gunboat had suddenly emerged from a silvery fog bank off the Manteo Inlet to Currituck Sound and opened fire. He knew he'd never forget the first time he had heard a cannon fired in anger. The *Staghound* was fast, much faster than that chunky little sidewheel gunboat now firing hurriedly at her.

All but one of her shots fell short, no more than raising harmless waterspouts in the blockade runner's creaming wake. The final shot came skipping from wave top to wave top and managed to hull the fleeing vessel near her mizzenmast's base. The sound of crackling wood and the snarl of canvas being torn and ripped by jagged flying splinters appalled Christian, as it did most of the blockade runner's crew. He reckoned he'd never quite forget the *thunk!* made by big pieces of wood landing on the deck. Suppose he'd been standing there? He began to understand what some men-of-war's crew, after having survived a fierce action, meant when they admitted having been scared "fit to shit their britches."

As it was, the mizzenmast had not been cut through; being well supported by shrouds and braces, it canted only a few degrees toward the starboard rail so the *Staghound*'s speed scarcely was diminished at all, since little time was required for her expert English crew to repair the damage.

As it was, only four days passed before the *Staghound* had cautiously negotiated huge sand bars off Manteo Inlet and steamed into the smooth, gray-brown waters of Currituck Sound and, in so doing, had frightened into flight countless thousands of waterfowl of many species, from saucy little ruddy ducks, skimming low over the wave tops, to gorgeous redheads, canvasbacks, and scaups flying in clouds so dense as to obscure the sun for a while. There were also snowy squadrons of majestic trumpeter swans, which took to the air like geese. Because of the deliberate beat of their great, pointed wings, these birds looked as though they were flying slowly, but just the opposite was the case — they overtook most ducks with ease.

There had been a great celebration once the *Staghound*, with a British ensign once more flapping from her maintop, tied up at one of several wharves studding Elizabeth City's ramshackle waterfront.

The populace, mostly poorly dressed, crowded about and offered these foreigners all the drinks they could absorb. What a curious lot, Christian decided, were these drawling, generally ill-shaven men, wearing broad-brimmed straw hats, rumpled seersuckers or once-white linen suits. Most of them spoke with so curious an accent it was difficult to understand them.

Soon a pair of Confederate officers wearing ill-fitting uniforms spotted by tobacco juice arrived. With them appeared a gaggle of importers, agents, government contractors, and local buyers. They shouted, yelled, and gesticulated as though prepared to sell their souls for what goods they required. Christian noted that medicines, handsome hand guns, and fancy dress goods fetched the best prices — things to be remembered.

Like his fellow crewmen, Christian for the next two days toiled from dawn to dusk, raising freight from holds, urged on by the Captain, his mates, and a burly, gap-toothed Scottish bo'sun who brandished his "starter" — a length of rope knotted at intervals — and wasn't backward about using it. Black stevedores only handled cargo after it had been deposited on the dock.

Naturally, Captain Blakeston refused to pay off the crew until the *Staghound* was homeward bound, deep under a dangerously huge cargo of cotton, having broken through Mr. Lincoln's "soapbox blockade" for a second time, outward bound for Bristol.

On the night before the *Staghound*'s announced sailing date, Christian Pitcher had realized he must make a critical decision. Should he jump ship? He had wanted again to tumble a pretty and saucy mulatto girl, but he had already parted with twenty cents — the last of his cash.

What particularly graveled him was the possibility that should the *Staghound* return safely to Europe, he would lose generous pay and the owner's bonus. Why, the meanest of the blockade runner's complement stood to gain at least one hundred pounds!

Of course, last week, during the trip down the American coast to North Carolina, there had been plenty of card games of various sorts, and Christian, ever deft with a deck, had nursed a modest sum which had come in handy; long since, he'd spent the last of that pitiful sum discovered in Kitty Hamilton's purse.

Kitty? Now there, he mused, was a rare fine wench. A damn shame it no longer seemed possible to capitalize on his knowledge of her mulatto mother, but he consoled himself with an experienced gambler's philosophy that "you can't expect to win 'em all." So, after his recent tumble with a giggling high-yellow whore, he indeed was penniless.

Despite everything, it shook the Bermudian to watch the *Staghound*, British flag aflutter, swing her pointed prow about and begin her run down to Currituck Sound. His only recompense, he reminded himself, was that here in this great, sprawling country nobody was likely to take him for an ex-convict. Besides, in this way he couldn't risk touching at Bermuda and being recognized.

Great flocks of waterfowl, like undulating spirals of dark smoke, returned to the river once the *Staghound*'s smokestack vanished beyond the tops of pines and huge white oaks lining the riverbanks. Anyhow, Christian felt better for having reached a decision; he'd never again willingly expose himself to cannon fire. It was just as well the future remained a closed book.

When he could sight no more of the blockade runner's smoke, he eased himself to the ground. Now what? He skirted a bedraggled-looking tobacco field and set out for Elizabeth City. Too bad he'd had to land just now in this great country, torn by a so vicious a fraternal conflict. It was difficult to get a straight answer to any political question; everybody spoke with reservations or in distorted, flaming partisanship.

He intended to seek a cheap rooming house near the edge of town, but even so he would have to enter this disorderly yet evidently thriving community. Before he had reached the edge of town, he realized something unusual must be taking place in Elizabeth City's dusty main square; a quantity of kerosene torches were tracing bright patterns like gigantic fireflies before the Town Hall, on the steps of which stood an improvised podium consisting of two superimposed office desks.

Because much of the *Staghound*'s cargo would be auctioned next day, this little port town and its scant accommodations were crowded to capacity.

Christian lingered at the edge of the square, finally making bold to ask of a yellow-bearded young sergeant in a smart gray uniform and a rakish felt hat adorned with glossy rooster's tail feathers, "What's up, Captain?"

The soldier, flattered by the title, grinned. "Well, friend, 'pears like we're going to listen to an important address tonight; officer's been sent down special from Norfolk." He pronounced it "Norfick." "His name's Lieutenant Taylor Wood, and they claim he's a grandson of old President Zachary Taylor himself. Claims he needs to round up some real seafarin' fellers for a secret and most impo'tant mission."

"Secret my ass!" Christian overheard someone growl. "All that fancy Dan wants is to recruit hands to help finish building the *Virginia* and then serve on her."

Considerably more or less good-natured jostling and liquor-heated voices were beginning to predominate, when a rangy, black-mustachioed young officer wearing a gray double-breasted uniform was shoved up onto the improvised podium. Lieutenant Wood held arms high and gesticulated, which didn't still the crowd until a trio of snare drums kept on beating the long roll and the speaker was able to make himself heard. Even so, Christian had to cup hands to ears to undertand what he was saying.

"Fellow patriots! I'm heah to urge all true-born Southrons to heed my message and to answer our country's call." Quickly the throng quieted. "Up in Gosport we're very close to completing a mighty vessel — an iron steam ram of great firepower. She can, and certainly will, smash those Yankee ships off Fort Monroe into splinters so small you could pick teeth with 'em."

A succession of ringing cheers made the chilly semidarkness resound. Oily black smoke from kerosene torches billowed up to create a dark stratum under which the crowd milled and shouted. Only a few remained glumly silent.

Christian was surprised that so few blacks, apparently house servants, were to be seen. But any resident of this town could have told him that large signs or notices were posted on all roads and even paths leading into the city's limits, reading, "Niggers, read this sign and run before the setting of the sun!" For signatures, there appeared skulls and crossed bones, since blacks, almost without exception, were illiterate but certainly could grasp the significance of the pirate insignia. Often, white passersby translated the import of such signs, if any doubt remained.

Pitcher, aware that he was facing a most critical decision, shoved, elbowed, and wriggled his way through the rough and ill-smelling crowd. Some cursed him but fell quiet after noting his English seaman's garb, his hair that had been roughly barbered, and the fact that he'd shaved no longer ago than yesterday.

At length, by squeezing in between two frowsy women, Christian found space below the speaker's rostrum. The Bermudian directed his attention to Lieutenant Wood, whose naturally strong voice steadily swelled over a rising tumult. He was young and hard-faced but not brutal-looking, wearing a well-tailored uniform of light gray.

Once the drums quit beating, he began again in carrying tones: "Fellow Southrons, I've come heah on a special and impo'tant mission, which is to recruit a party of volunteers — preferably seafarin' men and shipwrights — to speed completion of the armored and powerfully armed steam ram we're fittin' out over to Gosport. Ah expect you-all have heard plenty about this vessel which, sure enough, will sink or break the backs of the Yankee Navy's most powerful ships!"

Silence descended, in which the gabble of waterfowl out on the river clearly could be heard.

"What Ah'm heah for is to enroll at least thirty patriotic and able men ready to come back to Po'tsmouth with me tomorrow. Such recruits will be fortunate, since they'll be privileged to watch the pride of the Yankee Navy blown to bits! No doubt some of you'all are thinkin', 'What can one iron vessel accomplish 'gainst a mess of the best battleships afloat?' "

Apparently a skilled orator, Lieutenant Wood lowered his voice until people stopped shouting and strained to listen.

"Although this mighty fleet of our enemy lyin' off Fort Monroe grows in strength every day, we, on the other hand, have to oppose this armada with only our magnificent new ram, but . . ." He lowered his voice to a conspiratorial level ". . . within a few days the whole world will be shaken with the news that our single ironclad has destroyed the most powerful fleet the damn Yankees can assemble!"

Cheers broke out from the crowd, along with voices raised in an increasingly popular tune called "Dixie's Land." It really wasn't very new, but it had become a sort of unofficial national anthem after the outbreak of hostilities.

Using his sword's hilt, Lieutenant Wood banged on the makeshift rostrum. "Silence! You-all will hear plenty more good news from abler orators than me, predicting what will follow once the *Merri* — I mean the *Virginia* — sallies out to meet our enemy."

His manner changed. "Now, friends, let's get down to brass tacks, which will come in handy when it's time to nail down the lid on Abe Lincoln's coffin!"

He beckoned a soldier wearing sergeant's chevrons who, after pushing his kepi onto the back of his head, seated himself behind a card table placed below the rostrum and opened a portable writing case. "Now, fellow Virginians, Ah want every patriot who believes himself fit to help finish or to serve aboard our ironclad to step forward, give his true name and qualifications! Men accepted will enjoy pay much higher than ordinary seamen or dockside shipbuilder's wages. Now, my brave countrymen, step forward and enlist! One at a time, please."

Somebody said, "Ain't them damn Yankees doin' nothin' 'gainst this armored ship of ours? 'Tain't like those bastards. They're smarter and meaner than a she fox with cubs!"

"Yes!" Wood answered him. "They know they can fire a hundred cannon to our one. The *Virginia* mounts only ten pieces, but these guns are the finest in the world. Two of them are rifled pivot guns forged in Gosport on the design of a fellow named Ulrich. Now, come forward, anyone qualified to help our armored giant smash those Yankee goliaths!"

A few men from the local police force, with reinforcements from gawping nonuniformed volunteers from the Elizabeth City militia, managed to hold back a surging crowd in this square where tall trees dripped great silver-gray beards of Spanish moss. Lit by the flaring of torches and resounding with the cries of nearly three hundred people, a scene ensued that Christian would never forget.

"Come along, boys!" yelled a scrawny individual. "Come along, you look fit. Let's go win our share of glory!"

Releasing a gaunt female partner, he flung an arm about Pitcher's shoulder. Somebody else grabbed him on the other side, shouting, "Come along, Mister, we'll teach them damn Yankees who's top dog in America!"

Almost before he knew it, the Bermudian found himself standing, panting and disheveled, before the recruiting sergeant.

"Name?"

"Christian Pitcher."

"Where's your home?"

Christian hesitated a split second and almost told the truth. "I hail from Barbados."

"An Englishman!" Cheers arose. Almost everybody had read or been told about England's willingness to back the South.

Lieutenant Wood, who had descended from the rostrum to stand beside the recruiting sergeant, arbitrarily but politely turned down volunteers obviously unfit or hopelessly drunk.

"Any special qualifications, Mr. Pitcher? You look educated."

"Yes, sir. I've been at sea most of my life and hold a pilot's certificate," he lied, for only by a narrow margin had he failed to pass examinations held in the Chief Pilot's office back in Hamilton.

Lieutenant Wood's hard, steel-gray eyes narrowed. "Tell me true, Mister, you really *are* a qualified pilot?"

Christian suffered only a momentary qualm. "Yes, sir, but of course I'm a British subject." Instinctively, he hoped this would disqualify him, since he'd never pretended to have been cast in a heroic mold. But Lieutenant Wood turned to the recruiting sergeant.

"That makes no never-mind; nowadays it's a case of all grist that comes to the mill. Jennings, place this fellow on the top of the list. Mark him 'specially qualified'!"

He beckoned Christian to one side and produced a twenty-dollar Confederate bill, which he deliberately tore in half and passed one part to the Bermudian. "Keep this. When you board Number Three train for Portsmouth tomorrow morning, I'll give you the other half. Next!"

It hadn't escaped the crowd that this dark-featured, slight young man had attracted Wood's special attention, so he was patted on the back and a big blonde with liquor on her breath kissed him wetly, declaring, "Wisht I was a man!"

"Well, I'm damn glad ye're not!" Christian laughed, somehow infinitely relieved that his problem had been solved for him.

Before he knew it, he was borne along by an assortment of roughly clad, ill-smelling characters to a local tavern, with the woman still clinging to his arm.

Of what followed, nothing remained for Christian beyond disjointed recollections of cheers for Queen Victoria, cheers for Jefferson Davis, and strangely enough, of cheers for a Lieutenant named John Brooke, who was credited with having designed this invulnerable ironclad. Remembering what had happened to him in New York, Christian attempted to refuse drinks, but to no avail. Brimming glass after glass was thrust at him, until the world whirled about him much as it had in Poppy Smith's Saloon.

The following morning he was awakened on a lumpy corn-husk mattress by the big blonde, drowsily reminding him that the Portsmouth train was expected to leave before long.

Pulling himself together, he bussed his damp and raddled baggage out of gratitude for having roused him, then swayed out on the street to join a disorderly gang headed toward the railroad yard where, to his surprise, hatchet-faced Lieutenant Wood was telling off a detail of militiamen to keep back the mob and allow only volunteers to pass.

To his astonishment, the Lieutenant recognized him immediately. "Ah, there, Mr. Pitcher, Ah sure was hopin' you wouldn't let me down. Here's the other half of your enlistment bonus. Now, go aboard." He passed over a folded paper. "When you reach Gosport, give this to the Chief Pilot — might do you a world of good." Abruptly, he offered his hand. "Good luck, and may you help guide our great ship to victory and everlasting fame!"

23

"The Invulnerable Armored Champion"

"OUR INVULNERABLE ARMORED CHAMPION!" So wrote the Norfolk *Day Book*'s special reporter in describing that ugly, queer-looking warship hurriedly and painfully nearing completion in the Gosport Navy yard.

Immediately after detraining, the recruits from Elizabeth City for a brief while were permitted to linger on the granite graving dock's eastern side. Christian felt at once deeply impressed but nevertheless disappointed by the *Virginia*'s insignificant dimensions. Standing on cold stone pavement amid a tangle of timbers, iron plates, barrels of rivets, spikes, and other building materials, Christian quickly counted this extraordinary craft's armament; one pivot gun forward, another aft, and four along each beam for a total of ten guns, just as the Lieutenant had said.

From some of these ports protruded the muzzles of what undoubtedly were heavy guns — large broadside pieces, they looked like nine-inch smooth bores. Apparently iron port shutters had been called for by the designers, but thus far only the hinges from which such protections were to be slung were in evidence. All about the dockyard a state of noisy confusion prevailed.

Certainly, the C.S.S. *Virginia* in no way resembled any craft the Bermudian had ever beheld, and he had seen plenty at various times. He could appreciate the original beautiful lines remaining in the old U.S.S. *Merrimac*'s original hull that had been razed down to her berth deck; at that level an iron-covered wooden "raft" had been affixed, together with a short, wrought-iron ram at its bow end.

From the jackstaff forward of her single squat funnel she was flying a Commodore's red pennant and from her stern floated a brand-new Confederate ensign composed of two broad horizontal red stripes and one white stripe; seven white stars shone on a bright-blue field on the flag's canton corner. At once it struck Pitcher, as it would many others, that the Confederacy's ensign, when viewed from a distance, might readily be mistaken for that of the United States.

This late February morning was cold and clear but almost windless, so the ringing clang of mauls driving home red-hot rivets, the whine of saws, and continued hammering created such an appalling din that flocks of seabirds and wild fowl sheered away from Gosport in general and the graving dock in particular.

Lieutenant Wood pointed to the hull nearing completion. "Take a good look at her, boys. Some people predict she'll prove only an iron coffin for her crew, so if any of you think she will, you can fall out right now and Ah'll find other work for you-all; we want no faint hearts aboa'd the *Virginia!*"

Something inside of Christian squirmed at the prospect of being encased in that iron monster onto which creaking and groaning cranes were still lowering iron plates, angle irons, and other structural equipment. Her hull, of course, was wooden — that of the *Merrimac* — but her casemate was of four-inch iron throughout.

So this was the "juggernaut" the Northern press had been screaming about. Save for her casemate, this so-called steam ram didn't appear at all impressive. At a rough guess, Pitcher estimated the *Virginia* wouldn't measure much over one hundred and seventy feet in length by about seventy feet in the beam, amidships.

Quite a few others of the party looked downright uneasy, but no one fell out. Once they'd done staring at this strange, brown-gray vessel, Wood marched the recruits down to the Navy Yard Superintendent's office where, to the Officer of the Day, he explained these volunteers' special qualifications, if any. When he came to Christian, he motioned the Bermudian aside.

"Ah've been thinking about what you've told me. If you really *are* a qualified pilot, Ah reckon you'd be a heap mo' useful aboa'd some other vessel of the James River Squadron than on the *Virginia*. There'd be no space for you in her wheelhouse. Ah think you'd most likely prove mo' useful aboa'd the *Patrick Henry*. Her skipper, Johnny Tucker, and I were classmates in school."

Lieutenant *Tucker?* Christian blinked. Could this officer be related to the Bermuda Tuckers? They were a numerous family possessed of long-established connections with Virginia, as far back as when this State had been an English colony.

The young Bermudian swallowed hard as Lieutenant Wood searchingly scanned his lean, brown features. "Can you *really* read charts, and do you have a true pilot's feel for wind and weather?"

"Yes, sir, or so I've been told often enough."

"You'd better be right; these local waters are among the most difficult along the Atlantic coast. You'll have to learn a heap of various reefs, shoals, flats, and sandbars lying in Hampton Roads and off Newport News, and in a damn short time, too. Think you can?"

"Oh, yes, sir! I'm sure I can. The waters off Bermuda are very treacherous, too." Hell! He'd slipped up at last and mentioned Bermuda — of all fool things in this situation. Fortunately, the recruiting officer didn't appear to notice his admission.

"Well, come along. Ah'll let the Chief Pilot quiz you. Mind, you don't attempt to draw the long bow concernin' yo'self and your abilities, else you'll land in mighty deep trouble; the Chief is as sharp as a tack. If you don't measure up, you'll likely find yourself heaving coal aboa'd some little gunboat."

From somewhere the ex-convict drew a measure of reasurance. Nobody here could check his past; besides, he'd long been held the best damn apprentice pilot in the Islands. He pulled himself together and stood at rigid attention, thinking how much the Chief Pilot resembled a vulture, what with his reddish bald head, huge, hooked nose, and thin, deeply wrinkled neck, while he conducted a brief but searching and difficult examination. To his amazement, Christian discovered he knew a bit more concerning certain fine points of navigation than did this hard-eyed, tobacco-chewing fellow in the black-and-white-checkered shirt.

"Well, son," the Chief Pilot said at last, "if you ain't really as smart as you seem, you're a clever, first-rate liar. Since we-all are short of competent pilots, Ah reckon Ah'll assign you as relief pilot aboa'd — " he settled back in his chair and briefly stroked ginger-colored sidewhiskers — "lessee — mebbe Ah'll send you aboa'd the *Virginia* but mebbe Ah won't. One of her assistant pilot's been sickly, but he's gettin well fast, or so they say."

Christian's heart seemed to falter. Again, he knew he'd never willingly serve aboard that weird-looking ironclad. Instinct warned him that, if she floated at all, such a vessel, designed as she was, would prove sluggish in speed, difficult to steer, and probably dangerously unseaworthy in any kind of open water.

The Chief of Pilots accurately squirted tobacco juice at a cuspidor overflowing across the room. "Now, Mista' Pitcher, since mah friend Lieutenant Wood seems to favor the cut of yo' jib, Ah'll assign you for temporary duty as a relief pilot aboa'd our gunboat *Patrick Henry*, which is to be flagship fo' the James River Squadron. She used to be on the Norfolk-to-New Y⸺ a real fine steamer, biggest and fastest side-wheeler we ⸺ equipped with about twelve cannons.

"⸺g over a wide, cluttered table, the Chief of Pilots sele⸺ed and well-thumbed charts. "Now, Mista,' just you go s⸺ ah charts till you can recite soundings at any given point in H⸺ads or off Newport News in yo' sleep. Ah'll grant you two days ⸺ what's needed, then come back heah. If you satisfy me, and ⸺ yo Ah'm damn' hard to please, Ah'll recommend yo' to the *Patrick Henry*'s head pilot. His name's Joe Richardson and he's a fire-eater so y⸺'d better be prompt in answerin' correctly any question he puts."

Unexpectedly, he offered a tattooed and bony brown hand. "Well, Mista' Pitcher, heah's luck to you. You'll damn' well need plenty of it."

Perhaps it was due to Pitcher's nimble mind and retentive memory, added to the Chief of Pilot's "good luck" wish, or more probably, due to the Chief's influence, that three days later the ex-convict readily passed a searching and difficult examination and was hired, but not enlisted, in the service of the Confederate States of America as Second Assistant Pilot aboard the swift and graceful C.S.S. *Patrick Henry*.

Christian Pitcher guessed he'd never felt so happy, so supremely confident was he of what the future might hold in this great land.

24

"Ericsson's Folly"

FOR THOSE WHO HAD PLANNED and labored so long and hard on "Ericsson's Folly," it seemed too good to be true that on the 25th of February, 1862, she should be formally accepted and commissioned as a third-class screw steamer in the Naval Service of the United States of America. To a man, her crew of hand-picked volunteers were intensely excited. Ira vaguely recalled someone's observation that only nitwits, woolly-minded idiots, or potential suicides would volunteer for such admittedly hazardous duty.

Only two days earlier, Ira had reported aboard for duty as Third Assistant Engineer, which sounded like a pretty insignificant post until knowledgeable persons became aware that in this tiny vessel of only 766-ton displacement, more than two dozen small and newly designed independent steam engines, serving a variety of purposes, had been seated in the *Monitor*'s cramped hull. They were intended to operate ammunition hoists and to drive bilge pumps and ventilation blowers which had been built to force drafts designed to serve two horizonal vibrating lever-driving engines, delivering some 320 horsepower upon a single propeller shaft and thus driving Ericsson's invention at a top speed of possibly twelve knots.

Once he had found his sleeping quarters, Ira discovered they were very dark and measured exactly eight by four feet. There was only a wash stand and a narrow bunk, on which he had been forced temporarily to deposit his scant baggage.

Later, Ira came to marvel over the supreme ingenuity exercised by the great Swedish-American inventor in utilizing every square inch of a hull, all of which — except for the turret, a collapsible smokestack, two blower intakes, and a tiny, iron-covered pilothouse near the bows — were situated safely below the waterline.

Even her anchor, when installed, lay completely protected in a well built into the bows; her hook, therefore, could be raised and lowered from below without exposing a single man to shot or shell. Ira blinked as he noted that in the ceiling of this hutch was situated a small, round deadlight of heavy glass, which in fair weather might be opened to admit a little light and fresh air. God above! Even with her blowers in full operation, this vessel's atmosphere was dark and smelled oily and stale.

Painful bumps and sometimes serious injuries would be suffered by anyone careless enough to make a sharp, unexpected movement. Even before coming aboard, Ira had heard reports that the *Monitor*'s single trial run had not been accomplished without a number of serious problems coming to light. For instance, among other flaws, she steered erratically, yawing to and fro, because her so-called balanced rudder hadn't been properly proportioned. However, like other errors, this one was soon corrected by the indefatigable Ericsson, who often worked twenty hours a day.

While unpacking after a fashion, the new Third Assistant Engineer smiled as he recalled the small farewell dinner party given by Captain Daniel Dexter in his honor. During a main course of roast wild goose, his host had pointedly inquired of Ira, resplendent in a dress uniform he might never wear again, what single invention, among the forty-odd patentable devices Ericsson had devised, he deemed the most useful. An impish impulse caused Ira to bow to David's father, and then reach under his chair to produce a small cardboard box which he had placed on the dinner table saying, "Here, sir, is what we all feel to be the most useful of Mr. Ericsson's inventions." Solemnly, he lifted out models of two curious pieces of mechanism.

Mr. Delamater exclaimed, "What in God's name is that damn thing?"

Captain Dexter had replied gravely, "As we all know, man needs food, which, when digested, must be evacuated. Here, my friends, are models of the two flush toilets built by my firm and recently installed aboard the *Monitor*. They operate by compressed air supplied by one of the engines — just how efficiently, we don't yet know."

The impromptu dinner party had exploded into ringing shouts of laughter. An aging Flag Officer roared, "Now, by God, I can go back on duty with an easy mind. For over forty years I've frozen or scorched my butt in a head, and now I'll be able to shit in comfort!"

Once the party had broken up and the last guests had departed amid a babble of liquor-enriched voices, Captain Daniel Dexter had placed frail, white, blue-veined hands on Ira's gold epaulettes. "Son — I hope you don't mind my calling you so, but right now, I've been feeling the need for one ever since David departed so abruptly two days ago."

Wrinkles had deepened across the old man's parchment-hued forehead. "Don't know why, but I'm badly worried about him. Seems to be something mighty important bothering him. He denies that there is, but I know better. Have you any idea what's wrong?"

"No, sir," Ira lied. "We haven't seen much of one another lately."

A long and sibilant sigh escaped the Captain's lips as he shrugged. "Well, now that's that, so let's change the subject to yourself. I only hope and pray this extraordinary little warship you've elected to serve in accomplishes even a part of the miracles a few smart people expect of her. Right now, Ericsson's invention puts me in mind of David carrying two guns, preparing to do battle with that armored Goliath the *Virginia* — no, the *Merrimac* — which we know mounts a battery of *ten* heavy pieces. Go with my blessings, and remember, Ira, you'll always find a home here."

"Thank you, sir, for everything. Don't expect too much of the *Monitor*, but Acting Captain Worden and the rest of us, down to the dirtiest coal heaver, will do our best."

25

Various Intrigues

As usual, the handsome Hotel Willard's huge main dining room, Washington's meeting place, was full to overflowing with a colorful assortment of uniforms. Most of the liberally bewhiskered patrons wore dark Federal blue, but there were also plenty of the colorful if not gaudy uniforms worn by innumerable militia and volunteer units, such as Duryea's Zouave Regiment, clad in French Army Colonial regalia composed of red fezzes, baggy scarlet pants, white gaiters, and blue gold-laced shell jackets.

There were plenty of prosperous-looking civilians, too, most of them boasting heavy gold watch chains, almost as thick as small cables, draped across ample paunches. But they were in the minority, these men who were mostly would-be contractors, seeking, by fair means or bribery, exclusive permits, lucrative positions, or contracts with the government. There were also in evidence quite a few foreigners, distinguishable by the cut of their clothes and hair and their continually animated gestures. Voluminous hoop skirts or crinolines of vivid hues worn by vivacious females of varying degrees of beauty and virtue circulated, adding vivid splashes of color.

As a result, David Dexter, although his civilian suit had been cut in London by one of the most fashionable tailors in Savile Row, felt somewhat like a jackdaw unexpectedly introduced to and associated with a flock of peacocks.

Moodily, David sought a small corner table and there slowly drained a tall glass of iced bourbon, while at the same time he reviewed an unhappy conversation he'd just had with an old shipmate, Paymaster Holmes Alexander.

On first sighting David, Lieutenant Alexander had halted dead in his tracks, dark eyes rounded in disbelief. Recovering and beaming, he rushed forward to bear-hug him briefly. Holmes, who hailed from a handsome plantation hard by the Culpeper estate, for years had been on intimate terms with the Ridgely family.

Alexander was wearing his uniform, but, although he didn't ask, he wondered why his old friend was not also in blue. Sensing this, David invented an evasive story of having been sent to Washington by the Navy on an important secret mission, to obtain evidence of corruption between certain powerful politicians and contractors.

"Now it's your turn," David said, concluding his fabrications. He inquired casually about the Ridgelys of "Gunner's Hill."

"First off," Holmes informed him, "you should know that since this damn war broke out, the Ridgelys have had a hard time. You recall Francis, Louisa's elder brother?"

"Of course. What about him?"

"Well, while he was serving under General Bragg in Tennessee, Francis was shot and killed in a silly little cavalry skirmish of no real importance. Pity. No glory in that, but he was just as dead as getting heroically slain in some great battle."

David had stared fixedly at the glass-marked marble table. So, Francis Ridgely was dead! How readily he could recall riding to hounds with him and his brothers, Charles and Peter; the third boy was only fifteen. How vividly he recalled various cotillions they'd attended, and the brilliant dinner parties they'd enjoyed before Fort Sumter had been attacked. Soon he had fallen deeply, hopelessly in love with Louisa Ridgely, that sparkling, nineteen-year-old beauty, whose bright and fine honey-colored hair shone like a glowing beacon.

David controlled his memories to inquire about what Charles Ridgely might be doing in this conflict.

Holmes shrugged. "I've heard through the grapevine that Charles has been made an aide-de-camp to General Pemberton and is serving somewhere out in the Midwest."

Gently, Holmes beat one fist against its mate. "You know, Dave, it's hell being so long out of touch with home. Imagine me, a Virginian born and bred, wearing Federal blue!" He gulped the last of his drink. "My own folks despise me and my fellow Union officers distrust me, but, even so, I'm so dead set against disunion and slavery. I've followed my conscience." Alexander tugged at a short and pointed brown beard. Narrowly he considered his old friend for a long instant. "With your background, you can't have had too easy a time of it either, Dave."

"Correct. Until recently I've been on duty in the Naval Attaché's office in London, but even so, I've heard nothing direct from Culpeper, let alone from the Ridgelys and 'Gunner's Hill.' So for God's sake, tell me about Louisa!" He stared at the chatterng, ever-shifting crowd of patrons. "I think of her night and day, and wonder how she feels about my remaining a Union man. I've had never a word from her."

Alexander took a deep swallow of ale, wiping the froth from the corners of his mouth. "Well, as you probably have learned long since, the Navy *Gazette* reported the U.S.S. sloop of war *Argus* lost last March with all hands. A short communication to that effect was reprinted in most Southern newspapers, Richmond included — or so I was told. Of course, I haven't been near home since before Bull Run, so all I've told you is hearsay."

"I suppose she believes I was lost in the *Argus*. How did Louisa take the report of my supposed loss at sea?"

"They say she fairly wept her eyes out, wouldn't eat, and locked herself in her bedroom and refused to leave it for three whole days. When she did come out, some folks thought she appeared five years older. She seemed subdued, although always agreeable. By every possible means she attempted to verify the *Argus*'s loss, but after the *Washington Post* and other newspapers in Norfolk and Richmond published formal obituaries for Lieutenant David H. Dexter, U.S.N., she gave up; the *Argus* undoubtedly had sunk off eastern Cuba while on antislave patrol duty."

"Please, Holmes, have you any idea where Louisa is now? How is she faring?"

Alexander cocked a slightly bloodshot eye at a gaslight chandelier glowing overhead — such illumination was still a novelty in private homes, except those of the very wealthy, and in certain important hotels and some public buildings.

Sensing the depth of David's anxiety, Alexander said quietly, "At the start, Louisa joined other local ladies in making bandages and sewing pledgets, but apparently that wasn't enough for her."

Elbows on the table, David leaned forward. "Go on, for God's sake, man. What is she doing *now?*"

"She's joined the Ladies Sanitary Commission and is a great help to old Dr. Lafayette Grundy at Miss Julia Anderson's Female Seminary near Brandy Station, where she's boarding, so as to be able to work around the clock."

So Louisa wasn't in Culpeper but at Brandy Station. Still, both places lay quite a little distance from Norfolk. With communication so uncertain nowadays, he couldn't be confident of locating her. Holmes's information admittedly was several weeks out of date, so while it might have been possible, somehow, to find official business to take him to Brandy Station, it would be difficult, if not impossible, to find his way north to the Capital and make his report on the *Merrimac*. Along that stretch of country, both sides were apt to shoot first and possibly talk later.

"Tell me, Holmes, can you think of any means of assuring Louisa that I'm far from dead? What happened is clear. The officer lost in the *Argus* and mentioned in the obituaries was a Virginian and went to Annapolis. His name and middle initial are — or were — the same as mine; but as near as I know, he was no relation."

"Bad luck, such coincidences. Lucky they happen so seldom."

Before Holmes could answer David's imploring question, their conversation was terminated as a pair of Alexander's friends, clad in the New York Fire Zouaves' outlandish oriental uniform — baggy red pants and all — insisted on joining them. David, overwhelmed by his thoughts, didn't mind. Where could Louisa be? For that matter, where would he be in another few days? He made his excuses, and after leaving his address with Alexander, he departed. At once, however, he was beckoned by a distinguished gentleman whom David recognized as an important official in the State Department's foreign service.

Quietly, he was conducted into a private sitting room where, in precise detail, the official, Robert Copperfield, explained what technical information David's espionage mission was expected to discover. But with that explained, a large question arose: how could he plausibly reach Norfolk, Gosport, and Hampton Roads undetected?

Every possibility had to be explored. If Confederate counterintelligence had the sense God granted astigmatic titmice, he would stand little hope of convincing an experienced interrogator that his new identity, Henry Dutton, was a sheet-iron contractor, or a shipbuilder — or the potential skipper of some blockade runner. Mr. Copperfield asserted that he was prepared to supply any sort of forged and convincing papers for him.

But the real answer came when David recalled his conversation with Lionel Humphrey. Why not claim to be a foreign and entirely neutral newspaperman? After all, his command of English was perfect, if just a shade Americanized, so why not pose as a correspondent from some Canadian newspaper?

Mr. Copperfield was mildy enthusiastic. Yes, that might do. Henry Dutton could convincingly pose as a correspondent for the *Halifax Gazette*. Nowadays, Halifax often figured in the news, that part of the Empire being considered, along with Bermuda, as a probable and important British base for naval operations in case hostilities broke out with the United States, an event that often seemed far from an impossibility in this year of 1862.

David Dexter, alias Henry Dutton, as an accredited journalist from a country openly friendly toward Southern aspirations, might well be allowed to roam about Norfolk and Gosport asking questions. Good. Tomorrow, his credentials would be in order.

Making his way through the lobby after this meeting, David again heard his name called, and was pleased to recognize Lionel Humphrey's tall, lanky figure, beckoning from a table at which sat Mademoiselle Arlette d'Aubrey, fashionably dressed and appearing more intriguing than ever.

"My dear fellow," Lionel said, in such warm tones that several of his fellow journalists turned in surprise to see him shaking hands enthusiastically with a tall young man of unmistakably military bearing.

Arlette lifted her lips and kissed him so warmly her lips left traces of red. "Oh, *mon cher* David! So often have Lion-el and I not wondered where the Fates might have directed you. Whatever are you doing in such *chic* civilian garments?"

"Well," he said in an undertone, "I would have been a hypocrite to go on wearing a Union uniform when, as you know, my heart lies Southward."

Arlette looked sympathetically; as always, the word "heart" touched her. Never had David seen Arlette look so expertly *soignée;* whoever was settling her accounts these days must be well heeled.

Without appearing to do so, the French girl studied her ex-shipmate and noted very slight aging lines radiating from his eye corners. ***Mon Dieu!*** David must have suffered greatly since they had parted up in New York.

An inspiration burgeoning, David excused himself after making sure that Lionel and Arlette *both* were occupying rooms at the Willard. Later on, a discreet inquiry and a generous tip to a reception clerk established the not too surprising fact that their rooms adjoined.

26

Enter Henry Dutton

For a few moments longer, David, now Mr. Henry Dutton, lay with fingers laced back of his head, staring at garish wallpaper. Certainly a vast amount of money had been spent on this hotel, although its furnishings and some decorations were not in the best of taste.

Seldom had he floundered in such a state of mental turmoil, but he thought perhaps he had discovered an answer to establishing a convincing new identity. Properly approached, he reckoned that Lionel Humphrey would prove of assistance. During the voyage from Bermuda, it had gradually become apparent that the Englishman, albeit unobtrusively, supported the Northern point of view. Apparently, Lionel was acquainted with a good number of those foreign war correspondents now swarming about Washington and its environs.

The problem was, why should a well-established if presently out of favor British journalist risk further trouble by vouching for him as a bona fide representative of the *Halifax Gazette*, a practically unknown Canadian newspaper? Possibly he might find out before a firing squad. But the scheme just *might* come off. What with his native Boston accent and the time he'd spent on duty in London, he reckoned he would pass convincingly for an English-born Canadian, except to a most discerning individual.

The beauty of this projected ploy lay in the probability that, as a presumably accredited neutral correspondent, "Henry Dutton" could be passed through both Union and hostile lines, since both sides were avid for favorable comments, credit, and equipment from abroad. The more he thought about it, the more David felt he had discovered the best way out of the dilemma into which United States Navy Intelligence had maneuvered him.

"Of course," as Lionel pointed out later, after agreeing, "we can't support you in any way should you become detected as a spy."

In hopes of ironing out possibly dangerous details, David invited Arlette and Lionel to join him for supper following the theater hour, although he had no notion of attending a play himself, but it seemed advisable to make this invitation appear impromptu. Much to his satisfaction, both of his companions declared themselves pleased at the prospect of a late snack. They would be delighted to rejoin their former shipmate in the Palm Room at eleven-thirty.

Lionel and Arlette, however, also entertained no plans to attend a theater; their own variety of entertainment was far more intriguing. Strange how, gradually, they had both grown to understand each other, with something more valid than a merely physical attraction. To Lionel it was astonishing that the two of them, aside from the bed, had discovered so much in common.

"A glass of wine, *mon cher?*" Arlette suggested, turning on the broad bed and exposing magnificent white bosoms, the like of which Lionel had seldom beheld even in the best seraglios of the Near East. How infinitely stimulating it was to view her, indolently propped up in the big double bed, all pink and glowing amid a nest of bolsters and pillows. Through experimentation they had discovered his bed to be more comfortable than hers next door. Arlette, however, took care to leave personal possessions in there, and should somebody knock, it wouldn't require more than a few moments to slip past through the connecting door, leaving behind no more evidence than the faint scent of "Abrabesque," her personal, distinctive, and stimulating perfume.

Sipping a light Chateau Margaux, she playfully tousled Lionel's wavy, sandy-brown hair, thereby earning a sleepy kiss.

Setting down a slim-stemmed glass, Lionel drawled, "Odd, wasn't it, our encountering David Dexter?"

"Yes, *mon cher.* But one thing I do not understand, why was he not wearing his Union-blue uniform?"

"I know why," he told her. "Tell you later. Now turn over, *chérie,* for a gentle spank."

"Plus tarde." She pulled up the bedclothes. "After you tell me why you suddenly looked so grim when that dispatch arrived from London this afternoon."

He emitted a rueful little laugh. "Well, my dear, as a result of its contents, our idyllic interlude may perhaps be nearing its end."

"Oh, *non! non!"*

Her eyes widened and she sat up in bed, more intriguingly curvaceous than before. "What is your meaning? Your newspaper has perhaps recalled you?"

"No. My editor on the *Telegraph* only indicated that unless I send in some really startling items of information before long, he will dispense with my services."

"Dieu! You are being threatened with — discharge?"

"To employ an American euphemism, I have not been really fired, but almost. That penny-pinching bastard, Brownlow, claims I've been sending in too many exorbitant expense accounts, despite, I may modestly admit, a goodly number of news items of the first importance."

"Oh, *non! non!* But this is serious?"

"Not quite, yet." Lionel reached for a well-worn briar pipe, loaded it but didn't light it, certain testimony that he really was perturbed.

"But, Lion-el, your record as a war correspondent in the Crimea was most distinguished, to say the least."

"Be that as it may seem to a stranger." He kissed her cheek. "Arlette, my dear, you can't possibly understand the peculiar standards of the newspaper world where, as we often grouse at Press Clubs, unusual ability and foresight all too often are their own reward."

"But — Lion-el, if you could send news of some outstanding event of great magnitude, would that not restore you to favor?"

"It just might, dear; but we shall have to see what we shall see. In the meantime, allow me to order up a few hors d'oeuvres before we go down to the Palm Room and seek our friend Dexter."

Arlette made no immediate reply, only stared fixedly at the brass footboard. "Do you know something, Lion-el, my love? I am achieving a growing sense of affection for this great if barbarous country. Here, before the law at least, everyone stands equal — or is supposed to. Here a person possessed of wits, energy, and courage can rise to great heights, no matter who his father or grandfather is or was supposed to be."

"I hope only that we are lucky enough to stay in it — if possible together, my little love," Lionel said, pulling her yielding body down to him.

27

The Palm Room

PERHAPS BECAUSE THIS WAS A SATURDAY and many officers and men had been relieved from a multitude of duties in and around Washington and its defenses, the Palm Room's walls reverberated and tobacco smoke billowed thick as burnt powder during a heavy skirmish. Voices mounted while drinks were emptied, often in reckless succession.

David at once noted several groups of officers clad in smartly tailored and gold-laced French naval uniforms. Several affected long, spike-sharp mustachios and pointed goatees such as those affected by Napoleon III. They were occupying a large round table and enjoying the company of a group of vivacious French and American-Creole ladies. What would they be doing here in Washington? By this time, he had learned that of the foreign officers seen about the capital, a majority of French, Austrian, and Russian observers remained in uniform, but British, Scandinavian, and other nationalities usually wore more or less well-tailored civilian clothes.

What now? Instinct assured him that if anyone really could help him accomplish his mission, it would be Lionel Humphrey, that generally affable and open-handed veteran journalist who had earned a considerable reputation during the Crimean War, often, as he gradually ascertained, through lavish spending in order to learn — and keep exclusively to himself — especially valuable matters of critical importance.

"Ah, *mon ami! Vous voilà!*" Arlette's rich voice, without rising, successfully penetrated the hubbub.

David started to shake hands, but demurely; she offered a warm and rosy cheek, so he had no choice but to kiss her, thus meriting envious leers from nearby tables.

The Palm Room became so noisy the three sat with heads held almost intimately together. In honor of the reunion, David offered champagne, but Arlette preferred an anisette, and Lionel a glass of fine old sherry. At first, the three reminisced about their unforgettable passage from Liverpool to Bermuda and New York, but soon it became apparent to David that Lionel and Arlette had been in and around Washington for some time.

No mention was made of Humphrey's precarious relations with the London *Telegraph*. As for David, when they pressed him, he conveyed the impression that he had decided to surrender his commission after becoming convinced that this war would prove ruinously long and costly; he had come to feel that perhaps the Rebels might have sound, if hitherto unknown, reasons for leaving the Union. That being the case, he had about made up his mind to take up journalism and head for the West Coast, there to start a new life where many worthwhile opportunities were reported available.

Arlette, well-skilled in interpreting nuances, suspected that neither of her friends' plans nor motives were entirely genuine. To her discerning eye, David didn't appear half as indecisive as he pretended.

He said, "Now that I'm a civilian again, damned if I don't try my hand at writing."

Lionel nodded. "Appears like a sound idea; you've a way with words, you've a military background, and you're widely traveled. I think I might find you a roving commission with, let's say, the *Halifax Gazette*, which has the advantage of being a neutral newspaper."

Arlette started as if struck by a hatpin. "David a newspaperman? *Jamais!* He is too honest for conniving and doing dirty tricks, such as some newspapermen adopt on occasion."

"I believe *you're* right, Lionel," David said. "I've talked with quite a few influential people who believe that, with my Regular Navy experience and service here and abroad, plus a knowledge of foreign affairs, I might, with luck, prove to be a useful correspondent. What's your honest opinion?"

After Arlette had left them, Lionel Humphrey tilted back in his chair after lighting his pipe, deciding there must be something promising about this. He had to respect the American's intelligence in selecting newspaper work as a civilian cover; especially as a neutral, he would be practically free to come and go. And his journalistic instincts swiftly appreciated that, quite possibly, as a former professional naval officer, David might be able to recognize and take note of pertinent but not obvious facts at Hampton Roads, which a civilian could not hope to do, thus transmitting facts which might escape even so expert a correspondent as William "Bull Run" Russell. And if he could follow Dexter's lead with a few special articles, rich in hitherto unknown information, Lionel reckoned, he might restore his present equivocal position with the *Telegraph.*

During the course of the next half hour, Lionel described solutions to problems an inexperienced war correspondent might encounter in rough-and-ready battle areas. While he did so, the Englishman's long and bony features remained expressionless. "Let me remind you that you have been accredited by the *Halifax Gazette,* which you haven't mentioned in public half often enough. Take care of that in the future! As it is, I've secured special introductions in Norfolk to certain newspapermen who should make our stay there a rewarding one — provided you use good sense and play your role to the hilt. I will furnish you with necessary information, even a letter I've forged in your behalf — on condition that you give to me, and to *no other* writer, everything and anything of importance you can learn about the *Merrimac.* Understood?"

"What about the *Monitor?*"

"That is entirely for your conscience to decide."

Like a warm tide following an icy current, relief flooded David. God above! Thus far, at least, matters seemed to be advancing far beyond his highest expectations.

Lionel continued. "As I've already said, with your near-perfect English accent, and especially since you can speak better than average French, you can readily pass for a Canadian. See any objections?"

For answer, David gripped Lionel's hand.

"I believe this is by far your best bet to go south," Humphrey went on. "This afternoon I'll see what can be accomplished in that direction. If the Royal Navy bigwigs are starving for accurate and detailed descriptions of the Confederate ram's armament, top speed, her ram, and possible inventions, tell them about your pretended shift of sides — as a patriotic gesture only. Shouldn't wonder but you'll straight away get a Rebel commission."

He stared hard at his companion. "One more thing — never for an instant forget that, no matter what your connections, you remain an out-and-out spy, and if you're exposed, you'll be executed straight away."

Next morning, as Lionel Humphrey had predicted, Captain Walker of the recruiting service, a saltwater Regular, came dangerously near to smiling when he said, "Very well, Lieutenant — Mr. Dutton. I will keep notes on the truth of your secret mission locked away, not to be seen by anyone else unless there arises a need to produce such evidence as may clear you of turning your coat." He offered a freckled and sinewy brown hand. "I expect much good will come of this venture. Let us pray all goes well with you."

28

His Imperial Majesty Napoleon III's Sloop of War, *Gassendi*

Somehow, it appeared incredible to David, now Henry Dutton, that what had been deemed a baffling Gordian knot could so easily have become undone — and without use of Alexander the Great's sword.

Next afternoon Mr. Copperfield arrived at the hotel to produce various convincing credentials from the *Halifax Gazette,* officially stamped by what purported to be the U.S. Army's Provost Marshal General's office. In addition, presumably the Provost Marshal himself had scribbled on the margin of an official letterhead:

June 3, 1862

To Whom it May Concern:

This is to request that every privilege and assistance be accorded a Canadian war correspondent of the *Halifax Gazette,* named Henry Dutton. In the opinion of this Department, Mr. Dutton has an entirely neutral point of view and is to be trusted.

Perhaps it was indicative of this Provost Marshal's sketchy education that his signature was all but unidentifiable except for a pair of bold flourishes drawn across two slants; people might not recognize his writing, but one and all could recognize that distinctive signature.

Over a light breakfast served in her room, Arlette could barely contain her happiness. Now that David was well on his way to Norfolk, the Ministry of Marine in Paris and Papa should receive some truly exclusive and expert reports about the true situation off Fort Monroe and Hampton Roads.

As for Arlette, she intended to remain in Washington and its environs, where a shrewd, perceptive, and experienced young woman could amass all manner of information which might prove of great importance to Monsieur le Marquis Edouard de la Villette in particular, and to the Ministry of Marine in general.

There were many eligible and well-mannered foreign officers on duty in Washington, a surprising number of them French. It was even rumored that Prince de Joinville was expected soon to arrive in America to serve as a high-ranking observer of this ever-spreading and costly war.

Lionel said, "With any luck, my love, before sundown David — that is Henry — and I should be aboard the *Pocahontas*. She's a speedy dispatch boat chartered for the benefit of official observers, journalists, military artists, photographers, and the like for a trip down to Fort Monroe."

But a disconcerting event occurred as Lionel and "Henry Dutton" were paying their hotel bills after booking passages on the *Pocahontas*.

"Good God!" cried the clerk. "What are you doing here?"

Something in the fellow's expression caused David to catch his breath. "What's wrong?"

"The *Pocahontas* received special orders and sailed an hour ago. Dunno why they changed her departure time, but she's sure enough sailed. Seems suddenlike. These damn civilian steamboats get more expensive and less dependable every day."

How in God's name could he and David hope to reach the vicinity of Fort Monroe in a hurry? Lionel thought. Apparently, a naval clash was imminent down there.

Smothering heartfelt curses, but wearing outwardly unruffled expressions, the two returned and sought Arlette's suite, where they found her fresh from a bath and clad only in an almost diaphanous negligee.

"*Mon Dieu!*" she exclaimed. "What are you doing here, you *vaux riens?* You should be on your way south by this time. I . . ." Arlette broke off short. Both correspondents appeared utterly downcast.

Lionel, as usual, belittling their mischance, explained that for some reason, still unknown, the *Pocahontas* had suddenly cast off an hour in advance of her advertised sailing time.

"But why, *mes amis?* Is it that some secret military or naval coup of importance is pending?"

"Don't know yet," the new Henry Dutton told her. "I reckon our best chance of getting there is by hiring some fast yacht to run us down in a hurry."

No one could have suspected that, for a different set of reasons, but chiefly on Lionel's account, Arlette felt badly shaken. Suddenly, her expression changed and, lifting a softly rounded chin, she snapped fingers loud as firecrackers. *"Tiens!* Possibly one has arrived at a useful solution to this problem."

Lionel's expression relaxed as, bowing, he kissed her hand. "And what is this solution?"

"Now attend me carefully. Early this evening I dine *en intime* with Captain Gautier, who commands His Imperial Majesty's sloop of war, *Gassendi*. It is possible one just might persuade the gallant Captain Gautier to carry you as journalists to Norfolk, where incredibly, there still remains a British Consul's office. Perhaps," she rolled her eyes a little, "with a bit of — persuasion, Captain Gautier will credit that, by accident, you two correspondents were left behind by the *Pocahontas* and that he would please me enormously should he agree to carry you writers down to the vicinity of Hampton Roads. I will see what can be accomplished toward helping you and Monsieur Dexter — I mean Monsieur Dutton — to sail aboard the *Gassendi* as strictly neutral observers."

After the tableware had been removed by an obsequious waiter, Captain Ange Simon Gauthier, before buckling on his dress sword and doing up a double row of glittering gold buttons, stepped back from the disordered dinner table and, with frank thoroughness, studied his hostess's svelte figure.

Laughingly, she said, "Will you oblige me in this certain matter, *mon cher* Capitaine?"

"And what is this again you wish?"

"I assure you, *mon* Capitaine, it is nothing of military importance or significance. Monsieur Humphrey is an Englishman I have known for a considerable time. Mr. Dutton, the other correspondent, is a Canadian newspaperman. I promise you neither will say or do anything to compromise or embarrass you for having transported them to Norfolk."

Captain Gautier gave her what he intended to be a significant glance. "You are most persuasive ma'mselle," he said, smiling. "A more charming bargainer I have never met."

29

Between the Rip Raps and Fort Monroe, Virginia

LONG BEFORE DAYLIGHT, Dexter, Lionel, and the other neutrals sought the *Gassendi*'s rain-soaked bridge, scanning the dim, blue-gray of the shorelines off either beam. Captain Gautier also did not sleep late, but for another reason. He was feeling nervous because his six-gun steam sloop had proved so speedy that by dawn the Roads already were visible, along with the running lights of ships anchored in or traveling along Chesapeake Bay.

Since it remained almost impossible for distant observers to identify for certain the tricolors of the Third Empire, Gautier had ordered large white flags for his mastheads, as a reminder that this was a neutral vessel. That was just as well, it appeared, as the sloop of war bore to starboard and headed for the Rip Raps, an artificial fortified island of stone built to defend the southern side of the entrance to Hampton Roads. Numbers of gunboats and armed merchantmen began to churn in the French vessel's direction, with guns run out and crews at stations, standing ready for battle. What really annoyed Gautier was the presence of the corvette H.M.S. *Rinaldo.* Once more the British had arrived first and anchored in the choicest observation point.

The *Gassendi,* having cruised these waters on previous occasions, was soon recognized by both the Confederate and Union gunboats before she dipped her colors, whereupon the threatening gunboats returned the courtesy by briefly lowering their own ensign before veering away.

Lionel mopped his high, faintly lined forehead. "Well, David — I mean

Harry, 'Henry' sounds too formal, don't you think — so far, so good. But the good Lord alone knows what sort of reception we'll get between the Rip Raps and Fort Monroe, off which the Yankees' main blockading fleet is supposed to be anchored."

Rapidly, the *Halifax Gazette*'s phantom correspondent began to make entries in a mental notebook about the positions of Union capital ships, powerful batteries, forts, busy dockyards, and supply vessels. Veritable forests of topmasts and spars bristled above the littered waters off Fort Monroe and, in fact, along most of a long, concave crescent of the shore, curving southward toward Newport News.

By now it had become general knowledge among the French and their guests that the *Merrimac*, reportedly armored and equipped with very powerful guns, was about ready to sally forth on a momentous mission — nothing less than to challenge the *Monitor!*

Under a borrowed blue watch cloak, David shivered. Studying Fort Monroe, he suddenly felt sick at heart. Good God! How many of these impressive men-of-war were familiar? Among them he recognized the *St. Lawrence* and the *Roanoke*, in which he'd served a few years ago in his midshipman days during a cruise around the Mediterranean.

Everywhere, the sky was clouded by waterfowl of all kinds, but what chiefly commanded everyone's attention was the presence of the *Merrimac*'s screw-driven sister frigates, the *Minnesota* and the *Roanoke*. David had already learned that the *Congress* and the *Cumberland* were lying out of sight, well up-river off Newport News. The heavy guns on these ships had nearly all been designed by Ulrich Dahlgren, and enjoyed certain improvements made by the English inventor John Brooke.

The Roads fairly teemed with traffic, both mercantile and military. All were showing Union colors and David felt more shaken than ever. If only his yearning for Louisa hadn't been so intense that it confounded patriotism. But had it *really?* His emotions were confused.

Presently a fast-armed tugboat churned up alongside and an officer in shirt-sleeves and suspenders shouted up to Captain Gautier, "Hi there, on the bridge!"

"Yes? What can we do for you?"

"*Monsieur*, follow me past the Rip Raps, where you'll pause until you've furnished the Commanding Officer there with satisfactory credentials, or you won't be granted the privileges of neutrals — like that damn'

British corvette, *Rinaldo* over yonder. She's nothin' but a Redcoat spy boat."

Before Captain Gautier's crew could acknowledge these instructions, the escort pulled away. Quickly and accurately David began to jot down in his brand-new notebook the names of major men-of-war comprising the blockading squadron, including their rig and estimated weight of guns. Lionel grinned. "I say, Harry, you've a shrewd eye about noting only important details; you might make a real correspondent some day."

By now David had observed a number of heavy batteries, recently constructed on Sewell's Point, and constituting the principal defense of Norfolk. Its docks and shipyards extending up the Elizabeth River created a smudged black line along the southern shore.

There was no doubt that Gosport, the huge former U.S. Navy yard and armory, were of vital importance to the Rebels, together with the great dry or graving dock, railheads, and supply stations. Nearly every foreign Naval Ministry, let alone Federal authorities, was aware that yonder lurked the armored craft conceived with amazing ingenuity by the physically handicapped Commandant French Forrest, along with Stephen Mallory, James Byers, and the Baker brothers.

All these must be itching for the rechristened C.S.S. *Virginia* to blow the powerful blockading Union ships to flinders. Her crew, David decided, must be real men, Rebels willing to risk careers, money, and lives at unpredictable odds.

That the long-anticipated clash was now imminent could be seen by a mounting traffic of vessels — dispatch launches, powerful tugs, and any number of small coasters, crabbers, and pleasure craft hurrying along on both shores of Hampton Roads. Only at the moment did David come truly to appreciate how beautifully proportioned were most regular American sailing men-of-war; the artistry evident in their lines and proportions could only be approached by French shipwrights.

David and Lionel were patiently moving their binoculars among the great wooden ships lying under the guns of Fort Monroe, searching for a glimpse of the fabled *Monitor*. Although reportedly small in proportion, the *Monitor* might prove to be a veritable giant, fit to face her much larger opponent, the ironclad *Merrimac*.

Once the *Gassendi*'s credentials had been scrutinized and unwillingly authenticated, and her anchor plunged into turbid waters close by and downstream from the Rip Raps, Captain Gautier relaxed sufficiently to order a hearty breakfast. He informed his guests, "Before long, *Messieurs*, it will be my duty and pleasure to go ashore under a flag of truce to present respects and deliver certain despatches to the Imperial French Consul. Should either of you two gentlemen of the press care to accompany me, I will assist, *provided,*" he paused and looked intently at one and then the other of the two newsmen, "you solemnly promise to commit no breach of the laws of neutrality. As English subjects, you are entitled to official protection and such other privileges as the Confederate authorities may care to grant you." Deliberately, he finished the last of a soufflé, then dabbed daintily at black, bayonet-pointed mustachios.

"*Alors, mes amis.* I propose to depart for Norfolk within the half-hour. Kindly be at the gangway." He drew himself up to his full height of five-feet-six. "*Messieurs,* I cannot emphasize this point too strongly. No weapons of any description are to be carried ashore by anyone."

His two correspondents, real and counterfeit, nodded solemn agreement.

30

A Change of Uniform

To DAVID, Norfolk appeared to have changed very little from the day when, as a midshipman on the U.S.S. *Roanoke,* he had first sighted this port. Clusters of rakish-appearing crabbers, oystering boats — bugeyes, skipjacks, and such — not to mention coasting traders; a few ocean-going ships and what obviously were blockade runners lay anchored off the teeming waterfront.

The only difference he could see was that there were only a few tall deep-sea sailing ships anywhere along the southern waterfront, and only a few lying at wharves close to the Elizabeth River's estuary. Through mingled smoke and haze, plenty of well-built batteries were visible on Sewell's Point, Pig Point, and other strategic locations.

Obviously, considerable excitement already had been evoked by the sight of the huge tricolor fluttering from the French man-of-war's maintop. With a large white flag drooping from its signal gaff, Captain Gautier's gig was promptly escorted by an armed tugboat showing the name *Teaser* painted across her stern.

A provost's guard stood at the Customs House lined up beyond the landing stage, and a civilian mob began to cheer, enthusiastically yielding to the illusion that the French Government finally must have recognized the Confederate Government as a belligerent power and as therefore entitled to international benefits.

All too soon, however, it became apparent that this pleasant assumption was erroneous. The landing party were not granted permission to scatter and wander about at large. On their way to the French Consulate, all of them remained under an escort of tough-looking Confederate troops.

How to separate himself from the rest of the landing party was David's chief concern. Both he and Lionel had been issued cardboard forms to be worn in their hatbands, proclaiming them as neutral observers. But someone in the crowd spread the word that two of the visitors looked like Englishmen, and again hopes soared that, at long last, England was preparing to grant the Confederacy a belligerent nation's rights on the high seas.

Soon both party and escort were engulfed in a milling, disorderly mob of Southerners of all ages and colors. An unmistakably English voice yelled, "Ye come a bit tardy, mates, but all the same, ye're welcome to Norfolk!"

In no time, shiny black slaves, seafaring folk, citizens of all stations and many nations crowded noisily about the landing party, offering plenty of liquid refreshment and such local delicacies as huge, luscious oysters, cold crabmeat cakes, and beaten biscuit.

Once the escort was dismissed by an official of some importance, it proved simple for David, while being entertained in a better-than-average saloon, to inquire the whereabouts of a toilet and then to unostentatiously slip out through the tavern's backyard. After removing his correspondent's identification card from his hatband, he mingled with the crowd and, through judicious questioning of a semidrunken sergeant, found his way to the headquarters of Major General Benjamin Huger, C.S.A., Commanding Officer of the Land Forces in Norfolk and vicinity. Soon he found himself in earnest conversation with Lieutenant Harry Ashton Ramsay, Chief Engineer on the C.S.S. *Virginia*, who was also a graduate of the United States Naval Academy some six years before Dexter's class.

Brow furrowed, Lieutenant Ramsay demanded, "Why the pseudonym, Dexter, and these civilian togs? Why would you, a Yankee and a former Federal officer, come down here in search of a Southern commission?"

"I can't explain quickly or easily, sir, but shortly after the fighting began, I was recalled from duty aboard. Last winter I decided for private reasons to change sides, especially after I realized the degree of greed and corruption prevailing in New York and Washington. I've become a newspaperman because it's now almost imposible for a Regular to send in his papers without facing all manner of charges of disloyalty, if not treason."

"I understand," Ramsay said, "I'll see what can be done."

So, in the Port Commandant's stuffy office next morning, a document was produced which Dexter, heart hammering, signed under the name of "Henry Dutton," and entered the Naval Service of the Confederate States of America.

When David commented on the speed with which his commission had been granted, Chief Engineer Ramsay grunted, "It's not for the love of your manly bearing, Dexter — I mean Dutton — that we have agreed to this unusual transaction, but what with our building and commissioning so many new ships, we're desperately short of navy-trained engineer officers."

As they were pushing their way toward the waterfront through jostling, noisy, crowded streets, dodging freight wagons and vehicles of all sorts, Ramsay observed, "I believe there's just the right post vacant for you."

"How so?" There had to be too much sheer luck in all of this not to have a catch lurking somewhere."What is it?"

"Our Third Assistant Engineer on the *Virginia* was stricken ill yesterday with an acute inflammation of the bowels, and he may not recover in time to be on duty when we get up steam and learn what our ram's capabilities really are."

"And when will that be?" David took care to appear casual.

"With luck, and the arrival from the Richmond Tredegar Works of some important engine parts, she should be able to attack the enemy inside of three or four days."

31

"Gunner's Hill"

Louisa Ridgely, uncommonly tall and slim for a woman of that era, smoothed long, golden-brown hair, kissed her mother and younger sister good-bye, and then, lips quivering, prepared to descend the long, broad flight of steps leading from the white colonnaded main entrance of "Gunner's Hill."

Already "Uncle" Peter, the aged black coachman who had served the plantation's owners since before any of the Ridgely children had first beheld the light of day, stood waiting, battered top hat in hand, beside the chaise, holding a pair of bony but carefully groomed mules, standing with lowered heads and long, furry gray ears drooping.

Mrs. Ridgely clung to her eldest daughter, about whom she'd been increasingly worried since the arrival of the news that her fiancé's ship had been lost with all hands in a hurricane off the eastern end of Cuba, news which had burst like a mortar shell over "Gunner's Hill."

Louisa's full, coral-hued mouth forced a smile before she paused and cast a backward glance at her home, which, like most other mansions in the vicinity, was beginning to exhibit signs of deterioration.

"How long d'you expect to be away, Weezy darlin'?"

"Only a few weeks, mamma. After all, Brandy Station don't lie near the end of the world; it's only little more than fifty miles from this spot."

Mrs. Ridgely choked a little, "Dear me, how I despise to see you go risking your life like this."

"But I'm not going for a soldier, dear."

"True, but there's so much suffering and sickness around, aside from the wounded and the crippled." Lorena Ridgely turned aside, blew her nose hard, and straightened. "Sorry to carry on like this, Weezy. Us Ridgelys always have done our duty the best we could. Thank God for those last letters from your brother Charles, sayin' he's well and about to be commissioned a Captain. What a good thing Peter is still much too young to enlist." She sniffed a bit, and wiped her eyes on the back of her hand. "Sure you're taking everythin' a well-bred young lady would need — plenty of underpinnin's and some old swaddlin' cloths for you know what."

"Why, yes. Besides I've got a hamper and basket full of bandages and pledgets the Compassionate Committee are sending. I hope you don't mind, Mamma, I even took some of Papa's warm clothing I found in the attic. After all, he's been dead nearly seven years and they're long out of style." Her long and narrow deep-blue eyes lowered themselves as she caught her mother close, murmuring, "Dearest, I ought to be back inside of a few weeks."

Skillfully managing billowing hoop skirts, Louisa got aboard the rickety old two-horse chaise; long ago, all sound or useful vehicles had been donated for military use.

"Uncle" Peter bowed, bobbed a balding gray head to hide sudden tears. Always he'd been devoted to the Ridgely clan — Miss Louisa in particular — and deservedly so. Hadn't they always been praised for the fair and humane treatment of their black chattels who, at one time, had numbered close on thirty souls?

When the creaking old chaise moved out, Louisa's hands tightened in black, knitted mitts as she straightened her poke bonnet's draw ribbons tighter before settling back on the lumpy cushions of black horsehair to gaze blankly over the beautiful rolling countryside; budding pale green and sunlit for the first time in several days. Was this an omen? Somehow, Louisa still could not bring herself to admit in her heart of hearts that the remains of her beloved David lay scattered among reefs at the bottom of the Caribbean Sea. Why she had clung so firmly to this conviction she couldn't explain, even though the Reverend Dr. Stockton had urged her to submit to Fate and devote her attention and abilities to care of the wounded.

Already there were thousands of them; every day hundreds more mangled men were being brought in, some hideously disfigured, and all in need of sympathy and encouragement in addition to the miserably inadequate medical care.

By the time a train of cars puffed to a halt in Brandy Station, Louisa had regained her poise and crisply directed a couple of gangling young Negroes to handle the especially heavy items in her luggage. If only she were arriving to attend David! Beloved David; what a wonderfully happy life they could have enjoyed.

As she climbed the wide set of stairs leading to the former Female Seminary, she recalled to the last detail David's beloved features — his wide, deep-set hazel eyes; strong, luxuriant, and wavy light-brown hair; long, straight, and narrow nose; and wide mouth, about which there always seemed to lurk a hint of mischief and humor. Six feet tall, the Yankee Lieutenant had towered above her own five feet and seven inches. All too well, she could recall their first encounter in Lord Winterbotham's impressive mansion, just off Berkeley Square.

Even at this moment she remembered his masculine odor, and the exciting prickling of the short mustache he was wearing, when for the first time she permitted him to kiss her on the lips.

One matter still tormented her. After she had received numbers of impassioned missives, with no explanation at all, not a letter from David had arrived after the outbreak of hostilities. No matter how often she wrote, care of his mother, she had no word from David nor from the United States Naval Attaché's office in London. Finally, weeks later, came the clipping from Washington that Lieutenant David H. Dexter, U.S.N., had been lost at sea.

Louisa ascended the steps of Miss Julia Anderson's Female Seminary, in front of which dangled a limp and none-too-clean white flag. Somewhat like a soldier gathering weight behind his bayonet's point, in preparation for making an attack, she drew herself up and inhaled a deep breath of clear air before stepping inside the building, where the piteous moans and whimperings of patients sounded a dolorous obbligato to women's voices.

32

James River Flotilla

It came to Christian as no great surprise that the pilots of the James River Flotilla, like those in practically every port of the world, were mostly civilians, for the sound reason that, should a critical problem in navigation suddenly arise, it must be the pilot, not the Captain, who would take command for the time being. Even before reaching Norfolk, the young Bermudian was relieved to hear that this rule of the sea was observed here as elsewhere.

Christian was not in the least keen about having to swear an oath of loyalty to the Confederate States. In Bermuda, he had never even been asked — at least in so many words — to swear fealty to Her Britannic Majesty. The best of his current situation was that he remained without nationality, although drawing a respectable salary from the local Naval paymaster. Yes, Christian Pitcher seemed to be playing his cards right — so far.

The so-called James River or Flotilla Squadron, except for the ungainly ironclad, consisted first of the *Patrick Henry*, a large and speedy sidewheeler, which previously had been employed in the lucrative run between New York and Norfolk. Of fourteen hundred tons and captained by John Tucker, she now mounted twelve small guns, mostly six-pounders whose only protection was breastworks consisting of a double thickness of four-inch live oak planks reinforced by cotton bales. They might prove adequate protection against small-arms fire, but were not stout enough to withstand shot of any real weight.

Other components of this grotesque flotilla were the gunboat *Jamestown,* the *Beaufort,* and the *Raleigh,* and a former tug now called *Teaser.* All had been armed with two cannon apiece, but these weapons were chiefly intended for morale purposes and could not be exposed or called upon to put up a fight; their real job was to service and assist the unwieldy *Merrimac* in every possible fashion. As for the *Patrick Henry,* flagship of the James River Squadron, she remained a very useful craft, although in want of needed repairs in several places; because she was a paddle steamer, she enjoyed much better protection for her boilers.

Diffidently, Christian studied the *Patrick Henry*'s wheelhouse, an ornate structure which had been built as high as possible above the waterline in order to afford her helmsman as spacious a vista as possible. The Bermudian was not the only pilot to foresee that a conspicuous and unarmored pilothouse would offer a prime target for enemy guns. Everyone afloat knew that a vessel's steering gear was of vital importance; without it she would be helpless.

He found Chief Pilot Philip Lubbock conferring with a gaunt, bald-headed individual whose long beak of a nose increased his resemblance to a hungry gray heron. Lubbock, wearing a tremendous black spade-shaped beard, glanced up. "Well, son, what d'you want?"

Although not wearing a real uniform with brass buttons, Lubbock certainly had attempted to copy one, in that his coat and pants were of dark gray, but showed no ornaments indicating rank on either his cuffs or collar.

"Sir, I've been ordered by the Chief Pilot's office to report to you for duty as an assistant or relief pilot."

Lubbock stared. "God! What will they send me next? You talk funny and don't hardly look dry behind the ears, yet you claim to be a qualified pilot?"

Christian looked about the swarming harbor. "Yes, sir, I've piloted craft of all sorts and sizes, both paddle and screw-driven, in and around Barbados, Caicos, and others of the West Indies for near six years, and some of those waters ain't extra-easy to navigate, sir."

"I know that, but wait'll you see Hampton Roads and the nearby waters. They're among the most difficult soundings you'll find along this coast. Mudbanks and sandbars can move a lot during a storm and they can shift quickly to where you don't expect 'em. Since all the buoys and channel markers have been took up by the Yanks, you'll have one hell of a time conning any sizable vessel through that tangle of shoals, bars, and reefs out yonder; mostly because they're hidden by muddy water."

The First Assistant Pilot, a man named Mayhew, inquired, "Mister, you ever seen a real good chart of these waters?"

"Aye, aye, sir. I've spent most of the last two days studying some and memorizing all I could. As you say, sir, Hampton Roads is a real trap for any vessel drawing more than twenty feet of water — or even less in a lot of places."

Briefly, the Chief Pilot stroked his forked, tobacco-stained beard. "You seem to have caught on quick, Bub. Dunno how come a foreigner like you can learn so much in so little time. Most pilots 'round here have spent the best part of their lives conning ships through these waters. Even so, they often go aground or get snagged. Which is no disgrace, provided no cargo's spoilt or the ship really hurt."

Abruptly, Lubbock concealed under a sheet of paper a section of a chart on the chart table. "Now yonder, as you can see, lies Newport News, with all them goddamn Union troops and batteries defending it."

He planted a black-nailed forefinger. "This here's Pig Point and yonder's the entrance to Norfolk and the Elizabeth River. Now tell me, where are the principal mudbanks and sandbars to be watched out for?"

Hesitantly, but accurately, Christian reeled off a dozen or more dangerous soundings. His inquisitors exchanged surprised glances. "Is it true, Christian, ye've studied these charts only *two* days?" Lubbock demanded.

"Yes, sir, give or take a few hours." He adopted a convincingly modest air. "Of course, I know I must have left out some important soundings and the shape of some sandbanks."

With engines thumping and her walking beam swaying to the rhythmic hiss-hissing of escape valves, the *Patrick Henry* moved along an hour later, with Christian expertly spinning her oak and brass-bound six-foot steering wheel. The First and Chief Pilots watched him narrowly, and gradually with a measure of admiration. The Chief Pilot clawed his untidy beard, then took the wheel himself, saying over his shoulder, "Maybe you'll do, Pitcher. Only one drawback. You *claim* yer an English subject?"

Christian brightened and his spirits soared. "Not English, sir. I'm a British colonial — from Barbados."

"I've yer Bible oath on that? Don't want any trouble with the Richmond authorities."

"Aye, aye, sir."

"Very well, I'll sign you on as Second Assistant Pilot aboard the *Patrick Henry*. You'll draw half-pay till you make the grade as a fully licensed helmsman, or get killed. Now." He sought a closet and pulled out a wrinkled and water-stained chart. "Fetch your dunnage, Christian. Go below, report to the paymaster, and he'll sign you on. Then you can stow your dunnage wherever you find room."

Suddenly glittering possibilities danced before the Bermudian's eyes as he signed on. Always a quick learner, he applied himself with such concentration and attention to detail that, within forty-eight hours, he had qualified as Acting Second Assistant Pilot aboard the *Patrick Henry*.

Often, he found it difficult to study, so deafening was the shouting of orders, and the rumbling of gun carriages being repeatedly run in and out until the raw, profane, and generally short-tempered gun crews had learned the basic elements of serving a cannon.

After supper, Chief Pilot Lubbock lit a thumping big cigar, beckoned to Christian, and sought the dew-wetted deck. "Hear that there hammering?"

"Yes, sir. I was wondering why they're working by flares and torchlight up there."

"Yep. You can thank yer lucky stars for that, Bub; at last somethin's bein' done to protect us poor bastards up in the wheelhouse, even if it's only with sap planking, two and a half inches thick."

"Only that much, sir?"

"Yep. A real cannon ball can be farted through that without trouble. Still, some protection's better than none. It should stop rifle bullets, minié and musket balls, and maybe cannister, if it's fired at long range."

Lubbock spat accurately at an overflowing brass spittoon. "Y'see, son, like I said before, any stupid son of a bitch of a gunner knows that the wheelhouse is the most vital part of any steamship — or sail ship, for that matter. Knock out the steering gear and she's helpless as a drifting snag. Funny thing those Navy shipbuilders haven't realized that yet."

Sudden queasiness gripped the new pilot as Lubbock continued, "Yep! Good pilots must expect to get shot at plenty, and maybe get wounded or kilt. That's why us fellers draw such a high rate of pay."

Here was something Christian hadn't foreseen. Up in a wheelhouse he stood good chances of becoming a casualty!

Lubbock patted Christian's shoulder. "Keep on the way yer headed, Bub, and you might even get to be a full pilot before this here scrap is settled." He buttoned up a patched and well-worn jacket against the cold, damp wind. "Tomorrow we're going to make another trial run out into the Bay; to make sure our engines work right, and that all hands, 'specially the gunners, have learned their duties. Just might run into some enemy ships and get our gun crews bloodied. Johnny Tucker, yer boss, will let you take the wheel through easy sections of the Bay, but if you believe in the power of prayer, better get busy. G'night."

Just after sunrise, the *Patrick Henry* cast off and rendezvoused with her consorts, *Jamestown* and *Teaser,* after having taken aboard off Tanney's Creek some hard-mouthed officers with the look of Regulars about them. By now, everybody aboard was aware that Norfolk and Elizabeth City had been in turmoil. Since daybreak, dense, curling clouds of black smoke had begun to rise from the waterfront loading piers.

Like lightning, rumors spread that the mighty *Virginia* was firing up and pretty soon should be on her way toward Newport News. Aboard the Jamestown River Squadron, excitement mounted. At last, here was a reprieve from tedious exercises, mostly with unfamiliar equipment.

Christian passed his initial test run with ease, seemingly able to sense obscure obstacles with almost uncanny accuracy. Even the Chief Pilot looked impressed. "Say, son, they must teach you Limeys extra-good down there. Ain't half-a-dozen pilots your age, or older, who learn as fast as you.

"Now, get you below and check the charts, especially the waters between Sewell's Point and the Rip Raps, also around Newport News. Hope the skipper shows our flag plenty plain, or else our batteries on Sewell's and Willoughby's Points will open up. Nowadays, since all those rumors about the Yankees havin' an all-iron ship of their own, our artillery men are as jumpy as a she-cat with new kittens."

Christian was well aware of the danger. Spied at any distance, the Confederate flag bore such a close and confusing resemblance to the Stars and Stripes that gunners might well make a mistake.

33

Replacements

BECAUSE OF THE EXPIRATION of many enlistments, deaths from illness, and a shameful percentage of desertions, the number of replacements aboard the U.S.S. sloop of war *Congress* totaled eighty-nine officers and men.

Hardly had seaman Dennis O'Day and other reinforcements lined up on the dock at Fort Monroe than a brisk, spotlessly turned-out Major of the Marines strode up and took over. One look at him convinced newcomers of the tension prevailing here.

The new men who made the best impression were a detachment from the Ninety-ninth New York Volunteer Regiment, sometimes referred to as the "Union Coast Guard." The rest of the volunteers, O'Day among them, slouched in ranks, gazing about in awe at massive granite battlements, batteries, barracks, and other buildings composing Fort Monroe. O'Day thought that the ponderous artillery in evidence here surpassed those on Ireland Island by a considerable margin. Others gazed at a motley array of armed vessels anchored close under the Fort's guns, or within easy range.

Dennis's eyes smarted, and momentarily his teeth bared themselves. His broad back, scarred by the "cat," had begun to throb. Long since, he had begun to worry whether anyone might find out about his service in H.M.S. *Tenedos,* during which he'd lost his temper and slapped an insolent midshipman who'd ordered him to pick up a handkerchief fallen from his cuff.

Again he recalled the agonizing impact of the cat-o'-nine-tails on his bare back.

For Dennis, it had proved instructive to watch regular American gunners at gun drill. Their movements were almost identical with those used aboard Her Majesty's ships of war. And he noticed that there were quite a few others whose backs showed broad, pinkish scars from floggings.

Krikey! Wouldn't it feel fine once again to tread the decks of a real man-of-war? Dennis, me boy, he'd warned himself time and again, from now on keep that temper of yours under a tight rein. Already it's made a hard life for you and ye're damned lucky not to have had your neck stretched long ago because o' them two fellers ye killed for sure up in New York. From now ye'd best learn to keep that devilish streak in yer natur' under control, he told himself. Already he'd learned that most American officers weren't harsh as the goddamn British, and that nowadays flogging seldom was resorted to in the U.S. Service.

Yes, it was exhilarating to look up at those towering masts and professionally squared yards, and clean paintwork. There were such swarms of small boats moving about or official launches and gigs busy on various duties and errands that he was reminded of a holiday weekend at Brighton.

He was recalled sharply to the present by the Marine Major's ordering the replacements to stand at attention and not sag about like so many pregnant females.

Holding up a sheaf of paper, he announced, "These are drafts for replacements required aboard various vessels. The frigate *Congress*, being the most shorthanded, will get the most of you unwashed heroes."

He beckoned a corporal. "If we've got them, experienced gunners will go aboard the *Minnesota*, nine will serve in the *Cumberland*, and three men will be detailed to service aboard the *St. Lawrence.*"

Once each detail was named, and formed into a single rank, the Major grunted. "Ye look a sorry lot, but thank God you've arrived in time," he said.

He pointed toward the dim outlines of Norfolk, across slate-brown waters over which flocks of pelicans, cormorants, terns, and other seafowl were swooping, wheeling, and occasionally diving. "Now, for your own sakes, pay close attention. Word has just been received at headquarters that the old *Merrimac*, renamed the *Virginia* by the Rebels, has been converted into an ironclad monstrosity of a ram and is getting ready to attack us very soon, so it's up to each and every one of you replacements to start learning your duties the minute you report aboard ship, and then drill till you can do what you're supposed to do in your sleep."

Ordinary seaman Dennis O'Day would long remember the first time he set foot aboard the *Congress*. She might be a trifle aged, but she remained beautiful and mounted fifty carriage guns of varying caliber. Before O'Day and the other replacements had been aboard forty-eight hours, they had already learned the rudiments of gun drill. Regular members of the crew looked vastly relieved to find their depleted numbers refilled.

An unidentifiable but welcome sensation gripped the tall, black-haired young Irishman as he boarded the *Congress*. B'God! right now he felt finer than satin again to be treading the deck of a real man-of-war.

Not much time was required for the frigate's Chief Gunnery Officer to spot him as an expert in the handling of heavy carriage guns. He was promptly told off to be head loader on Number 5 piece — a thirty-pounder, as were most of the broadside guns.

During the first two days, there was scarcely a leisure moment aboard the *Congress*, although on that sleek sloop of war, *Cumberland*, lying a quarter of a mile distant, a noisy party of some sort was taking place. Banjos, harmonicas, and the squeak of fiddles could be easily heard across the still, black waters off Newport News.

At sundown, Captain Joseph B. Smith realized his crew were so dog-tired as to approach inefficiency, and he issued orders that on the morrow there would be only a single gun drill first thing in the morning. After that, until late afternoon, hands not on duty would be permitted some time for themselves. Most badly needed to wash clothing, so before long, undershirts and drawers, trousers, jerseys, and such were hoisted to dry on the rigging.

Similar relaxations were visible aboard the *Minnesota*, anchored about a half-mile downstream. Like the *Roanoke*, she had been built as a sister ship to the *Merrimac*, which had been half-burned early last summer when the Gosport Navy Yard was lost to the Rebels under disgraceful circumstances.

By now, everyone aboard the *Congress* knew that the *Merrimac*, when water had been run into the Gosport graving dock, hadn't turned turtle, as so many self-termed experts had predicted. Right now she was reported to be making adjustments to her machinery, mounting her armament, and taking aboard ammunition, fuel, food, and other necessities.

As for O'Day, he decided to risk speaking frankly to Captain Joseph B. Smith, who followed the unusual practice of making himself accessible to any of his men whenever possible. He confessed he'd once served as a gun captain aboard H.M.S. *Tenedos;* also, that he'd been brutally flogged over a trifle and then condemned to serve his sentence in Bermuda.

"Tell me," Captain Smith remarked quietly (he had listened to several similar confessions), "is there anything else we should know about your past?"

"No, sir." O'Day felt no need to mention those two men he'd killed in New York. Luckily, both had been civilians.

"Things standing as they do," the Captain said, "I'll assign you, on probation, as captain of Number Six gun starboard broadside." Nervously, he bit the end off a cheroot. "I've been informed by the Bo'sun and gun captains that their crews are beginning to shape up, which is fine because, from all I hear, we won't be granted much more time for gun drills. Spies report that the Rebel ram's about ready to sail while we're only beginning to pull up our socks, so to speak."

His gaunt, bronzed features relaxed a trifle. "There are some experienced gunners aboard to serve the pieces, but they're few, so if many of them get killed or hurt, we're in big trouble; and that's when you might prove useful, O'Day, new aboard though you are."

By now, O'Day had learned that among the *Congress*'s company there were only a few Regular officers and men; the others were inexperienced merchant seamen.

On the morning of March 5, the Bo'sun's pipe shrilled. Orders were bellowed in response to signals from Fort Monroe. Shortly afterward, the U.S.S. sail sloop *Cumberland,* with twenty-four guns, upped anchor and was towed up the James to reanchor close to batteries protecting the little town of Newport News and Camp Butler's huge military establishment, its defenses fairly studded with emplacements, mostly for pieces of heavy caliber.

On this nearly windless morning, there seemed small point in wasting coal or making sail for so short a move from Fort Monroe, so when the *Congress* appeared, she too was under tow until she could drop her hook a quarter of a mile off Newport News.

34

"Cheesebox on a Raft"

THAT THE 6TH OF MARCH 1862 should prove relatively mild was a considerable relief to the *Monitor*'s crew since, even now, most of the hands barely understood all that was expected of them, or even knew where some essential items of equipment were kept aboard this diminutive ironclad.

Of one thing Ira Thatcher and other engineer officers had become quickly aware, and that was the amazing ingenuity of John Ericsson's designs. Everyone had soon utilized to maximum effect every square inch of space below decks in one way or another. Since no machinery was above the waterline, everyone had learned to make no quick or unexpected movement for fear of bashing someone or getting hurt himself.

Although seas remained moderate, two serious defects in the *Monitor*'s design became apparent. First, her tiny pilothouse, only four by three feet, was continually being submerged by waves breaking over the bows, which had a freeboard of only a foot and a half. Secondly, it was situated so far forward that if her guns were fired directly in line with the bow, the resultant concussion would render that vitally important post untenable.

An American jack — blue-fielded and white-starred — was hoisted to her jackstaff and streamed out as flat as though it had been cut out of tin. In midafternoon the night chill of early March had not begun to be felt, in spite of the wind.

Sure enough, the three men on duty in the wheelhouse, Captain J. L. Worden, Lieutenant Dana Greene, and a brawny quartermaster, sweating and wrestling over the steering wheel, were forced by sheets of water continually soaring over the bows to desert temporarily the sodden pilothouse and seek the turret's top. Armored by closely interlocked railroad iron, it was already becoming crowded.

Among others gathered up there for a breath of fresh air was Second Assistant Engineer Lieutenant Ira Thatcher, who kept an anxious eye on the giant paddle tug *Seth Low,* plunging and rolling at the far end of a six-inch-thick towline, but still making steady progress despite mounting seas.

Off Sandy Hook, New Jersey, about 4 P.M. a large pilot boat came churning out so fast everyone wondered what was up. On signal, the *Seth Low* slowly lost speed until there remained just enough tension to prevent the tow rope from being fouled by the *Monitor*'s big nine-foot propeller.

A glance at his watch told Ira that almost exactly an hour had passed before the wildly plunging pilot boat arrived to grind alongside the ironclad's almost invisible beam. Everybody cheered on the turret top while, a quarter of a mile off either beam, appeared two scantily armed escort gunboats, *Currituck* and *Sachem,* which dipped their colors in salute. From the lively way some official jumped — heavy sea boots, slicker, and all — onto the *Monitor*'s wave-sluiced deck, everyone reckoned this fellow was risking his life to deliver orders, which therefore must be of prime significance.

Once heavily bearded Captain Worden's blunt, stubby fingers had ripped an end off a waterproofed envelope and he had scanned the single sheet of official paper it contained, his fingers began to tug at his beard — a mannerism of his when matters grew tense. Dana Greene and Ira crowded close, silently swaying to the *Monitor*'s violent heaving. Finally, Captain Worden, bracing himself against the motion (already he was half seasick) shouted over the engine room noises, "I'll read this dispatch from Naval Headquarters, Washington, to you all. It says,

> PROCEED AT BEST PRACTICABLE SPEED TO HAMPTON ROADS. YOUR PRESENCE THERE IS OF THE VERY FIRST IMPORTANCE. SIGNED, GIDEON WELLES, SECRETARY OF THE NAVY."

The pilot nodded, wiping spray from his whiskers."Reckon you boys are like to find yer hands full pretty soon, if even half of what they claim about what that there Rebel ram can do is true."

The pilot lifted a leather-peaked civilian cap, and wrung Captain Worden's hand, as though expecting never to see him again. "Ashore, we pray this here contraption of yours is able to do even half of what's expected of her."

Sea boots clumped down an iron ladder, and then, with considerable agility, the pilot sprawled onto the pilot boat's frothing deck. His craft began at once to plow toward the *Seth Low*. Good idea, Ira told himself silently. Only she can help us carry out instructions. Soon the *Seth Low*'s huge paddle wheels began to thresh and sprew spray far and wide until the towline snapped out of the sea and quivered like a frightened horse, flinging water far along its length. Signal flags were set up, warning other escorts to proceed at top speed.

The *Monitor*'s Chief Engineer, Alban Stimers, exhorted his black gang mightily, and soon fountains of black fumes and dazzling streamers of flame began to burst from the *Monitor*'s collapsible twin funnels, blowers driving forced air through the hull. These blowers were situated aft of the smoke stacks, which were six feet tall and sited abaft the turret.

The most reassuring sound to be heard was the steady *clunk! thump! clunk! thump!* of the two main caloric engines. No matter how this ungainly little craft plunged and twisted, their strokes remained steady as the heartbeat of a healthy man. Whatever the *Monitor*'s faults, John Ericsson's main engines could not be criticized — nor, thus far, could any of the accessory engines he had designed for various purposes.

After gulping a meal in the wardroom, far more elaborate than any that would be tasted for a long time, Ira lurched toward his small cabin, situated just aft of the starboard storeroom. He was still finding it difficult to credit that fifty-eight officers and seamen could be crowded below the waterline into so cramped a space. Air from the engine blowers sent warm, oily-smelling drafts beating irregularly through his Venetian-blind door.

Ira lifted a box of books off his bunk, shoved his valise beneath, and, heaving a sigh of relief, extended his body, already aching from unaccustomed stresses. He clasped hands beneath his head and at the same time thanked God that, so far, he'd never suffered seasickness. Already, Captain Worden and not a few of the crew had been forced to spew into buckets secured for such emergencies at convenient points.

By now, even though it was just past midnight, Ira was ready to believe that the events of March 7th, 1862, would linger in his memory for as long as he lived. Fortunately, he could not foresee that events taking place on the 8th and 9th would make the voyage down to Hampton Roads seem like a pleasure cruise by comparison. As he lay gripping the sides of his bunk, he continued to wonder whether or not this clumsy iron craft would manage to remain afloat if the seas worsened, or would it capsize, or at least lose the use of some vital element in her machinery and so head for the bottom. Sea noises grew steadily louder. In spite of them, the hairy and unshaven men occupying the berth deck, worn out from forty-eight hours of continual exertion, were beginning to snore in their hastily rigged sling hammocks.

Ira would have felt much more confident if the *Monitor* had experienced a real shakedown cruise instead of an unsatisfactory one-day trial run off New York. Had her battery, only two huge eleven-inch breech-banded Dahlgrens occupying the turret, ever been tested by firing shot? They had not. Therefore, pursuant to rigid Navy Department regulations, *no more than fifteen pounds* of powder could be used on each discharge, although these pieces had been especially constructed to handle charges of twenty or twenty-five pounds of powder. A multitude of doubts and questions swarmed about Ira's tired mind, like bees around a disturbed hive.

As for the crew, about the only thing this ship's company had in common was almost complete inexperience with the handling of the vessels' intricate and mostly novel equipment. As Third Assistant Engineer, however, Ira had found (or made) more opportunities to examine, after a fashion, the more intricate mechanisms.

So far on this harrowing voyage southward, the *Monitor*'s machinery of all sorts had functioned surprising well. But despite efforts of the powerful twin blowers mounted aft which could inject some two thousand square feet of air per minute, the air below decks remained fetid, reeking of steam, hot oil, and other unpleasant odors.

From an increase in the ironclad's violent motion, Ira guessed that the wind must be picking up. He could only hope a real gale wouldn't rise before the *Monitor* passed the entrance to Chesapeake Bay, when Hampton Roads would lie in sight. Weary as he was, he couldn't fall asleep. He asked himself again, as he lay staring into the semidarkness created by a heavy glass deadlight let into the deck just above his head, what *could* have occurred of such importance that the Secretary of the Navy himself should have forwarded orders as he had? Common sense convinced Ira that only the appearance of the dreaded *Merrimac* could have inspired so urgent a signal.

Briefly, he pondered on what might have happened to David Dexter. All he'd been able to discover, without risking a breach of security, was that David must have been ordered from New York to Washington so suddenly he had not even found time to take leave of the Captain. Ira half suspected, and felt ashamed of himself, that David just might have seized some unexpected opportunity to go South and maybe even turn his coat. Normally, Ira knew, David was a cool and rational fellow, but by now there could be small room for doubt that on the subject of Louisa Ridgely, his lovesick friend had become almost demented. What a paragon among females that Virginia belle must be, if even half of what David had said was true.

He'd never forget the way old Captain Dexter had one day driven down to the *Monitor*'s dock, and, stone-faced, had entrusted him with a cardboard box and a letter for his son, saying, "This box contains an ensign we flew when Commodore Perry's men-o'-war first showed the Stars and Stripes to the Japanese heathens back in 1854. We didn't have to fight 'em, but we so overawed those little yellow rascals that they respected our rights and obeyed the Law of the Sea."

Ordered to report as duty officer at four o'clock, Ira for the first time used one of the two flush toilets manufactured by David's father — that invention of Ericsson's over which he and the rest of the *Monitor*'s company had endured so much joshing. He had intended to visit this utility whenever action impended; it wasn't a good idea to have a full bladder under battle conditions — or so his father and other veterans claimed.

Across the berth deck, a candle was glowing in Acting Paymaster William F. Keeler's minuscule cabin. What a strange mixture he was. Even on the brink of exhaustion, he could turn his hand to almost any problem, but no matter what chanced, he wrote every day to his wife, Anna, a letter full of color and detail. To earn such devotion, she must really be a fine woman.

At the moment, Paymaster Keeler was scribbling:

                            Aboard the U.S. Steamer *Monitor*,
                                    7 March 1862

Our decks are constantly covered with a sea of foam pouring from one side to the other as the deck is inclined, while at short intervals a dense green sea rolls

across with terrible force, breaking into foam at every obstruction offered to its passage.
Now we scoop up a huge volume of water on one side &, as it rolls to the other with the motion of the vessel, is met by a sea coming from the opposite direction, the accumulative weight seeming sufficient to bury us forever.

By the time Ira crawled under the single coarse, woolen army blanket covering his bunk, he was aware that, by all reckoning, a storm was making up for which the *Monitor* certainly had not been designed to cope. John Ericsson had never intended his invention to serve as an oceangoing man-of-war; she was fit only to operate within sheltered bays, rivers, and estuaries, of which there were many south of Chesapeake Bay.

Once more, Ira lamented that he couldn't write to his mother. She had become such a bitter, religious fanatic after her husband's death that the real world no longer appeared to exist. Probably at this moment Emmeline Thatcher was on knees calloused through long hours of prayer, imploring the Almighty to save Christianity; only on occasion would she remember especially to pray the Lord to keep her only child safe and sound.

Just after an early twilight on the 7th, water, cascading down six-foot twin smokestacks and blower gratings, began to permeate the hull with such poisonous gases that many of the crew, gasping for pure air, were forced to abandon their duties and seek relief on the already crowded turret's top. Nobody aboard the *Monitor* would ever forget that night. Time and again, even skeptical Catholics got out rosaries, and kneeling Protestants, lurching like drunken men, made knuckles crack by the intensity with which they joined sunburned and often tattooed hands during fervent prayer for survival. Even daylight did not ease their fears.

Finally, at four on the afternoon of March 8th, the little convoy of four oddly assorted and sea-battered United States naval vessels sighted low-lying Cape Charles, marking the northern entrance into Chesapeake Bay. Not long afterward, the vague, blue-gray outlines of Cape Henry, down in Virginia, also became visible. It was dusk when the *Seth Low* finally towed her unwieldy charge into the relatively calm waters of Chesapeake Bay.

Once real darkness fell, several strange phenomena became apparent. First, everyone heard what seemed to be irregularly spaced, low, rumbling sounds like that of a great but distant thunderstorm. A few of the old seamen growled, "Stow that, you goldurned ninnyhammers, them ain't thunderclaps — it's cannon fire and a damm lot of it!" Soon, on the southeastern horizon, there showed a throbbing scarlet-golden radiance, which, inexplicably, waxed and waned.

Ira asked Acting Paymaster Keeler, "What d'you make of that?"

Wearily, Keeler put down his pen. "All I can imagine is that either Norfolk's on fire or else Fort Monroe is blowing up." He shoved forward a box of slightly mildewed chocolates. "Take a couple, friend Thatcher — soothes the nerves." He popped a square between thin, straight lips. "See? Now, I'd better go on writing, else Anna will be disappointed."

Thanks to these calmer waters, most of the crew, gaunt-cheeked and long unshaven, were roused and dispersed, trying to discharge duties about which all too many were still puzzled how to perform. Officers and petty officers, hollow-eyed, did their patient best to render at least some help to gunners, engineers, and ammuniton passers.

On the evening of the 8th, having cast off the towline and now under her own power, the *Monitor* steamed toward Fort Monroe, off which she arrived at 9 P.M. Boats appeared from all directions, some conveying officers of high rank. To a man, these men appeared tired out; they looked grim and uncertain of their instructions, which often appeared to be contradictory. Just before dawn began to break, a swift picket boat came charging away from the Fort's main pier "with a bone in her teeth."

"Sir," the officer it carried said, "General Wool, commanding this area, presents his compliments and orders that you at once proceed up the James River and assume a position best calculated to protect the *Minnesota* and the *Roanoke* from Rebel attack. Yesterday we lost the *Cumberland,* and the *Congress* is a flaming wreck; she'll be blowing up anytime soon. They are, or were, two of our finest ships. Further such losses cannot be tolerated; therefore, you will get under way immediately for Newport News."

Lieutenant Greene demanded, "But, sir, how could two such powerful men-of-war be destroyed by a single enemy?"

"Both were attacked by that damn armor-plated ram the Rebels have finally got into action. She seems invulnerable to any kind of shot and carries ten heavy guns."

Brief silence settled over the *Monitor.* Everyone stood peering up the James, where, off Newport News, great sheets of flame were soaring hundreds of feet into the sky amid enormous incandescent billows of smoke and sparks.

From men doing lookout duty on the turret — all others having been ordered below to their stations — burst volleys of curses. Far upstream the *Congress*'s main magazine finally blew up with such violence that the concussion could be felt at Fort Monroe, and even beyond. Flaming sails, yards, and topmasts soared into the moonlit heavens even before thunderous reports reached Fort Monroe.

Lieutenant Greene, in charge of the *Monitor*'s two enormous Dahlgren guns, explained, "That would be her principal powder magazine going up."

Soon it would become known that some three hundred and sixty men who had been serving in the *Cumberland* and *Congress* would never again see their homes.

35

The U.S.S. *Cumberland*

OFFICER OF THE DECK Lieutenant Tom Selfridge, pacing restlessly on the U.S.S. *Congress*'s spotless gun deck, counted nearly sixty Union vessels anchored off Newport News. How satisfying it was to enjoy such a peaceful Saturday morning, like everyone else. Selfridge had been without real rest for hours. He was nearly played out, but didn't dare show it.

From the direction of Newport News now appeared a swarm of commercial craft, fetching a wide variety of food, delicacies, liquors, and items of clothing not issued by the United States Navy. Under an unseasonably warm sun, washing done aboard the *Congress* began to dry rapidly. Booms were rigged and small boats lowered, prepared to accommodate shore parties for a brief visit to and for a variety of entertainments.

By now, the always gregarious Dennis O'Day had identified not a few compatriots among the crew, and these lads who had formed a "Gaelic Gang," were preparing for a real frolic ashore.

Band music came drifting across the water from that huge tent city called Camp Butler, lying behind a series of batteries defending Newport News. Everywhere on the North Shore floated Union colors, while bands blared such patriotic airs as "Hail Columbia, Happy Land," the "Star-Spangled Banner," and "Columbia, Gem of the Ocean." Then, like a sudden clap of thunder, sounded the staccato report of a signal gun. Another and then another, roared out. Ashore, drums beat and bugles blared. The bands quit playing.

Carefully, Captain Joseph B. Smith, timing intervals between reports, understood at once that these were genuine alarm signals. Accompanied by Lieutenant Selfridge and others, Captain Smith sought the forepeak and employed field glasses to scan the Elizabeth River's mouth in the direction of Craney Island and Sewell's Point. Soon he made out a procession of tall, thin funnels and stubby masts, unmistakably those of gunboats proceeding under a cloud of smoke in the direction of Newport News.

In their midst towered a curious-looking vessel. A deck hand laughed, yelling, "Say, look at that big barn with a smokestack in the middle of its roof!" Even as he spoke, the strange ship's funnel began to spew impressive clouds of coal-black smoke. Aboard other Union ships, alarm guns, bugles, whistles, and speaking trumpets spread the word: "Look alive, everybody! Looks like that there damn *Merrimac*'s comin' out at last!"

In no time, hands aboard Union naval vessels, amid a brisk rattle of drums, ran to battle stations; Marines swarmed to the fighting tops or manned light guns. At last! At long last!

Tom Slade, loader for Number 5 gun crew of the *Congress*'s starboard broadside, had an especially good view. Yes, far across the river — a long mile and a half wide at this point — more and more steam vessels, trailed by weaving ribbons of smoke, were heading in the direction of the three big warships lying off Newport News.

"Notice something peculiar about yonder flotilla?" Lieutenant Selfridge inquired.

"What?"

"They've got that armored contraption they're escorting *under tow!* Can something have gone wrong with her steering gear?"

"God alone knows. Let's pray so," Captain Smith growled. "One thing's certain. She's just been cast off by her tug, and unless I'm mistaken, she's making for the *Cumberland* instead of us, very slowly but under *her own power,* dammit." He uttered a barking laugh. "That's where her people are going wrong. Though she may rate as only a steam sloop, the *Cumberland* mounts twenty-two nine-inch Dahlgren guns and nine-inch rifled pivot guns on her stern and bow. They're among the most powerful guns in our squadron."

For some inexplicable reason, the James River Squadron advanced with great deliberation. The fact was that Christian and other pilots were finding their hands full, for these waters were a veritable maze of scarcely visible bars, flats, and shoals.

Selfridge concluded there must be some pretty smart pilots aboard the *Patrick Henry* — the Rebel's acting flagship — if that long, red pennant fluttering from her forepeak meant anything.

Aboard the Union men-of-war orderly confusion reached a peak. Veteran officers, some in wonderment and some with contempt, scanned this curious steel-gray, low-lying creation steaming slowly but steadily in their direction. A few compared this enemy with a half-submerged crocodile and were relieved to observe that apparently her engines seemed unable to turn up better than five knots at their best. But they weren't sure. Might this be a trick? From the *Merrimac*'s jackstaff fluttered a plain black flag to indicate that the Commodore of this heterogeneous flotilla was aboard. Why in the world the Southern Commander had selected black, the color of piracy and "no quarter," for his personal flag, nobody could explain.

By contrast, the design of the Confederate national colors astern sparkled crisply in the midday sun. Disputes arose over the number of white stars showing against a blue field in the ensign's canton corner. Otherwise, there were two broad red stripes separated by a single equally broad white one. Eventually it was agreed that there were seven stars — and would remain so until Kentucky, Maryland, and Tennessee joined the Confederacy. The stars were arranged in a circle, perhaps intentionally reminiscent of the first American flag.

When the enemy were still about a mile distant, the Union packet boat *Zouave* fired six rounds from her thirty-pound Parrot gun, thus opening a conflict destined to shape the armament of the world's navies for generations to come.

Everyone could see the brief white columns of water raised by her round shot falling short. Promptly, the *Merrimac*'s escorts fired a few rounds which fell even shorter than those of the nearest Union vessels, and then, in no great hurry, they retired to hover among a heterogeneous squadron off Sewell's Point to protect shipping collecting along the James's southern bank.

Since there was no wind at all, the *Cumberland*'s executive officer and acting commander, Lieutenant George U. S. Haines, shouted through his megaphone for tugs to tow his ship about so that the shattering power of her starboard broadside might bear on this advancing, outlandish-appearing, very-low-in-profile, and smoke-spouting enemy.

The fifty-gun frigate *Congress*'s first volley skipped wide or landed short, although a few of her shot passed over the enemy, missing the target by a narrow margin. Her deck whitely awash, she opened fire with her bow rifle as she advanced, but the Confederate ram paid no need, plowing slowly ahead, straight for the *Cumberland*, which now was maintaining a furious, thunderous, and incessant cannonade. Soon the enemy's forward pivot gun was in a position to rake the frigate, and did so, killing most of the *Cumberland*'s pivot gun crew. Huge, jagged splinters shattered other crewmen, more effectively than shell splinters. Terrible screams and howls arose.

Experienced Union artillery men gasped and groaned as they watched their heaviest round shot glance off the *Merrimac*'s dully gleaming, rivet-studded gray-brown armor, like "so many India rubber balls," as one gun captain growled.

Quickly the ear-torturing thunder of cannon fire swelled into a roaring tumult audible for miles. Because there was little or no wind to carry off the rotten-smelling burnt powder fumes, lung-searing, dense billows of smoke swirled about, blinding many of the *Cumberland*'s complement.

Now that the Confederate vessel was within close range, the *Congress*'s thirty-pound starboard broadside bellowed again, but nothing much resulted except that a great, jagged hole was punched through the ram's single squat funnel, while her flagstaff, boat davits, and most of the gear exposed on deck were bent or carried away — in fact, anything unprotected by the *Merrimac*'s dully gleaming casemate was flung far and wide.

More and more furiously swelled the cannonade, but although both the *Congress* and the *Cumberland* fired their heaviest solid shot, the *Merrimac* kept churning slowly, relentlessly, toward the beautiful sail frigate lying at the extreme southern tip of a Union line stretching at intervals down the James from Fort Monroe. The din became almost unbearable.

Aboard the *Merrimac*, David Dexter, now Acting Third Assistant Engineer, felt his head ring like a hard-beaten brass gong; his eardrums seemed ready to explode. Several gunners, he noted, seemed dazed, and some showed trickles of blood seeping from ears and noses. And still the slow but steady thud-thudding of the ram's engines continued without interruption.

Men in the wheelhouse could now see the *Cumberland* lying broadside-on, presenting as choice a target as any naval gunner could dream of beholding. Beyond her lay the *Congress,* nearly obscured by her own gunsmoke. With each passing moment, the frigate seemed to magnify magically in size and height.

"Grab a good hold of something solid and brace yourselves!" David yelled over the rumble of carriage wheels and the clang of metal on metal. "We're about to ram!"

Somebody cried out, "For Jesus' sake! Why don't we tackle the *Congress* first? She's the best ship the Yanks have."

Someone else answered, "Don't be such a goddamn fool! Cap'n Buchanan knows what's what! The *Cumberland* mounts a lot fewer guns, but they all fire heavier shot than any aboard the *Congress!*"

Christian Pitcher, in the *Patrick Henry*'s wheelhouse, was infinitely relieved when signal flags ordered the ex-ferry to retire. Obediently, the ship steered to port, her officers cursing the fact that their armanent was of such small importance it couldn't possibly affect the conflict's outcome. Meanwhile, on the *Merrimac,* the gun captain swung back the heavy iron port cover of the *Merrimac*'s stern pivot gun — one of the ram's few pieces presently enjoying such effective protection. So far, only a few shots from the bristling array of Union shore batteries were raising miniature geysers in the *Merrimac*'s vicinity while she threshed onward at her maximum speed of five knots, her engines wheezing and groaning like those of some antique ferryboat. Cannonading from batteries along the Union shore of Hampton Roads had increased until the sky seemed to shake, but all of their projectiles fell far short of the targets.

Dexter — momentarily he had forgotten his alias, Henry Dutton — watched the outlines of the *Congress* grow larger. Some of her rigging was still grotesquely aflutter with laundry. Her crew were at battle stations, and powder monkeys were racing, while crewmen were taking in booms and casting loose the ship's small boats, stowing essential gear as swarms of seamen sought to reach their stations.

Captain Buchanan turned to his lantern-jawed Chief Pilot, "Mister, I want you should take a course across that frigate's stern. There's no wind, so she's helpless to maneuver without help."

"Aye, aye, sir. She's sure a sitting duck if ever I've shot at one!"

While the ram churned slowly past the *Congress*'s stern, her gun pointers had time to fire six heavy shells apiece, and these missiles effectively raked the Union vessel from stem to stern. By now it was hard to hear anything aboard her above the crackle of timbers and screams rising from beyond a blinding curtain of gunsmoke. The deafening roar of the frigate's forward pivot gun's discharges were stunning, and the resounding *b-o-o-m* made by her heaviest shells glancing off the ram's iron casemate was exceeded only by the more frequent *clang* and *clash* of equally ineffective blasts of shrapnel and cannister.

The three men occupying the *Merrimac*'s pilothouse observed with satisfaction through drifting smoke the tangled canvas, torn rigging, and general wild disorder prevailing aboard the once beautiful old frigate. Commodore Buchanan, commanding the *Merrimac*, was at once incredulous and astonished by the appalling results obtained from his ship's guns when several of the frigate's yards snapped or began to sag or give way, causing fearful havoc among the enemy's crew as they fell.

The mortally stricken *Cumberland* was assuming an ever more ominous list to port. Ridiculously, some sailors' washing still floated in her rigging. As the ram swung sluggishly and headed toward her, the Union ship's mangled but still powerful batteries increased their rate of fire.

Everybody aboard the *Merrimac* could hear the resonant impact of shot striking the iron casemate. Incredibly, most of the Federal gunners continued to fire grapeshot and cannister, probably in anticipation of repelling enemy boarders. These rattled futilely, like gigantic hailstones, against the *Merrimac*'s four-inch armor.

Then came a terrific blast as the muzzles of the *Merrimac*'s Number 1 and Number 3 guns were shot away; flying steel splinters killed two Confederate gunners outright and severely wounded several more. Their awful screams and shrieks penetrated even the infernal din prevailing within the casemate.

David, having never been involved in action of any consequence, was astonished to find himself unbelievably self-possessed, perhaps an inheritance from generations of ancestors who in various wars had fought and died for the Union. Somehow, he couldn't imagine a Dexter lurching aside and vomiting, as some men — and officers, too — were doing.

Abruptly, the tumult ceased as the ram now steered straight for the frigate's unprotected starboard side and bilges. Her guns could no longer be sufficiently depressed to be useful. Word bellowed down from above, "Brace yourselves! We're about to ram!"

Forgetting the *Merrimac*'s huge tonnage momentarily, David thought quickly that it shouldn't be too damaging to ram at only five knots. His thoughts were shared by the ship's executive officer, Lieutenant Catesby, who muttered, "If *only* we had a little more speed."

A gale of small-arms fire pattered against the armor all about them while the ship's engineers, purple-faced and sweaty, struggled to coax a few more revolutions out of the admittedly inadequate and undependable engines.

As though they were in a too-vivid dream, David and the crew at their stations gripped what handholds were available and, through the open gunport, watched the wooden side of the *Cumberland* draw close, and closer. Then came a tremendous grinding, crunching sound, as though a hundred wooden forage wagons had suddenly collided, as the cast-iron ram struck home.

Aboard the *Merrimac*, the effect of the impact was relatively small, strangely enough, but the *Cumberland* shook as though under the influence of a marine earthquake, then heeled so far over to port that water gushed into her lower gunports before, sluggishly, she righted herself. Amid the grinding, crackling, and rumbling of the stricken Federal ship, gun crews fought to free their tackles, but failed to break loose any guns.

Shouts and triumphant yells broke out on the ram as, very slowly, she backed away, leaving a huge hole in the *Cumberland*'s side, large enough to drive a horse and carriage through. A strange brief silence fell. An order from the wheelhouse to continue reversing came down, and David jumped for the reversing lever. The laboring, hissing engines reluctantly responded, and the *Merrimac* succeeded in backing free of the frigate's shattered side.

So much for iron against wood, thought David, while the ram continued to retreat slowly over the debris-littered gray-brown water. Then she altered course in the direction of the *Congress*. But not for several moments did anyone aboard the *Merrimac* become aware that this last maneuver had cost her dearly, because her twelve-foot cast-iron ram had been broken off clean from her hull and was wrenched away. Torrents of water began to rush through her partially smashed bow. Captain Buchanan promptly ordered all the men not actively engaged in essential duties to run aft, bringing any pieces of heavy equipment that they could move in a hurry. As a result of this order, within minutes the influx of water into the ironclad's hull diminished to unimportant spouts.

Once the steam bilge pumps had begun to whine, lowering the water still further inside the ram, an officer scrambled below. David heard him shouting through cupped hands, "Steady, you-all, *Cumberland*'s going down. Now we'll go finish off the *Congress!*"

Orders were relayed with difficulty along the dank, dark length of the ship. The men could scarcely believe it, and David, who had been making mental notes for the attention and evaluation of the Union Navy's Department of Engineering, if he ever got the information to them, could hardly believe what he had seen. But he couldn't help cheering along with the others, although every breath drawn rasped throats and lungs with burnt powder fumes.

David was amazed at himself, how he could forget his true identity and mission, and think only about keeping these worn-out old engines running. Briefly he wondered how he could possibly cheer for a victory over his own people. Union men had died on the *Cumberland,* and his ship had killed them.

But now the Confederate ram, her shot-away ensign replaced and secured to the already riddled smokestack, was churning on toward her second enemy, the huge sail frigate *Congress*. Sweating, half-deafened and dazed, David felt a swell of pride in realizing that the *Cumberland* had sunk on a more or less even keel, with battle flags still flying from her mastheads. She'd been sunk, all right, but she hadn't surrendered!

The U.S.S. *Congress*

To most of the *Congress*'s crew, including Seaman First Class Dennis O'Day, what had just taken place was utterly incredible. No one would have believed it possible if they hadn't been eyewitnesses to the fact that an ironclad vessel mounting only ten guns had defeated a regular U.S. frigate armed with ponderous cannon, had raked her cruelly and then rammed and sunk her.

Now the well-drilled Union gun teams on the *Congress* fired salvo after salvo. Everyone could watch their projectiles go skip-skipping over the surface. In these calm, nearly windless waters, shot seldom was aimed directly at a small target, but this unprecedented enemy offered such a miserably low profile that Union gunners had to train their pieces to fire low over the surface.

The effectiveness of the Union fire reminded David of the flat stones skipped by small boys across a tranquil millpond. Federal hopes of scoring a solid hit were increased by the fact that everything unprotected by the ram's casemate by now had been shattered or carried away. Her funnel had been pierced again and again by shrapnel until it resembled a colander and now supplied only feeble drafts of air down to the ram's gun deck and the engines laboring in the nearly unbearable heat of the stokehold.

Once more the *Merrimac*, achieving a raking position, since the valiant Union tugs hadn't been able to free the *Congress* or to push her any distance, continued to pour roundshot and shell into the battered but astoundingly defiant *Congress*. Aboard the steam frigate, her bulwarks, gun ports, spars, and other top hamper snapped and crackled like great kernels of popcorn in a hopper.

Fearful screams, shrieks, and howls of agony arose from all directions as raking shots from the armored vessel killed or wounded an entire gun crew. From below, shouts began rising. "Making water fast!" The frigate's single steam-engine water pump did its best, but inexorably the water level continued to rise.

Surgeons, splashed red as butchers, toiling below decks, labored until water rose to the level of hatch covers hastily improvised as operating tables. A number of seriously wounded men pleaded for help and threshed feebly about until they drowned.

On deck, Dennis O'Day, heart hammering, ran to the nearest cutlass rack and, screeching like a banshee, joined a handful of staunch Marines who had formed up amidship to repel boarders, and still were firing brass swivel guns in the direction of the smoke-veiled ironclad now lying almost alongside, but with no effect.

For all his violent nature, Dennis prayed to Jesus, Mary, and Joseph and assorted Saints that never again would he have to behold such horrors and destruction wreaked by the enemy's roaring guns.

The crashing of broken spars falling onto the deck increased, as did the sound of splintering bulwarks. Jagged sections of these swept the frigate's deck amidships and caused dozens of the most dangerous and painful wounds seamen could suffer.

Dennis, sweating like a coal heaver and splashed here and there by shipmates' blood, couldn't make himself heard, so great was the crashing roar of artillery. Using the flat of a cutlass, he led or drove a staggering handful of dazed, blackened, and often bleeding figures in an effort to reman the forward pivot gun. Only then did he realize that, beyond question, this once-beautiful frigate was being reduced to a shapeless wreck and already had become a floating shambles, from which rivulets of gore streamed down her scarred and shattered sides.

An officer on the *Congress*'s quarterdeck shouted something through a speaking trumpet, and a seaman began climbing toward the thus far undamaged mizzentop. Shortly afterward, a white flag was broken out, supplanting the Stars and Stripes.

A blackened gun pointer exclaimed, "B'God, damn if some dirty yellowbelly ain't give up the ship!"

A string of dreadful memories flashed through O'Day's mind. Soon, it seemed, he would be a miserable prisoner again!

No one was astonished when, out of the bitter-smelling murk, the ram drew up alongside, like some prehistoric monster, with gunsmoke curling out of her gunports once their protective iron covers had been triced back. Onto the *Congress*'s half-awash deck streamed groups of wild figures, mostly not in uniform, waving pistols and brandishing cutlasses, swords, and even Bowie knives.

A hatless Confederate officer bellowed through cupped hands, "Avast fighting! This ship is surrendered! Disarm and send all prisoners aboard the ram! Do your best for the wounded. Tell 'em they'll be cared for as soon as possible. Let no one say us Southrons ain't honorable fighters!"

Dazed men still on the *Congress*'s deck watched as more powder-blackened, wild-eyed men scrambled over the frigate's battered rail. "Surrender! Surrender!" they yelled. Nobody on the *Congress*'s littered and gore-streaked deck made a move until after a shell screamed over from one of the Union land batteries, and another burst harmlessly nearby. Evidently, the white flag, obscured by battle smoke, had not yet been sighted ashore.

A red-faced officer in a checkered red-and-black shirt yelled, "Seems those Yankee sons-of-bitches don't recognize a signal of surrender. Secure all possible prisoners and wounded and hurry 'em aboard before we finish this job for good and all!"

At that point, no one manning Camp Butler's and other Union batteries realized that dense powder fumes had rendered invisible the white flag hanging, limp and lifeless, at the surrendered frigate's mizzentop. Accordingly, they resumed firing. Furious, the Confederates and their prisoners scrambled aboard the *Merrimac*. O'Day had taken care that he wasn't among them.

"Down to the gun deck," Flag Captain Buchanan shouted. "The only answer to such dishonorable behavior is red-hot shot. Get some ready in a hurry!" Then, in a bizarre act which startled everyone, he snatched up a carbine, ran out on deck, and commenced firing blindly at the shore batteries until a bullet pierced his thigh and he collapsed onto the deck grating.

"Aye, aye, sir," David heard someone shout — he had been aboard so short a time that he knew scarcely a dozen officers and men by name. "... and be prepared to send hot shot into that pirate!"

"She's no pirate," protested a prisoner. "The *Congress* is regular Navy."

Hoarse and loud, a voice rang down from the wheelhouse, "Any warship flouting the laws of war forfeits nationality. Ahoy, down there! Be sure to wet your wads well, boys — don't risk any prematures. I want that damn frigate set ablaze in jig time!"

The *Merrimac*'s crew complied.

Further talk was drowned out by volleys fired while the ships were still lying not fifty yards apart.

For O'Day it was incredible to watch the heaviest cannon balls glance off the *Merrimac*'s armored and rivet-studded casemate, because they'd been laid at plates inclined to a forty-five-degree angle. Meanwhile, shot after shot from the enraged Confederates smashed the mangled frigate from stem to stern. Soon smoke began to rise through her hatchways, while her deck shook from the impact of Rebel shot striking with devastating effect. There was no need for dozens of voices to yell, "We're on fire!"

Already the *Congress*'s deck was assuming, slowly, an increasing tilt toward her bows. There followed a brief lull in the cannonading, during which all hands helped the wounded, many of them unconscious and spattering the gun deck, sending puddles and streaks of crimson dripping onto tugs which braved soaring flames to lie alongside.

"Sure and didn't we surrender?" O'Day asked a dazed Captain.

"You bet we did. Twenty minutes ago, dammit!"

"Then why should the Rebs keep on attacking like goddamn pirates?"

"Got me."

"Damn'd if I'll quit!" roared Joseph B. Smith, Acting Captain because his brother, Commander W. B. Smith, the frigate's actual commander, was on leave. Just then, Confederate guns resumed heavy firing. Under the impact of their shot, the *Congress* reeled, rocked gently a few times, then began to go down by the stern. As water started to boil up through her ammunition hatches, an officer, unrecognizable through his blackened features and singed hair, shouted, "Get to hell out of here, quick! Help the wounded."

Bitterly, Dennis flung aside his cutlass, snarling, "Criminently! Ain't going to get to use this pretty hanger after all."

Through drifting smoke, he glimpsed a young midshipman whose right arm had disappeared above the elbow. He jerked off his scarf, knotted it, and using a long splinter to create a crude tourniquet, he turned it as tightly as possible. "Listen, sir," he panted to the chalk-white youth, who was staring with unseeing blue eyes, "till you get to a real sawbones, remember to ease this contraption a little for a minute or two every now and then, else ye'll likely get gangrene."

Dennis joined a weird column of figures staggering and slipping on spilt blood as they groped their way across the littered deck toward the bow, away from slowly rising water.

Once again, comparative silence descended because, convinced that she had destroyed her second enemy, the *Merrimac* began to back off sluggishly amid dense smoke and gathering darkness. In so doing, she offered Union gunners ashore an even less satisfactory target than ever.

The ram's single funnel was leaning crazily and oozing heavy black smoke from a dozen-odd ragged punctures. Otherwise she appeared undamaged, except that the muzzles of two of her nine-inch Dahlgren guns had been shattered by the *Cumberland*. Now, consequently, her ensign was secured to a pike staff, everything else vertical above water having been shot away.

O'Day reasoned that there must have been a good many untrained or ill-disciplined artillery men on shore. They had fired on a surrendered vessel and now were filling the air with futile cannister, which often struck the burning *Congress*, as well as a disorderly swarm of small craft attempting to take off survivors, and valuables such as the ship's papers and pay chest. The age-old order arose aboard the shattered frigate, "Every man for himself!"

Hurriedly, Dennis lowered and almost dropped a wounded and half-conscious midshipman onto a floating hatch grating which seemed large enough to support several men. Just then a piece of cannister casing struck his leg so hard that he collapsed and fell into the water, luckily near enough to the grating to be hauled aboard. His right leg began spouting blood below the knee, but it could still feebly obey his will. All the same, Dennis guessed he would never again walk without a limp, or be able to do an Irish jig.

At the end of a week in the Station hospital, however, Dennis for the first time in his life seemed to be pretty sure about his future when it turned out that his wound, although painful, was not too serious to prevent continued service in the U.S. Navy. Only able-bodied men were accepted on shipboard, but he would be welcome in noncombatant service such as the commissary or the medical corps in order to release able-bodied men. After that, he reckoned, he would take out American citizenship, and with enough pay money and the proceeds from certain shady deals, he would buy a saloon — a business about which he had acquired plenty of knowledge over the years. And maybe he would marry some local Catholic girl with money, and maybe he might settle down for keeps.

For the first time in years, he felt at peace with himself and confident of the future.

Armored Duel

Like almost everybody else aboard the *Monitor* on the night of March 8th, as soon as the anchor had plunged from its ingenious shotproof well, Ira Thatcher collapsed and slept like a dead man, as did all the crew, except for those unfortunates designated to stand watch. The voyage down from New York had proved harrowing beyond belief; twice it seemed improbable that Ericsson's invention could remain sufficiently buoyant to reach Hampton Roads, Virginia.

Again, there was much confusion because the *Monitor*'s men, having been assembled in such a hurry, were mostly unfamiliar with even the major driving engines, let alone numerous lesser engines designed for special purposes. Few even knew each other's rank or name, or the exact nature of their duties, and what might be expected of them should an emergency arise.

Since the crew was composed of only sixty-odd men, it soon became obvious that any officer or enlisted man capable of discharging more than a single duty would be rewarded by increased pay and possible promotion — a cause of satisfaction to the late Captain Scott Thatcher's son. Not only was he experienced with a wide variety of steam engines, but he was also an expert on the service of several types and sizes of a man-of-war's carriage guns. In fact, he had won a few prizes for proficiency in that direction. Aboard this extraordinary craft, he was rated only as a Third Assistant Engineer. Who knew what advancement might not result from good gunnery, once battle was joined?

At first light on the morning of Sunday, 9 March 1862, all hands were roused by alarm guns being fired aboard the towering frigate *Minnesota,* close to which the *Monitor* had cast anchor about midnight. It was incredible to see how quickly the exhausted crew of the *Monitor* roused. Some had to tilt water over bleary heads before, by dim lantern light, they groped to locate posts and duties to which they had only recently been assigned. Men who had fallen asleep in the strangest places and in the most uncomfortable positions roused when they heard the shout down from the turret's top, "Battle stations, all hands! Rebel ram's coming this way." Wisely, all hands save the *Monitor*'s senior officers had been spared harrowing details of the bloody ravages caused by the *Merrimac*'s mangling of the *Cumberland* and the *Congress.*

Because the Rebel ram's top speed was so sluggish, it gave the *Monitor*'s men the opportunity to gulp scalding coffee and test their teeth on iron-hard ship's biscuit.

Below, in the engine room, the "black gang," as the stokers were nicknamed, were frantically occupied in getting up steam. Coal passers didn't have too much to worry about because, incredibly, the *Monitor*'s bunkers had been designed to accommodate no more than eighty tons of coal. She had been designed to operate only in shallow waters along the coast, where no more would be needed.

Unshaven, wild-haired, and often only half-dressed, the crew speeded to battle stations. Already the *Minnesota* had begun firing a series of deafening, ear-shattering broadsides which proved just as ineffective against the *Merrimac* as those fired by her companion ships, the *Cumberland* and *Congress.*

Orders soon came to up anchor. In the *Monitor*'s tiny and vulnerable pilothouse, Acting Captain Worden, Lieutenant Greene, his Executive Officer, and Pilot Howard felt the first throbbings of the *Monitor*'s huge engines after she had upped anchor and started moving away from the towering frigate in whose lee she had spent only a few hours.

Since nothing whatever could be seen from below the *Monitor*'s deck, and his responsibilities in the engine room were in order, Ira seized the opportunity to climb an iron ladder for a quick visit to the turret. Squeezing between the breeching of the two huge eleven-inch Dahlgren guns, he had a partial view of tan-colored water and a gaggle of armed, converted merchantmen raising dense clouds of smoke while escorting what must be the dreaded *Merrimac* away from her anchorage off Sewell's Point.

Ira was just beginning to get a good view of the enemy flotilla, when suddenly the escorting gunboats fired a few futile shots at the Rip Raps just before returning to their anchorage. To Ira it seemed utterly incredible that a craft as small as the *Merrimac* could have evoked such hysterical, terror-stricken reactions in the Union press.

At first, the Rebel ram continued toward the *Minnesota,* but when the *Monitor,* a midget by comparison, emerged from the frigate's lee and headed in her direction, the Confederate man-of-war altered course to intercept.

From the more or less accurate drawings and descriptions of this ungainly craft that had circulated in many Northern publications, most of the *Monitor*'s crew had long known that the *Merrimac* mounted a total of ten guns, with two rifled pivot pieces at bow and stern. Her broadside guns, all eight of them, had been reported to be nine-inch Brooke smooth bores.

As usual, dense clouds of wildfowl filled the air, while small craft, such as oyster boats, skipjacks, pungies, and cargo boats employed sweeps or ludicrously small rowboats to try to pull themselves away from the scene of the impending conflict. That there would be no wooden craft from either side around to complicate maneuvers was much to Acting Captain Worden's relief. To Pilot Howard he snapped, "Make for the enemy's bow!" Next, he shouted down a speaking tube leading to the turret, "Mr. Stimers, prepare to open fire!"

Ira Thatcher lingered long enough in the turret to watch brawny, eight-man gun crews run out the two huge Dahlgrens and he made a mental note of errors committed in handling them. All of them were minor, but should the action grow intense, collectively these mistakes might cause serious trouble. Cursing his fate for not being able to remain in the turret, Ira returned to his station in the dimly lit and stifling engine room.

Soon the two armored vessels closed in until they were separated by no more than a quarter-mile of turbid water. Then they opened fire. Shells from numerous shore batteries protecting Camp Butler screamed and howled overhead, bursting impartially over both ironclads. Their fragments, however, dealt neither combatant more harm than so many handfuls of popcorn.

Correspondents and neutral observers aboard the French *Gassendi* and the Royal Navy's sturdy sloop of war, *Rinaldo*, leveled telescopes and a weird assortment of binoculars. Conversation diminished and died out as they watched the two ironclads converge. Wild cheering from both shores of the Roads could be heard, now that most guns had quit firing and the duelists maneuvered for position.

Not for a moment did Acting Captain Worden forget that his principal responsibility was to protect the Union's stately wooden capital ships. In no time at all, it became apparent to even the most innocent observer that the *Monitor* could run rings about the *Merrimac*, whose officers more wholeheartedly than ever were cursing the feebleness of her engines and the ram's appalling lack of maneuverability. Thirty minutes were required to turn her completely about. Still, the fact remained that she mounted ten very heavy guns, all well protected by iron plates.

The Confederate opened fire with her forward pivot rifle, but missed the very small target presented by Ericsson's ship. Without a moment's hesitation, the *Monitor*'s turret revolved and fired, flinging a pair of heavy solid shot squarely at the *Merrimac*'s casemate, but to those watching it was a sharp disillusionment that neither of these two solid shots, which had struck squarely, had penetrated, but had only cracked or slightly dented the ram's armor.

As Ira and other experienced gunners had foreseen, those half-charges ordered for unproved guns by over-cautious ordnance officers at the Navy Department, following the *Princeton* disaster, precluded effects which to any other ship would have proved fatal.

Still, the impact of the *Monitor*'s solid shot was so severe that several of the *Merrimac*'s iron plates were broken. Some of the gun crew members were stunned or dazed, staggering about as though drunk. Many had blood trickling from their nostrils onto huge mustaches.

At that moment, Acting Captain Catesby R. Jones reached an unpleasant decision. Attempts to sink the *Minnesota*, then the *St. Lawrence*, and the *Roanoke*, must be postponed.

While the *Monitor* churned ever closer, the *Merrimac* trained all the guns which would bear on this strange new menace. Acting Captain Jones then ordered a full broadside fired at "Ericsson's Folly," as it had been derisively called. Time and again huge geysers of water were raised, and although several hits were registered, they caused the outlandish little craft no visible damage.

In the *Monitor*'s pilothouse, it long since had been appreciated that their ship would cruise easily twice as fast as the enemy, and could turn about far more quickly. If only, Worden thought, while the turret was being revolved on a broad brass ring let into her deck, some weak section in the enemy's armor could be detected.

Following the impact of heavy solid balls fired by the Yankees, the ram's casemates rang like fire alarm signals. Men fell, briefly stunned by the impact and choked by swirling, burnt powder fumes. Two other broadside guns had had their muzzles shot away and made useless. Although none of the enemy's shot actually penetrated the casemate, everybody could hear the resounding snapping of broken iron plates and the *clang!* caused by pieces of falling metal, and the crackle of splintering wooden beams supporting them.

Aboard the *Monitor,* things went better, notwithstanding that few of her crew had been able to snatch more than a few hours' sleep since Sandy Hook had been left astern two days earlier. But conditions below deck approached the incredible. Heat and gas fumes almost gagged the "black gang" shoveling furiously to keep the horizontal, vibrating-lever engines running and both boilers supplying 320 horsepower to the propeller's single shaft to the single nine-foot propeller.

Both vessels were briefly lost to sight to observers aboard the *Gassendi* and the *Rinaldo,* anchored at a discreet distance from the action. French officers and reporters, not often quiet, now discharged duties in thoughtful silence. Among other observations, Lionel Humphrey, a little later, recognized this Gallic calm in really tense moments; he had noticed it in the Crimea.

Just as the sun approached its zenith, a shell from the *Merrimac*, by pure mischance, exploded directly in front of the *Monitor*'s tiny and thinly armored pilothouse, driving tiny fragments of iron through its observation slit and sending blinding, choking, burnt powder fumes onto the faces of those on duty inside. In an instant, all three officers were discolored as black as Negro minstrels.

Although badly shaken and nearly blinded, Acting Captain Worden nevertheless ordered the *Monitor* into such shallow water that the *Merrimac*'s pilots dared not follow. There, at a safe distance, a reasonable estimate could be conducted of damage the *Monitor* might have sustained. However, no injury of any real importance could be discovered.

Strangely, Pilot Howard, although still half-dazed, discovered to his amazement that the steering wheel in the nearly wrecked pilothouse was still functioning perfectly, but the speaking tube connected to the turret had shattered so badly that from now on orders would have to be relayed by the voices of noncombatant officers, such as Paymaster Keeler.

Once the shaken and all but sightless commander of the *Monitor* had been helped below, Lieutenant Greene assumed command in the pilothouse, and while the ship's guns were being reloaded, he ordered Ira to duty in the turret and commanded the helmsman to head for the Confederate ironclad, in an attempt to override her very low unarmored deck and run her down.

During this brief period of readjustment, the *Monitor*'s blower engines were ordered to bring speed to maximum velocity; steam and gas generation from her imperfectly insulated engine room were having serious effects on the engineering crew. Already several men had fallen unconscious and had to be hauled up to fresh air atop the ever-swinging turret.

As for Ira, he was delighted to be ordered to the turret, even though the events that had just been occurring there were frightening enough. A gunner's mate who had happened to be leaning against the turret's armor at the same instant a Confederate shell struck outside it had been knocked unconscious and badly hurt.

While the *Monitor*'s twin Dahlgrens were firing away at intervals of no more than seven or eight minutes, the ship put on her best speed of twelve knots and rapidly closed in on her enemy. But then word was relayed from below that the coal supply was running dangerously low, and must soon be replenished.

But before he interrupted the fight, Acting Captain Greene, his jaw tight, ordered a pair of parting shots fired before the *Monitor* turned back toward the *Minnesota* in order to refuel from a coal barge lying in the frigate's lee. To the pleased surprise of everyone aboard, no answering shots came from the enemy.

Not until later was it discovered that the *Merrimac* was also ready to break off the engagement. Her smokestack had again been riddled, and so largely shot away that her engineers reported a shortage of draft air so that she could barely maintain steerageway. Besides, the ram's ammunition was reported to be running so short that Acting Captain Jones decided that, for the time being at least, discretion was indicated. Consequently, he ordered the ram to break off the engagement and painfully thresh her way back to Sewell's Point — a critical fact noted and commented upon by foreign and native reporters alike.

"Well," Lionel Humphrey remarked to a colleague, "seems as if the incredible has just taken place."

"What's your meaning?" someone asked.

"Why, sir, the Rebels actually are quitting the field."

A gunner's mate, his face streaked like a tiger's as sweat ran through a coating of smokey steam, asked, "Mr. Humphrey, do you think that ram will come back and renew the engagement once she's been resupplied?"

"She will if, as I've been told, a certain Henry Dutton is aboard and holds any real authority."

"No doubt the *Monitor* has been more than holding her own," observed a reporter from the *Chicago Tribune*.

"Maybe so," Humphrey admitted. "The heaviest Confederate broadsides just seemed to bounce off her turret like so many hailstones."

He was proved right in the long run. Although the *Merrimac* was repaired and later on appeared in the Roads a few times, her Commander was never permitted to engage the *Monitor*. Both sides now understood that an ironclad's presence was the only real assurance of protection against naval attacks on the respective capitals of Richmond or Washington.

38

Critical Decision

DAVID DEXTER, like most of the *Merrimac*'s company, was fully occupied when the dented iron ram, with the aid of several tugs, had limped back into Gosport. Because the damage she had suffered soon proved to be relatively unimportant, aside from the blasting away of her smokestack and some cracked armor plates, plus the loss of her iron ram, the ship remained quite as formidable as ever. Those two broadside guns whose muzzles had been shot off by the *Cumberland* could be quickly and easily replaced.

In his quarters ashore, David made sure his door was bolted before completing a list of injuries suffered by the *Merrimac*, as well as recording the possible weaknesses where plates had been cracked even though her casemate had not been penetrated.

Then, like the professional he was, David described in meticulous detail how efficiently the ram's broadside guns had been handled, as well as the system employed in supplying ammunition for them.

For the moment he decided there was nothing further he could do about collecting information while repair crews sweated and swarmed over the *Merrimac* like ants about a disturbed hill. Of course, he had been very close-mouthed the whole time he had been aboard. By some miracle, nobody so far had recognized him as a former Federal Naval officer.

Everybody from bootblacks to bankers was talking about the outcome of the *Virginia*'s battle with the *Monitor*. Local newspapers, of course, ran banner headlines proclaiming a great victory for the Confederacy despite the inescapable fact that it was the *Monitor* which had been left holding the field of action.

Many high-ranking officers commanding ports and defenses farther south were demanding vociferously that a definite showdown action between the two naval ironclads should be brought about as quickly as possible. To the fury of the fire-eaters, however, dispatches came down from Richmond forbidding another duel, for the time being at least. The *Merrimac*, it seemed, served a far greater need as a blockade ship denying Union troop and supply vessels passage up the James River to supply McClellan's and Butler's armies, now on the verge of laying siege to the Confederate capital.

Although only a few top Union generals were aware of it, very similar orders had been sent from Washington, forbidding the *Monitor* from sallying forth and challenging her rival. Should she be sunk, it was argued, the Confederate ram would then be free to steam up Chesapeake Bay, to bombard and lay siege to the Union's capital.

For the time being, then, both ironclads remained vigilant and ready to get up steam at short notice, but were forbidden to make any decisive move against each other.

David viewed the tangled waterfront along which more and more brown and white cotton bales from massive stacks were being loaded on blockade runners of all types. So far, he still had to encounter any local who knew for sure where Culpeper might be, let alone knowing of a fine plantation named "Gunner's Hill."

How could he go about seeking his heart's desire? He was still in search of a workable solution when, like a welcome bolt from the blue, he was ordered to report at once to Naval Headquarters.

Entering Captain Buchanan's office, David clicked heels and snapped to such rigid attention that the older man smiled faintly. "At ease, sir," he said, then unlocked his desk and presently produced and passed over a large official-looking envelope, heavily sealed with blue wax at various points.

"This, Mr. Dutton, contains a list of requisitions urgently required to complete repairs on the *Virginia*. With all possible speed, I want you to deliver these requisitions to Secretary Mallory's office in Richmond."

The Captain's voice deepened. "Make sure to impress upon the officers at our Navy Department that my demands are to be fulfilled with all possible speed." He shoved back his armchair and elevated bushy red-brown brows. "I have been observing your bearing, Mr. Dutton, and for some reason feel confident you understand how to tactfully approach gentlemen holding high and responsible positions."

Captain Buchanan, waving aside a persistent halo of flies, got to his feet. "Therefore, you will take the train for Richmond early this afternoon. Never forget that time is of the essence, Mr. Dutton, in securing these supplies." He tapped the sealed envelope, and added gravely, "Pray present my sincere compliments to Secretary Mallory and assure him that we are most impatiently waiting to receive orders to attack and destroy the *Monitor* as soon as possible."

"Aye, aye, sir. I'll do my best." David, smart in his unfamiliar gray naval tunic, felt himself to be walking on air. Through this totally unexpected stroke of luck, he now would be free to travel to Richmond, and once there, it should not prove too difficult for him as a Confederate naval officer, presumably on leave, to find transportation to Culpeper, a way station on the Orange, Charlottesville & Rapidan Railroad.

Secretary of the Navy Stephen B. Mallory accepted the requisitions, scanned them with care, and then frowning, observed, "Old Buck seems to need — considerable. Too bad some items he calls for are utterly impossible to fill, and least of all in a hurry, but I'll see to it personally that what supplies we do have are dispatched with all possible speed."

David hesitated. "Sir, I hate to mention it, but since I arrived in Norfolk I haven't drawn any pay. Would you be so kind as to give me a draft for funds to cover my expenses? I can't travel very far on the few dollars I have."

"Of course." The Secretary scribbled a message on a note pad. "Present this chit to the bursar on the floor below. How many months' pay are due you as an engineer-lieutenant?"

David thought fast. "Why, sir, it's only for three months, but I'd be grateful to receive even a half of it."

Fortunately, so many clerks and aides were swarming about the paymaster's office that David, without answering too many questions, soon found himself in possession of three hundred dollars' worth of crisp and handsomely printed Confederate bills. Privately, he would have preferred even a quarter of this sum paid in United States greenbacks.

* * *

He was fortunate enough to find a worn rattan seat in one of a pair of passenger cars attached to a troop train en route to duty in the vicinity of Fairfax County Court House. Gradually relaxing, David listened to the chatter of civilian passengers with growing concern. Apparently, the impact of this war was now really beginning to be felt personally. Women were complaining about shortages of all kinds of luxuries and a number of necessities. Apparently, Mr. Lincoln's "paper" blockade must be proving more effective than people were inclined to believe.

At all stops, and there were many, more troops wearing all manner of military uniforms and headgear, some pompous or outlandish, but mostly in gray or butternut-tinted coats and pants, swarmed into coaches closer to the locomotive. The military cars were soon overflowing. By the time the train clattered into Orange, some officers were forced to seek accommodation in the crowded and ill-smelling civilian coaches.

David immediately recognized one of the new arrivals as Captain George Oliver, who owned the property adjacent to "Gunner's Hill."

"Well, if it isn't David Dexter!" He offered a lean, brown hand. "Glad you had the sense to change your coat to the color of justice, States' Rights, and prosperity. But why choose the Navy? All the glory and promotions go to the armies nowadays. Oh, I forgot. Didn't you serve in the old Navy?"

David at once removed the carpetbag he'd bought in Richmond and motioned Oliver to join him. The Captain was young, only about thirty, but there were lines about his eyes and mouth which deepened as he described what war on land was really like — snakes, alligators, a variety of dangerous fevers, let alone Yankee sharpshooters. This angular young Captain had fought at Manassas and engaged in a couple of particularly bloody skirmishes.

"You've got no idea how rough this land war can be. Till last week I was detailed to serve in, and to improve, some of the forts defending Pensacola Bay. Wish I were in the Navy."

"Don't try to jump from the frying pan into the fire, Captain. War at sea can be just as miserable. On land you can always retreat, if necessary, but you can't retreat from a crippled or a sinking ship." Drawing a deep breath, David took the plunge and, heart hammering, inquired quite casually, he hoped, "How are things around Culpeper?"

Oliver's deeply tanned features tightened above his brief yellow goatee. "I've already lost a brother, and last I heard from Pa, he's a Lieutenant-Colonel, stationed in Vicksburg to design and build emplacements for a lot of heavy artillery. I heard that two months ago. The mails nowadays are simply terrible; lots of important letters get lost and are never delivered."

"You were speaking of your neighbors. How are my old friends the Ridgelys faring?" Again David's breath checked in his throat while he awaited the reply.

"Ridgelys? Oh yes, *now* I remember where I met you. You stayed with them a couple of times before this damned war started. Reckon you were beau-ing the lovely Louisa."

"Aye, that I was." He thought it wise to change the subject. "What about her brothers?"

"Well," drawled the cavalryman, pulling out a golden-brown plug of tobacco. Noting David's expression, he explained. "Lots of us fellows have taken to chewing on account of there's no flame to show the enemy where you are."

"Makes sense. What about the Ridgely boys?"

"Major Charlie Ridgely got himself killed leading a charge at Philippi; his brother Francis died last fall from wounds he got in a cavalry skirmish somewhere in Tennessee."

Finally, David inquired, "And how are the Ridgely ladies faring?"

"Why," said the cavalry officer, twirling his drooping mustaches, "heard tell from somebody who'd just come down from home they're doing their best to keep up 'Gunner's Hill' with the help of Peter, who's too young to . . ." Then the chuffing noises of the laboring wood-burning engine seemed to fade as David inquired, "What about Louisa?"

"Oh, last I heard," Oliver said, "Louisa is way up in Brandy Station, nursing wounded men in a hospital converted from a female seminary up there."

"She-she's well?"

"Last I heard, she was. They say she's still as pretty as a picture." Captain Oliver paused, and used a little finger to dig a cinder out of his ear. "There's a dreadful lot of disease breaking out, now the weather's warming up. Plenty of diarrhea, mumps, measles, and typhoid about, too."

Firmly, David pursued his subject. "The last you heard of Louisa — how long ago was that?"

"Oh, must be nigh on a month. You'll be pleased to hear that the hospital staff declare Miss Ridgely's a very fast learner and that she makes a competent and conscientious nurse."

Rapidly, David recalled this train's route. Culpeper village, if he remembered correctly, lay not far removed from Brandy Station, so it shouldn't prove to be any great problem to get transportation to that village. He wondered what the war might have done to the joyous beauty he'd danced with on the balcony of Lord Winterbotham's town house in London.

Distinctly, he could recall not only the exact shape of Louisa's mouth, but a strangely stirring, tiny line of blonde fuzz along her upper lip.

The train clanked noisily onward. Obviously, on most Southern railroads, rolling stock and locomotives alike stood in urgent need of repair. Right now the engine was wheezing like a tired old man climbing up a steep hill.

Hours later, the train rattled into Culpeper and clanked to a halt. At first glance, this pretty little place hadn't changed appreciably since he'd last beheld it, but after alighting, he noted differences. So many buildings stood in serious need of paint. Again, there was hardly an ablebodied man in sight who wasn't wearing a uniform of some description. Captain Oliver pointed out that the militia's handsome old red brick drill hall, which dated back to the Revolution, had been converted into a warehouse, at present crammed with tobacco, kegs, and barrels of various sorts.

They were in search of a conveyance when a third man, a sergeant, who said his name was Griffin, recognized David. "Why, if 'taint Misto Dexter! We-all heard you was dead — drowned or somethin'." Glancing at Captain Oliver, he raised a brow. "Suppose you've heard the bad news?"

"Lately, I've heard little else," Oliver remarked. "Well, Griffin, what's happened this time?"

"Why, it's the Ridgely gal. She took sick and died last week of dysentery up to Brandy Station Hospital. They buried her up to 'Gunner's Hill' graveyard yesterday afternoon."

David's heart missed several beats, and he felt frozen. "You don't mean Miss Louisa Ridgely?"

Sergeant Griffin had witnessed that paling and crumpling of features before, and would witness it many times more before the war ended. "Yes, suh. Everyone claims Miss Louisa were a mighty fine female; did a lot for the sick and wounded."

For a long moment, David stood rigid, motionless as a post. "You're *sure* it was Miss Louisa?"

"Yes, suh. Ah've known that family for a long time." He turned aside, saying, "Say, suh, you ain't Captain Oliver of Silver Springs, are you?"

"Yep. I'm on my way over there right now." He turned to David. "You want to ride out with me as far as 'Gunner's Hill'? My property lies only 'bout three miles beyond."

For the life of him, David couldn't endure the prospect of facing the bereaved family. After all, he wasn't really "family" yet, and now never would be.

Starting toward a rickety buggy standing outside a public stable, Captain Oliver said, "Sorry, Dexter. I'm eager to get home. How about you?"

Stunned though he was, David reached a quick decision. "Can't. I'm on important government business at Fairfax County Court House, so I reckon I'd better stay on this train till it reaches Fairfax."

Captain Oliver appeared a trifle incredulous, and wondered briefly about what sort of duty would send a naval officer as far inland as Fairfax County, which lay close to the fighting front. But there was no point in asking; nowadays nobody knew much about what was going on, even a few miles away.

After an exchange of courtesies, the three men shouldered their way through a milling crowd of people, hopeful of boarding the train. Nowadays schedules scarcely meant anything. Would-be passengers often were forced to wait half a day or even longer to board some already jam-packed cars. With a great effort, David forced a smile as he shook hands with Captain Oliver and Sergeant Griffin.

"You're *sure* it was Miss Louisa they buried?" he asked once more.

"Certain sure, suh. And more's the pity. She were real sweet and kind to everybody — even niggers!"

In a daze, David climbed back aboard the train, and completely numbed, collapsed onto a vacant seat even as the locomotive sounded a series of asthmatic whistles.

Louisa dead? It didn't seem possible; she had been too vital, too lovely for this to happen. Long-cherished and lofty dreams collapsed. He still could not accept his loss. Should he go seek her grave? No. Common sense warned that this was no time to appear at "Gunner's Hill," especially since, on his last visits to the plantation, he had been wearing Union blue.

Following a final gasping blast on its whistle, the locomotive, bright sparks rising from a bell-shaped smokestack, began to puff. Volunteer brakemen released brakes, coupling chains rattled, and freight and passenger cars began to lurch and sway, resuming the uncomfortable journey northward.

While the train gathered speed, David felt confused, as though all his essential mental props had been pulled away. He had to face the hard fact. Louisa was forever vanished from his life. Flashes of precious, joyous recollections continued to harass his peace of mind as the train gathered speed.

39

C.S.S. *Patrick Henry*

During most of the action off Hampton Roads, billows of gunsmoke on occasion obscured both the *Monitor* and the *Merrimac,* so that the Confederate steamboat *Patrick Henry*'s Captain continued to keep his big side-wheeler circling as close as he dared along the outskirts of the duel. In fact, so close did he venture that quite a few spent shells and solid shot raised brief white geysers barely short of the speeding ex-passenger ship. Several times shells burst close enough to splatter her deck with iron shards, but the missiles' velocity already had been spent, so no damage resulted.

Christian Pitcher, gripping the six-foot wheel, experienced a spasmodic griping in his bowels even after the thunderous explosions stopped, and the resultant smoke had drifted lazily away. Glancing at the gun crews, crouched behind breastworks of cotton bales, he marveled that human beings facing death at every minute could remain outwardly as calm as these Confederates.

Silently, the Bermudian vowed, "O great Lord, spare me this time, and I vow I'll never again set foot aboard a ship of any kind."

All the same, not ten minutes later, under Captain Johnny Tucker's orders, he was steering the *Patrick Henry* closer to those whirling, boiling clouds of gray-black smoke through which, from time to time, burst brief, bright flashes of cannon fire, punctuated by ear-torturing reports. Then a heavy shell fired by a Union shore battery burst at the base of the *Patrick Henry*'s two long and slender smokestacks. There was a terrifying explosion, and amid the sounds of shattered timber, roaring spouts of steam shot skyward. The ship's long, diamond-shaped walking beam wavered to a halt, whereupon her huge, dripping paddle wheels stopped turning, so that the *Patrick Henry* could only drift helplessly.

From below, somebody's voice was screaming louder than the rest. "Christ Jesus! Our steambox's been split apart!"

During a short interval, only the whistling roar of escaping steam could be heard — steam which for several minutes mercifully concealed the *Patrick Henry* in a dense and humid fog.

Pitcher was on his way below from the pilothouse to fetch a special chart when the crippling shell exploded. The Bermudian sagged onto the deck, with bright red blood spurting from a small splinter wound in his upper thigh. From below were rising terrible screams and cries; later it became known that five of the engine room's crew had been suddenly scalded to death, and that several others of the steamer's black gang had also been gravely injured.

Even before the flagship of the James River Squadron lost way completely, a tug chugged alongside and Christian, still in shock, heard, as from a long distance, harsh voices arranging a tow. Then he lost consciousness. He could never recall being lugged ashore on a gore-stained canvas hammock.

Only late in the afternoon did he recover consciousness, stabbed by the pain of a surgeon's probe digging into a slash low alongside his testicles. He fainted again as the doctor dropped a short, jagged iron splinter into a small wooden bucket. While compresses were hastily being applied, the doctor turned aside, muttering, "I might be wrong, but if this fellow ever walks straight again, it will be a miracle. Pity. He's so young and good-looking, but I'd venture plenty of girls are going to look aside from such a cripple."

Christian, recovering a measure of strength days later, reached a new conclusion. Whichever government eventually won control of the bustling port at Norfolk, competent pilots must always be in demand. He decided to take up that profession, and silently renewed his vow never again to set foot aboard a ship of war.

He stared out into the bright spring sunlight. With many men being killed every day, why shouldn't he, being wise about women, induce some settled female possessed of plentiful means — and harboring no desire of rearing a family — to marry him?

40

Dispatch to the London *Telegraph*

ONCE THE *Merrimac* had limped slowly out of range, Lionel Humphrey went below decks to pour himself a double cognac which, since the ship was French, proved to be the only distilled drink available aboard His Imperial Majesty's sloop of war. Gradually his head cleared, and his ears stopped aching, as he sorted out and listed by categories his impressions of various aspects of what he quite accurately perceived as an epic-making action.

A French newspaperman sat across the sloop's tiny but spotless mess room, composing a dispatch so rapidly and with such intense excitement that frequently his pen's steel point dug deep into the paper and splattered this tentative draft with constellations of minute black specks.

Lionel paused, absently tugging at his sandy side-whiskers, a mannerism which in the past had calmed him and restored his thinking to its usual constructive pattern. But, great Caesar's ghost — it wasn't going to be easy this time. The veteran correspondent's every instinct led him to believe that the results of this duel inevitably would result in revolutionary changes in naval construction. But how could he get ashore to wire the *Telegraph*'s New York office that they must dispatch his report to London by the fastest means available? How could he get such vitally important news on the wire before rival reporters dispatched this critically important story? If he did get through, that hostile editor in the Home Office no longer would dare to quibble over his expense account. By now Lionel had learned that by all accounts the nearest reliable telegraph station with Northern communications was in Fort Monroe, whose mighty battlements lay frowning across the James.

An opportunity to solve his dilemma arrived when, presently, a small cutter manned by Army men pulled up alongside and a lanky civilian pilot, evidently in charge, pleaded in execrable French for a tow over to Fort Monroe; he said there were several severely wounded men aboard.

Captain Gautier remained polite yet firm. *Hélas,* for the *Gassendi,* His Imperial Majesty's warship, to assist either combatant at such a time as this constituted a serious breach of neutrality.

"Hell, sir!" shouted a brawny sergeant, "we've got to have help! Some of our wounded here on the footboards have been so hard hit they mayn't live long!"

Quietly, Lionel stepped up and addressed Captain Gautier, "If it's all right with you, sir, may I go ashore and help the wounded? Having witnessed a good deal of action in the Crimea, I've learnt something about the rough dressing of wounds. Possibly I could be of some use, and still in no way contravene the Laws of Neutrality."

"That being the truth, and I hope for us all that it is, Monsieur Humphrey, you have my leave to depart." Captain Gautier seemed infinitely relieved when, ostentatiously swinging a canvas bag of medical supplies, the gaunt, red-faced Englishman descended a rope ladder and dropped into the cutter bobbing alongside. His suitcase landed a moment later among the oarsmen. Oars were thrust against the *Gassendi*'s beam and, flying a less than clean white cloth from her bow and a dingy little Stars and Stripes at her stern, the cutter started in the direction of Fort Monroe.

To the Englishman's astonishment, the *Gassendi*'s company yelled, *"Vive l'américain!"* a diplomatic cheer since *both* belligerents were American.

41

Letter Home

Washington, D.C.
March 22, 1862

Respected Sir,

Trust you long since have received a communication from the Navy Department explaining the truth lying behind my apparent change of allegiance during this War, informing you that I only did so on order to facilitate a detailed examination of the *Merrimac*'s present armament, machinery, her capacity to maneuver, and at what speed.

Today, thank the Good Lord, my Commission in the Navy of the United States has been reinstated; also to my surprise, including warm words of praise for the discharge of my responsibilities in connection with the engagement between the *Monitor* and the other ironclad.

If only we might see each other, beloved Father, even briefly, that I might convey the results in detail to you, as a man so knowledgeable in engineering matters, of my mission to Norfolk! These include Southern estimates of the *Monitor*'s future usefulness. The Rebels now are fully aware that Mr. Ericsson's invention presents enormous possibilities and is very dangerous to their cause.

This must be the case, for I have just heard on excellent authority that U.S. Government contracts for no less than *ten* craft embodying most of the *Monitor*'s basic design have been let to various shipyards. This type, tentatively to be called the *Passaic* class calls for an almost invisible deck or a very low freeboard and at least one revolving turret. I hear rumors are circulating that some are being designed to support *two* turrets and, if all goes well, could be ready for action come a few months' time.

On the other hand, the Rebels, or so our spies inform us, are building — we don't know yet how many or where — more or less exact copies of the *Merrimac* — the *Virginia*, so-called by them — although this craft, so far, never yet has dared to come out to challenge the *Monitor*.

Although I have requested a brief leave that I might come to New York to pay my respects to you, Dear Captain, it has been refused because I am expecting orders to report to the Commanding Officer of the Western River Flotilla. I believe its present headquarters lie in St. Louis or, perhaps, in Cairo, Illinois, where several stout river ironclads have been constructed by a Mr. Eads.

This morning, of all coincidences, who should I bump into but Ira Thatcher! We had only time to converse briefly because he also is about to receive orders sending him out to join the Western River Flotilla.

Ira believes he is for duty in the U.S.S. *Carondelet,* which at last report is lying somewhere along the Ohio River or perhaps the Mississippi River. Precisely where, nobody knows.

He looks fit and promises to communicate soon, extending to you, Sir, his most sincere respects and regards. He swears he will never forget your many kindnesses toward him in New York last winter.

While awaiting orders I have taken quarters in a modest boarding house situated not far from the Willard Hotel. It was recommended by several Service friends who have patronized this establishment.

Of old friends, I have encountered only two in Washington; the charming Mlle Arlette d'Aubrey and Lionel Humphrey, the English newspaperman — the same two who, last winter, crossed from Bermuda with Ira and myself in the *Princess Royal.*

Humphrey, like myself, inhabits a boarding house. For a Britisher, he appeared somewhat excited over some good news he has just received from his publishers; he promised he would give me details tomorrow when we lunch together.

Please, Respected Sir, describe the true condition of your health. I feel much concerned in that a mutual friend who, at his request shall remain nameless, saw you not long ago and was shocked at your appearance. Loving you so deeply as I do, Sir, I feel much worried.

Pray present my regards to Manuel should he still be in your employ. I trust by this time Mother's Father is much improved, and that she is home taking care of you, with my dear sister, to both of whom I also send my love.

I will save the details of how I escaped from the South, which was easier than I feared it would be, until we are reunited.

I will telegraph as soon as I receive orders, and forward you my postal address as quickly as I can determine it.

Your ever dutiful, loving, and respectful Son,
DAVID

42

News, Sweet and Bitter

LIONEL HUMPHREY returned to Washington following an absence of nearly a month during which he had dashed off a note to Mademoiselle Arlette d'Aubrey, reporting that he had been instructed to linger in the Hampton Roads area, based on Fort Monroe. He was to remain there until all likelihood of a renewed action between the "Armored Giants" — as he had come somewhat whimsically to term the *Merrimac* and the *Monitor* — became unlikely.

Then he had received curt instructions to return at once to the *Telegraph*'s Washington bureau. So, in all probability, his dismissal had been decided upon, and he now, for the time being, supposed himself to be unemployed, although he had succeeded in filing his dispatches about the great battle.

The lanky Englishman reasoned that with his Crimean War accomplishments still glowing he might not encounter too much difficulty in obtaining fresh assignments elsewhere. But to his vast astonishment, when he reported to the *Telegraph*'s Washington bureau, he was welcomed with open cordiality by its hawk-faced chief, who remarked, "Well, Mr. Humphrey, it would appear that your graphic accounts of those bloody battles off Hampton Roads between the Confederate ram and those Union wooden men-of-war — what were their names?"

"The *Congress* and the *Cumberland,* sir."

"And then your astute description and your estimate of the significance of that duel betwixt the ironclads, the *Monitor* and the *Merrimac,* have met with our managing editor's most enthusiastic approval. Indeed, Mr. Humphrey, he was so pleased by your dispatches — envied by his rivals — to the extent that he has authorized your salary increased to one hundred pounds per month, plus expenses. My sincere congratulations."

"Thank you kindly, sir."

"Pray, step into my office, Mr. Humphrey, where we can talk privately about a fresh assignment which must prove of considerable importance. From what I can learn, it will be ticklish diplomatically and, possibly, dangerous to your person, since this war is becoming bloodier and less predictable by the day. You accept?"

"Wouldn't I be a fool to do otherwise, sir?"

"I expect so; good reporters seldom have good sense."

"When do I depart, sir, and to where — if that's not a military secret?"

"It's not. In due time you will travel to Cairo lying in some state bearing the barbarous Indian name of Illinois, and there become attached to the headquarters of a General called U. S. Grant, presently commanding the Federal Armies out there. Good luck to you, sir. Somehow, I feel you're going to require a plentiful ration of the same."

Once the door to her small but well-appointed sitting-room had closed behind the tall, broad-shouldered and well-tailored figure of Mr. Herbert Morrison, President of Morrison, Selby & Putnam, of Manchester, New Hampshire, wholesalers of hardware of all descriptions, Mademoiselle Arlette d'Aubrey went over to a window and peered down at the busy street and the brilliantly sunlit square below.

Never had she been so torn by such a complexity of crucial decisions, such an intense conflict of profound sexual emotions. Matters wouldn't have reached such a critical pass if Lionel Humphrey had only not reappeared a few days earlier, as dryly whimsical as ever and so very endearing in his inarticulate but sincere British fashion.

Eyes moistening, she arrived at what seemed to be a most practical if not the most heartwarming of decisions. Now that Lionel was back, they would enjoy the best dinner Monsieur Hugo, the Willard's Swiss chef, could devise. They would enjoy sherry, Chablis wine, champagne of a famous vintage, fancy hors d'oeuvres, fish, and squabs *rôti à la Reine*. For a certainty, this reunion deserved the chef's best effort. Unless she was hopelessly in error, tonight would mark a major turning point in both their lives.

Seldom had Arlette devoted more skillful attention to her toilette. Every curl of her coiffure was trained just so, and in the latest mode; tactfully, she donned a modest little necklace of seed pearls that Lionel had once bestowed, which emphasized her evening gown of mint-green chiffon, cut low enough to reveal an intriguingly deep cleavage between those breasts he'd always admired and loved to caress. Her billowing hoop skirts artfully hinted at the intriguing proportions of long and slender white legs. Arlette donned frilly garters of chip diamond-studded yellow silk — a gift last year from her late benefactor, the Marquis de la Villette — to support champagne-hued silk hose. Arising, she sought a tall mirror and surveyed her ensemble, ending by making a little *moué* of satisfaction. Even a *duc*, let alone a well-experienced British newspaperman, should prove entranced.

Come to think of it, Lionel in his last letter hadn't sounded like himself, it was not quite as light and witty as his previous missives. She had arrived at the reluctant conclusion that Lionel must have received further editorial criticism about the newsworthiness of his recent communications.

On recognizing their private signal — two, then three taps on her door — her heart surged. For a moment, Arlette felt strangely panic-stricken, almost like a schoolgirl caught *in flagrante delicto*. Rallying, she hurried into that little sitting room she lately had been able to afford, thanks to Mr. Morrison's unsolicited generosity. *Mon Dieu!* That well-mannered gentleman, quite unostentatiously, oozed wealth from every pore.

Cautious inquiries on her part had attested to the huge extent of Mr. Morrison's fortune, but seldom did anyone know the true amount of it. In Washington nowadays, one had to be careful. There were so many clever charlatans and persuasive but penniless *poseurs* strutting about town, not to mention hordes of *demimondaines,* or clever prostitutes possessing various degrees of charm, sophistication, and greed.

Why, only the other day, up-and-coming General Joseph Hooker, the Army's Provost Marshal in the capital, had announced that drastic steps were about to be taken, by force if necessary, to transport the most objectionable and generally diseased whores (gonorrhea and syphilis were becoming almost epidemic and so were a serious threat to the efficiency of troops stationed in or about the capital) beyond the limits of the District of Columbia. Hence, common strumpets soon became known as "hookers." Needless to say, most of these brazen creatures reappeared in the capital almost overnight.

"Ah-h, Lion-el, *mon coeur.*" She flung herself into his arms ardently. He was delighted especially when she kissed him, using her tongue as only Arlette knew how. Finally, she backed off a little, peered into the Englishman's startled and deep-set brown eyes as he almost gasped, "My word, Ducky, and to think I never suspected you were capable of missing me so intensely!"

"But I have, Lion-el! Did you miss me as much, *chéri?*"

"Of course, m'dear. Saw not a female even a tenth as delectable as your sweet self." Resettling his cravat, he looked about and smiled. "I perceive, Ducky, you've not experienced too great hardships during my absence, so let us celebrate our reunion in unforgettable fashion. Only then I will confide news which at once is excellent but still chancy, affecting, as it must, only the two of us. The matter can wait so — come here." He kissed her fervently, and welded her body to his for several moments.

"Hein?" Although still out of breath, she formed a radiant smile, which faded gradually. "How strange this is."

"Why?"

"Because, dearest Lion-el, I also have tidings both sweet and sad, but as you've just said, this matter can wait. So now, *mon coeur,* let us celebrate our reunion. Like the excellent *sommelier* you are, will you pour us what, let us hope, will prove the first of many bottles of *Cordon Rouge!"*

"Shall do!" For the first time in years, Lionel felt hopelessly disoriented. Now, colorful as a hummingbird, Arlette was darting about the candlelit sitting room, skirts fetchingly asway, effectively rousing urgencies too long suppressed. God Almighty! Would he ever again encounter a female even half so desirable? Somehow, he doubted it.

By the time pleasurable transports had calmed temporarily, Arlette's supper had chilled, but the great, soft bed remained delightfully warm. After a while, Arlette tenderly held the Englishman's bony features between her dampened yet still stimulating and fragrant hands. Still breathing rapidly, she sat up, bolstering herself against a pile of pillows and pushed aside disordered, moist ringlets. In a voice almost shockingly matter-of-fact, practical, and devoid of passion, she said, *"Alors,* Lion-el, suppose you give me your good news before the sad? Then I, too, will confide a sober decision I recently have arrived at, though not without profound consideration and suffering much pain."

"So be it, my sweet," he said, when they had done kissing for the moment. "First, my good news. It appears that my publishers and their editor in chief in London finally have been pleased by my coverage not only of that battle between the two ironclads, but by my descriptions of the loss of the Union ships *Congress* and *Cumberland,* and the heroism exhibited by both their crews. I don't know why, but my accounts of these actions have been reprinted many times, not only in London and in the counties but also in Paris, Berlin, Stockholm, and even in Russia."

He reached out to swallow a sip of cognac. "The result has been that not only have I been highly commended, but my salary has been increased to a hundred pounds a month, plus expenses — to them, and to me also, a princely reward for a quill-pusher like myself."

"Bravo! Bis! Bis!" Arlette clapped hands so hard her breasts jiggled. She lifted her champagne. *"Magnifique!* Oh, I am *so* happy for you, *mon bien aimé."*

She sobered abruptly. "And your bad news?"

"Only today, my beloved, I received orders to report to the headquarters of Major General U. S. Grant, who commands certain Federal armies out in what Americans loosely term their Midwest. Alas, I have had no information exactly where this General's headquarters lie at present, only that they are situated somewhere in the western part of a state called Tennessee. Friends also warn me that my assignment to his staff is likely to be difficult, to say the least. Newspapermen, it would appear, are not welcome around his headquarters. Several reporters, he believes, have misreported his decisions and tactics. And we scriveners are no more popular with Grant's second in command, Major General William T. Sherman. Therefore, Arlette, my darling, although I had hoped to render our romance a legal one, thoughts of marriage — should you be willing — must be postponed indefinitely."

He felt genuinely miserable, and kissed her lingeringly. "And now, my dear, it's your turn to hold the floor — or bed, which I presume would be a trifle more accurate."

Arlette got up, as naturally and beautifully nude as Phidias's Aphrodite, and swayed across the room to fetch a fresh bottle. Once she had refilled their glasses, she said smiling, "Whatever the future holds, dearest Lion-el, here is luck and love to us both!"

"Hear! Hear! You were about to confide?"

Arlette spoke in soft yet suddenly unemotional tones. "Strangely, my story, *chéri,* comes close to being the counterpart to yours. First one enjoys security, then uncertainty and then . . ." She paused and watched a succession of frost beads descend her glass's stem.

"Last week I was advised by the Marquis de la Villette, the Assistant Minister of Marine, that my intelligence reports have proved to be lacking in value. Much of the information I forwarded already was known to the Ministry."

"Sorry. Know just how you feel. Then what?"

"I have been recalled, which I know means that my liaison with Monsieur le Marquis, unofficial though it was, is near an end, and also his support of me. I have been informed by my brother that my unhappy father has been declared bankrupt and has fallen so gravely ill he is not expected to live very long."

She peered steadily at him. "Under such conditions, is one not forced to be practical? Since, *mon cher,* you were nowhere to be located, I accepted invitations to a number of gay but very select dinner parties. At one of them, I found myself paired with a tall, good-looking gentleman named Herbert Morrison. If I have been correctly informed, he is a very important textile manufacturer who is in Washington to negotiate important contracts for various sorts of hardware required by the Union Armies. Amazingly enough, Mr. Morrison speaks good Parisian French and has spent much time in Lyons and other cities — on business affairs, naturally."

"He is well-born and educated, I presume? Single?"

"No. Divorced. His wife eloped a year ago with an opera singer."

"Please continue."

"Although Mr. Morrison has lived in Chicago for some time, his family comes originally from New England, a state called New Hampshire. He also is a graduate of an American college which I think is called Harvard. You have heard of the place?"

Humphrey suppressed a grin. "Rather. I've heard much about that institution of higher learning, also about another such called Yale. I'm told they are supposed to be as outstanding in America as Oxford and Cambridge are at home, but are by no means comparable to them by the best European scholastic standards."

Arlette resumed: "Upon receipt of Monsieur le Marquis's message, I became aware I had received my *congé*. So what was I to do? Should I return to France and humble myself before de la Villette, who is a difficult taskmaster in more ways than one, or should I be forced to seek a new *patron*, probably one of a lesser rank." Briefly she bit her lip. *"Hélas,* as one of an ancient noble family, pride renders such a step as an impossibility.

"Alors, even though I thought constantly of you, Lion-el, as I've already said, I decided to attend various diplomatic social invitations, but," she shrugged, "I met with no success in advancing certain ambitions until I encountered this Monsieur Morrison who, as I have explained, speaks excellent French and knows a great deal about the economy of my country. Besides, he has a sense of practicality which is almost Oriental.

"Almost at once I felt attracted to him, more and more intrigued by his good manners, his quick intelligence, and erudition...." She smiled and stirred among disorderd and body-dampened pillows. "I was even more attracted when I found that Herbert Morrison is only forty and divorced from his wife not long ago. He is also very rich and is of a most pleasing personality. I feel sure you would like him."

"Undoubtedly, dearest Arlette, since evidently he appeals to you in so many ways. And now . . . ?"

"I — well, I accepted his attentions, always of the most discreet, and only two days ago I accepted an apparently well-considered and sincere offer of marriage. Like so many Americans, Herbert appears much impressed by my family's very ancient title. But enough of this — are *we* not together for perhaps the last time?"

"Yes. In the foreseeable future, at least. Recall that old saying? Man proposes, God disposes."

"How true, *mon aimé."* Fervently she kissed the disheveleled Englishman. "You understand my position, *n'est-ce pas?"*

"Naturally. Odd, isn't it? Both of us are now forced to exercise that least common thing called common sense." Gently, he stroked her smooth, hot cheek. "Who knows but that once this ghastly war ends, our paths may not cross once more?"

A little wearily, Arlette nodded. "Who knows? But now let us agree that for the moment matters may have worked out for the best."

Lionel shrugged. "Yes. Even with my rise in salary, I could scarcely keep you in the style you know and deserve."

She started to interrupt, but he held up a hand. "Never forget, my dearest, that my profession is demanding, uncertain, and sometimes dangerous. You know by this time that, at a moment's notice, I can be assigned to duty in Kamchatka, Pondicherry, or Zululand, and be gone for God knows how long — which would never do. Therefore, as you have so delicately pointed out, we are only acting like sensible and essentially practical people." He drew her close, and stroked the memorable softness of her back and buttocks. "Therefore, my poppet, why not make hay while the sun shines?"

Arlette giggled. "Of course, but what a pity we are not in Norway or Sweden, or in some land where sunlight can be enjoyed at midnight!"

Her body slid slowly downward to meet his.

43

Western Rivers

AFTER HAVING MET by agreement at Naval Headquarters, where they both had reported for reassignment, Ira and David sought the newly christened Monitor Saloon. Inevitably, the place was proving wildly popular.

Ira reported that he had orders to report to Commander Henry Walke at Cairo, aboard the U.S.S. ironclad *Carondelet.* Following a drink or two, David confided that he had been issued orders, first, to deliver, with all possible speed, a number of all-important contracts to Brigadier General Carl Brebner, Q.M.C., Missouri Volunteers, in St. Louis, and then to hasten down the Mississippi to Cairo, Illinois, where he was to report for duty to Colonel Charles Ellet, now commanding the Western River Flotilla's steam ram division.

"Colonel!" Ira's straight brows rose. "Why would a Regular Navy officer be reporting to an Army Commander?"

"Early in the war a strange arrangement was arrived at for activity on the Western rivers," David told him. "All but Regular Navy vessels, such as those Farragut commands downriver in and around New Orleans, are owned and partially operated by the Army, but the Navy supplies them with some officers — mostly ordnance types, gunners, Marines, and as many regular seamen as required to man cannon, maintain discipline, and insure sound communications."

"My God!" Ira flung both hands in the air. "I wonder who thought of anything so insane."

"So you're for Cairo, too," David said. "Why shouldn't we travel together as far as East St. Louis?"

Ira hesitated, slowly revolving his glass over the spotted tablecloth and, without looking up, said, "Tell me, Dave, what's back of some crazy rumors I heard a while back about your having turned Rebel? What's the real truth?"

David glanced quickly about and then bent forward, lowering his voice. "Of course I've your word of honor you'll not breathe of this to anyone?"

"Of course not, but why all the mystery?" Ira leaned forward, grim of expression. "You've known me long enough to be certain of that."

Jaw muscles rigid, David said, "Well, to tell the honest truth, I accepted a spying mission to go down to Norfolk not just to discover the *Merrimac*'s true capabilities, but also because it was my only hope of seeing my Louisa in the foreseable future."

"You — you saw her?" As few others, Ira Thatcher had a long and intimate knowledge of the couple's mutual devotion and the profound and intense nature of their love.

"No, Ira, I didn't. I couldn't. She died the same day the *Monitor* fought the *Merrimac*."

"Died?"

"Yes." In a toneless voice, David continued, "She died of some disease — like all too many others — that she contracted while she was nursing wounded Confederates."

Words failing the classmates, they gripped hands fiercely below the table. Nothing was said until a tired-looking waiter had fetched a menu. With an effort, David shook off his memories and reverted to the present. He joined Ira in ordering mighty corned beef sandwiches, pickles, and a pot of coffee strong enough to float an ax head. Once the coffee had been generously laced with bourbon, David actually smiled and inquired, "Well, Ira, how are you doing with the girls these days? Keeping out of trouble?" He chuckled. "My God, shotgun weddings are so frequent around here they sound like a brisk skirmish."

Abruptly, Ira's expression sobered. "No, David, it ain't as though I haven't had plenty of opportunities — you know what Washington's like these days — but there was one pretty young widow I was growing damned fond of and she acted so extra-eager to get spliced, that I wondered why. She told me her husband had been killed somewhere in Kentucky only a few weeks earlier, and that he'd been mighty rich. Then she admitted she couldn't inherit his estate unless she had a child by him, and since he was beyond doing that, she'd picked me as a quick substitute."

A brawl broke out amid a crash of broken tableware, effectively drowning out conversation for a moment.

"Why didn't you take up her offer? You've always had plenty of push 'em up, I've noticed over the years."

A small laugh escaped Ira. "Well, old boy, I'm not quite the frozen-toed career worshipper some people imagine me, so time and again I did my best to help Pauline earn her inheritance. When nothing happened, I looked up a newly arrived German specialist who was supposed to be an expert on such delicate matters. He discovered the cause of my sterility." He gulped his coffee. "Thank God it's not impotence. I've satisfied my share of the fair sex often enough."

"What was the explanation?"

"This doctor inquired if I'd ever contracted mumps after I was an adolescent. I said I had and remembered it damn well because it was so painful when my knockers swelled to the size of oranges.

" '*Mein Herr,*' says he, 'you can take at least some encouragement, despite your impairment. A good many men, famous in history, were sterile: Julius Caesar; Sir Henry Morgan, the great buccaneer; Sir Francis Drake; I believe Alexander the Great begot no children; and even your great President Washington was childless, to name but a few.' "

A grating laugh escaped Ira. "So, Dave, let's hope I'll become a world-famous admiral by way of recompense. Perhaps service with the Western River Flotilla will do it. I'm told it's so different from all we were taught and trained for at Annapolis. It may be that when I'm freed from the toils of red tape, it will allow me to exercise a latent military genius."

The locomotive's whistle shrilled several times, whereupon the brakemen assigned to various cars ran out onto platforms and commenced unhurriedly to revolve cast-iron brake wheels until the local on which Ira and David were moving westward was switched onto a siding and came to a shuddering, clanking halt to permit, before long, the passage of an express train roaring along the single line right-of-way. It vanished amid a whirling tornado of sparks, cinders, and smoke.

Ira asked, "What about this flotilla of so-called steam rams you mentioned? What sort of craft are they?"

"All I know is that the Government Commissioner, a well-known civil engineer named Charles Ellet, was directed late last month to purchase a number of fast new river steamers and fit them up to serve as rams — how, I've no idea as yet. At the last report, this Mr. Ellet, who's been commissioned a Colonel in the *Army*, has bought four powerful side-wheelers and three stern-wheelers. The only description of them I was shown stated that the hulls of these ex-river steamers had been strengthened by solid timber bulwarks twelve to sixteen inches thick, running fore and aft. Also, it stated that a lot of heavy wrought-iron rods ran across the hull, and so secured one side solidly to the beam."

"What about the engines and the boilers?"

"They're supposed to be protected by white oak walls two feet thick."

Ira stared at the car's ceiling. "Now, as God's my judge, I've heard about the craziest craft ever to join a civilized Navy. How near complete are these monstrosities?"

"Nearing completion, even though they were thrown together in six weeks' time. All they need now is to have iron beaks fitted to their bows, then they'll be off to join the Eads ironclads lying somewhere below Cairo near a place called Fort Pillow. That's where I figure you'll be sent. Any idea which ship — I mean boat, as they call 'em here — *you'll* be aboard?"

"Surprisingly, yes. It's the already famous *Carondelet* — you know, she was the ironclad which performed so well earlier this year during the capture — in February, I think it was — of a couple of Rebel forts. Can't remember their names."

"One was Fort Henry lying on the Tennessee River, the other, and more formidable one, was Fort Donelson, which was supposed to defend the Cumberland River. I've learned that much about it."

While the local train clanked on, the two talked until, late that night, people attempting to doze on cruelly uncomfortable seats complained in no uncertain and often obscene language. They fell silent; after all, several hours of daylight must pass before they parted at East St. Louis Junction.

44

Kitty's Diary

EVEN NOW it wasn't easy to contemplate making another entry, yet Kitty Hamilton forced herself to open that gilt and morocco-bound diary, complete with golden key, that Mrs. Markham so earnestly had advised her to keep, saying, "No female, least of all one dependent solely on her wits and charms, should go without one. Lacking security, I have learned that a diary can become a highly useful and remunerating utensil by enabling the writer to recall just when, where, and with whom she was on a given date, and if advisable, to describe in ladylike detail exactly what chanced and what was promised."

Thank heavens, mused the willowy Bermudian girl, she'd possessed sufficient wit to follow Adah Markham's advice. All her spelling was of the phonetic variety, to say the least, and her syntax and punctuation elemental, though often she worked late into the night attempting to correct such deficiencies.

Nevertheless, to herself at least she managed to convey what was important. Tired or not, she invariably scrawled at least a few lines before retiring but, more often than not, adding to these the next morning when her memory and senses were clearer.

Now she was seated before a window opened to admit an early spring breeze off the Mississippi into "Edelweiss," the somewhat garishly furnished yet surprisingly spacious cottage which Brigadier General Carl Brebner had presented to her, together with the deed registered in her own name, to dwell in it until at least the year of mourning for Augusta, his deceased wife, prescribed by society, had passed. Too many important people were still sticklers enough on that point to ignore it.

Her little property lay discreetly at no great distance from "Himmelschoch," Brebner's imposing neocolonial mansion on Goethe Street. "Edelweiss" was just far enough distant to reassure all save the most inveterate of gossips. The darkly lovely and well-mannered niece that Carl had fetched from back East was at first cast in the role of nonresident housekeeper, and later as temporary hostess until such time as the General might feel free to marry once more. Most people did not question this arrangement. What with the terrible bloody war spreading ever wider and disrupting more and more lives, families, and fortunes, nobody really cared too much about General Brebner's private life, except for his only brother, Heinrich Dietrich Brebner, and his horse-faced wife, who, having produced a pair of gawky, red-haired nephews, breathed and lived their correct circumscribed beings in Cincinnati, where Heinrich represented skillfully enough the ever-growing interests of Messrs. Brebner, Denton, Levine & Co., wholesale dealers in textiles and hardware, whose army contracts with each passing month were growing ever more lucrative and impressive.

For this time of year, the evening was surprisingly warm, so before she began to write, Kitty absently parted and blew down the front of a diaphanous French negligee Carl had purchased for her only last week. Lord, almost as quickly as she had donned it, he'd been as impatient as a young bridegroom to watch her remove the lovely garment of billowing yellow gauze and parade its fragility by executing a few whirling dance steps.

It was queer, almost macabre, how often dear Carl continued to dwell on his defunct daughter's charms. Later, while lying alone, as always, in her marvelously comfortable bed in "Edelweiss," it occurred to her that perhaps her protector's infatuation for her might be due to the gratification of possible incestous memories.

'4th April 1862

'Deer Dairy,

Forgive me for having negleckted you these last few days but this towne reely is in an uproare. Troupes and ships supplie keep coming and going all the time. Bussiness is booming or so Carl konfides when he cums Home for supper. Always he is tired but not too weary to enjoy A little frolick later on if I am not "off the roof" or "having the flowers," as they describe that affliction in these parts — in Bermuda we call it "Curse of Eave."

Last night my deer Carl informed me that tomorrow he expects the arrival of an Officer from Washington baring big orders for Goods and Supplies beyond all expecktation. This Officer must be on a most important mission for my beloved Carl gave me only a Fatherly kiss and a quick, half-harted tumble before retiring and leaving Roscoe, his black body servant, to eskort me back to my comfortable cottage called 'Edelwise' spelt something like that — down by the Rivers Front.

Kitty paused and pursed full, dark-red lips to lick her pencil's point before continuing her entry.

Ah, deer, deer Carl. I am growing to LOVE and adore you more every day. You are so Genrus and understanding and never ask questions about my family. You are so Fatherly and yet so passionat a bedfelloe you seem like two men in one Body.

Deer Carl always is well mannered, swears by everything Holey he really intends to marry me once the prescribed period of Morning for his late wife comes to an end.

Still I feer and wonder what would happen should my Protector ever discover that this beloved Kitty in truth is but the Bastard daughter of a Gentle-bread Bermuda lady and also that she had a BLACK slave for a grandmother. Thus far, no one has even Suspeckted there is a touch of the tar brush in my blood as they say here in America. I pray my luck holds.

Well, deer Diary — only Time will tell if deer Carl will marry me should he learn the truth. I trust so, for with all my soul I reely and deerly love Carl Brebner — NOT for his wealth but for his unfailing tenerness towards Me, and so goodnite, Deer Dairy.'

45

Assassination?

DAVID SOON DISCOVERED that Carl Brebner, Quartermaster General of U.S. Missouri Volunteers, and his partners, Matthew Denton and Julius Levine, occupied spacious but always busy offices on the second floor of a substantial brick warehouse fronting a wide wharf jutting well out into the Mississippi's swift coffee-colored current.

Discharging freight onto the crowded dock lay a trio of large, sturdily built stern-wheeled freight steamers, whose tall, iron-crowned twin stacks were sending lazy black clouds of smoke curling skyward. On and around these and other boats tied up nearby swarmed roustabouts and black dock workers, loading or discharging an amazing variety of freight wagons, wooden cases, barrels, and bales of all descriptions, besides a significant number of wheeled field guns and caissons.

Along St. Louis's long and teeming waterfront, similar activities were going on, and in the distance could be heard the continuous resounding *clang! clang!* of iron plates being riveted into place, and the dull thudding of mauls driving spikes into wooden timbers.

At a snap guess, David estimated that at least a dozen shipyards were busy in the immediate vicinity. All of this created a deep impression on the emissary from Washington. Lord above! Hereabouts shipbuilding was proceeding at a speed seldom attained, let alone sustained, in the busiest of Eastern yards.

After ascending a flight of gritty, well-worn stairs and encountering a steady stream of messengers, clerks, and other employees headed in opposite directions, he reached the second floor. David paused long enough to check his overcoat's buttons, then straightened a beaked Navy cap and dusted a sadly travel-rumpled dark-blue uniform before a ground-glass door marked "General C. F. Brebner, U.S.V." Above it was affixed a less freshly painted sign, "President's Office." About a hot and smoke-filled waiting room lounged at least two dozen more or less roughly clad individuals.

Once David had knocked, a large, loutish blond youth stuck his head out and brusquely demanded to know this Naval officer's business. Obviously the fellow had become so accustomed to uniforms he wasn't in the least impressed by braid or brass buttons.

"What's yer business with the General?"

"Say 'sir,' you clown, when you address me or any other Regular Navy Officer!"

"Why-why yes, *sir!*" The fellow goggled.

"That's better. Now go inform the General that Lieutenant Dexter, of the Regular Navy, has come direct from Washington to see him on urgent business — and don't you dare to keep me waiting, Buster."

"No, sir! He'll see you just as soon as the General's finished doing business with Mr. Tremayne." The yellow-haired youth ducked his head and retired, hurriedly straightening bright red sleeve garters as he went.

A burly fellow wearing an ill-fitting and well-worn civilian suit surged to his feet, roaring, "Hey, you Navy spit-and-polish! You'll wait yer turn. I've been waiting here a long while. I got . . ."

He got no further, for from the General's office sounded two short, sharp, and flat-sounding reports such as those caused by a double-barreled derringer pocket pistol.

The men awaiting General Brebner's attention stood openmouthed and frozen in ludicrous attitudes, but David plunged toward the office door. Before his hand closed on the knob, the door flew open and a stocky fellow wearing wide mustachios and a pointed goatee burst out, brandishing a still smoking weapon, knocking David sidewise off balance and at the same time pulling out a second nickel-plated derringer.

Eyes glittering, the man bellowed, "Outa my way, unless you want the same as I give that great crook in there, sure's my name's Tremayne!"

Lunging toward this apparition, David ducked just in time to escape a bullet which knocked off his cap and grazed his scalp but drew no blood. Before he could straighten amid blinding clouds of gunsmoke, the assailant kneed him a glancing blow in the groin. No one else made a move while the gun wielder's boots clattered below and ceased to be heard.

Only then did some of the waiting crowd, collecting themselves, produce pistols and Bowie knives with astonishing speed. Only then did they start in pursuit, shouting obscenities. Others, less valiant, merely flung open windows and bellowed for the police. David, meanwhile, staggered into the president's still gunsmoke-dimmed office to find General Brebner's rotund figure collapsed across his desk. His fingers were working spasmodically amid a welter of spilled ink and scattered documents such as invoices, bills of lading, and other printed forms employed by the Government. David flung open a couple of windows. The office boy had vanished and so had various clerks. Some hovered fearfully outside the office door.

"*Nach Hause* — fast — send runner for Doctor Ashdown — "

It was evident that the industrialist had been shot twice in the lower abdomen. Blood was flowing freely through a heavy gold chain draped across a bulging red-and-black grosgrain waistcoat.

"Where d'you live, sir?"

"*Funfzehn*, Goethe Street. *Ach! Mein Gott! Schnell! Schnell!*"

Of the visitors, only one, apparently a real friend of Brebner's, had remained in the outer office. He ran in crying, "You! The Navy feller. Try to staunch the bleeding — you should know how. I'll go fetch the nearest doctor — then get his carriage."

A tumult steadily swelling outside attested that news of the attempt on General Brebner's life was spreading fast.

Slowly, the General's bulbous pale-blue and long-lashed eyes opened, gradually focusing themselves on David. In a surprisingly stronger voice, he wheezed, "*Ach, dot* Tremayne — *ein echte Kerl* — always hot-tempered — greedy — claimed I cheated him — last few contracts — Didn't. I — always — *immer richtig!*"

"Never mind, sir. Where are you hit?"

"Look! In the belly — *mein Freund.*" He made an effort, then again straightening momentarily, spoke more distinctly. "Take me *zu Haus* —

home only — no hospital. *Ach Gott! Der Schmerz ... der Schmertz ist ... unerfräglich!"*

Obviously, the friend who had first appeared had dispatched a swift runner to Brebner's solid and handsome if unimaginative mansion on Goethe Street. By the time the General's glossy carriage rolled up its white-graveled driveway, a group of servants wearing a variety of uniforms stood milling under the portico. A handsomely coiffed, slightly built and olive-complexioned young woman appeared to be the only person present capable of keeping her head and assuming authority.

Once the carriage horses had been pulled to a halt, this young woman rushed forward, face contorted, hoop skirts wildly swaying, crying, "Oh, Carl! My own darling Carl! What has happened to you?"

Over one shoulder as he helped Dr. Ashdown get the wounded man out of the carriage, David snapped at this gracefully moving young female he mistook for a daughter or some other member of the General's immediate family, "Please, Miss. Make those idiot servants stop gibbering and order a small, well-upholstered armchair to be brought out at once!"

Here, at least, the Navy blue and gold of David's uniform commanded respect, and it wasn't long before the groaning, putty-faced master of the house was placed in an armchair and carried upstairs to a huge bedroom dominated by a handsome fourposter. There Doctor Ashdown, impressive in his white square-cut beard and square-lensed, gold-rimmed spectacles, snapped to the girl who obviously was no stranger to him, "Kitty, I want plenty of clean hand towels, a pot of near boiling hot water, and a lot of bandages if there are any; otherwise tear a clean sheet in long strips. But first, send these useless servants away."

While unpacking a battered black bag, over one shoulder he cast a glance at David. "And who might you be?"

"Lieutenant David Dexter."

"Why have you taken charge?"

"No one else seemed capable and I was there when the General was shot."

David went on as briskly as though he were on a quarterdeck, "Only yesterday I arrived from the East, so I haven't the least idea what lies back of this business. I only chanced to be in the General's waiting room on official business when he got shot twice by some fellow who called himself Tremayne, and for good luck fired at me while he fled. My cap and a few singed hairs were the only casualties."

The doctor nodded toward the young woman who was sobbing beside the now unconscious General. "Mr. Dexter, isn't it?"

"Yes, sir."

"This is Kitty Hamilton, the General's very capable housekeeper, and please don't get any wrong impressions about her position in this household. Miss Hamilton is as fine and capable a young woman as I ever encountered."

"I shan't. Please go on, sir."

While snipping off the wounded man's sodden shirt and undervest, the doctor continued, "All of us close friends and most other people agree that Miss Hamilton, to an incredible degree, resembles the General's late daughter, Hildegarde."

Doctor Ashdown applied clean pledgets to the ugly still-welling holes in Brebner's rotund but nearly hairless belly and expertly bandaged them into position. "Now, Lieutenant, or is it Mister — ?"

"Only on shipboard or on duty are we referred to as Mister."

"Very well, Lieutenant, please help me turn the patient on to his side, then if Miss Hamilton will bring a fresh nightgown and leave the room, we will get the patient completely undressed and so render him more comfortable until . . ." Gold-rimmed spectacles flashing, Doctor Ashdown momentarily averted his gaze.

" 'Til?" David prompted when Kitty, ignoring them, rushed in bringing with her an aura of delicate fragrance, and bent low over the bed.

"Until? And you a Navy officer! Ever hear of a gut-shot casualty recovering? All I or any of my profession can do is to administer sufficient laudanum to ease such a patient's passing."

"Oh-h! But Doctor Ashdown! Carl — I mean the General — simply can't leave us," gasped Kitty, dark eyes overflowing. "He's the best — the kindest man that ever was."

But Brigadier General Brebner never recovered consciousness. He died late that evening, after whispering only loudly enough for Kitty and David to hear (the elderly doctor had gone for a rest in an adjoining room), "Never forget, *Liebchen* — deed to Edelweiss — registered — *your* name — and two hundred — month till — till — you find some man you can make happy — as me. *Auf wiedersehen* —" he muttered, and departed into eternity.

David noted Kitty's sincere tenderness. No trace of false sentiment was visible in this handsome young woman with the gleaming gold-brown hair who crouched at the great bed's side, emitting deep, heartrending wails which held a curious eerie foreign pitch.

Doctor Ashdown had closed the dead man's eyelids and, collecting his instruments, said kindly, "Should the strain prove too great, my dear Kitty, just send me a message and I'll send you something to tide you over the worst of your grief." He bowed to David. "Good night, Lieutenant, and thank you for your able assistance."

Suddenly, Kitty swayed to her feet and raised tear-streaked features, staring at the blue-clad officer as though he represented the only element of stability at what was undoubtedly the most ghastly hour in her distinctly checkered career.

"Just tell me, Miss Hamilton, what d'*you* think should be done — right away, that is?"

"Tell you soon," Kitty sniffled, then sought the door and called in a choking voice, "Claudius! Come up here! Tell Bella to find a length of black cloth — any sort will do — and to hang it on the door knocker."

Claudius, the General's dignified butler, answered, "Yes, M-Miz Kitty, ah means. Ah'll do that straight away! Anythin' else?"

"Oh yes! Don't admit no one who's not on official business — police, doctors, the coroner, and military officers."

"Yes'm, Miz Kitty."

As if to bear out her instructions, a hubbub arose below and a loud, gravelly voice Kitty at once recognized as belonging to Matthew Denton, the murdered man's older partner, spouting curses, came pounding upstairs to, as he announced, "take over." He stared blankly at David, whose face remained still slightly black, speckled by the derringer's blast.

"Who the hell are you? What're you doin' here?" he panted.

Self-controlled, David explained to this overbearing fellow the circumstances of his presence, also the necessity of his immediate departure tomorrow in compliance with War Department orders.

Ignoring Denton, Kitty ran to his side, "Please, please, Mr. Dexter! Don't go *now*. I-I need you — you're so dependable!"

"Sorry, Miss Hamilton." He stood very straight but his voice wasn't so steady. "I have no choice but to leave St. Louis tomorrow on the first boat going downriver."

By now Kitty had learned the inviolability of such commands.

Using fingers to comb still singed and rumpled hair, David assumed his quarterdeck attitude. "Mr. Denton, does the General have close family residing in St. Louis, or nearby?"

Denton, still breathing hard and mopping a huge, domed and shiny pink brow, replied in a much less aggressive tone. "No, not that I know of. Carl has — had — many real and loyal friends in this part of the country, but as for immediate family, all I know for certain is that he has a younger brother, Heinrich Dietrich, who lives in Cincinnati and has very capably managed our firm's interests out there for a long time. I've hardly met the fellow except when he came to attend the General's wife's funeral."

"What about him?"

The partner looked unhappy. "I found Heinrich to be, at best, a nosy type. He was — damned suspicious of," his eyes shifted in Kitty's direction, "of Miss Hamilton's status. However, he and his wife eased up a bit on learning that Carl hadn't mentioned Miss Hamilton in his will, but they took it with ill grace when they found out that in a separate deed, he gave Miss Hamilton a cottage for her own, outright, together with a modest yearly income until she should marry."

"I think I begin to understand," David said. "And how did Mr. Brebner digest that?"

"Sourly. I hope his deed of gift was well drawn — foolproof."

Denton rearranged a gray silk cravat, and then ran nervous, slim fingers through his thinning gray hair. "Yessir, Carl sure doted on her, and to tell the truth, Miss Kitty did — does — so resemble my partner's daughter, Hildegarde, dead now, that it's uncanny."

Even under the circumstances, for David to devote renewed attention to Kitty Hamilton was natural. Even with lustrous and naturally curly golden-brown hair, blue-green eyes, and short, straight nose, hers was a quiet and not a flagrant quality of beauty. Furthermore, she moved with unaffected grace. It was Kitty Hamilton's complexion which most intrigued David, however. It was just a shade coppery under what might be a deep tan. But then, there was also a trace of some faintly unfamiliar inflection in her speech which seemed familiar. Where had he heard it before? Where?

46

The Western Flotilla

IT WAS THE IMAGE of Kitty Hamilton that remained in David Dexter's mind on the morning the steamer *Cincinnati Queen* slipped away into the muddy, rolling waters of the Mississippi, her prow cleaving the river in the direction of Cairo. Try as he might, and he felt no compelling reason to do so, he could not get out of his thoughts the slim perfection of her figure, the way the light glinted in her golden-brown hair, even the enchanting mole lying beside her left eye.

He would never forget that last evening with her, the night before. Distraught as she was, she had somehow contrived to gain control of herself, to thank the General's partner, Matthew Denton, for coming so quickly to her aid, overlooking with quiet dignity his aggressive arrival in the bedroom where her protector, Brigadier General Carl Brebner, now lay in the waxen stillness of death.

With a sudden new calm, she had ushered Denton and David out of the room, closing the door quietly with a quick backward look at the still form on the bed. To Denton, she said, "You can be of most service to me, Mr. Denton, if you will, by making arrangements for the funeral. I'm sure you know the General's wishes in the matter. He once told me there were full instructions in his will. But I shall leave it to you, with my grateful thanks. I will take care of matters here, and you may find me at Edelweiss tomorrow if you wish to consult with me about details." There was a quiet determination in her voice that told both men Kitty Hamilton was the mistress of herself as well as the house.

Denton recognized that tone, and said respectfully, "Don't worry, Miss Hamilton, I'll take care of all the details, and I'll call on you tomorrow afternoon to discuss the arrangements." Turning to David, he added, "I hope you'll forgive the way I busted in on you today. I was considerable upset, as you can imagine." He paused. "The General was a fine man. We had our differences, but I'll miss him. I'm glad you were here today, Lieutenant, and I wish you could stay longer."

"Thank you, Mr. Denton," David said. "I was happy to be of service to Miss Hamilton, and I wish I could do more, but I have my orders."

"We all have our orders, don't we," Denton said sententiously. They shook hands, and the late General's partner hurried off, leaving Kitty and David alone together.

As they moved slowly toward the door, David was acutely conscious of her presence beside him, the feminine smell of her, and the way she seemed to lean toward him.

"I must ask a favor of you, Mr. Dexter," she said, pausing, her blue-green eyes heavy with the tears still unshed. He looked down into those eyes and felt that it would be difficult, perhaps impossible, to refuse her anything she might ask.

"If it's within my power, I'll be more than happy to grant it," he told her, trying to keep a rush of emotion from his voice.

Kitty essayed a little smile that curved her lips briefly. "I believe it is not beyond your powers," she said. "Would you come back this evening to Edelweiss, the cottage nearby where I live, and have supper with me? I-I know I have no right to ask so much of your time, especially when you must leave tomorrow — and to ask it of someone who was a stranger to me until today . . ." She broke off, biting her lip. "Nevertheless, I have the courage to ask just a little more of your presence, Lieutenant. I-I can't explain it, but it seemed to me today that you were the only human being in the world I could rely on. Your strength has given *me* strength in this terrible hour, and I need, so much, a little more of it to prepare me for the next few days, especially when I know I must face them without you."

David could hardly speak for the emotions that surged inside him, but he managed to say, "It would give me the greatest pleasure to be with you tonight, Miss Hamilton," he said. "No man could be more complimented than I by your confidence in me. I hope I will never do anything that might cause you to think it misplaced."

He held the slim, white hand she extended to him — for such a lengthy time, unaware of what he was doing, that when he realized how long those lovely fingers had lain against his own, be blushed and dropped them abruptly. She lowered her eyes and he imagined — could it possibly be? — an answering blush on those slightly coppery looking cheeks. "Until tonight, then, about eight." Again he heard the strange, lilting cadence in that voice.

David had parted from her then, his head whirling from the events of the day. In a few hours, he thought incredulously, I have seen a man killed and have fallen in love with a woman who may have been his mistress. Yes, there was no use in denying it. Kitty Hamilton had completely conquered him in the space of an hour or two, and unbelievably, it had happened at a moment when the terrible event in which he had played so unexpected a part must surely in any ordinary situation have completely excluded any other emotion than the most penetrating grief on the part of Kitty, and no more than pity from him.

As he put together his gear in preparation for the trip to Cairo, David could not help himself from speculating. He could understand his own reaction well enough. It was simply that he had met the woman, possibly the only one he might ever see, who could erase from his mind the still warm and tender memory of his lost fiancée, Louisa Ridgely. He had believed that would never be possible, but then he had not seen Kitty's golden beauty, and even though he had seen it in a moment of terror and agony, nothing could diminish the response that had overwhelmed him.

He flattered himself that, even as distraught as she was, Kitty had felt it too, otherwise how to account for that unmistakable blush as they parted with lingering hands. But how could it be — a woman who had just lost her close companion in the most terrible of circumstances, giving any thought, especially of so intimate a nature, to another man? David knew nothing of the circumstances of this relationship which had ended so tragically, but there was reason enough to suspect it was not a usual one. There was the obvious great distance in their ages, and then Denton had talked of Kitty's resemblance to the General's dead daughter. It was not likely she had been only the General's housekeeper, but he burned to know more about it — to know more of Kitty.

She told him that night, or at least enough to confirm his suspicions. In the glow of the candlelight which reflected softly off the linen in her simple dining room and lit her eyes with pale flecks of light, a sight from which David could not avert his own eyes, Kitty began to tell him something of her life in a calm, controlled voice.

She did not tell him everything, of course. And what if I did? Kitty wondered. If she told this tall, handsome young Lieutenant who had come to mean so much to her in a few hours, told him that she was really a quadroon, a Bermudian who had fled the Island in the company of desperate characters and ended as a — well, not exactly a whore. Kitty could never bring herself to think of her time with Mrs. Markham as anything so crude. It had all been discreet, in such good taste, and the gentlemen callers had never been anything less than gentlemen. Still, she doubted whether Lieutenant Dexter would understand and she did not intend to test him. If he came from a good family (she was certain he did), he might be repelled by such a story and she would never see him again. Already, although she could scarcely believe it, that was a prospect she could not face. It would be harder to endure, she had to admit, than life without dear Carl.

Discreetly, then, Kitty did not speak of her early life in Bermuda, nor of her escape from the Island, nor of Mrs. Markham's establishment, except to say that she had met the General at a party in the home of a dear friend, which was true enough.

"You heard Mr. Denton say that I greatly resembled Carl's daughter Hildegarde, who had died not long before," Kitty said, in a voice so low David had to strain to hear. "It would be foolish of me to deny that this was why he was so attracted to me, and why he insisted on bringing me out here as his housekeeper. His wife had recently died, and he meant to marry me as soon as he decently could."

"And would you have married him?" David could not help asking.

"Yes," Kitty said evenly, "I would have married him because I owed everything to him. I had no money and nowhere to go when he met me, and when he brought me here, he gave me all the love and consideration a woman could ask."

David leaned forward. He simply couldn't restrain the question: "And all this time he treated you as — as a daughter?"

For just a moment Kitty considered. Should she tell him the truth, or at least an honest part of it? Something told her that if she lied now, she would live to regret it.

"I was his housekeeper as far as the world was concerned, and his hostess as well when he entertained. How much he may have confused poor Hildegarde and me in his mind, I don't know, and neither does any mortal man or woman. But in private, he treated me as a wife he couldn't wait to marry, and I loved him for it. It wasn't the kind of love I always thought I'd feel for a man I meant to marry, but I loved him all the same." Kitty ended defiantly, her chin up, eyes proud and serene.

David averted his head. "I had no right to ask you such a question, Miss Hamilton," he said. "My profound apologies to you."

"But you *did* ask it, Mr. Dexter," Kitty said softly. "Why did you?"

It was David's turn to consider whether the truth should be told. He hadn't really sorted out his feelings, but there was something driving him now, and it was the same kind of force that had made Miss Louisa Ridgely the center of his life for so long. His hesitation was only momentary.

"I had to know everything about you that I could discover, Miss Hamilton," he burst out. "I-I know it will be impossible for you to understand how such a thing could happen, but from the first time I saw you today — I can scarcely believe it was only today — I have been able to think of nothing or no one else but you. Please try to forgive me for saying these things at such a time — believe me, I'm shocked to hear myself saying them. But I also had such a loss as yours, and today, for the first time since then, I could feel that another life was possible for me." He put his head in his hands despairingly. "How can I talk to you like this — so selfishly, when I know what you must be feeling tonight."

Kitty put out a slim hand and touched his arm lightly. "You speak from honest feelings, and I prize that more than anything," she said. "Will you tell me something about — your loss?"

"It was my fiancée, and I loved her as you loved the General — no, more, because she *was* the woman I had always dreamed of marrying."

David went on to describe how he had met Louisa, how he had thought her lost to him, and before he knew it, he was pouring out the whole story of his confusion over loyalties, and of his discovery at last that Louisa had died. Through it all he was conscious of Kitty's lovely blue-green eyes fixed on him, at first with an innocent wonder, and then with something coming into them that he thought at first must be pity and sympathy. But it was more than that, he could see. She was looking at him with the same intense fascination that he had been regarding her, and there was a warmth in her eyes quite beyond what his story demanded.

He stopped at last. "There's nothing more to tell, until I met you today. I say to you again, Miss Hamilton, I cannot believe all that has happened since I opened my eyes this morning. Do you understand anything, or believe anything, that I have been telling you?"

Kitty nodded, and now there were tears again in her eyes. "I understand and believe everything," she said, "because of what my heart tells me." She lowered her eyes and her breath came quickly. "I have no more right to say what I'm saying than you do — and I mean no disrespect to dear Carl's memory, but when you told me that today you felt another life was possible for you — well, that is how I've been feeling tonight."

Abruptly, David was overcome by the intensity of his feelings. He took Kitty's hands in his and drew her slightly toward him, her body moving with a kind of breathless expectancy.

"This is no time for me to declare my intentions, Miss Hamilton — Kitty, if I may. But when your affairs are in order, I will return and ask your permission to declare them."

"You will have it," Kitty breathed, "and you may be sure I will listen."

He gripped her hands tightly and held them against him, white on the blue of his uniform. "You understand that I am under orders, and it may well be that when I get to Cairo, I'll find myself about to go into battle. I may not return. You understand that." She nodded, her eyes wide and her face close to his. "That's why I have the courage to tell you now that I love you, and at the first moment it's possible, I mean to marry you — if you'll have me."

"David — David . . ." Her voice was so full of emotion that she could not speak for a moment. "I can't believe something like this could be — to have happened so fast. I feel so disloyal to poor dear Carl. But I can't help it, David, I *do* love you, and when you ask me, you can be sure of the answer I'll give you."

At last her full red lips lay against his, and he could feel the rapid rise and fall of her breasts against his body, and the tautness of her legs against his own. They broke apart, and he held her hands while they spoke for a time in low voices, passionately, endearingly, until it was time for him to go.

As they walked to the door, his arm around her, David said, "I'll come back to you at the first moment I can. When that will be, I don't know. And I don't even know where I'll be, so that you can write. Please be patient and wait for me, Kitty darling."

"Yes, yes, I'll be as patient as ever I can, David. God keep you safe for me."

They held each other tightly again for a moment, and he was gone.

Standing on the deck of the *Cincinnati Queen,* watching the nondescript wooden structures of St. Louis slipping away from him, David relived those last moments again, still scarcely believing what had happened to him. One doubt gnawed away. He remembered what Matthew Denton had told him, how the General had given Kitty the title to her handsome little cottage, Edelweiss, and a respectable sum of money, both to be hers until she married. Could he ask her to give up all this for the kind of precarious life that lay ahead of him? If he was lucky enough to be alive when the war ended, could he go back to New York and begin again? How he was still regarded there, he didn't know. Did people think of him as a man who turned his coat? His father knew the truth, thank God, but would he ever be accepted again? The future stretched ahead of him as mistily as the great river, from which the morning moisture was ascending in long, vaporous clouds.

Back at Edelweiss, where Kitty was preparing for the General's funeral, there were doubts too. Still glowing from her newly discovered love, in bittersweet contrast to the mournful ordeal before her, Kitty could not help wondering what would happen when David came back to claim her, as she was certain he would — surely God would not let him die now, when they had found each other. She would have to tell him that she had a black grandmother and a mulatto mother, and only by the luck of inheritance did she look like her blue-eyed, white father. She must tell him, too, about her escape, even about Adah Markham's house. If she didn't, Kitty thought, she would always live in terror that they would meet someone from her past who knew the truth, and everything she had hoped for, embodied in the person of David Dexter, would be lost. For now, there was nothing to do but await his return, and although Kitty had never been a particularly devout woman, she now spent every night on her knees before she climbed into bed, praying for her Lieutenant, wherever he was sleeping.

But as the *Cincinnati Queen* approached the docks at Cairo, David was thinking less of Kitty than of what lay before him immediately, and he would soon know what that might be. His new assignment would have to wait until morning, however. It was well into the evening before the hawsers of the *Queen* were safely wrapped around the capstans and David stepped off into the busy dockside of Cairo, his gear slung over his shoulder.

The dock was ablaze with lanterns, both moving and stationary, and alive with the movement of men, loading and unloading ships. Cairo was now the naval station for all the Federal gunboats on the river, and they had to put in here for supplies and repairs. The station was so crowded that ships had to line up for the work to be done on them, and some had to be repaired while they were afloat since there was no room for them on land. Peering about, David could see that a veritable forest of vessels clogged the waterside as far as the lanterns stretched — old steamers, wharf boats, tugs, flat-boats, rafts, and small craft converted into gunboats.

There would be time enough to examine all this in the morning, he thought, when he came down to report for duty. For now he needed a place to lay his head and recoup his strength for the morrow.

"Say, there, beg your pardon," he hailed a seaman passing by, dragging a coil of rope behind him, "d'you know if there's a hotel anywhere nearby?"

The seaman took in David's officer's uniform with a quick glance of his sharp eyes, but he showed no particular respect for it.

"There's the Cairo House just up the street there, and that's it. There ain't nothin' better, and a couple that's worse."

It was on the tip of David's tongue to say, "Is that the way you talk to an officer," but he caught himself. In this rough town, hectic and jammed with the men and machines to make war, and the enemy not far away, the distinctions of Washington and the East somehow didn't seem so important. "Thank you," he said curtly, and strode off up the street.

The Cairo House was not hard to find. It was on a main street thronged with all kinds of people even at this hour of the night — sailors, soldiers, civilians, men and women of every kind. Some were drunk, others hurrying along on private errands, and from them rose a babble of voices, crying out, importuning, yelling, or just conversing as everyone strove to keep clear of the carts and wagons moving noisily along the muddy thoroughfare, the horses straining under the whips of the teamsters.

David pushed his way into the lobby of the three-story wooden building, which was also crowded with men talking together, and a few women, some of them plainly night ladies seeking customers.

"We've got one room left in the house," the clerk told him. "Take it or leave it, mister."

Another time David might have resented this renewed lack of respect for the uniform, considering that he was about to risk his life to protect this man and the other inhabitants from the Confederates just down the river, but again he held his tongue. He was in no mood for an argument; he wanted only to stretch out, collect his thoughts, and renew his energies.

As he walked across the lobby, room key in pocket, a familiar voice hailed him: "I say there, Lieutenant Dexter!"

Turning, David beheld the lanky figure of Lionel Humphrey, red-faced as ever, his drooping blond mustachios and yellow side-whiskers framing a wide smile of greeting. In these drab surroundings, hemmed in by rude characters, Lionel's stylish clothes and aristocratic manner made him stand out more than ever, as though he had just stepped from the offices of his London *Telegraph* into a street crowd.

"I'm delighted to see you, old chap," Lionel said, seizing David's hand enthusiastically. "I had no idea of finding you here. Thought you must be in St. Louis."

"I was until the steamer brought me down just now," David told him, returning the correspondent's greeting with as much enthusiasm as he could muster. He was, in fact, glad to see a familiar face. "I thought *you'd* be at the front, wherever that may be."

"I *have* been at the front, Lieutenant, and I've seen things I never expected to see in this war." He gave David an odd glance. "I also have news you may not have heard, and it's best I tell it to you over a drink." He hesitated. "I see you've just arrived. Why don't you meet me in the saloon next door when you've stowed away your gear — say, in about twenty minutes?"

David would have refused from sheer weariness, but there was something in the tone of Lionel's voice when he mentioned the "news" he had to tell that aroused the young Lieutenant's curiosity, and somehow sent a little shiver of apprehension down his spine. He decided quickly that he must hear whatever the correspondent had to tell him. "Thank you, I'll be right along then," he agreed.

A half-hour later as they settled down over their whiskey in the saloon next door (another crowded, noisy, smoke-filled place), Lionel Humphrey seemed strangely reluctant to impart the news he had mentioned, regaling David with irrelevant observations about the problems of the correspondents in covering the war in this tumultuous frontier.

"I'm much interested in the news you have to tell me, Mr. Humphrey," David broke in somewhat impatiently, as soon as he decently could.

"Ah, yes, I mustn't delay any longer," Lionel agreed. His long, rugged features were suddenly less animated, settling into what David, puzzled, could only think of as melancholy. "Have you heard recently from you friend, Lieutenant Thatcher?" he inquired, staring intently at David.

"Never a word since I've been out here," David said. "I don't even know where he was assigned." Again he felt the ominous chill down his spine. "Have you seen him? Do you have any word of him?"

Lionel was not looking at him now, but seemed to be regarding the table with absorbed interest as he went on. "Yes, I've seen him, and it's lucky indeed I found you tonight because it's likely nobody else would be able to tell you the news about him as I can do it." He paused.

"I must tell you this much first. As you may or may not know, the Union river fleet came into being late last year and early this year as the result of a contract made between the Government and a man named James B. Eads, of St. Louis, who built seven ironclad steamers. One of them was a ship named the *Carondelet;* she looked a bit like that cheesebox on a raft you knew so well in Hampton Roads. Her commander was a remarkable man named Henry Walke, and it was to him that your friend Lieutenant Thatcher was ordered to report."

"Ira was on the *Carondelet?*" David exclaimed, and a powerful apprehension began to seize him, like a slow paralysis. He had heard tangled reports in St. Louis about that ironclad and her sister ships and what had happened to them scarcely two months before. The newspapers had carried incomplete accounts, but enough to alarm David now. "Did you see the action at Island No. 10?" he demanded

"Saw it, indeed," Humphrey said, raising his eyes again. "I was lucky enough to be on that gallant ship last April, with your friend Ira. Permit me to tell you what happened, Lieutenant."

Ira could smell danger in the air when he joined Commander Walke's staff on the *Carondelet*. At the first meeting of staff officers he attended after he came aboard, Walke had been blunt about it. His long, thin face, chin ending in a rather wispy goatee, and high forehead rising bald above his thick eyebrows, seemed more gaunt than ever as he explained their situation.

"Gentlemen," he said, "as you know, General Polk has moved to Island No. 10 with a hundred and thirty of his big rebel guns. Here they are." He unfolded a large map, and the staff bent to peer over his shoulders. "On the upper bend of this big double curve in the Mississippi, just about forty miles below Columbus, Kentucky. General Beauregard had already fortified this place before Polk got there, and the Rebels think it's strong enough to stop anything we've got from going any farther south. We think otherwise. Now here's the town of New Madrid, on the Missouri side. The Rebels held that with heavy guns and breastworks until last month, when General Pope and our fellow Unionmen took it.

"What does all this mean, gentlemen? It means that we've got Island No. 10 isolated. Our gunboats are above it, and General Pope's men are below it along the Missouri shore. Nothing but impenetrable swamp to the east, and as you know, Pope had occupied New Madrid. There is only one escape route for the Rebel troops, and that is this road here," he drew a long finger down the map, "which runs south to Tiptonville. If we can secure that road, there will be nothing for Island No. 10 to do but surrender. There are a number of batteries guarding that road, however, and *they* are the problem, gentlemen. Our flotilla commander, Commodore Foote, has come here this morning to explain it to you further."

Commodore Andrew H. Foote rose to speak, his bearded face rising out of powerful shoulders as he stretched his substantial frame. Ira regarded him with respect. Foote, soon to be a Rear Admiral, was already a legend in the Navy, known to many as the Stonewall Jackson of the West. His reputation had been established years before in Far Eastern waters, and he was well known for his fierce efforts to suppress the slave trade. Like that other Stonewall, he was a deeply religious man who was known to preach in churches wherever he happened to be; he had done so in Cairo after the fall of Fort Henry. He was already an old man, and an ill one besides; Ira could see that in the pallor of his face, with its sharply etched lines. In another year, he would be dead.

"I have a solemn duty, gentlemen," Commodore Foote began, his voice sounding old and tired. "As your commander, I have the power to order you on an important mission that could well mean the destruction of this ship and the others in our little fleet. God alone knows our chances, and in that respect we must put our faith in Him. But I cannot bring myself to force you into so perilous a situation. General Pope believes it's possible for our fleet of gunboats to run the gauntlet of Island No. 10's batteries. I do not. We know there are at least fifty cannon guarding the passage, and it is my opinion that an attempt to run them would be suicidal. I am here to ask *your* opinions, and I will poll you one by one."

The commanders of the ironclad gunboats were all present, and Foote turned to each of them in turn. From the bearded lips of all these men — the chief officers of the *Benton*, the *St. Louis*, the *Cincinnati*, the *Pittsburgh*, and the *Mound City* — came the short, terse verdict; in various ways, they said, "We agree with you, Commodore." Walke was last. When Foote turned questioningly to him, the voice of the *Carondelet*'s commander was firm and clear: "I believe we can do it, sir. In my opinion, it's worth the chance."

Foote hesitated, obviously taken aback. A certain shrewdness came into his eyes as the others almost literally held their breaths for a moment, waiting for him to speak. "Would you be willing to try it with your vessel alone?" he asked at last.

"Yes," Walke agreed without hesitation.

Again there was a breathless pause as the two commanders confronted each other.

"Very well, then," Foote agreed at last. "You are to be commended for your courage, Captain Walke. I hope you won't live to regret your decision. We'll discuss the details this afternoon. That's all for this morning."

As the meeting ended in a rumble of voices, the ships' officers drifting off in excited groups, Walke said to Ira, "Report to me in an hour, Lieutenant, for further orders."

Ira was in a high state of excitement as he tried to keep himself busy during that hour. I'm going to see real action! was the thought that kept racing through his mind. The broad conflict between *Monitor* and *Merrimac* might pale before this concentrated act of sheer daring. A surge of pride welled up in him, to be a part of this ship that was daring to go where the others refused to venture, and to be under the command of such a hero as Walke. Ira realized, as he viewed the coming ordeal, that he was committed to a venture that might end in his death. But, he thought grimly, my prospects for a happy civilian life are none too good if I'm lucky enough to survive the war. What woman would want a man who couldn't give her children? Far better, if that was his fate, to go in a burst of glory, doing his duty for the cause he was sworn to support. His father would have understood that.

When he reported to the Captain's cabin, he found Walke operating with the cold, brisk efficiency for which he was well known in the service.

"Lieutenant, you've had some experience with ironclads in Hampton Roads, I believe, isn't that true?" said this craggy-faced Captain as his blue eyes surveyed Ira with keen calculation.

"Yes, sir," Ira said, "I was Second Assistant Engineer on the *Monitor* in the action we undertook against the *Virginia*."

"Good. I'm relying on your experience to help us prepare for running the batteries at Island No. 10." He glanced quizzically at Ira. "You have no qualms about my decision, do you?"

"Oh no, sir," Ira assured him, with more passion than he intended. "I believe we can do it, sir, and do it well."

A thin smile appeared on Walke's taut lips. "You and I may be in the minority on that point, Lieutenant, but I'm happy to know you're with me. Now, I want to place you in charge of preparing the ship for our run. She must be well protected, as well as we can possibly make her. Sit down with me and let's discuss the problem."

That was the beginning of a week of tireless effort on the part of Ira and the *Carondelet*'s crew to make their squat, almost ungainly craft ready for its hazardous mission. To Ira, she looked like a large rectangular raft with an upside-down box rising from her waterline, and a rather makeshift superstructure thrusting up squarely from it, distinguished by parallel smokestacks forward. To protect her for the run, Captain Walke and Ira had devised an elaborate plan, which the young Lieutenant now began to carry out.

Around the exposed pilothouse and other parts of the vessel that seemed vulnerable, large chains, hawsers, and cables were wrapped. On the side where the ship's iron ended, leaving the magazine dangerously open to gunfire, a coal barge heavily loaded with coal and hay was brought up and lashed firmly; it seemed dense enough to absorb a cannonball — but who could tell?

The smokestacks presented a difficulty at first. If the puffing of the engines, usually clearly audible through the smokestack, were permitted to be heard as usual, there was no chance of approaching the batteries without being discovered well in advance; consequently, the steam escape was directed through the wheelhouse and out the other side. Captain Walke ordered arms issued to the seamen so they would be able to resist boarding parties — if the Rebels got that close — and a special detail of sharpshooters was deployed at strategic points on the ship.

While all this was being brought into place on the *Carondelet*'s busy deck and interior, Ira one morning heard a well-remembered voice hailing him.

"I say, old chap, you do remember me, don't you?"

Ira turned quickly to see with surprise (as David was to do later in Cairo) the lanky figure and long-nosed countenance of Lionel Humphrey.

"Mr. Humphrey! I'm certainly surprised to see you here." Lionel grinned, showing his equine, slightly yellowing teeth. "We newspaper chaps are likely to turn up anywhere, you know. I have a letter to yur Captain from his superior, Mr. Foote, introducing me. Where will I find him?"

"His cabin's there," Ira said, pointing. "You aren't planning to stay aboard, are you?"

"That's my intention," Lionel said cheerfully.

Ira was about to say, They'll never permit you to do that now, when he caught himself. It wasn't his decision to make. "You'll have to speak to Captain Walke about that," he said. "But come and talk with me when you're through with him."

Less than a half-hour later, the correspondent emerged from the Captain's cabin, wearing a broad smile.

"I'm sorry, old fellow," he observed to Ira, "I'm not only going to stay aboard, but I'm afraid you'll have to put up with me yourself. The Captain has placed me in your charge."

"He *did?*" Ira exclaimed incredulously. "Did he tell you what we're getting ready to do?"

"I'd already heard about that from my interview with Captain Foote, and I came with his permission in hand to be the only correspondent aboard when you go down the river, if your commander approved. He has."

"I can't protect you from being killed," Ira protested. "The Captain doesn't expect me to do that, does he?"

The Englishman laughed his booming, hearty laugh, which Ira had first heard in Bermuda so long ago, and replied, "He certainly wouldn't give you such an unheard-of responsibility, Mr. Thatcher, and I wouldn't expect it. No, he merely instructs you to answer any reasonable questions I might have, and to tell me where to stay out of the way if there's trouble."

"There'll be trouble, all right, Mr. Humphrey, don't worry about that," Ira said, unable to respond to the Englishman's customary good spirits. "You can be sure, though, I'll do all in my power to help such an old friend as you."

"God bless you," Lionel responded heartily. "I won't try your patience, Lieutenant, any more than I have to."

He had kept his word on that score, Ira thought later. As the hours and days passed, in an atmosphere of increasing tension, the London *Telegraph*'s able correspondent stayed out of the way, asked a few questions from time to time, and mostly observed the feverish preparations in which everyone was now engaged.

The time for the *Carondelet*'s dash through the Rebel gauntlet had been carefully chosen for the night of 4 April. Everything was in order by late afternoon of that day. The men had been thoroughly briefed on what to expect and what they might be called upon to do. After the sun slipped down into a heavy bank of clouds, the order was given to start engines, and the *Carondelet,* steam up, backed quietly away from shore, swung slowly around, and pointed downstream. In the gathering darkness, Ira could see from his position on deck the tall, gaunt figure of Captain Walke, silhouetted in the wheelhouse. Lionel had chosen a position where he was surrounded by bulky coils of cable and other heavy impedimenta, out of the way and presumably safe from cannonballs.

It was a close, still night, very warm for early April even in those latitudes, and the moon, riding high, soon disappeared in gathering clouds. Ira was suddenly conscious of Lionel at his elbow. "A dark night, Lieutenant," the correspondent remarked.

"Just right for our purposes," Ira said, "and I believe a storm may be making up. I can smell the rain coming. That should help too."

As though to substantiate his words, a distant mutter of thunder trembled in the breathless night air, and a far-off pulse of lightning beat in the gathering clouds.

Shortly after ten o'clock, the command came: "Half-speed ahead." Slowly the bulky ship, bound around with its many protections against the Rebel cannon, began to slide down the river, into a night that by this time was impenetrably, densely black, save for intermittent flashes of lightning on the horizon.

As the ship moved more rapidly through the water, now traveling at full speed, Ira strained to see some identifying mark on the shore, but he could discern nothing. He had no idea how the veteran pilot who had been brought aboard that morning could guide them. A puff of wind stirred the canvas wrappings on deck, like a long sigh in the dark, and a heavy rumble of thunder sounded straight ahead, where the sky suddenly split with a vivid, vertical bolt of lightning. Damn it! Ira thought, if we're going to have a real storm, that lightning will give us away. The batteries on the Island would be sure to see them. The storm swept down on the *Carondelet* with fury, and Ira saw that, indeed, there would be no hope of secrecy. The whole sky was lit with almost constant flashes of lightning, and the shore stood out in sharp relief; Ira was sure the defenders of Island No. 10 would have no difficulty in seeing the ship's bulky silhouette, tossing about on the substantial waves that were now undulating and slapping over the low deck.

For a few more minutes the gunboat steamed ahead, all eyes aboard her trained apprehensively toward the shore. Then a dull boom could be heard above the roar of the storm, and a flash of light on the shore, which even Nature's artillery could not dim, confirmed that they had been discovered. A soughing whistle above the ship marked the passage of the first shot from the Island's batteries. The other cannon erupted instantly, and the *Carondelet* was soon moving through a curtain of artillery fire and the night was fragmented with light from above and below. Mingled with it was the glow from burning powder, as the *Carondelet*'s gunners responded to the order from Captain Walke, "Fire when ready!"

That brave and determined Commander had described his bulky craft earlier in the day as looking "just like a farmer's wagon," with all the improvised protection girdling her, but Ira could see that it wasn't the coal barge with its cargo or the chains and hawsers that were protecting the ship from the fury of the Island's batteries. He was aware that the fire from shore was whistling harmlessly overhead, and realized, with the knowledge he had gained both at the Academy and elsewhere, that the *Carondelet* must be running so close to the Island that the gunners could not depress their pieces low enough to get her into range.

The ship's gunners were under no such handicap. They could see the fort plainly enough now, and their pieces were concentrated on it, spreading a curtain of fire and death. Some of the shore cannon were still firing as the *Carondelet* moved just beyond the fort, but it was clear that many of Island No. 10's guns were already silenced.

A subdued cheer went up from the crewmen as they understood that they had not only run the gauntlet but disabled the fort as well. Lionel appeared from his shelter and began to move across the deck toward Ira. "You've done it, old boy," he shouted against the uproar of sound that still prevailed. At that moment, one of the last shells from shore, falling short in what was now a long trajectory, whistled toward the ship and disintegrated directly above it, having been faultily made by harassed Confederate suppliers. The fragments rained down on the deck in devastating iron splinters. Cries of anguish suddenly rose from the part of the ship where the fall was heaviest, testifying that this last desperate thrust had done some damage.

Lionel plunged forward to the deck, and lifting his head a moment later, saw the tall figure of Ira staggering drunkenly toward him. The young Lieutenant was holding his hands against his face, but they were not enough to stem the tide of blood that flowed from a gaping hole in his forehead. He stopped, swayed as though a stiff wind were blowing him, and fell to the deck.

Springing forward, Lionel half-caught him and eased his descent. "Lieutenant! Lieutenant!" the correspondent cried, and holding the bloody form of his friend, he screamed to the crewmen now pouring out from everywhere, "Get a medic at once!"

Ira stirred slightly in Lionel's arms and his lips moved. Bending, the Englishman heard him whisper, "Tell David we did it. He'll-he'll" — the whisper began to fade — "be happy we did it."

In the noisy squalor of the saloon next to the Cairo House, David heard Lionel Humphrey pronounce those words, and they rang in his heart like a tolling church bell. He only half-listened to Lionel's final accounting: "He died in my arms, Lieutenant, a brave man, a hero like all those other splendid fellows." He paused and went on: "The *Pittsburgh* came on down two nights later, but there wasn't too much for her to do; the *Carondelet*'s gunners did their work well. But then the two ships put all the Rebel batteries completely out of commission, Pope's army crossed over, straddled the Tiptonville road, and the Rebel garrison surrendered on the seventh, with seven thousand men taken prisoner."

David scarcely heard this satisfactory ending. He was fighting to keep back the tears that welled in his eyes. First it had been Louisa, and now his best friend — both victims of this terrible war, while he was the one who remained alive and well. Maybe that, too, would change now; perhaps his assignment next day would bring him to the same kind of fatal voyage that had ended Ira Thatcher's brief career. He put his head in his hands, scarcely feeling Lionel's comforting arm on his shoulder. Mingled with his grief for Ira was the awful thought that he might never again see Kitty Hamilton's lustrous, golden hair and look into the depths of those blue-green eyes. It was an insupportable thought, and there in the rough, murky atmosphere of the saloon, a deep sob escaped him in spite of all he could do. He cried now for himself as much as for Ira, and he dreaded what the next day might bring.

47

Battle of Memphis

It was a weary and grim-looking David Dexter who appeared on the Cairo docks next morning. Not even the warm sunshine of late May could fully overcome the chill that had enveloped him the night before when Lionel Humphrey told him how poor Ira had died.

David regarded the tangled waterfront scene with distaste. It was even more chaotic than he had thought it the night before, when the lanterns had failed to disclose the general disorder in what the Government was pleased to call its naval station. Craft of every description clogged the piers and docks. Along the bank were buildings just as varied, some wooden and some brick, in which, David supposed, the repair and refitting tasks were being carried on. He had no idea where Headquarters might be; none of these structures looked particularly official.

At least he would soon have settled the question that had puzzled him ever since he had received his orders. His instructions were to report to Colonel Charles Ellet, Jr. The name meant nothing to him, but the title made him wonder if some mistake hadn't been made in Washington. Why should he, a Regular Officer of the United States Navy, be asked to report to a Colonel in the Army? It made no sense. David took out the papers and read them again, as though he might somehow have made a mistake himself in the dozen times he'd read them before. No, it was clear enough: Colonel Charles Ellet, Jr., was the name, and the place was Naval Station Headquarters.

Where might that be? He approached a carpenter who had rigged himself a small shop under canvas beside a dock, and was busy sawing lengths of timber.

"Can you tell me where I might find Naval Station Headquarters?" he inquired.

The carpenter stopped sawing and straightened up, which did not take long because he was short and built like a block, with a face on which the map of Ireland had been plainly outlined beneath his red hair.

"Sure, now, ye might be finding it anywhere," he observed good-naturedly, "but if ye'll just turn yer head, Lieutenant, you'll be afther seein' it in front of you."

David followed the man's stubby forefinger, pointing to his right, but he saw only a large, rectangular, two-story brick building, obviously with an attic above, with two large doors at one end. Next to its entrance on one side, a small, low, one-story brick shed had been attached to the main structure at right angles.

"That's Naval Headquarters?" David exclaimed, hardly believing it.

"Not the big one now," the carpenter warned. "It's the little one, where ye see the small cannon in front."

David thanked the man, and still disbelieving, approached what seemed to him little more than a shed with a tin roof. There was no guard at the door, so he walked in and found himself in a small reception room, where a young ensign sat at a plain pine desk which was littered with piles of paper the officer was sorting as he wrote on them. The rest of the room had been partitioned into offices, most of them with their doors closed; through one still open, David could see that the officers here had no better quarters to work in than anyone else.

"Yes, sir," the ensign said, looking up, "may I help you, Lieutenant?"

"My name is David Dexter, and I have orders to report to Colonel Charles Ellet, Jr."

"Oh, yes." The ensign pushed away his chair and stood up. "He's been expecting you. Right this way."

He knocked discreetly on one of the closed doors, and at the invitation to come in, he ushered David into a room that was painfully plain, decorated only by a Union flag leaning in one corner, four chairs spread about haphazardly, and a desk, behind which sat the Colonel.

"Lieutenant David Dexter, U.S.N., reporting, sir," David said, saluting smartly. In spite of his blue Navy uniform, he somehow felt compelled to add the "U.S.N.," so there would be no mistake.

Colonel Charles Ellet, Jr., stood up and, unlike the squat Irish carpenter outside, that took some time because he was a tall, slender, six-feet-two, with a thin, slightly hawk-nosed face as commanding as his frame. David thought he exuded a kind of restless energy.

"I was hoping you would arrive no later than today, Lieutenant," he said, returning David's salute lackadaisically, but extending his hand, which his visitor considered an unusual gesture even as he shook it. "Sit down, please. We have a great deal to talk about, and precious little time to do it."

To David, there seemed to be a slight edge in the Colonel's voice, although his manner was entirely courteous, even austere. There was something very reserved about Charles Ellet, David thought, as though he had little trust in his fellow man.

"I assume you're wondering what you're doing here," Ellet said, stretching his long frame more comfortably in his chair as he leaned back.

"I must admit, sir, that I couldn't understand why a Navy oficer should be sent to report to a Colonel in the Army — and then find him in a Navy Headquarters."

Ellet smiled, a thin, remote smile. "You might well wonder, and I'll explain to you briefly why I'm here, because that in a sense is why *you're* here. I am not a military man, Mr. Dexter, but a civil engineer — of some reputation in that field, I flatter myself. For a considerable time, I have been trying to persuade our Government to construct a small fleet of ram-boats for use in warfare. I made similar proposals to the Russians for the relief of Sevastopol, but with small success, I must say. Nor did I have much success in Washington, for that matter, until the *Merrimac* showed our War Department what a ram could do. I understand from the Department that you know something about that ship."

How much did he know? David wondered quickly, but there was no time to ask. Obviously, some word from Washington must have preceded him, and the whole story must be known to this tall, strange Colonel. He would have to take a chance on that; there was really no choice.

"I was Third Assistant Engineer on the *Merrimac* — that is, the *Virginia* — in the action against the *Monitor,* sir," he said quietly.

"So I understand," Ellet nodded, showing not the slightest surprise. "The *Merrimac* and the *Monitor* were not exactly the kind of ram I had in mind at the time, but they were enough to demonstrate the possibilities and convince the War Department. Two weeks after the engagement in Hampton Roads, I was commissioned a Colonel in the Army and directed to prepare a fleet of ram-boats which would be capable of clearing the Rebels out of the Mississippi. Secretary Stanton ordered that I be subject only to his authority.

"As a Regular Navy man," Ellet went on, with a touch of irony in his voice, "you may not appreciate the little fleet of four rams that I assembld on the Ohio. I admit they are a motley collection — old side-wheelers and stern-wheelers they are, for the most part, but I've put iron strength into their bulkheads, protected their boilers with more iron and oak, and I guarantee, Mr. Dexter, that when those bows with their heavy metal sheathing strike one of those wooden Rebel ships, it will be like slicing a piece of pie. They've just finished the refitting here in Cairo, and it is our intention to set off tomorrow. My orders are to join the gunboats of the western flotilla somewhere between Fort Pillow, which has surrendered, and Memphis. Together, we hope to clear out the last of the Rebs at Memphis, and the way will be clear to New Orleans. Does all this interest you, Mr. Dexter?"

David was confused. He had thought to find himself on one of the larger gunboats, like the *Carondelet*. What did he know about these little rams, of which he had heard no more than rumors.

"I'm happy to serve you, sir," he said diplomatically, "although the little knowledge of rams I've managed to pick up may not be of great use to you."

"I need men with experience, no matter how brief, and I don't have to tell you how hard they are to get," Colonel Ellet said. "I know of your European experiences, as well as your duty on the *Merrimac,* and I assure you, Mr. Dexter, you'll be the most experienced man in the fleet besides myself and two or three others. But you have a right to know that, even though you've been assigned to me, you are permitted to refuse the assignment. Every man aboard these rams must be a volunteer, by order of Secretary Stanton."

"May I ask the reason, sir?" David inquired, even more confused.

Colonel Ellet's countenance set in a look of grim determination that David would soon come to know better.

"First of all, and most important, because these ships will be unarmed except for squads of sharpshooters. No cannon. We are *rams*, Mr. Dexter, following a tradition as old as the history of naval warfare, and our object is to overcome the enemy vessels by ramming and sinking them, not by firepower. That entails a risk which seems extraordinary to many men — above and beyond the call of duty, so the Secretary believes. Consequently, he insists on the volunteer force. I must say, we have had no difficulty in manning the ships."

David tried to collect his wits. Everything he had been taught in the Navy led to warfare aboard armed vessels; to go into battle with no other weapon except the ship itself was not only contrary to his training, but made him wonder about his own role in such an action. Then a quick thought came to him: Ira had served on the *Carondelet,* and it certainly must have been far from the kind of craft he would have chosen. True, he had no opportunity to refuse, but knowing his friend, David believed that Ira had gone to his assignment with the same instinct for service that had led them both into the Navy. He made up his mind.

"I will be happy to volunteer, sir," he told the Colonel.

Ellet rubbed his hands with satisfaction. "That's what I wanted to hear," he said. "You will be Deck Officer in charge of the crew on my flagship, the *Queen of the West.* Our kind of warfare is a war of maneuver, and it is essential that every man do his job efficiently. It will be your task, Lieutenant, to see that they do. I count on you."

Ellet stood up and they shook hands. "We will have a meeting of all the officers promptly at one o'clock. Report to me then. Meanwhile, bring your gear onto the *Queen.* She's tied up with the others just down the road there."

David saluted and walked out, his head whirling. He was going to see action, all right, but of a kind he would never have anticipated in his wildest dreams. It still seemed incongruous to him, a Regular Navy officer careening down the river on an unarmed ram commanded by an Army Colonel. On the other hand, it looked like a glorious adventure, an opportunity to see real action again, and every instinct in David Dexter's youthful body responded to that challenge.

Outside again, he walked quickly to the waterfront and looked for Colonel Ellet's fleet. There they were, appearing as Ellet himself had described them — motley. He saw the *Queen of the West* at once, a converted sternwheeler covered over with armor plate, her bow ugly and menacing with its heavy load of metal. Near her was her sister ship, the *Monarch,* slightly smaller, under the command of the Colonel's younger brother, Alfred. The two others, *Switzerland* and *Lancaster Number Four,* were no larger, but David had to admit they looked menacing and efficient, even though they had lost whatever gracefulness they might have had in their original state.

He hurried back to the hotel to get his gear and in the always crowded lobby encountered Lionel Humphrey, who appeared to be in just as much haste.

"Sorry I can't stop to talk, Lieutenant," he said, "but I've just received permission to join the ram fleet. They're headed for Memphis, and I've been promised a hell of a fight."

"I hope so," David told him, "because that's exactly where I'm going, too."

The correspondent seized David's arm in his excitement. "You don't mean it! Are you by any chance on the *Monarch?*"

"No, the *Queen of the West.*"

Lionel swore under his breath. "The flagship! That's where I hoped they'd assign me, but Colonel Ellet is a hard man, as I've been told. He swore there'd be no correspondents on his ship, although he made no objection to his brother having one, I notice. In any event, Lieutenant, we'll be in it together."

He caught himself short, and the buoyant enthusiasm faded for a moment from his long, ruddy face. David knew they were thinking the same thing — that Lionel and Ira had started out together on a great adventure only a few weeks before, and now there was only one of them to go into a new battle. How strange and yet how right, David thought, that he should be taking Ira's place, so to speak.

"At least we'll be on sister ships," David said, impulsively clasping the correspondent's shoulder, "so you're right, we'll be in it together."

They were so close next morning, in fact, that David had to smile, remembering his remark of the day before. The four rams stood out in the river, two by two, the *Queen* and the *Monarch* lying close to each other, the others a little behind them. David, in the wheelhouse, looked across to see Lionel waving a greeting to him from the bow of the *Monarch,* and they exchanged salutes. Colonel Ellet, meanwhile, was carrying on a brief conversation with his brother across the few yards of open water that separated them. Then abruptly he called up to David, "We're ready, Lieutenant. Full steam ahead!" David conveyed the order to the engine room and the tiny flotilla moved off, hardly majestically but with honest purpose, down the river.

As the *Queen of the West* led the way, David, in the pilothouse, was entranced with the sheer beauty of the scene that lay before him. It was a June morning of the most shimmering loveliness on the river. Under a benevolent sun, the great stream slid along between banks which sometimes rose sharply into bluffs, then ebbed away into marshes and flatlands. Forests came plunging down to the water at some points, trailing overhanging branches into the water. Clouds of birds circled overhead from time to time; kingfishers patrolled the surface looking for the next meal. It was hard to believe that not far ahead there were determined men, ships, and guns waiting for the advancing rams and the gunboats they were soon to join.

The iron craft moved along through the day without incident. At one point they came to the great bend in the river where Island No. 10 lay quietly now, safe in Union hands. David regarded it somberly as they slipped by, his thoughts full of Ira and the many days they had spent together, in so many places. With fists clenched and tears in his eyes, he vowed silently, "I'll carry on for you, Ira Thatcher, just the way you would have done."

The *Queen* came to the top of the bend, passed that other hotly contested stronghold, New Madrid, and then turned south again, beyond Point Pleasant, where the Mississippi straightened out once more and rolled directly southward toward Memphis. Night fell and a great moon illuminated the scene with such a full light that both shores could be seen as clearly as though it were day, rippling the water with a silver path and making the trees on the banks stand out sharply in silhouette.

As another bright, clear day dawned, they approached Fort Pillow. Standing with Colonel Ellet in the pilothouse, David could see smoke rising from the bluff where the fort stood. He had been briefed, along with the other officers, about what had taken place there only a short time before. The same gunboat fleet that had forced the surrender of Island No. 10 had sailed on down the river, and for two weeks had bombarded Fort Pillow at long range. They were challenged at last by a Confederate fleet known as the River Defense, commanded by Captain J. E. Montgomery.

In the battle that ensued, David was glad to hear, with a touch of mournful pride, that the *Carondelet* had distinguished herself again. She had come to the rescue of the *Cincinnati,* which had been struck on the starboard side by a powerful side-wheel steam ram, the *General Bragg,* leaving her virtually helpless. At that point she was rammed again by two other Rebel craft, the *General Price* and the *Sumter.* But now the *Carondelet* had come steaming with full power to the rescue, her guns firing as fast they could be loaded. One of those fifty-pound Dahlgren cannonballs had struck the *Sumter,* ripping open her steam chest. With the steam pouring out in great clouds from her casemate, the crew had leaped for their lives. The more fortunate fell into the water; others were either scalded to death or burned badly as they fell to the deck under the impact of this faceless, boiling enemy.

Over that fearful scene of conflict, smoke had drawn a billowing gray curtain. At last came a lull in the firing and, as a gentle wind began blowing away the pall, the Union officers could see what remained of the Rebel fleet drifting down the river toward Fort Pillow. The Union ships withdrew about a mile upstream, and for the next two or three days contented themselves with lobbing shells from long range at the enemy craft, which now lay huddled beneath the protecting guns of the fort.

That was the scene as Colonel Ellet and his little flotilla of rams came into view of the Union gunboats, stationed only a mile or so above the fort. The Colonel viewed them with a kind of grim jocularity as he stood on the deck, David at his side, inspecting the fleet through his glasses.

"They're good enough for regular fighting, Lieutenant," he observed to David, "but wait till they see what my rams can do."

Discreetly examining his commanding officer's craggy profile, David realized that for this intense, driving man, the purpose of the battle that surely lay ahead of them was not so much to drive the Rebels southward and clear the river for an advance toward New Orleans, but to prove the superiority of the rams. So had it been with Ericsson, he mused. For the volatile Swede, the meaning of that engagement in Hampton Roads was not to embarrass the Southern fleet but to establish the superiority of his armored giant, the *Monitor.*

"There's the *Benton,*" Colonel Ellet remarked, focusing his glasses a little more sharply. "She's the flagship, if you can call it that. You'll be meeting Flag Officer C. H. Davis sometime today, I have no doubt. You should know, Lieutenant, if I haven't already made it sufficiently clear, that we are operating directly under the orders of the Secretary of War. My instructions are to cooperate with Mr. Davis, and that we shall do, but we are not subject to his orders. *I'm* in command here."

"Yes, sir," David said, conscious once more of the singular character of this Army Colonel Fate had cast him, an Annapolis man, to serve. He felt a surge of excitement inside; it *was* going to be an adventure, no doubt of it.

The *Benton* was surrounded by the fleet's other gunboats, the *Louisville,* the *Cairo,* the *Mound City,* the *St. Louis,* and that ship David never would forget, the *Carondelet.* Toward them, but maintaining a discreet distance, the ram "fleet" moved slowly, the *Queen of the West* in the lead, followed by the *Monarch,* with *Switzerland* and *Lancaster Number Four* trailing behind. They pulled up two by two near the gunboats and cast anchor. David saw the familiar lanky figure of Lionel Humphrey on the deck of the *Monarch,* and they exchanged a friendly wave.

But David had no more than turned away again to resume his duties when the air trembled with the shock of a powerful explosion. It was followed by others until the very atmosphere appeared to roll like the ocean waves. The little rams shuddered for a moment or two. From all the Union craft, gunboats and rams alike, crew and officers tumbled on deck, gazing toward Fort Pillow, from which tremendous clouds of black smoke were now rising into the serene June day. Captain Ellet reappeared with his glasses, but he scarcely had need of them. It was clear to everyone that the Confederate troops in the fort were blowing up their powder magazines, which could mean only one thing — they were evacuating.

A straggling cheer rose from the men on the Union ships, particularly when they saw the River Fleet making rapid headway downstream. Flag Officer C. H. Davis resisted the immediate temptation to pursue them. Time enough for that, he thought.

Next morning a party of officers and men from the gunboats went ashore to inspect what remained. The Rebels had done a good job of it.

Fort Pillow was in ruins, and also nearby Fort Randolph. Smoke still rose from the rubble, and the devastation was so complete that even the earthen breastworks had been torn apart. Commodore Davis stood beside the ruins and gazed down the river with satisfaction. The only remaining obstacle now was the River Fleet itself, which had retreated, he was certain, no farther than Memphis. By eliminating those ships, the way to New Orleans would be clear. Signals fluttered from the *Benton* as soon as he returned; the officers were summoned for a council.

Colonel Ellet, his brother Alfred, and David were rowed over to the meeting in a dinghy. They were greeted with reserved cordiality by Commodore Davis, a short, sandy-haired man, normally laconic but today fairly bubbling with enthusiasm and energy as he sensed that his fleet was closing in for the kill. His intense blue eyes fairly snapped as he told his brother officers:

"Gentlemen, we've got the Rebels where we want them, I believe. It's plain to me that the River Fleet means to make a stand at Memphis, but they'll get no support from the shore there, because the city is not fortified. We can wipe them out and clear the whole blasted Mississippi. I mean to start doing just that tomorrow morning. Now, let's discuss the details."

David felt this energetic officer's enthusiasm elevating his already high state of excitement still further. He was ready for the promised battle. But were his men? That was a troubling thought, for sure. These young volunteers were willing enough, but like David himself, they were unsure of their way about the rams. None had ever fought this kind of war before, and in spite of his experience at Hampton Roads, David could prepare them for what lay ahead with only a minimum of assurance, because he felt little more at home than they did on these armored projectiles, as he thought of them. There was nothing to do now, he thought, but hope that determination and courage would somehow make up for experience.

Next morning the gunboats, with the rams trailing a little distance behind, began to glide down the river toward Memphis. It was another perfect June day. In the radiant dawn, the river stretched before them like a vast ribbon of glass, marked by the wake of the iron monsters whose smokestacks cast small black pillars into the cloudless sky. On the ships, men and officers were on deck and a virtual holiday atmosphere prevailed under the banners that trailed above them in the windless air. They joked and laughed among themselves, and David could only think it was like going on picnics when he and Ira were at the Academy. All that was missing were the girls from Annapolis town, with their heaping picnic baskets. He had to remind himself that all this gaiety could end in death tomorrow for any one of them.

But he cast aside this morbid thought. How could anyone think of death on such a splendid day? It was far better to watch the gently undulating shoreline and think of Kitty Hamilton, of how her body had felt against his that night at Edelweiss, and the soft pressure of her lips. What a strange turn of the cards it was that had led him to St. Louis and to General Brebner's office on that particular day and hour — and how unbelievably fortunate. The image of Kitty now filled that aching, empty place left by Louisa's death. With just a touch of guilt, he considered how quickly devoted allegiances could change, but the experience had been overwhelming. One minute he had been a young man grieving for a beloved fiancée, forever lost, and a few hours later his life was filled again with the face and figure of a woman whom it seemed he had loved all his life. David sighed. When would he ever see her again?

In the early evening, the Union fleet cast anchor at the lower end of Island No. 45, no more than a mile and a half above Memphis. There was little sleep on the ships at night; every man was conscious that next morning the River Fleet would come up to give them combat. If they had only known, there was no more repose on the ships lying in the lee of the Memphis bluffs, most especially on the *Little Rebel*, the River Fleet's flagship, where her commander, Commodore Montgomery, tossed restlessly in his bunk. He had already made his decision, and it had taken considerable courage to do it. His eight rams were not the equal of the Union fleet, as he was well aware. One of them carried four guns, and all the rest could boast only two. The *Cairo* alone, in the Union fleet, carried three cannon forward and four on each side. They were badly outgunned, Commodore Montgomery knew, but nevertheless there was no choice. His River Fleet was all that stood between the advancing Union gunboats and the Gulf. His duty was as clear as the orders he had already received, and that was to stop them if he could.

At dawn, as the clear June light began to flood the river over its high banks, David stood with Colonel Ellet in the pilothouse. As the bluffs became more clearly visible, Lieutenant Dexter could not repress an exclamation: "My God, sir, look at the bluffs."

The morning light pouring over the hills threw into clear silhouette the shifting, milling figures of thousands of people — citizens of Memphis who must have risen in the dark and hurried to these vantage posts on high ground to witness the impending collision which they, as well as the combatants, knew was inevitable.

"They've turned out to see the show," Ellet observed, his voice thick with the tension of the moment, "and by God, we'll give 'em one."

"All hands to quarters," came the signal from Commodore Davis, on the *Benton,* and David sprang to work as the ships came alive with activity, the men hastening to their stations. While they did so, there was a forward movement in the River Fleet.

"Here they come," David half-whispered.

The *General Van Dorn* led the way, followed by the remainder of Montgomery's undergunned rams — the *General Price, General Bragg, General Jeff. Thompson, General Lovell, General Beauregard, Sumter* (hastily restored to duty), and *Little Rebel,* which soon took over the advance, as the flagship.

At David's signal, the Union ships began to move down the river toward them, the *Louisville* and *Cairo* dropping below the *Benton* at first, with the formidable *Cairo,* its eleven cannon at the ready, slightly in the lead and pointed head-on toward the Rebel rams. But then the *Benton* signaled that Commodore Davis wanted the lead, and took it.

As the *Little Rebel* reached a point opposite the upper limits of the city, the morning air, already shattered by the pounding of the engines, resounded with a dull reverberation from one of the Confederate ram's cannon, firing the first shot. It passed over the Union gunboats, but fell perilously close to Colonel Ellet's rams, which were in the rear. David watched with fascination and a growing excitement as a spout of water cascaded up from the impact, shimmering in the sunlight.

To Colonel Ellet, it appeared to be some kind of private signal. Springing forward on the hurricane deck of the *Queen,* he shouted across to his brother Alfred on the deck of the *Monarch,* lying only a few yards away: "Round out and follow me! Now is our chance!" He shouted his order to David: "Signal full steam ahead, Lieutenant!"

With their power and small size giving them greater speed, the four rams plunged swiftly into the clouds of smoke that were surrounding the action as all the ships on both sides began to fire. Standing on the hurricane deck, David peered into the swirling billows and saw that the rams were beginning to pass the gunboats and emerge on the other side of them, with the Rebel ships dead ahead.

Above the constant heavy booms of the cannon all around, David could hear Colonel Ellet shouting, "We'll take that one first," pointing toward the *General Lovell*, almost in the center of the Confederate battle line. The Rebel ships were continuing to fire, but already were beginning to drop back a little. On came the *Queen*, rapidly closing the gap of water between her and the *General Lovell*, which maneuvered sideways to bring its guns to bear. But the gunners never had an opportunity to aim properly, so fast was the *Queen* cleaving through the water.

"Brace! Brace!" David shouted to his crewmen. It was the one lesson Colonel Ellet had most impressed on him. The mission of a ram was to ram, the Colonel had emphasized over and over, and at the moment of impact, it was highly important that every man be braced against some solid part of the ship, otherwise injury, or even death, would be the result.

David held on tightly as the two ships approached each other. The *Queen*'s sharpshooters were popping away at the *Lovell*'s gunners, and men could be seen falling here and there, while frantic efforts were being made to get their cannon lined up on the swiftly moving target.

It was too late. With a roar of metal grinding on metal, the iron prow of the *Queen* struck the enemy gunboat squarely amidships, cutting her nearly in two. Screams and yells rose from the men of the stricken craft, which seemed to emit an agonized groan itself as it lurched to one side. The *Queen* reversed engines and backed off. As she turned away, her attack completed, David could see that the *General Lovell* was beginning to sink quickly. In a few more minutes she would be on the bottom, carrying with her many trapped men who could not jump over the side.

Maneuvering deftly under orders from Colonel Ellet, who stood on the hurricane deck, a commanding figure seeming to rise out of the battle smoke, the *Queen* turned toward the *General Beauregard* and, like the *Lovell*, that ship began to maneuver to take the blow. In doing so she was luckier, or more agile. Again the *Queen* rapidly closed the gap between them until they were so close that David could see plainly the faces of the seamen and officers who were firing both pistols and rifles. With a sudden shock, David realized, "They're firing at me! They mean to kill me!" He drew his own pistol for the first time and began firing with the others of his crew; Ellet himself held a smoking gun in his hand as he continued to yell orders.

With another grinding crunch of metal the *Queen* struck once more, but it was only a glancing blow near the stern of the *Beauregard,* and she escaped with little damage. The impact apparently had done more damage to the *Queen;* David saw a tangle of men and hawsers and machinery at one side of the main deck and leaped forward. He could see that some of his inexperienced crewmen were obviously confused by this kind of warfare. There was reason to be confused, he thought briefly. Great billowing clouds of smoke swirled over the action, through which ships could be seen dimly maneuvering, and completely annihilating the peaceful quiet of this June day was the grinding roar of metal on metal, the resounding booms of the cannon, and the incessant sputtering of small-arms fire. A scene straight out of hell, thought David, as he moved toward his crewmen.

Dimly, he heard Colonel Ellet's voice penetrating the din: "Watch out, Lieutenant! Brace!"

Glancing up, he saw that the *Beauregard* had taken advantage of the *Queen's* momentary loss of momentum after her missed strike, and turning quickly, was bearing toward the little ram, which it far outweighed. Chimneys flaming, the two ships bore down on each other, the *Queen* desperately trying to maneuver herself into better position. Just before the moment of impact, David saw a young seaman near the rail of the gun deck. He could have been no more than eighteen, was the quick impression in Dexter's mind, and he was obviously completely bewildered, his arms raised to his head, not knowing which way to turn. When the ships struck, he would either be thrown into the water or against the iron side of the ship.

"Brace!" David yelled at him, but the boy could not hear him clearly above the noise, apparently, and simply turned his stricken face toward the young Lieutenant, who was only a few years his senior. Instinctively, David leaped forward, seized the boy, and made a frantic grab for the nearest support. Too late. The *Beauregard* struck the *Queen* a shattering blow near her stern and both men were sent hurtling through the air to crash sickeningly on the deck, the seaman falling on top of his rescuer.

David felt a blinding pain in his left leg and suffocating pressure in the ribs on his left side before he lost consciousness. When he rose to life again a few minutes later, the young seaman was huddled on the deck beside him, holding David's body half against him, shielding him from the rain of rifle and pistol shots around them.

"Are you hurt, sir?" the seaman inquired, peering down at David anxiously. David tried to get up, tried to say, "We'd better get off this open deck," but no words came. He was unable to move or to speak.

"I'll get you out of here, sir, as soon as I can," the seaman said in his ear, making himself heard above the constant roar around them. He appeared to be unhurt, his fall broken by David's body.

David lost consciousness once more, unaware of the drama surrounding the ship. As the *Queen* floated away, disabled but still able to make some headway, Colonel Ellet's brother Alfred, aboard the *Monarch,* had seen what had happened to the *Queen,* and started to the rescue. A rebel ram lay in his path, and the *Monarch* struck her a glancing blow in passing, but in doing so, found herself momentarily between two of the Rebel ships. Before any damage was done, however, her expert sharpshooters, firing as fast as they could load, picked off most of the rebel gunners as they worked at their ports, preventing a deadly series of broadsides that would surely have sunk both the *Monarch* and the *Queen.* Some of the Confederate ships were momentarily out of range of the rams by this time, but the Union gunboats were pouring in volley after volley upon them. The *Switzerland* and *Lancaster,* Ellet's other two rams, were doing good work as well, but the latter, in a backing maneuver too close to shore, drifted into the bank, knocking off her rudder and putting her out of action.

In escaping the trap, the *Monarch* had slid down below the scene of battle, but now moved up again, aiming directly for the *Beauregard,* which Captain Alfred Ellet guessed correctly was preparing to finish off his brother's ship as soon as possible. The *Beauregard,* seeing the *Monarch's* swift approach, tried to shift out of the way, and in doing so, with her crew blinded by the drifting smoke clouds, struck her sister ship, the *General Price,* a heavy blow on the side, breaking off the *Price's* starboard waterwheel. Disabled and careening wildly, the *Price* made for the safety of the Arkansas shore, sinking nearly out of sight just before she reached it as the crew tumbled overboard and swam to solid ground. While this was occurring, a broadside from one of the Union gunboats demolished the *Lovell,* and she became the second Rebel ship to sink beneath the Mississippi's turbulent surface.

But now the deadly duel between the *Beauregard* and the *Monarch* resumed, as the former made for her enemy once more. Captain Alfred Ellet, a man as calmly daring as his brother, saw her coming this time, and by a dexterous evasion avoided the charge. Before the *Beauregard* could position herself again, he sent the *Monarch* steaming at her full tilt. The Union ram struck its Rebel counterpart on the bow with terrific force, opening a tremendous hole below the waterline. As the *Beauregard* began to fill with water and sink, her crew and officers gathered on deck, fluttering anything white they could find in token of surrender.

Captain Alfred was not through with his day's work, however. He turned the *Monarch* toward the *Little Rebel* and came at her with full steam. Commodore Montgomery was a prudent man as well as a brave one. Knowing that his ship, slower and not as well armored, would hardly be able to stand up to this powerful Union ram, he turned the *Little Rebel* toward the Arkansas shore and fled, with the *Monarch* in hot pursuit. Captain Alfred came within a hundred yards of winning the race, but the *Little Rebel* suddenly ran aground in shallow water. Montgomery and his crew tumbled over the side into the water, swam frantically to shore, and fled into the forest that grew almost down to the water's edge.

Seeing his prey had escaped, Captain Alfred Ellet demonstrated that he could be magnanimous as well as intrepid. He sent the *Monarch* steaming back to the middle of the river, where the *Beauregard* was now settling rapidly, white cloths still fluttering on the deck. Coming alongside, the *Monarch* took on the crew of the stricken ship, cast a towline to it, and pulled it into shallow water, where she quickly settled down into the mud, the water up to her boiler deck.

Four Confederate gunboats had now been rammed and shot out of commission. For other four, seeing the day lost, turned tail and fled for their lives. With the Union fleet closing in on them, three of these turned toward the Arkansas shore, hoping to accomplish on land the escape they had been unable to accomplish in the water. Leading the others, the *General Jeff. Thompson* reached shore first and ran hard aground, after which her officers and men splashed their way to land and vanished into the trees. Minutes later, a shell from one of the Union gunboats landed squarely on the deck of the abandoned ship, setting her afire. She burned to the water's edge.

The *Bragg* and the *Sumter*, following behind, were able to reach safety, at least for their officers and men, who abandoned ship and melted into the heavy forest with the others who had preceded them. Of the entire River Fleet, only one remained, the *General Van Dorn,* and with the pursuit of the others distracting attention from her, she managed to escape downriver. The triumphant Union ships did not pursue.

Meanwhile, aboard the *Queen of the West,* David Dexter remained largely oblivious to this momentous Union victory. As the ship drifted apart from the action a little way, her crew continued to fire their hand arms briskly at any Confederate ship that came near enough, but the *Queen* was unable to carry on. David swam hazily in and out of consciousness as he lay on the gun deck, struggling with almost intolerable pain and shock. Once he became aware that another figure, a very familiar one, lay not far from him. Turning his head and straining to see, he realized that it was Colonel Ellet, his knee shattered by a pistol shot, unable to rise but still giving orders to the crew of his stricken ship.

David heard his gallant Captain give a final order, "Take her into shore, boys; we can't do any more," and then he lost consciousness once more, collapsing into the arms of the young seaman whose life he had tried to save.

48

Fresh Starts

WHEN DAVID DEXTER WOKE again, he opened his eyes and had no idea where he might be. He was lying in bed, in what appeared to be a large open space; there were murmurs and cries and conversation around him, but it was certainly not the horrendous sounds of battle which were his last memories. A hospital? Possibly, but he felt motion, which could only mean that he was still on a ship.

Cautiously, he turned his head, and for the first time realized that this left leg was in a cast, and his entire left side appeared to be bound up. Even the slight movement of his head made him wince with pain, and he found it hard to focus his attention. He saw that he was lying on one of a row of beds, and next to him lay a figure he recognized as Colonel Ellet, eyes closed and presumably asleep — not dead, he hoped fervently.

There was a stir of movement near the foot of his bed as figures approached, one of whom swam hazily into his range of vision. Focusing a little more clearly, David saw a large, heavyset man with a thick black mustache bending over him.

"How are you feeling, Lieutenant?" the man inquired, in a brisk military voice.

"I-I'm not sure," David said. "Who are you, and where am I?"

"My name is Dr. Charles Mitchell, United States Navy, and you have the good fortune to be on the U.S.N. *Hospital.*"

Even in David's confused mental state, that name was one he knew. He had heard about this hospital ship and in fact had seen her anchored during his brief stay in Cairo. She had been a Confederate transport called the *Red Rover*, sunk with five others and a gunboat by the Rebels when they abandoned Island No. 10. General Pope had ordered all the transports raised, and the *Red Rover* had been quickly fitted out to be the hospital ship of the Mississippi Squadron, under the command of Lieutenant W. R. Wells. This old river steamer was a spacious ship, with roomy cabins and wide decks, easily converted into a comfortable (if comfort was possible) hospital, which usually housed the fever and dysentery cases so prevalent in the Union Army forces consigned to this unfamiliar climate. David had been told she was to come along behind the rams, in anticipation of the battle.

"Where are you taking me?" he managed to inquire weakly.

"To St. Louis, where you'll get better care than we can give you here," Dr. Mitchell said. "We thought to pick up a great many casualties, but fortunately there are only four. However, we have a God's plenty of fever cases aboard, so we're making a run to St. Louis before we come back down."

"How long . . ." David started to stay, but Dr. Mitchell interrupted.

"Everybody wants to know that. I have to tell you, Lieutenant, that for you the war is over. You'll recover, to be sure, but it will take some time and I'm afraid you won't be in condition to serve again. You have a badly fractured leg and four broken ribs, as well as a fairly severe case of concussion. You're in even worse shape than your brave commander here," he gestured in the direction of Colonel Ellet. "His knee is in rather poor condition, but I believe we can mend it, with a little luck." He suddenly smiled. "From all accounts. Lieutenant, you fellows fought a splendid fight and won a great victory. I'm sure your friends back home will treat you like heroes. They should, at least."

David tried to smile, but the effort was too much. He lapsed into unconsciousness again.

There were confused days of pain that followed, days when David was not certain whether he was dead or alive. Wild dreams floated through his head, dreams in which Louisa, Ira, Lionel, and Kitty Hamilton were inextricably mixed, and other dreams in which he could hear the guns once more, smell the burning powder, and feel the deck shuddering under him. He was only dimly aware that he had been taken off the hospital ship and now was lying in a real hospital, in a place called — where was it the doctor had said? — how could he have forgotten — St. Louis, where his strange journey had begun.

St. Louis! The thought brought him abruptly to a sharper consciousness. Kitty was nearby, unknowing that he lay wounded, so near to her. He must pull himself together and get word to her. For the first time, David could feel real life returning to him. His body hurt and ached, but not as intolerably as before, and at the thought of Kitty, he was acutely conscious of the world again.

But how could he get word to the one person he so longed to see, more than any other. While he was trying to muster his thoughts, footsteps approached the bed and a voice he could not forget greeted him.

"So here you are, Lieutenant!" It was Lionel's hearty voice. "How are you feeling, old boy. Had a devil of a time finding you."

"Mr. Humphrey — Lionel!" David greeted him happily, seing in him at once the solution to his problem, but at the same time rejoicing in the reappearance of a man he must now consider an old friend. "What happened to you on the *Monarch* — and how did you get back here?"

"I had the best seat in the house for that show you fellows put on," the correspondent declared, sitting carefully on the edge of the bed. "The *Monarch* saw more action than any of the other ships, I think — and acquitted herself nobly."

"Tell me what happened," David asked. "I've yet to hear any details, and I seem to remember very little of what happened after the *Queen* and I were put out of commission."

"I'll give you a firsthand report, just as I gave it to the dear old *Telegraph*," Lionel said, and proceeded to describe the events that David had been only dimly able to sense as he lay on the deck of the *Queen*. "And," he concluded, "I was in at the death, so to speak. When the battle was over, I joined up with my colleague from the *Cincinnati Commercial*, Charlie Miller. We went with Commodore Davis into Memphis, and saw the Mayor surrender the city to him. There were a few who cheered our arrival, but I gathered that most of the inhabitants were Rebels, and it was a sad day for them, especially because so many of them had seen the River Fleet virtually destroyed with their own eyes.

"Charlie and I went up to the telegraph office afterward," Lionel went on, "hoping to file our stories. There wasn't a soul in the place, but the operator left us a note. Here, I've still got it in my pocket." Chuckling, he reached in and pulled out a crumpled piece of paper. " 'To any Federal Lincolnite,' " he read. " 'I leave this office to any Lincolnite successor, and will state that, although you can whip us on the water, if you will come out on land we'll whip you like hell.' He signed it just 'Operator.' Fortunately, Charlie Miller knew how to operate the key, and we got our stories out."

"They'll never whip us on land, either," David said.

Lionel laughed. "You must be feeling better, Lieutenant," he said. "You sound belligerent enough to fight again."

"I'm afraid not," David said ruefully. "The doctors tell me that my cracked ribs and broken leg will heal properly before long, but I won't be fit to fight again in this war — unless, may God forbid, it goes on for a good many years."

"Well, at least you'll get a hero's discharge," Lionel said cheerfully, "and that's a damn sight better than being at the bottom of the Mississippi, where you might otherwise have wound up. Still, I know it must be a shock to you to be out of the action, and you have my sympathy. Perhaps it will cheer you to hear a bit of good news. It seems that the *Telegraph* isn't the only paper to be pleased with my dispatches. Somehow they've come to the attention of a bright young man named Joe Medill, who's the general manager of a paper in Chicago, the *Tribune,* which I understand is the most up-and-coming newspaper enterprise in this part of the country. Well, Mr. Medill has made me a handsome offer to leave the *Telegraph* and come with him as one of their correspondents."

"Would you leave England for good then?" David inquired.

"Yes," Lionel answered soberly. "It's a large decision to make, but I've come to be very fond of this country, and I mean to make it my home — if I survive the war."

David sighed. "I believe you will," he said, "and I'm happy to know the future looks so bright for you. I wish I could say the same."

"My dear boy, is there anything I can possibly do for you?" Lionel asked solicitously.

"As it happens, there is," David said quickly. "There's a young lady in St. Louis named Kitty Hamilton, who lives in a cottage called Edelweiss. It's well known; anyone can tell you where to find it. If you could possibly find a piece of paper for me, and something to write with, I want to set down a short note to Miss Hamilton and entrust it to you to be delivered."

Lionel grinned and winked conspiratorially at David. "Ah, this can only be romance." Then he suddenly sobered, remembering once more his own lost Arlette d'Aubrey, who had never been far from his thoughts since they parted in Washington. For a moment he was silent, lost in his memories, then was just as suddenly himself again, resolutely shrugging off the vain hopes that David had unwittingly renewed.

"I'll be most happy to carry out this assignment for you, Lieutenant," he went on, with something of his old cheerfulness. "And you've come to the proper man for writing materials." He picked up his dispatch case, which he had left on the floor, opened it, and brought out the tools of his trade. "This is what you need, I believe."

David took the paper and pencil gratefully. It was still not easy for him to write, but he managed to scrawl: "Kitty my darling — I have been wounded in action and am here in the military hospital. Come as quickly as you can. Your loving David."

He handed the folded message to Lionel, and lay back on the pillow weakly, exhausted with even this effort. Humphrey regarded him with sympathy writ large on his long, ruddy face. "You're still in bad shape, I see, Lieutenant, but don't worry. I shall look to it that the lady gets this immediately."

The two men shook hands warmly, Lionel strode away, and David fell back into his usual half-waking state.

Outside again in the busy, congested streets of St. Louis, Lionel considered a moment. The quickest way to find Edelweiss, he decided, was to ask the clerk in the Somerset House, where he was staying — a new hotel, fated soon to burn down to the ground, but at the moment the best quarters to be found in the city. Lionel walked quickly toward it, cursing the deep mud that splashed over his boots whenever he crossed the street, and keeping a wary eye out for large drays whose plunging horses, urged on by harassed drivers, were not likely to be concerned about mere pedestrians.

Entering the lobby, Lionel was walking quickly to the stairs when he heard a voice he thought never again to hear in this world: "Lion-el! Lion-el!" Before he turned, he knew it could be no one else, no one but his love, Arlette d'Aubrey.

Unbelievably, there she came toward him, arms extended from her lovely, petite body, her coarse chestnut hair framing that unforgettable pale, sharply oval face. They clutched each other for a moment, staring with such undisguised joy that those around them were rude enough to watch.

"I simply can't believe it's you, my dear," Lionel murmured. He could hardly get the words out as emotion choked him.

"But it *is*, my dear Lion-el. You can believe it is I who have come half across the country to find you."

They clutched each other by the arms, wordlessly. Lionel glanced about. "We can't have a proper reunion here, with all these spectators. Come up with me to my room."

She hesitated just a moment. "Would that be proper — for these people to see me going upstairs with you?"

"Devil take propriety," Lionel murmured to her. "I want to hold you in my arms."

Taking her elbow, he piloted her to the stairway and they ascended together wordlessly, while curious, amused, knowing glances followed them. They were oblivious, conscious only of each other.

Once inside Lionel's room, they threw themselves breathlessly into each other's arms and exchanged a long kiss, their bodies responding with thrusting warmth as they had those nights in New York and Washington.

"My darling," Lionel said into her hair, "I thought I'd never see you again — and not a day has gone by that I haven't loved you and missed you."

"I, too, Lion-el. I have been only half a woman since you left."

He drew apart a little. "But what are you doing here? You must tell me what's happened."

She gave him a coquettish look of mock dismay. "Ah, you gentlemen of the newspapers are always so curious, always asking questions." But then her charming face sobered again, and she said; "Oh, Lion-el, I thought when we talked last that I was doing a wise thing, something that had to be done. But as soon as you were gone, I began at once to regret it. I had not listened to my heart, *chéri,* and if I had, I would never have done it. I love only you, Lion-el."

"But what of Herbert Morrison, this rich and attractive man you had agreed to marry?"

"Alas, I found I could not do it. It would have been a great hypocrisy. I could not truly love him as long as you were in my heart, and there I knew you would always be. I was tormented, *mon coeur,* but I knew what must be done. I told him my feelings, and he was a true gentleman — he released me from my promise. And then, my dearest, it was as though it were fated. The very next day there came word from Paris that my father had died, and now there was no reason whatever for me to return. I was free, and there was no one in the world for me but you."

"Arlette!" Lionel held her tightly again, murmuring endearments against her lips and cheek. "But how did you find me?" he asked.

"For a woman in love, it required only persistence," she laughed. "I inquired at your office, and they told me that you would not be going at once to see this General Grant you spoke of, but had been instructed to go first to the battles they expected on this river — the, the, what is it you say — Mees-ess-eepi? Oh, Lion-el, it is so hard to pronounce! They told me that at some time you would be in this town with the French name which is not at all like France, and I decided I would come and wait for you here. Every day I would inquire from the Army people of your whereabouts, and I — I hoped and waited, Lion-el. I was certain you would come back to me."

He held her again, and this time every thought was blotted from his mind but the need to hold her smooth, naked body in his arms. He began to fumble at the fastenings on her dress, and she laughed the low, throaty laugh he loved to hear in the dark.

"A moment, Lion-el. I will help you."

They were warm and close in bed a few moments later, and the world outside dropped away.

Later, they murmured and giggled together, exchanging endearments. Lionel pulled himself on one elbow and looked down at her. "My dearest," he said, "I've only now thought to tell you my news," and he related the circumstances that had led to his new assignment.

"Let us marry here as soon as possible," he concluded, "and I'll take you to Chicago with me. I'll have to go wherever Mr. Medill chooses to send me after that, but as soon as this blasted war is over, I'll come racing to you and we'll never be parted again."

"Except when you have another assignment," she teased.

"You've chosen a newspaperman's life when you chose me," he said.

"I know, dearest heart, and I would have it no other way," Arlette d'Aubrey told him. They clung together again, feeling new excitement stirring in them. Much later they fell asleep in each other's arms.

Lionel awoke first next morning, with the disturbing feeling that something had been left undone the day before. He looked down fondly on Arlette's sleeping, naked body and thought, My God, it's a wonder I can think of my own name.

But then he remembered, with a quick pang of guilt. There *were* other loves in the world besides his own, incredible as that might seem, and he had faithfully promised poor, wounded David Dexter to deliver a note to a lady he obviously yearned for. He bounded out of bed and began to dress. Arlette stirred sleepily.

"What is it, my darling? Must you go out so soon?" she asked softly.

"Only for a short time, my sweet. You remember our friend, Lieutenant David Dexter? Well, I found him here yesterday in a hospital. We were in a battle together on the river, and he's been seriously wounded. He asked me to deliver a message to a lady, at once — and I'm afraid I forgot it, my dear, in all of last night's excitement. I was inexcusably selfish, and I must take this note at once. I'll return very soon." Then he dashed from the room, fastening the last buttons as he left.

It had been a virtually sleepless night for David. He had expected that Kitty would be there within an hour, perhaps, after Lionel left, and his whole body ached with an anticipation as sharp, almost, as the pain he had felt before. But the hours dragged slowly by, and there was no Kitty. Daylight faded, the lanterns were lit, and she did not come, nor when all but a few of the lanterns were turned down for the night.

Shifting restlessly in his bed, the unthinkable possibilities floated before him. She had gone away and Lionel had been unable to find her. But then, he would certainly have returned and reported that fact. Or she had found another man, even in the brief time he had been away — after all, what he had thought of as a great love had flared between them in a few hours, and if it hadn't been wholly sincere on her part, she could have been as quickly attracted to someone else. He could not entertain that thought for long, not only because the idea was unbearable, but because it was beyond his ability to believe that Kitty had not felt for him everything she professed. No, something else must have occurred, but what?

So he tossed in torment through the night, half-waking and half-sleeping, until daylight streamed through the windows. Breakfast arrived but he could not eat it. Anxiety enveloped him as though he had been wrapped in a blanket, and he began to sweat. He heard footsteps approach his bed in the long ward, where fifty men were being cared for, and raised his head hopefully, but it was only the orderly with the morning's mail. There was one letter for him, and he recognized the precise scrawl of his sister Abigail. Hastily, he tore it open; there had been no word from home since he had left New York on his secret mission.

> Dearest brother, [the letter began] I have discovered where you are through repeated enquiries at the Navy Department, and so have learned of your heroic conduct, which is no more than I expected of my David, and of your injuries, which I have been assured are painful but no bar to your complete recovery in time. You have my dearest sympathy and good wishes. How I long to see you again, but there seems no means to accomplish it.
>
> Having said as much thus far, dear David, I can hardly bring myself to write what I must now tell you. Two weeks ago our dear father died in dreadful pain, after a terrible struggle, and while the loss almost overwhelmed us, it was but another manifestation of God's mercy that he was so relieved and taken beyond his pain. He was scarcely in his grave before dear mother, who had suffered greatly through father's last days, fell to her bedroom floor unconscious. I found her and summoned the doctor at once, and he pronounced her the victim of a heart attack. Dear David, how can I tell you, but I must — she died no more than an hour later.
>
> As you may well believe, I have been prostrate with grief, but you must also know that I have been greatly solaced by my fiancé — yes, my dear brother, my fiancé! Not long before father's death, I had consented to be the wife of Captain Robert Carter, U.S.N., who is in the Navy Department at Washington. You need not worry about my welfare then, dear brother. It is I who worry about *yours*.
>
> I am informed that you will be discharged when you are able to travel again. Will you return to New York? Alas, it will not be to the house you knew so well, where we grew up together. It is being sold, and I shall soon be married and living in Washington with my Captain. I feel it is my duty to warn you that if you should return to this city, there will be those who still look upon you as a turncoat, not understanding your mission to the South, which father told me about before he died, so that I would be as proud of you as he was, which I am, dear David.
>
> I am sorry to be the bearer of so much sudden, bad news, but there are better things to tell as well, and . . .

There was more, but David let the letter fall to the bed. A sense of loss and loneliness gripped him. Never had he felt so alone in the world — his father and mother dead, Abigail about to be married and enter upon a new life, no longer sure of a welcome from his friends at home. Ira dead, too, and no word from Kitty, the one person left to him. A dark despair enveloped David Dexter, and he felt that he might better die on this hospital bed than rise from it and try to face an empty world. David closed his eyes; it was the lowest point in his life, he thought, and perhaps the end of it.

A few moments later there was quick, light rush of footsteps, and he felt himself surrounded by an unforgettable feminine fragrance. Warm, soft arms embraced him, and a tangle of curly golden-brown hair fell about his face.

"David, David, David!" he heard Kitty saying, her eager lips covering his face. In a rush of unutterable relief, he held her against him, unable to say anything but her name, over and over, as she had said his.

"I came as quickly as I could when I received your message this morning," Kitty said, drawing apart a little.

"I sent it to you last night," David said, "and I thought you weren't coming, that I'd lost you."

"You will never lose me, my darling!" Kitty assured him passionately. "But tell me how you are, and how you came to be here? Are you hurt badly? When can I take you away?"

David laughed, the first real laughter he had been able to muster for a long time. "One question at a time, dearest Kitty." He proceeded to tell her the story of his adventures since she had last seen him, until that morning. Picking up the letter he had abandoned, he handed it to her. "Please read it," he said, "and you will see that I have no future but you."

She read it quietly, tears beginning to flood her eyes, until she had to put it down and lay her head against his chest. "I am so sorry, David, so many dreadful things have happened to you. But I am with you now, dear heart, and I will see that you are never lonely."

He gripped her shoulders with hands that were now surprisingly strong, and gazed steadily at her. "I want you to marry me, Kitty," he said, "but you must realize that I have no particular prospects. I'll be a discharged Navy officer with a pension, and no immediate job prospects. But *you* will be sacrificing a great deal — Edelweiss and the monthly sum

General Brebner left you until you married. How can I ask you to exchange so much for so little?"

Kitty Hamilton laughed gently. "You may ask me, David, because there is nothing in the world I would not give up for you. I've managed to save quite a bit — Carl was a very generous man, as you know — and we will have enough to live on for a while."

"I expect that I'll inherit something from my father's estate," David said, suddenly cheerful, "and there's always work for an engineer in a growing country like this one. Oh Kitty, my darling, you *will* marry me then?"

"Yes, with all my heart," she said simply, and they held each other in a long, searching kiss.

But then she drew apart, and a troubled look came into her eyes that puzzled David. How *could* she have forgotten, Kitty thought. Even though all her happiness in the world might depend on it, she could not bring herself to marry David unless he knew the truth.

"There is something about me you must know, David," she said, gripping his arms, "and when you have heard it, if you wish to take back your proposal, I will understand that you have every right to do it."

"Nothing in the world could possibly make me do that," he assured her.

"Don't say that until you've heard me," Kitty insisted. Slowly, carefully, she told him the whole story, beginning with her Bermudian mother and British Army officer father, her life on the Island, her escape from it — and, with a catch in her voice, she bravely told him enough of her life with Adah Markham so there would be no doubt of what it was.

Watching her, David felt curiously detached, as though he could see himself hearing these things which were contrary to everything he had been brought up to believe could be accepted. What would his family have said, if they had known that he was considering marriage to an illegitimate half-mulatto woman who had once been a high-class whore in New York? There was no doubt whatever; even at so remote a distance, even knowing both father and mother were dead, he could easily imagine their horror.

But as she talked on, Kitty Hamilton's face came into sharper focus in his consciousness and he understood that no matter what she had been or was, it made not the slightest difference. He would love her with all his heart until he died.

Kitty stopped and looked at him, expectantly, fearfully, her eyes dark with anxiety. David kissed her and, holding her tightly again, said, "Nothing that you have told me changes my love for you in the slightest way. I love you with all my heart, and I want to marry you as soon as possible."

They held each other and murmured together for a while, until David said, "When I'm discharged from here, and from the Navy, and we're married, let's make a completely new start. We'll leave your life and my life behind and start fresh. What would you say to San Francisco? I hear it's a growing place that might need engineers."

"I think it would be wonderful, David," Kitty said. "Anywhere we're together would be wonderful."

Their kiss was a promise of days to come.